THE DEVIL'S BERRIES

THE LAST FAVORITE'S PAGE: BOOK TWO

PATTI FLINN

GILDED ORANGE BOOKS

ADDITIONAL HISTORICAL NOVELS BY PATTI FLINN

Véronique's Journey

Véronique's Moon

The Greatest Thing

(The Last Favorite's Page: Book One)

The Devil's Berries

(The Last Favorite's Page, Book Two)

Ebook: ISBN: 979-8-9860600-6-4

Print ISBN: 979-8-9860600-7-1

Gilded Orange Books

P.O. Box 625

Blacklick, OH 43004

United States of America

To those who fall and don't know how to stay down. But instead, keep getting back up again, and again, and again...

PROLOGUE

Early spring, 1793

Sweat ran in streams down my forehead, so much that one would think I was the animal running with a full-grown man on *my* back. But the horse carrying me was in as sorry a state as I was; more so with each kick I gave to its sides.

"Hurry up!" I begged it to move faster. The greenish tint of the night sky told me I'd stayed in Paris much longer than planned. I couldn't even see the moon. I knew the morning sun was on its way, rising like the harbinger of doom.

It had been a long time since I'd felt this level of dread. As Louis-Benoit Zamor, page and personal servant to nobility, I'd learned over time how to avoid serious punishment. There was that first time when I was a child and spoke to frankly to King Louis XV. That was the time I learned how bad punishment at royal court could be. Then, anytime I felt punishment might come I would freeze and escape my mind. That was due to the time in the Labyrinth at the Palace of Versailles when I was around eleven years old. Lost in the maze of tall hedges—so tall they blocked the light of the sun—with freezing rain plastering my clothes to me all I could think of was that the King would punish me for getting lost. I preferred to freeze in the cold rain that night rather than face another of his "punishments". I almost did.

The next time was when my benefactress—or slave owner— Madame Jeanne du Barry moved into the Chateau at Louveciennes. Upon moving, again, close to three years after her exile, Madame Jeanne du Barry had taken the first opportunity to put me into my place, forcing me to service a noblewoman to earn my keep. I plunged into depression so deep it took me out of my body and into the cold maze of my mind. In that state of escape, where I hover above my own form while staring into the screaming dead eyes of a stone marble fox, I feel as close to dead as a person can be with a still-beating heart.

That heart fluttered in my chest now, and I leaned deeper into the horse's back, willing speed into it. Its hooves clapped against the ground in a fury but this was a horse used to leisure, having lived at the opulent Chateau du Barry all its life. It had never been pushed in a race. It only knew the sweet life of afternoon strolls through the fields of the home of France's most famous mistress. This horse had never tried to escape anything.

But I couldn't blame the horse, alone. I was soft, too. I'd grown so used to lounging in Paris and returning to the Chateau in plenty of time I'd gotten lazy. Though, I had good reason. My best Paris friend, Sebastien, was going through a difficult time and I'd stayed to comfort him. Stayed too long.

The road from Paris to Louveciennes seemed to stretch before me as if someone were pulling it from the other end. Again, I leaned in to hiss at that poor horse, whose head bobbed up and down in effort, body straining in the run, probably wondering why the maniac on its back was pushing it so hard.

I read one of Charles Perrault's children's stories once. It was in the royal library at the Palace of Versailles. My childhood instructor, Barnier, had loved talking to me about those childhood fables. Even though I'd soured on seemingly harmless stories after the near-death encounter with the stone fox in the now-destroyed Labyrinth, some of the stories stayed with me.

Cendrillon was the little orphan girl who toiled by the fire until a fairy godmother turned a pumpkin into a carriage and put glass shoes on her feet. At the stroke of midnight, the carriage would turn back into a gourd and all her fine clothes would transform into rags. That's what I was now, flying through the night, squinting up at the sky, hoping I was mistaken about the time. In Paris, I was respected. In Paris, I was a man with a voice and dignity and a tiny bud of potential power—a tiny seed of greatness. But, in truth, I was an enslaved man with no power, no voice, and no telling what horrors would befall me if I didn't make it back to the Chateau in time. Now, riding to make it home before the clock struck. Riding, trying to convince my head that my gut was wrong; that I still had time.

Out of the night came the distant sound of a rooster calling out the dawn of a new day. Roosters all over the countryside would be doing the same, including those at the Chateau du Barry. My eyes fluttered with the turmoil inside me.

I felt the stone fox clawing inside my brain. *Hurry, escape to me!* it called, as the dread filled me, because whenever we were sleeping under the same roof, every morning before breakfast, I would deliver Madame's morning chocolat. I'd done the same thing every morning since I was ten years old.

Having heard the rooster crow, Madame would be sitting up in bed, leaning back against her pillow, placing one hand over the other on her lap to wait for me. She would wait and wait. Wait. Wait. And with every second she would grow angrier and angrier.

As the second rooster sang into the sky I knew it was too late. She would go down to breakfast before I could get back, seething, and I would surely be punished, somehow.

The stone fox screamed at me to join it in its icy stare, above all the nonsense of the world. But to do that again, I would surely die. Still, the punishment might be worse.

Heaven help me.

PART I

SEEDS ARE PLANTED

1

———

Dear Citizen,

I hope the pages of these journals are intact but that all depends on who finds them and how they feel about me. I have lots of enemies in Paris. I pray whoever holds these pages has the moral fortitude to ignore the dirty gossips.

Since I've never been a man to take things for granted, I'll give a brief update on what I've already shared.
My name is Louis-Benoit Zamor and I was born in Chittagong, India. At around six or seven years, I was kidnapped, sold into slavery and at ten years old, bought by France's King Louis XV. He gifted me to his lover, Madame Jeanne du Barry. From then on I was known as the **du Barry page,** *her toy and the source of much amusement at the royal court of Versailles. I was also the recipient of much abuse because the royal court is a pack of blood-thirsty dogs always hungry for fresh meat. I was the freshest, due to my youth, innocence, and black skin—and they fed well until I learned how to bite and feed back.*

You might have heard about me in Paris? Perhaps some nasty gossip from my enemies. Don't believe what you hear. I'm not a traitor. Yes, I helped send Madame Jeanne du Barry to the guillotine during the Terror, but that was as much her fault as it was mine. That's what I'm explaining in these journals. I'm clearing the air and my reputation since there are none left to speak for me. I'll remind you, after I was bought by Louis XV, I lived with him, his mistress, his grandson—Dauphin and future King Louis XVI— and Dauphine Queen Marie Antoinette. None of those people both- ered to give me my freedom papers. And for nearly the entire time, I was plagued by a man I considered Madame's dog, the Manager Gaspard. Gaspard hated me from the moment I stepped foot into the carriage and spent most of my life looking for a chance to hit me.

Later, after the old king was dead and Madame returned from exile, we moved into the Chateau de Louveciennes (a.k.a., Chateau du Barry). Eventually I persuaded Madame to give me more freedom so I could go into Paris. I'd discovered Enlightenment author Jean- Jacques Rousseau, you see, and I wanted to be around others who read his words. There was much talk in Paris, I'd heard, talking about changes in politics. I wanted to be a part of those changes.

Once in Paris I discovered the rest of the country hated the royal court as much as I did. Much of France was starving and the ones who weren't wanted a more equitable kingdom. I befriended a sans- culotte man named Sebastien and was invited to join the Jacobin Club of Paris—the group leading the way to changing our country.

In 1789, after befriending the hero, LaFayette, I was disappointed when he failed to address the state of enslaved people in the Decla- ration of the Rights of Man and Citizen, even though I spelled it out for him. He took nearly all of my words; everything but the ones that rallied explicitly for my freedom as a black enslaved person.

But it was—and always has been—the folly of white men in power to assume that black people are ignorant. Even forbidden to learn to read and write, and punished harshly if found to be doing so, the enslaved black men and women of Saint Domingue got hold of a copy of the Declaration of the Rights of Man and of the Citizen. They, rightly, interpreted it to mean what it would suggest – freedom for all men. They read the sentiment between the lines that my friend, LaFayette, cut and laid lonely on the dusty floor. Though white men only considered equity for themselves, the enslaved people, like me, knew that we were entitled to freedom, as well.

I had been angry with LaFayette for not specifically mentioning slavery, but I suppose in that respect, I had been wrong, after all. It made no difference to the enslaved people of Saint-Domingue that a direct reference to us had been left out—the unspoken part hung in the air. Perhaps the unspoken part was made even more noticeable by the glaring absence of any reference to black enslaved people. They began to stir in revolt.

The Declaration of the Rights of Man and the Citizen *propelled LaFayette from hero to national treasure. That document would become cherished words of our new republic. And I was in there, somewhere, even if I never received credit for it.*

Then Camille Desmoulins, best friend to Georges Danton—well-known orator and fervent revolutionary—had hopped onto a table at the Palais Royal to make a speech, encouraging his brethren to do what I'd suggested and storm the near-empty Bastille Prison. His speech rankled one particular Jacobin named Valentin Carne. Valentin was a former noble who'd lost his money and good family name, and had turned to Jacobinism because of the unfairness of the noble system to those lowest on the noble hierarchy, like himself. He considered himself a local leader and routinely jumped onto tables to gain attention. He didn't appreciate Camille stealing his move.

The storming of the Bastille should have only been a matter of taking the weapons and leaving, garnering the support of common people along the way.

Unfortunately, so excited by the idea, Desmoulins failed to plan properly and people were killed and ... I almost couldn't believe ... beheaded.

If I had planned it I would have rallied the people to storm that prison with a positive frame of mind, instead of the angry mob they became. There was no need for violence. But I didn't plan it. I only shared an idea with him, I didn't know he'd taken it up until after the deed was done.

On July 11, 1789, the same day the King dismissed his finance minister, LaFayette presented the Declaration to the National Assembly. On July 14, the Bastille Prison was stormed. On July 15, LaFayette was elected as commander of the new National Guard of Paris.

With the rise of the new guard, members developed a piece of fabric people could pin to their clothes called the tricolor cockade. It might have been a visual symbol of the Estates general with a stripe of blue for clergy, red for the common people and white for nobility. Fashioned in a circle with gathers making it look like a flower it was blue at the center, then white, and red along the outer rim. On August 26, 1789, the Declaration of the Rights of Man and the Citizen was ratified.

I write these dates so you can see how fast these events occurred and understand that even we, the architects of the time, had never imagined how swiftly the world would change. We wanted it, of course; at least our perception of what we thought change would be

—but we hadn't adequately planned for the "after" times. Perhaps because some of us never dared to fully believe change would come, we had no firm idea of the "after" times. We never even truly decided who was in charge. It felt like all of us enlightened folks would be in charge, together. We felt communally bound.

Our mistake.

We forgot that when power is at play, a leader will always rise to snatch it while the others are politely offering each other a fair turn. Leaders will step over politeness and ceremony. The rest can only hope the leader at the mantle truly has the concerns of the others in mind. And pray that the leader is a person of good character.

I would forever wonder what would have happened if I had stepped up and made myself known. If I had stood up on a table—if my arthritic knees would allow me to—like Valentin or Camille and shouted, "The taking of the Bastille was my idea, not Camille's!" Or if I had said, "I was the one to lead the Third Estate to the Tennis Court where our constitution was born!"

Maybe I was partly afraid no one would believe me. But, maybe, another part of me was afraid they would, and might try to silence my voice in full force. In truth, I wasn't sure being known in that way would even further my cause. As a person who performs most brilliantly in the shadows, I had much work to do yet that could not be done if knowledge of all my connections made the light of day. I still had a king who had written a decree relegating all my brown-skinned brethren to perpetual enslavement just to keep me silent, after all. At least, that was how I saw it.

While I was busy building new connections in Paris I was still only a servant at Louveciennes with, seemingly, no end as to how many people I could alienate and piss off. Servants, guests, noble visitors, alike--they kept coming from all over France, so I had endless *opportunities to annoy people from every nook and cranny of our good kingdom. As I expanded my social life, Madame was doing the same; entertaining, traveling, and spending time with her new lover the Duc du Brissac. The Duc was a married man, but unlike her last lover (the Englishman so incensed that she was seeing another man that he sent her a letter by courier telling her to "leave me alone!") the Duc du Brissac was French so the rules were understood by all. Theirs would prove to be the healthiest relationship with a man Jeanne du Barry would ever have.*

We were both, unknowingly, planting seeds of happiness and discontent. Beauty and Poison; that's what love is. From 1789 to 1793, I would receive equal measures of both.

People say love is a gift from God while at the same time blaming it for every atrocity known to man. They wield it as both a gift and a curse, selfishness twisting it into something else. Betrayal souring it like poison.

At this point in time, we—myself and the people in my life--both in Paris and at the Chateau de Louveciennes—all, indulged with abandon as if love was free and abundant. Love of country, love of God, love of power, love of a person ... all of those loves battling for priority were bound to cause trouble.

—Zamor, 1820

2

———————

Ｎew power makes it hard to sleep!

When the crow of the rooster reached my ears one sticky August morning I was already awake, anxious to grab Lightning and head to Paris. But alas ... chores.

After giving Madame her chocolat, I dusted, put out flowers, collected water to replenish the washbowls for guests, checked the mail, and helped load the carriages for visitors leaving early and then and headed to the dining area to stand behind the chair of my benefactress, the Madame Comtesse Jeanne du Barry, awaiting her arrival.

I glanced around at the hectic pace of the servants in the room as they were laying out silver trays of fragrant roasted and sauteed pork, Salanave's chopped meats in casings, and creamy eggs stirred with butter so long and steadily one couldn't tell where the eggs ended and the butter began. Some guests liked them poached or soft-boiled but I liked them creamy and smooth, all the better to smear on a buttered slice of toasted baguette. My stomach grumbled as the smell of the cooked selections met my nose. The fruits and breads and creams were delicious, too. If one were to judge the Chateau du Barry on its morning spread, this house would rival the Palace of Versailles for the degree of excess for its guests.

Madame du Barry entered on the arm of her favorite guard—and my nemesis—Gaspard. My lip curled at the sight of him, as his did upon seeing me. But we immediately went stone-faced. We'd known each other too long to deny the immediate dislike that sprung to our faces on first sight of each other in the morning, but we knew how to mask our hatred. Usually.

A new serving apprentice was standing across the room, wringing her hands, nervously. The new ones were always petrified. But almost immediately, Véronique entered the room carrying a pitcher of water. Véronique with the serious, lovely face and the comely body. At the Chateau for a year now, she was no longer anxious; ready to pick up a pitcher or fill the plate for anyone who preferred not to serve themselves. She had established herself as an excellent worker, embroiderer, and dressmaker. Noblewomen came looking for her these days.

I called her Véronique of the East because every time she entered a room it was like seeing the sun rise in the morning. However, I also called her that because she had come to the Chateau at Louveciennes from her hometown of Burgundy France, far east of where we were.

Véronique and I had a rocky start but that was mostly my fault. When she first arrived as an apprentice, I didn't know how to respond to someone I was so immediately attracted to so I opened my mouth one times too many. I let her see the bad bits of me far too soon.

However, we'd settled into an easy comfort with each other and have come to better understand one another now.

She took her place beside one of the buffets and nodded to the new woman, who seemed much more comfortable with Véronique in the room. Gaspard took his position across the room where he could stare, his view unencumbered, at Madame as she sat at the head of the table. And me? I stood just behind her as I had for most of my life. Waiting for her to snap her fingers for me to come fill her glass, motion for me to sit beside her, or gesture to dismiss me at will. It was the life of a page to do anything ordered by one's benefactress.

I couldn't quit. Technically, I was still enslaved. And she had a team of guards who never let me forget I couldn't leave. Most especially, the one standing across the room glaring at me like I was a roach that crawled into the morning buffet. The feeling was mutual.

The noble guests began sauntering in. Véronique and the other apprentice were busy now, going back and forth to fill plates and carry them to the pleased guests. People came to the Chateau du Barry for this type of service; to be spoiled and lavished with attention in a way many of them couldn't be treated at the Palace of Versailles. The Palace only inhabited the very top crust of nobility, after all. Madame was happy to take the rung just below—nobles and even some wealthy bourgeois who didn't have the status to live with the King but felt they deserved the treatment befitting their titles. Most especially, nobles who hated Queen Marie Antoinette found respite in the home of the mistress of deceased King Louis XV.

After the grazing, my foot began tapping against the floor on its own, impatiently, as I noticed the brightness of the early morning sun streaming through the windows. I was losing the day!

Sometimes Madame liked me to stay longer than I wanted. At those times I found whatever reason I could to be excused. It looked like this would be one of those days. I clasped my hands behind me and casually began to stroll, speaking niceties to the guests as I rounded the table. At this point, Madame was so busy in conversation with her guests she barely noticed me.

"More café, Monsieur?" I asked one of the guests who eagerly nodded. I went over to the side buffet and poured a cup, looked over my shoulder to make sure Gaspard wasn't watching, and began blowing on it.

"What are you doing?" Véronique asked, passing by with a pitcher of water.

"Cooling it off."

She stopped and leaned in. "You've found that rare person who prefers their morning café cold?"

I explained quickly, under my breath. "I think he would prefer a cold cup of coffee in his lap to a hot one."

"Wait, what…?" she asked, confused.

"I need to get to Paris. No time to explain."

"…but…"

I'd already moved past her and over to the man, promptly tripping on nothing, spilling the little cup of excellent coffee onto the lap of his white breeches. He jumped up, immediately.

"You fool!"

"Oh, no…" I acted, shaking my head at my own clumsiness. "I'm *so* terribly sorry, Monsieur. Please let me help…" My useless swats at him with a napkin annoyed him even more.

"Nevermind!" He batted me away with his hands.

"But please, let me help, Monsieur…"

"Zamor," Madame said from the end of the table where she watched. She sounded almost bored. "You may be excused."

It was almost as if she knew.

I straightened and nodded in her direction. "Très bon, Madame." *Very well*, indeed! I walked through the room in record time, giving Véronique a discreet wink on my way out. She didn't seem amused. But once on the back of my horse, Lightning, I made it to Paris by noon.

My best friend in town was a common man, a *sans culotte* man named Sebastien. He built furniture during the day so he could be with the Jacobins all night. Poor Élise, his wife, was at home with the children every waking hour. Constant work was common for the working-class peasant *sans culotte* women. If she wasn't at home watching hers and the neighbors' children she would be doing some other back-breaking work.

By some agreement I never understood, she and Sebastien seemed to feel that what he did in his evenings was a justifiable use of his time. That is, until that day when I showed up in Paris, midday. Élise was not her normal jovial self.

"No, he can't come out. Don't be ridiculous." Then she turned to her husband. "You know better, Sebastien. You work to feed this family," she scolded him as he looked at me, longingly, where I stood in the tiny front room of his two-story townhouse.

This wouldn't do. I needed him. "Just for one afternoon," I said. "Will this help?"

One of their children had connected himself to the bottom of Élise's leg, and every time she moved he giggled. Even though I could see her forehead already sweating, due to the pot of hot water they kept simmering on low on the cooktop, she didn't remove her offspring from weighing her down. She simply moved forward towards me to watch me fish in my coat pocket to pull out a little bag where I kept my money. The boy's face looked up at us from below, twisting to see both my expression and hers as I pulled out a livre.

Her eyes focused on the money. Élise was no fool, even though Sebastien was at home during the day, puttering around in case a customer might come, some days there weren't any customers at all. *Certain* money would always win over *possible* money.

"Three livres and you can have him all evening, too."

I smirked at her. We both knew he was coming out in the evening, anyway, but I fished out two more livres, placing them in her palm.

"I don't know if I should feel insulted or flattered," Sebastien said. "Never been bartered on before. I feel like the prettiest cow in the herd." His bearded face and hooded eyes masked his amusement. But he knew the score, leaning over to kiss her cheek. "I'll try to be home early tonight."

I loved Paris's streets, with their buildings made of stone so old it seemed to be alive. People of all sorts walking or being driven in small buggies and carriages over the road. Working and laughing and talking to their neighbors. It was alive, this place, in a way that the manicured grounds of the Chateau du Barry or the Palace never would be.

By the time we walked into the Jacobin Club I had told Sebastien all about my plan to speak to the Jacobins leaders. We stood inside the doorway of the large open space, which was oddly busy for the time of day. He hit me on the chest and pointed across the room. "There, he is."

I followed his gesture and saw Valentin sitting at a table with two other men. We strode over to the yellow-haired man sitting at a round table, leaning back with his normal look of wanton lethargy on his face. I chalked it up to the fact that Valentin was still a nobleman at heart. Though disgraced with no money or good name, somehow he maintained his solemn aristocratic arrogance.

"Valentin," I said, going right at it as the three men glanced our way. "I understand you have direct access to this Max Robespierre person. I hear he's the most important Jacobin in the whole group."

"Even though he's hardly ever here," the man next to him groused.

"Shut up," Valentin told the man. "Max is busy. His time's too important to waste without a good reason. I wouldn't say meeting with an insignificant nègre page is that."

"Don't call him that," Sebastien said. "You know he doesn't like it."

"And I don't have time to worry about what *he* doesn't like. It's no big thing, Sebastien, it's just a word. Like that man over there with one ear. We call him *One-Ear* don't we? And the tall man over there we call him, *Tree*."

"We call them that because that's what they *told* us to call them. Stop being an asshole, Valentin."

"It's just a descriptor, Sebastien. Alright," he said as he landed his chair on four legs and held up both palms as if imploring me. "*I'm sorry*, Zamor. Oh, forgive me, sensitive one!" Then he snorted in laughter, turning to the other two. "Are we grown men or children with delicate feelings?"

Valentin was a bastard. My eyelid ticked. I smiled, brightly.

"So, you're not going to help me, then, brother?"

He went back on two legs again, rocking his chair, languidly. "I'm doing you a favor, page. Max doesn't tolerate nonsense. He's the most principled man I know. They don't call him Max, *The Incorruptible*, for nothing. He smells bullshit and he'll get a whiff of yours before you walk into the room. You're my friend and I barely tolerate you. He'll chew you up and spit you out."

We weren't friends. I would chew *Valentin* up and spit him out—he didn't even know—but I was here for a reason and it wasn't to play around with this man. A muscle in my jaw ticked. I looked at the other two men and tried an old, simple tactic: Wound his pride.

"Perhaps one of you two gentlemen can get me in to see Max since Valentin can't."

"I didn't say I *couldn't*..."

"I would only need a few minutes," I went on as if I couldn't hear the blond man at all. "Perhaps if one of you impress upon him the benefits of meeting someone who frequently visits the Palace. Explain the uniqueness of my position as a black enslaved man with close proximity to the King. Or whatever way you feel telling it will work. An enterprising man could figure out how to work this in their favor since it's apparent the ponytailed idiot here, can't."

Two sets of eyes quickly swung Valentin's way.

"What'd you call me, page?" Valentin's chair legs hit the ground.

"I called you a ponytailed idiot," I repeated, louder. "Useless. Cowardly. Forgettable. Without the ability to think broadly. With a ponytail." Someone snickered. "Don't take offense to the *idiot* part, Friend. It meant nothing. It's just a descriptor, *that's all*." Several men laughed and Valentin stood up and walked away, his face red, his back stiff. "Bonjour, Valentin," I called in a singsong tone, without turning around to watch him leave. He'd taken up enough of my time.

"He was your best chance," one of the men said. "We're not far enough up the chain to have access to Max."

But as we walked away, Sebastien said to me under his breath, "Don't worry. You pricked his ego. He'll get you that meeting if only to prove to you he can. Mark my words."

Though I had no meeting on my schedule in the near future I wasn't done that day.

The answer had come to me the night before. Lying in bed, I realized I was missing a solution that was right in front of me. For as long as I could remember, someone was regaling me with stories of my own deeds, whether true or not. Since I'd been coming to Paris I'd discovered pamphlets were being printed that detailed all these salacious rumors, and then some. The stark truth was, all of France would continue to write lies about me as long as there were pamphlets to be printed and money to be had from the selling of them.

But I could write, *too*. Very well, in fact. It was time for the turnabout to be had. I had these little feeders in me—a fact Salanave, the cook, had taught me as a child—that fed on the despair of others. Those feeders could make me strong. They could also make me financially comfortable if I used them correctly.

Of course, I didn't go into all of this with Sebastien, I simply told him I wanted to write. We were friends but sometimes I didn't know how he would feel about the less pleasant side of me. Véronique didn't like it much.

We walked through town to a small seating area behind a bar.

"He's the one to talk to." Sebastien pointed to a diminutive man sitting at a table nursing a small glass of dark liquid and staring intently at what appeared to be a little pad of paper. He wore a scarf wrapped around his head. Unlike Véronique's headwrap, his wasn't neat at all, with one end loose, so he kept flipping it with his arm. "His name's Jean-Paul Marat. He used to be a doctor but now he writes for one of the local presses. I hear he might be starting his own paper soon. He can help or introduce you to other printers."

"You're a wealth of information, Sebastien. I think I recognize him from Versailles." I was willing to take whatever opportunity revealed itself to me.

Sebastien hung behind, leaning against the corner of the building, his dark hooded eyes scoping the street while I made my way over to the man.

"Monsieur," I said to gain the man's attention. "I'd like to start writing and I hear you publish."

He glanced up with large, plaintive, watering eyes. He had one of those faces, full of lines and dents that people denote as being of "character". My approach stopped his writing, and he still held his pen, mid-stroke. He laid it down and squinted at me. "Have I met you before?"

"I feel I might have seen you at Versailles. My name is Zamor."

"Ah, the Palace... haven of the depraved. Yes, I used to visit occasionally in my work for the King's brother. I used to be a doctor."

"So, I've heard. But I'm told you're now one to speak to if I want to write."

"Well, depends...what is it you write?"

"Whatever pays."

"Ah, you mean the filth pamphlets, then. Sinning and romping and who's cheating whom. There's plenty return on that if you've got a clever tongue and a good supply of spite."

"Lucky me, I'm blessed with both. But I would need anonymity."

"Of course you would, everyone who deals in smut does! Well, Zamor, I won't help you publish trash. But when you decide to write something worth reading under your own name, I'll be here."

I was annoyed with his comment because I wanted to take him up on the offer. It was easy for him... to sit there and judge me so quickly.

"It's not as if we all have the freedom to write what we like," I said. "Some of us have practical needs."

"You look like your practical needs are met just fine," he said, eyeing me dubiously.

"Never mind, you don't understand, and you don't have to. Just give me the name of the smut peddler I should speak to. Can you introduce me to the publisher, or not?" I asked.

"All right, all right. No need to get in a snit. Come back Tuesday and I'll take you to him myself. He'll be pleased with me for bringing him new meat. Okay then, bonjour, monsieur."

I lingered, and then, when he looked up again, plunged ahead with what was on my mind. "I *can* write other things, too. I want to write other things, I just can't do it under my name yet. No one can know I'm writing."

"What's the point of writing if no one knows it's you? A writer should want to claim his words." His smile was crooked as if I were asinine. He would think so. People like him, arrogant and self-absorbed.

"The point is to express what needs release, whether or not you can put your name on it. Sometimes things need to be said, even before they can be said freely."

The following Tuesday this strange man did introduce me to a printer willing to take on my anonymous gossip. Learning that I had intimate access to the Palace of Versailles his eyes lit up with possibility and greed.

While Paul Marat had no interest in the salacious writing that was going to fund my future he was very interested in my political ramblings. One day, after reading some of the notes I carried around in my bag, he asked me to write pieces for him, here and there, and said that he would pay handsomely to publish under *his* name (funny how quickly his moral outrage changed when he read my words).

I agreed, immediately! I couldn't publish under my own name—yet—so it was the best of both worlds. I was free to express even my most radical views and take none of the barbs in response. And Paul seemed to love my boldest pieces. My fiery words brought life to his somber image—people began to think an inner fire burned inside of him. He soon earned respect for his new, fearless voice. I preened with every stroke to his ego.

I spent my evenings writing by candlelight, penning the most scandalous, de-basing fictional stories of my noble enemies at the Palace and the Chateau. I put poets to shame. The more scandalous the stories the more thrilled the publisher was with me because the more he could charge. He found a cartoonist to put ridiculous illustrations to my gossip and those rags were selling like the most delicious baguettes, for the consumption of the hungriest deviant minds. I collected that money, hiding it under my bedding along with the stolen silverware and small jewelry pilfered from the visiting nobles. Someday the writing of trash would fund my new life.

But when I wasn't writing trash I began to write words that mattered.

I bought a larger leather satchel to keep my writing and a hooded light wool cloak to help me walk around more freely in town without worrying about being recognized. Zamor, the writer and revolutionary, began to take shape.

3

Dear Citizen,

I became one of many hundreds of Parisian writers and journalists that led the increase in the volume of literature, the likes of which the world had never seen. Publications took over Paris.

I thought of my black-skinned brethren who weren't allowed to read. I thought about how, if we all could read, we could share words over the water. But that's precisely why they wouldn't allow enslaved people to read and write. If we could communicate with each other we could pool our resources and find a way to freedom. As long as white people held black people captive, they would never allow the freedom I had to speak my mind, even if I had to do it anonymously. The two went hand-in-hand. It was one reason I was so upset that LaFayette removed any reference to slavery.

All at once, it seemed the whole world was reading and writing and trading written works out in the open and underground. The general illiterate began to learn to read so they could partake in this explosive new "medium" of publications. For a society where the

*common man was barred from having any real knowledge of poli-
tics or economy, the thought that regular people might be privy to
this information opened the door to a long-simmering desire for the
commoners to have a say in what happened to them.*

*You understand, ours was an absolute monarchy where the King's
word was law. Opposition was treason. So, the very idea of this
type of open communication was tantamount to treason, itself.*

*The King's secret police and censors were still out in force, but they
couldn't keep up with the sheer volume and speed of print material.
The most critical words against Louis XVI were printed in secret;
printers would hide their machines during the day and uncover
them at night after all the curtains had been drawn and no one was
around. The underground presses were born.*

*The term, Freedom of the Press, was spreading through Paris. I
didn't realize it had already spread through other parts of Europe.
We Jacobins began to discuss how a free and just society demanded
the voice of even its least powerful. It was a tenant of Enlightenment philosophy, after all, that every man has a voice. We believed
that a society that can't raise its voice to power isn't just unjust. It's
unnatural.*

--Zamor, 1820

There was a single, tiny cake on the kitchen sideboard covered with whipped cream and topped with a burgundy cherry. It was an evening spent at the Chateau after I'd been spending a lot of time in Paris when I saw the pretty little cake. I stopped to look at it and, like magic, Salanave appeared. She always managed to catch me when I was about to eat something in the kitchen.

"No, you don't. That cake's for Véronique."

"Véronique, alone? Why?"

"The other laundresses have bandied together to shirk their duties to make her pick up the burden. And today they conveniently disappeared when a load came in from the new visitors. The laundry manager isn't about to punish them, she wants Véronique gone as much as they do..."

"Why?"

"Why what? Why does that group of reprobates hate being shamed by one little woman from Burgundy who actually takes pride in doing a good job? Or why does the laundry manager prefer the reprobates over Véronique, who already knows enough to do *her* job? They're jealous! They will work her to death if they can. The other servants look at her like she's their hero, but they aren't going to put themselves in a bad way by defending her. On top of that, Madame dropped off bolts of material for Véronique to make her some new clothes. Véronique is barely sleeping and doing all the sewing by hand, alone. She asked me if I could lock the clothes up in the locked pantry when she's not working on them because she's afraid one of the other workers will sabotage her work out of spite. And today, being her birthday, I just wanted to show her that someone around here notices her hard work."

Her birthday?

Salanave gave me a sneaky look while she wiped the counter. "Would you like to give it to her, petit?" It was her childhood name for me that she delivered with a smug look.

"What? No, you should give it to her. You made it for her."

"It could be our gift to her together. The two of you are friendly now, oui?"

"No, I don't want to give it to her," I said. She deflated a bit. "I mean, we are sort of friendly. But ... maybe, I'll give her a gift of my own."

The cook actually smiled. "You'll give her a gift? What will you give her? Tell me."

I shrugged. "I don't even know. I only found out two minutes ago,

Salanave. What do you give a woman like her? I have jewels, I just don't think she'd like stolen goods around her neck."

She clapped with a self-satisfied smirk on her face. "You are not so much of an idiot after all, I'm glad. Véronique is a working woman like me. What would be the point in jewels? You must give her something from your heart. Something special to you. Make her feel like she is important to you. Share a book of poems or a hair tie. Or help with her chores."

"Important," I scoffed, "who said anything about her being important?" I snuck a glance to make sure I was throwing her off the scent.

I would help Véronique with her chores any day of the week, doing so wouldn't be special.

I caught up with her that evening after dinner. Salanave was right, she looked exhausted.

"Oh, bonsoir, Zamor," she said, bustling by me.

"Do you have a moment? A few moments, I mean?"

She put a hand up to tuck a piece of her hair into her wrap. "Well, it's been a long day. And I'm mad at you. That stunt you pulled the other day with the coffee – who do you think has to clean that up? Took me an hour to get the stain out of that man's pants. *White* pants. I'm going to bed."

"I'm sorry, I didn't think about it. You should have saved it for me, I'd have done it. Look, I won't keep you long, I promise. Just a few minutes."

"Zamor," she drawled. "It's been a long day."

"I just need you to come with me to the Pavilion for a few minutes. Salanave told me today is your birthday."

"Salanave is wonderful. She made me a little cake just as if I were at home with my family. I ate it for dinner and washed it down with red wine. I shouldn't have had the wine, though, because now I'm sleepy and can't sew. And I'm a little drunk."

She was flushed, and the way she said it told me she hadn't been drunk enough in her life. She always surprised me with her lack of worldliness, and that was saying something since I'd been cloistered at royal court for most of my life. "I have a gift I'd like to give you," I said. "Nothing big, just a small thing."

She smirked, "...if that's how you want to refer to it, then. I admire your honesty." She laughed at her own joke under her hand. "I'm sorry, I couldn't help it, you led me right to it."

"I'm being serious," I whined. "While I'm certain the gift of me would be more than rewarding I meant something else. A real gift I would like to give you."

She stopped laughing and sobered a bit, looking at me in a new, vulnerable way that clenched my heart. "A gift ... for me?"

"Nothing much," I repeated. "It's at the Pavilion, all right?"

"Well, all right, then."

I put out my arm for her to loop hers into and, together, we walked over the grass and through the trees. It was still hot enough that without putting out much energy I managed to work up a light sheen of sweat. At least, I thought it was the heat. It might have been my nerves that rumbled more with each step.

Véronique was looking at the moon like she wanted to touch it. She stumbled but I pulled her up, quickly. My heart made another leap, feeling how she trusted me to keep her upright. A moment later when I stumbled, she did the same, her arm going around my waist, quickly. Laughing, we managed to make our way in the dark past the manicured grounds, through the trees, to the adjacent property. The next section had another majestic green platform flanked by walking paths on either side, leading up to the building built in the classic architectural style. The moon was so bright the white stone reflected its glow in the night. We slowed to a stop.

"Close your eyes, please," I said. She laughed awkwardly, but followed my instruction.

Leading her up the steps, past the columns, and into the ornate main room, the shuffle of our feet seemed the only sound in the world and I thought how nice that was. A world with just Véronique and me would be a splendid place, indeed.

I had set some candles on the mantle and on the surface of small tables against the walls throughout the main ballroom, sitting her down on a chair I had placed in the center of the room. Though I would have liked a fire in the fireplace it was too hot. As it was, earlier I had come and opened the tall, tall windows that went all the way to the ceiling. It was a hot night but there was a breeze coming in off the Seine River that caused those many yards of sheer white silk to float and flutter. Sitting there, a gentle whisper of a breeze must have brushed her cheek because her face relaxed and her normally furrowed brow smoothed out.

"I smell water," she said.

"We're next to the river."

"May I open my eyes now?"

"Just one moment." I ran over to retrieve her actual present. My violin leaned against the wall, and I picked it up along with the bow. Then, I remembered the bunch of flowers I had taken from the gardens of Versailles an hour ago, went to pick them up off a table, came back and laid the bouquet in her hands. She felt the stems, with her fingers, grasped the bouquet in her lap, then brought them to her nose and sighed with the sweetness.

"Lovely," she said.

By that time I had placed my instrument into position under my chin. "All right, you may open your eyes."

She did just that.

I couldn't have said what she thought, seeing me standing there, but she didn't laugh, which I felt was a good sign. Her eyes moved around the room, and with each thing she saw her face brightened even more.

In the candlelight, the mirrors, gilded walls and sconces, painted ceiling and long panels of silk curtains that fell from high ceilings down to the shiny black and white marbled checkered floors were aglow in gentle light. But those few candles reflected off the tall, tall mirrors and the glass doors, lighting up the space with, seemingly, a thousand candles. It was a beautiful place, of that there was no denying.

"I haven't had a chance to see the Pavilion from the inside," she breathed, looking around with large eyes. "It's so beautiful. You say there's water close by?"

"The Seine. You can't see it in the dark but during the day you can go out back and it is laid out there behind us."

"Really? I haven't been back there. I would like to see it in the daylight. Maybe the morning at first light when the world is still and quiet. Except for the machine, of course." The 'machine' being the Marly Machine, the giant wheel contraption that sat just north of us on the river and pumped water to the Chateau and the Palace. The sound of its gears moving against each other was horrible but after you were at the Chateau for more than a week you no longer even noticed it. Véronique looked enchanted with the idea of seeing the river, but my movement with the bow caught her attention. "What are you doing with that?"

I had to smile. "I told you, I'm going to give you your birthday present." At her doubtful look I added, "Don't laugh at me, I'm serious."

And I was. Suddenly I was nervous and my eyelid began to tic, I wanted so much to impress her. I felt as shaky as a child with their first instrument but when I closed my eyes, took a deep breath, and drew the bow across the strings ... the sound was smooth. The smoothness was the sign of a well-cared for machine and a bow that had grown accustomed to my hand after years of use.

I'd never played for anyone other than myself and some of the servants during the holidays, though I played well. Now, my playing echoed through the room like the only sound in the world. I started a solo piece by the black composer, Josephe Bologne. Though my eyes were mostly on the instrument, I glanced at Véronique from under hooded lids to see how my performance was being received. And to watch *her*.

She wore a dress the color of oatmeal and a headwrap of soft butter yellow. Her bodice was embellished with an insert of brilliant purple and golden embroidery, which I knew was her handiwork. Her skin in the candlelight was warm chestnuts. Her lips, full and slightly parted as if she were about to speak. Quiet throughout and as still as if in church. Her eyes turned glassy and her stillness was a meditation of the night.

I played with my eyes closed from then on, to concentrate. Only my bow pulling across the strings sounded in that space. The sound was like the sweetest sigh, carried by sweet melody to her ears. The music wrapped us both in gentle warmth.

But soon enough, the song was over. I ended on a long note and when I pulled the violin from under my chin and steeled myself to look at her, the flowers were lying in her lap and her hands were clasped in front of her, under her chin, as if she didn't know what to do with them. She smiled, her eyes still glassy.

"Was it all right? I can play something else...?"

"Yes, I'm all right. It's just that no one's ever done anything like that for me before. You play like the professional musicians I heard in the noblewoman Martin's salon. She is, was, the woman I worked for who sent me here. Occasionally she would let me listen in the salon. What you played was better than anything I've ever heard. It was magnificent, Zamor. Truly magnificent."

Heat suffused all of me and I was both relieved and embarrassed that I cared so much.

"It's not much of a gift but I tried to make it decent."

"It was beautiful. I can't even describe... it's the nicest gift anyone's ever given me in my life. Truly."

We fell into awkward silence. Without the music the Pavilion seemed large. Suddenly, my gift seemed highly personal and inti-mate. I put the violin and the bow down on the chair. Even in the low light I could see a blush on her cheeks. Standing up, she held the bouquet with one hand while smoothing her skirt with the other.

"Well, I'd better get back," she said.

"I can walk you," I said.

"No, that's okay. I know the way. Just walk opposite the river, right?"

"Straight ahead."

"Straight ahead, that's right. And you need to blow out all these candles before the place burns down."

"Of course," I said. I turned away, my head tucked in embarrassment as she gave me a quick, awkward smile while walking past.

Then, I heard her footsteps stop and come back. She stood before me, looking unsure, before finally saying, "From now on I don't believe I'll ever be able to see a candle and not think of you, Monsieur Louis-Benoit Zamor. Thank you for making this day so special." She then quickly leaned in and before I knew it had kissed my cheek and … lingered there for a moment so my hand lifted on its own accord—I suppose to cup her head or stroke her cheek—but she had already stepped away. By the time I realized what had happened she had picked up her skirts and left out the door.

I stood in the candlelight, replaying that kiss on the cheek. I'd been with plenty of women in my life but that kiss on the cheek was more intimate than any kiss I'd ever shared with anyone. That kiss, the scent of her when she leaned towards me, the softness of her lips …

I turned to stare at the empty doorway long after she left and felt that perhaps my world had changed. I'd always liked and wanted Véronique but this was something more. It was something I had never even dared to dream.

4

———

Dear Citizen,

The writer Jean-Paul Marat introduced Sebastien and me to his artist friend David, and the three of us took to sitting together when we were at the Jacobin Club. Sometimes Valentin would join us. We were an odd group, but our excitement was palpable. We could feel we were at the start of something fantastic. And there we were ... in the middle of a movement that would bring our country from the dark ages into the future.

--Zamor, 1820

I'd been neglecting my Chateau friend, stable hand Henri, and sought to rectify that by bringing him with me to Paris.

We walked into one of the taverns the Jacobins liked to frequent, with its back room full of activity. If Henri made a good impression, perhaps he could become a Jacobin, too. Then we'd have more in common.

All eyes in the room swung our way the second we entered, and it felt like the air dropped a good twenty degrees. Like an apparition,

Sebastien appeared in front of us as quiet as a wraith, his dark eyes focused on Henri.

"Sebastien, I want you to meet a friend of mine. This is Henri from the Chateau."

"Hello, Henri," Sebastien said, but he forgot to smile. Henri did plenty of smiling for both of them.

Henri had something of a nervous habit where his hand or fingers would tap against his leg, a table, a wall ... just a little thing you grew accustomed to very quickly. It was like the noise of the Marly Machine, after a while you didn't notice it at all. But I saw Sebastien's eyes swing to that hand tapping against Henri's thigh.

"Very happy to meet you, Sebastien. What a busy place this is." He looked around as if he'd never seen a tavern.

Henri was from Paris and despite his boyish looks, a boy from Paris couldn't afford to be boyish of mind. I felt sure his instincts on dealing with this indicated a less-than-warm welcome in a Paris tavern.

"Where are you from, Henri?" Sebastien said, voice gruff.

"Not too far from here. I live near the docks."

"And you work at the Chateau. Quite an accomplishment. Long way from home."

"It's not so far. Sometimes I stay there overnight when I don't need to return home."

"And why would you need to go home? Wife?"

"Papa, and siblings. My papa isn't healthy so I work to help with the household."

"Decent money working at the Chateau, I hear. Your family couldn't be too far in dire straits."

"It takes a bit of money, Monsieur, to keep six fed."

I looked at Henri's face. I thought there were four total in his family. Sebastien instantly noticed my look, his eyes quick and observant. "You didn't know that he's got six to support?" he asked me.

"I'm sure he told me," I said. "Sometimes I'm not a good listener."

"I might not have told him that," Henri said. "My other sister and her little one are living with us now."

"I see," I said. I didn't know what the big deal was, but Sebastien had gone from cold to downright frigid. Henri kept talking.

"I've worked with horses my entire life. I'm good at it. That's why I took the job at the Chateau."

Sebastien nodded.

"Come, let's grab a beer," I said, heading towards the bar. Henri started forward but Sebastien hung back. "Sebastien, don't tell me you don't want a drink. I'm buying."

"Maybe later," he said. "There's someone I need to speak with. You and Henri go on and enjoy your time."

I looked at him, not quite able to understand the tone in his voice. "Okay. Later then."

He turned and walked away to the far corner of the room. I watched as he spoke to one man in passing and then settled, alone at a table in the far corner, so hunched over as to hardly be seen. It was similar to the time before we knew each other. He had become a silent watcher again.

Henri and I sat at the bar and chatted about nothing. He spoke to everyone who sat near him until they got up and left. He tried to engage the bar owner. The owner was a Jacobin I knew in passing, and every time Henri spoke to him the owner would take a second to look at me as if needing my permission to reply before responding, all the while avoiding eye contact with my friend.

Henri addressed the owner of the bar. "This is a great place, how long have you had it?"

Eyes swung my way. Then, down to the bar he was wiping with a rag. "Not long. Couple of years perhaps."

"It's amazing in here," Henri said, looking and craning to see into the back doorway. "What's back there? Can I go back and see?"

The bar owner's eyes swung to me again. Then to the glasses he was putting out, his hands more impatient with every moment.

"No, that's private space, back there," I said.

"Ah," Henri said. "Have *you* been back there...?"

I ignored the question and asked the barkeep for Chartreuse, as if I had not heard Henri's question. When the vivid green drink was sat on the bar before me I was grateful to have something to take my attention. At some point it became so uncomfortable I decided to put an end to it. I lied and told Henri I had to meet someone in town.

"Are you okay to get back to Louveciennes on your own?" I asked Henri.

"Of course I am, Zamor, I'm not a baby. I go back and forth to Louveciennes every day all by myself. I walked and talked all on my own before I met you, you know."

There was a bite in his voice that was the first indication he felt the discomfort of the evening. But then he smiled. "It's been fun. I'll leave you now. Thank you for bringing me out."

After he left, I stood up with my drink to head back toward Sebastien, who was sitting like a giant bear, head back like he was asleep with a frown on his face.

"Sebastien, wh—"

He gave me a quick, pinched, look ...a shake of his head before gesturing to someone by the door, snapping and pointing his finger towards the street. The man stood, walked over to the front door and peered out. It seemed like every eye in the place watched him, without a sound. When he turned back and nodded, everyone relaxed and began talking again.

"What was that?" I asked.

Sebastien told me simply, "Your friend set off the alarms of every Jacobin in the place. Eyes everywhere and voice too loud. And that tapping with his hand and counting ... he's reckless, that one, or stupid. Either way, this isn't the place for either. Don't bring him back here."

"He taps, it's a nervous habit. Is that a crime?"

"I don't care about the tapping, I care about the curiosity. You were nervous, too, the first time you came out. But you were smart enough to be careful. He's from Paris, he said? He should know better than to behave that way in a tavern where everyone is on edge. The King is still sending around his Secret Police, picking people up off the street. Or, raiding taverns like this for no reason. We *have reason* to be raided so we are doubly sensitive. A Paris boy should know better. Come on, stop being mad and sit."

I was mad. I had brought Henri, expecting him to be treated as the friend he was.

A half-drunk Valentin sauntered from the back room with a full glass of something dark brown in his hand that sloshed when he tried to point at me with the same hand.

"Is the coast clear? Did you get rid of the Secret Police? I wasn't coming out while he was here. I should have known *you'd* bring the King's men down on us. Being a double-agent like you are. Had a few drinks back there. You, you clever bastard, you... playing both sides..."

Yes, he was drunk for sure.

"Did you see what they're building over at the Place de Louis the... the..." he struggled to remember.

Sebastien gave me a look and tapped his head, signifying the futility of Valentin's effort. "Fifteenth?"

"Yes!" Valentin pointed to him, splashing brandy on Sebastien's annoyed brow. "That's the one." The finger swung back my way. "Your papa!"

"Some people should be barred from drinking," I said.

"They're putting up a massive bridge. Have you seen it? Huge! Made with a thousand broken stones from the Bastille. I tried to get one of those stones but they had all been taken. Isn't that a crock? Me, who started the whole thing, and I couldn't even get a memento ."

Valentin had told everyone the storming of the Bastille was his idea. He'd worked so hard he'd eventually convinced himself, too. It didn't matter to me. I was happy not to be blamed for it.

"A bridge at the Place de Louis XV would cross the river and end up directly at the National Assembly headquarters," Sebastien said, with raised eyebrows. "The Assembly on one side and the statue of Louis XV on the other. That's poetic."

"A beautiful sign of future harmony," I said, raising my glass. "I'll drink to that." I took a sip of my drink. "I would like to be in the Assembly, one day, to see it in action."

Valentin was laying back in his chair and pulled on the length of his ponytail. "How about tomorrow?" Then he smiled.

--

Sebastien was right. Valentin loved to show his power.

The next day a sober Valentin ushered Sebastien, Paul, David, and me into the balcony of the National Assembly proceedings. Once there he explained how all the noble members of the new Assembly preferred to sit together while most of the bourgeois and sans-culottes did the same.

"See, those aristocrats are always on the right. The rest of us over there on the left."

"Do they have to sit separately like that?"

"Have to? No. But doesn't everybody want to be with their own?" Valentin replied.

"Bourgeoisie, sans-culottes, penniless nobles like me, and clergy who aren't very high on the ladder. The third estate representatives and we misfits, we are all on the left. The right and the left think much differently. They'll be starting soon so let's go on up above where we can hear and not be seen."

Over the next hour we witnessed the members of the assembly discussing politics and the world's events as if the men in that room were the world's deciders, while men stood along the hallways and around the doorways scribbling furiously.

"What happens here is written down and printed, spread in papers across France and even as far away as the Americas. Can you imagine, that power?" Valentin mumbled, as enraptured as I was.

My skin prickled with excitement. I immediately thought, if so many in the Assembly were Jacobins, how difficult could it be to get into the Assembly?

"I see the wheels turning in your head," Valentin whispered. "Only *citizens* are allowed to be representatives in the Assembly."

Just like fucking Valentin to throw a bucket of cold water on my excitement.

"Well then, maybe this Assembly needs to have more discussion on who should be a citizen," I grumbled.

Back at the Chateau, Henri found me and asked when he could go back into town with me.

I felt responsible for Henri's safety, now. All the men of the club weren't as upstanding as Sebastien so I knew I couldn't bring Henri back to the tavern.

"There's nothing more worth seeing, but maybe. Soon."

I was sure he could tell I was lying. He took it with the fatalism that lingered over him like a cloud. Henri would perpetually be a man-child; never surprised by life's difficulties yet childishly surprised by life's wonders.

5

Dear Citizen,

On any given day at the Palace of Versailles I was often the only person with black skin. I knew there were black nobles but I never met any at the Palace or the Chateau. Though visiting foreign leaders of many different colors came to meet the King, they were only there for a short time, and too far above my station to even speak with. Sometimes aristocrats would bring black servants who would also leave soon enough and I'd be alone again. After a lifetime of this, sometimes I craved proximity to brown-skinned people.

When Véronique arrived in 1788 she had certainly been welcomed for that reason. Even though we came from two different worlds I never had to explain to her what it was like moving through the world, on a daily basis. The insults and degradations. She was never shocked by the level of disrespect leveled at me. We understood those instances when our skin color resulted in uncomfortable circumstances. But she was only one person, and one with whom I tried to stay on my best behavior.

So it was that when black men were introduced to me, not as a
servant, but as a man meeting another, it was hugely special to me.
And I will forever be grateful to Jacques Brissot.

--Zamor, 1820

I was meeting Brissot at a tavern for an introduction and fully expected to meet a white member of the Society of the Friends of the Blacks. I never imagined he'd walk into the place with a black man by his side, let alone the black man it was. A gens du couleur—a person born of a white landowner and a black enslaved woman—the man walked in with the bearing of someone who has been loved. Something about the way he walked told me he was privileged.

But I knew his face from more than a decade past when he'd played the violin in the salons of the Palace of Versailles. It was the very man whose music I'd just played for Véronique just two weeks earlier, and now here he stood, as if I had summoned him. Many people at royal court whispered that he was the best violinist in all of France, maybe even all of Europe. Rumor had it that a rising musician named Mozart was taking bits of this man's music for his own.

When Jacques Brissot sought to introduce us I interrupted.

"—Excuse me, Monsieur. I know this man well," I said. "And I know your heart through your work. I had the pleasure of hearing your music when you played for the Queen at the Palace of Versailles just after you were robbed of the directorship of the Paris Opera. You are Josephe Bologne, Chavalier de St. Georges. A more horrendous crime was never beheld than when they denied you that post, but I'm grateful the crime brought you to the Palace so I could hear you play."

The premier post in question was as composer of the Paris Opera. He would have had the position were it not for the refusal of the two top opera singers to be directed by a "mulatto". Instead, Marie Antoinette invited him to play in her salons, a small token that didn't make up for the loss of the opportunity to be the first black man to conduct an opera house of its caliber. He might have been known by all the world. Instead, he had to settle for being known by the guests of the salons at Versailles during the lifetime of the Queen. And known by me.

"Your music inspired me, monsieur to teach myself. I hounded my childhood instructor, Frederick Barnier, to find me an instrument, which he did by scouring the back of the royal opera stage. He found the instrument and some of your music. And though I made mistakes reading music, I was excellent at remembering sound."

"I remember the impression of a young black man who, like smoke, would disappear once any attention was directed towards him. You were very young then, correct?" Josephe Bologne inquired.

"Fourteen or fifteen, before I moved to the Chateau de Louveciennes."

"Are you the infamous Zamor? The du Barry page everyone talks about? It's thrilling to meet such a well-known person as yourself. And now that I know you also have an excellent ear, your praise almost makes up for having lost the position."

"I sincerely doubt that." I felt a blush moving over my cheeks. "I taught myself to play your music the best I could," I added, quickly, like an anxious boy fawning over a crush. "I mean, I'm not ... anywhere near as good as you, of course. Many of the written sheets were too advanced for me so I've mostly been going by memory, and when I started I didn't even know how to read music but I learned enough to get by. And then I tried with my clumsy hands to re-create the sound."

"I'm sure your re-creation did the music great justice."

"Not at all," I said. "But it was worth it to be able to preface every little concert I gave in the servant's quarters for two years with 'inspired by the estimable Chavalier de St. Georges'." The two men laughed.

"Yes, music does inspire. It will always be my first love but we all must keep ourselves fed, oui?"

"Every fox has to survive its own hunt ... and all that," I agreed.

"Yes, exactly."

Brissot supplied, "Josephe was born in Guadaloupe. Now he's a member of the Society of the Friends of the Blacks, but he's also been asked by the Assembly to lead a troop of black soldiers called the *Légion Nationale des Américains & du Midi*." He clapped Josephe on the back.

"A troop of black men?" I asked, wonder filling my brain. "Fighting for France?" If I had a thousand words I couldn't adequately describe how much I wanted, at that moment, to join his army. I opened my mouth to volunteer and then remembered my crooked back and creaky knees. But my arms were strong. My brain was strong.

"We fight for our country. And I will always fight for the rights of gens du couleur. We have the support of the National Assembly as part of the republican army," he continued. "The support of the new Assembly is significant. And with Brissot here, championing for abolition, we'll make headway soon, I'm sure."

"Do you really think so?" I asked, eagerly.

White people said a lot of words. I liked Brissot but his words and actions didn't seem to match up. To be able to speak to the Chevalier was a different thing. I wanted to hear affirmation from a person with some stake in the matter. He looked at me, soberly, I believe understanding my need.

"Truly, I do. Here's my second in command, now. Thomas…"

Josephe Bologne raised his glass. Brissot and I followed his eyes to another black man walking towards us. This second man was as tall and as handsome as Josephe, with a bushy black mustache over his lip. Josephe stood to greet the man, who clasped his hand warmly and came to sit.

"Brissot, you know Thomas but our guest may not. Thomas-Alexandre Davy de la Pailleterie, this is Zamor. I'm sorry, Zamor, I didn't catch your surname?"

I stood, "I'm called Louis-Benoit Zamor."

"And I'm Thomas Dumas, which is fine," the newcomer said.

"Then, Thomas Dumas, it is. It's a pleasure." I shook the man's hand and we all sat. I suddenly felt out of place among the two gens du couleur who would lead an army. My appreciation of what they wanted to do was bittersweet.

Thomas signaled to the server for a drink.

"Thomas's roots are also in the colonies, " Josephe said. "We met some years ago when I taught him to fence like a proper gentleman. Before that, he was swiping his sword left and right like a crazy man hoping to hit something."

The three of them burst into laughter and Dumas took the teasing in stride. He winked at me.

"Josephe likes to think he's the best at everything," Dumas said. "But I remind him, so what if you're a master fencer and a master composer and master horseman ... *why, by all that's holy,* are you so bad at chess?" Dumas said. He seemed a jovial man and I liked him immediately.

"Well, maybe I'm not a master of everything, after all," Josephe smiled, graciously. "But I look forward to showing the world how well we can represent France. Making this country stand up and see us for our value to society."

I heard hope in his simple statement. I heard in this man, this son of noble birth, a desire for recognition similar to my own.

"Oh, they see our value," I said. "As slaves contributing to the economy."

Thomas asked, "Zamor, were you born on the mainland or did you come after your birth, as we did?"

"I was born in India."

That took them all by surprise. "India? There are Africans in India?" Josephe asked.

"There are. My parents and their parents. As a child in a community of black people, I had no idea how much of a minority we were. Unfortunately, the very people who would have explained it were stripped from me when I was very young. Or, rather, I was stripped from them."

"I'm sorry to hear that, Zamor. We, both of us, know what it's like to be separated from your mother. There's no pain like it. But tell us, what are your plans for the near future and how did you meet this man?" He gestured toward Brissot, who answered.

"If I may? His plans are to further the republic. Zamor is a Jacobin," Brissot said on a smile, as if hearing the news would come as a surprise.

"A Jacobin?" Josephe looked surprised. "But aren't you the royal page?"

"I used to be. Now I'm just the page of Madame Jeanne du Barry."

Thomas looked surprised. "Do you still frequent the Palace? How do you manage to be on good terms with the royal family *and* be a Jacobin?" All three looked at me, curiously.

I said, honestly, "Why, very carefully, of course."

I was serious, but the three of them laughed boisterously until my obvious discomfort caused their mirth to die down.

"We mean no disrespect, Zamor," Josephe said. "But you speak so plainly about activity that could put you in peril."

"Perhaps, but sometimes you have to do something that might put you in peril to improve your life, don't you? If all I have is my intellect and my voice, I will give both to the new republic and the future of black people."

"A natural orator! I like him," Thomas said to Brissot. "His courage is twice the size of him!"

"You call it courage, but those who know me call it other things. Audacity, arrogance, insufferable inability to shut up..."

"Would you want to fight with us?" Josephe asked. "Do you have any combat experience? Can you handle a gun?"

"I've never held one," I admitted, feeling thrilled to have been asked. "As you can see, I'm not physically impressive but what I lack in body strength I make up for in intelligence. Do you think you might take me in your black army?"

"We can always use men willing to fight. You can be taught to shoot and wield a sword. How about we teach you, Josephe and I? While you consider."

6

———

I convinced Véronique to take a short break with me. She'd been walking around like she was partially dead, so obsessed with making nice clothes for Madame it looked like she'd lost some weight. I thought if I could get her to take a little break both her mind and body would be the better for it. I used Rousseau to occupy her mind.

We were at my favorite spot behind my favorite tree on the far end of the property. Véronique lay on her stomach reading *The Social Contract* while I ate an apple. Sheltered from the heat and in our own little world.

"So this Rousseau talks of men, men, and more men. The nature of man, the desires of man ... blah blah." She twisted around to look at me. "In Rousseau's world, are there no women?"

I shrugged, "Of course, but..."

She sat up. "I know. We don't figure much in his world, do we? We never figure much at all to men until they need something. But the world wouldn't turn if we weren't holding onto the spokes and leaning into the wheel. Show me a philosopher that respects women and I'll consider giving him the time of day." She tossed the book onto the blanket and reached for the apple that I handed to her, taking a bite. I was glad she was eating.

"But you can't look at it like that," I said. "You can't throw away everything he says because one aspect of his thinking is flawed on a particular component. You have to look at the greater good."

"Ah, so he *does* speak of women. I'm guessing not in a very complimentary manner, or you would tell me what he says. These male philosophers are all the same. Meanwhile, women are more frustrated every day, trying to make food out of little more than stones and water. Feeling the stress of daily life more than men ever will."

"But this is just a start. He's come the closest of any philosopher I've read to understanding how I feel. For that, he has my respect."

"What's in that satchel you carry around all the time?"

So, she'd been watching me, too.

"Just my papers. I like to jot down ideas. My own thoughts."

"Like Rousseau jotted his?"

I blushed. "Something like that."

"And what do you do with your thoughts?"

"They're just notes. Usually, I end up tossing them into the fire to keep my room warm. There's really nothing to do with them. And I don't want anyone finding them so I burn them. Eventually."

She said nothing but quickly reached over and plunged her hand into my satchel, pulling out a page

"Véronique...!"

She read a bit from the page and then looked up at me. "*L'Ami du Peuple*," she read. "Why does Monsieur Jean-Paul Marat sound like you?"

"You're mistaken," I said, taking it back and shoving it into my bag.

A bird was inching closer to the torn baguette that lay on the blanket. She pinched some of the bread and tossed it, sending the bird diving for it. "Is this what you talk about with your friends in town? All that time you spend with them is to talk about politics? What about other things?"

"Other things like what?"

"Life? Happiness? The future? Family? The things people talk about?"

I was quiet.

"I see. You go there for a reason, and it is not to make friends."

"I have a friend," I said. "His name is Sebastien. And ... there is Paul."

"The publisher of the *L'Ami du Peuple*, that Paul? Are Sebastien and Paul readers of Rousseau?"

I was quiet and she laughed, softly.

"I tell you I'm fine and you convince me to come out here and eat an apple and sit around doing nothing when you know how busy I am," she said.

"You can't just work your fingers to the bone, you'll make yourself sick."

"Meanwhile, you spend every waking moment either working for Madame or running around talking politics. Reading politics. Writing politics. Nothing about what you do is good for your health. You have to have people who know you and love what you love beyond the popular writer of the day."

"When I earn my freedom I'll have all the time in the world to make friends and do things that are good for my health."

"You say "when" and not "if" as if you know it will happen. Like you're certain of it. Is it the people in Paris? I hear they're being called revolutionists, against the monarchy. Have you been working with them to secure your freedom?" She was sharp like a tack.

I had to respond. "Now that you're here, living in the Louvecienne bubble, you can't see what's going on out in the world. You should come into town with me one night. Just to get out of the house."

"When? I'm spending every waking minute sewing." She held out her hands. I saw that they were red and chapped, her fingers blistered and cut.

"Your hands," I said as I took one gently.

She started to pull it back. "I know, they're hideous."

"No, they're strong. Strength is beautiful. But you need to take breaks or you'll drop. I'm sorry now that I pointed Madame in your direction."

She hesitated a moment, as if trying to decide if she should pull her hand away. It probably wasn't proper for her to let me hold it, but she let it remain in mine. I hid a smile, the pleasure flowing through me.

"Don't be sorry," she continued. "This is the chance I've been waiting for all my life. The chance to sell my dresses is truly the only reason I came here in the first place. Sure, I wanted to learn how to run an aristocratic household but only so that I could be paid more and afford to be a master seamstress on my own. And I wanted to gain the skills and the reputation to work for myself. The fabric Madame buys, I've never touched anything so fine in my life. Now I want to work with it more and more. French silk is heaven. Satins and laces and velvet ... it's a dream come true." The fire in her eyes was back and I was glad that it was still there under the layers of weariness.

"The tailors and their associations will come after you if they find out."

"Yes, I know. There are lots of things women aren't legally allowed to do, but we do them, anyway. I may never have a sign hanging over my door for customers, I can still do it, discreetly."

I smiled at her, and she returned it. "I'm glad to be here to see your dream come true," I said. She finally pulled her hand away and I fought the urge to grab it back. I didn't want to be greedy.

She started a yawn, talking through it. "But I would like to get out of here once or twice. Salanave and I go out to church sometimes, but... I'll go to Paris with you for an hour or two, sometime. In a couple weeks after I finish the dress I'm working on. But you have to promise we won't spend the entire time talking about Rousseau."

I perked up. "Really? You'll go out with me? To Paris."

"If you meant it when you asked me, that is?"

"All right! I can talk about other things. If you want. But you should know, outside of the Chateau they're doing a lot of talking about the state of things."

"I know." Her brow furrowed. "And those people you meet in Paris are the ones everyone says is trying to change the government, aren't they?"

"You can't ask me that. You can never say what you just said to me out loud again. You can never suggest to anyone that I'm doing *anything*. Promise me."

She gave me one of those bunched-lipped serious looks, putting a line on the smooth skin of her brow. "Should I be worried?"

"No, you don't need to worry at all. But if anyone tells Madame ... let's just say she won't let me go to Paris. Promise me you won't say anything to anyone."

"No one will hear a thing from me. It's tiring, isn't it?"

"What?"

"Being a reactionary. All the time, reacting to the world as it changes, with no consideration of the least among it. But I have hope. As long as I'm alive I have hope for all of us. And for you. I'll hold it for you even if you have none for yourself."

She stood up and touched my hair briefly before walking back toward the house.

"I have hope!" I yelled to her, but she kept walking. I said, softly, "And you are not the least among it."

7

"Man's first law is to watch over his own preservation; his first care he owes to himself; and as soon as he reaches the age of reason, he becomes the only judge of the best means to preserve himself; he becomes his own master."

--Jean Jacques Rousseau

September, 1789

I was in the back room of a tavern. Sebastien couldn't come out and I wasn't going to spend more money to buy his time. Besides, I needed to think about where I would take Véronique.

I was sipping my shockingly green Chartreuse liqueur at a little table by the fire, jotting down ideas—would she like the theatre? The Opera Garnier?—when a shadow fell over me. Glancing up I saw Valentin standing next to a man I'd seen that day at National Assembly. Valentin motioned the stranger to the seat opposite me.

"Zamor, this is Maximilien Robespierre. I told him about your lively conversations with us over the last few months and that you wanted to meet him. He was gracious enough to allow a few minutes."

Maximilian Robespierre! Sebastien was right about the power of Valentin's ego.

"Bonsoir, Monsieur Robespierre," I said, shuffling my papers into my satchel to clear the table. I raised one hand and a server rushed over with a drink for the man without him even ordering. I looked around and noticed everyone's eyes on us.

His eyes were keen and perceptive. He was a small man, all sharp angles and jerky movement. But quiet. Very, very quiet.

"Max is fine. Valentin," the man nearly mumbled. "Give Monsieur Zamor and me a chance to speak, privately."

Valentin looked like he wanted to stay but at one look from Max, he walked away, taking a seat next to the door.

For a long moment, the man said nothing. I started to become uncomfortable but I knew this game. He was testing me. However, I was as used to those games as I was to breathing. We sat in silence until, finally, he broke it with a blunt question.

"Was the storming of the Bastille your idea, Monsieur Zamor?"

I choked a little on my drink. "Just Zamor is fine. Why, what did Valentin tell you?"

"That it was his idea, of course. He's been spreading that lie all over town. Which is, I believe, why he sits over there watching us and hoping we're not discussing this very thing." Robespierre raised his glass to Valentin, who nodded, his expression highly uncomfortable. "He's been talking about doing something spectacular for the better part of three years. It wasn't until the royal page appeared that something actually happened."

I shrugged.

"It was a brilliant strike at his Royal Highness's dignity and a wound to his pride to see just how quickly people rallied to the side of the revolutionaries. And it gave the people something to root for. Valentin doesn't have the thought process to come up with that. He doesn't truly understand the sans-culottes, him born a nobleman."

"I only had a very basic idea that any strike on the Bastille would make a statement, I never imagined the rest. I would have done it differently to avoid bloodshed. I'm a simple enslaved man, I don't know these things."

"Ah, I see. Play the simpleton and no one will see you? I suppose that's how you've survived your circumstance. I didn't know you were still enslaved. There aren't supposed to be slaves on the mainland, it's a violation of French law."

"Yes, well, the King can't break a law against himself. There's no proof that I'm a slave and yet I'm on no registry of free men and I'm no citizen. So where do I stand? What rights do I have even over my own person? And what is that if not slavery?"

"So here you sit, owned by the King."

"Madame du Barry."

"Same thing. But clever man, you've managed to get yourself an introduction to a leader of the Jacobins in a very short amount of time. Let's cut to the chase: I can get you onto the registry of free men. Perhaps, even citizenship. That's what you want, isn't it?"

That was exactly what I wanted! I flushed from the sound of those words and licked my lips as my heart began galloping in my chest. "*...And* the abolition of slavery for all black-skinned French people? I've been talking to Jacobins for months but it seems the thing I want most isn't a priority."

"Yet. Not a priority *yet*."

"'*Yet*' is when we need it, Monsieur."

"*Never* is when you'll get it if you're not in the circles that are creating the laws for our new constitutional monarchy. Someday, I'll be in charge of the Jacobins, this I vow. Slavery is a travesty and a blight on our country and all who participate in it. But most French people don't care so long as we have sugar for our tea and spirits to warm us in the winter. But you know how terrible it is, don't you? You must have been very young when you were taken."

He wasn't going to make me into a mass of slobbering tears to maneuver me into doing what he wanted. I changed the subject. "What do you do for a living, might I ask?"

A small quirk of his lips told me that he'd caught my not-so-subtle shift. "I'm an avocat." A lawyer. "Does it matter?"

"It makes sense. With all due respect, you're asking me a lot of questions but I've yet to hear what you are prepared to do. I'm a selfish man, I want freedom now. I want to tell my children about the ancient history of slavery and a time they'll never know as free citizens. I want to die having been integral to the cause of freeing my brethren. I want to be a voice as important to the French people as Rousseau or Voltaire. I want to speak before the National Assembly and be heard, for once in my life. Can you give me that?"

"Can I give you an idyllic life? Hero worship? I would like that life myself. No, I can't promise that, but I can get *your* freedom. Eventually."

Eventually? My hopes fell. This was just the type of word games I'd heard all my life. At my expression, he went on as if I weren't hearing him properly.

"Don't be a fool, page, how long will freedom take *without* the support of the Jacobins? Change is coming. The Americans are establishing themselves as a king-less society as we speak, bound only by a constitution and the will of the people. They are the first to try this radical experience and damned if they aren't succeeding. France needs to relate to them in the new ways, not the old. We can't simply marry families together to broker peace treaties – they have no royal family to marry! The world is fast becoming a new place and up to now we've had both feet firmly planted in the past. We stay still at our own peril. *You* stay still at your own peril."

"You don't need to convince me on the value of a constitution, I think it's an excellent idea."

"And we're behind. England switched to a constitutional monarchy long ago. Even though we're going broke because we just paid for the United States to win their war against England, the United States has very little allegiance to us. We are a kingdom stuck in the past. We need to keep up with modern times! With Louis XVI representing us and a constitution governing us, we will take back our power on the world's stage. We'll be able to borrow the money we need to pay our debts at a reasonable rate once the world sees we have a stable government. We'll finally start taxing nobility and the church. We'll be able to feed our people, and our people will be able to vote and have a say in how our government runs. And after a while we'll no longer need to rely so heavily on slave labor."

"What you say would take years. A lifetime."

"Then you change it, Louis-Benoit. Become an active participant in this new movement."

"I can't be in the Assembly if I'm not a citizen."

"Your single-minded focus on citizenship fails you. Let me tell you something," he leaned toward me and poked the table with his finger to make his next point. "You need to prove your dedication to this movement to earn trust. You either have people supporting you or you're just one lone black man trying to survive in a world that doesn't want or need you. You have no power here, page."

"I've been taking care of myself my whole life, no matter who wants or needs me. I've been struggling to survive my own hunt and now you tell me I'm supposed to jump through *more* hoops before we can even begin the conversation of my freedom?"

"I don't take time out of my day to visit every new Jacobin. I truly wanted to meet a man who lives in the intersection of so many aspects of our society. We need people like you. But we need to know you are loyal to us, first. You are still living the life of a royal, after all. It's fair for us to want certainty of where you stand before we put our necks on the line."

He was acting like he was some low-level republican who could somehow be hurt by anything I could do. "Your neck? You're the leader of the Jacobins, you take no risk but ask me to throw myself off a cliff with no guarantee you'll be there to catch me," I said. "All I have done so far, I've put myself in harm's way with no return. And you still want more."

"What kind of future will you have without the new republic fighting for you? Our kings have hobbled the future of even free blacks on the mainland: no marriage of free blacks to enslaved blacks. Children of enslaved and free blacks deemed enslaved at birth. No citizenship. Restricted from owning property. Restricted from marriage with whites. Should I go on? Any risk you took by becoming a Jacobin is only for your own good, not for the general good of the republic."

"My own good as a man *is the same* as the general good of the republic. Every individual in this society is a natural part of the general good of the republic."

"Ah, now you will throw Rousseau at me," he smiled. "The fact remains that you need us more than we need you, and you have a limited period of time to be of use. The age of absolute rule by kings is dying and the new republic doesn't need royal pages. Where does that leave you? Some nobles have been leaving the country since the storming of the Bastille. They detest the National Assembly and refuse to answer to it. If your Madame leaves, will she take you with her?"

Whenever Jeanne du Barry left France she did it without me, every time. I never minded the break from her, but I also never asked myself why? He pressed on as if he could sense my weakness in this area.

"More importantly, if she *does* leave and take you with her, you'll not find a network like the Jacobin Club anywhere. You'd have to start from scratch with nothing and no one."

"I understand my situation."

"Do you?"

"You clearly have the upper hand. You're the leader of the Jacobins and I'm just a—

—a simple man, I know." He gave a mirthless smile. "There's talk of blacks planning revolts in the Americas. Well, to be fair, there've been small revolts for years but the chatter is different now. More ominous. And now it's not just the slaves, I hear even the gens du couleurs are becoming more radical every day. France is afraid of radical black people, no matter if they're full or half-black, it's all the same to white French people. All are threats. Royalists and republicans alike get nervous when there's talk of revolt. With things the way they are, it might not be practical to free all slaves at this moment. But you're one person on the mainland and you are ... *safe.* No one's afraid of you."

"Maybe they should be," I snapped, my ego wounded.

"Yes, maybe. With easy access to the King, you could be our secret weapon. It's helpful for us to know what he's thinking, and you can find out. You can be our eyes and ears at the Palace. You can also be our voice to plant information into the King's ear. I hear you've been doing it for the Queen and Madame du Barry for years. And, speaking of Madame du Barry..."

"...one woman with no power."

"Who's chosen to continue her rivalry with the Queen by hosting foreign dignitaries and entertaining the wealthiest men in Europe. She's simply an extension of the royal court—a misbehaving daughter the monarch has sent to her room for talking back to her mother—still part of the family all the same. It's helpful for us to know who comes through the Chateau and what's being said, as much as at the Palace." He leaned closer. "We're getting closer to what you want, Zamor. Work for me and we'll abolish slavery together for the next generation. Or don't, and the matter will fall to the bottom of *everyone's* list. Brissot and his Society members are few compared to the numbers of slave-owning colonists in the Assembly. You don't have the numbers for your cause, friend. You need the might. You need the alliance of those in power. *You need a mountain.* Imagine, with your unique way of looking at the world and my intelligence and power, what we could do together."

I thought I could contribute my intelligence, too, but this man obviously thought he was the more intelligent between us. And maybe he was, because he was convincing me to be his stooge. He was right. If the determination of slavery were left to majority rule, enslaved people would never be free.

A woman came through with a bottle to refill my glass with the shocking green liquid. Robespierre watched, bemused.

"I want my emancipation, first. Before anything," I said.

"No." He sat back, crossing one hand over the other, resolutely. "Quid pro quo. What can you give me in good faith to speed your cause along, friend, to earn your emancipation?"

I felt a flash of discomfort; usually I was the one setting the terms for quid pro quo. What I wanted was right, it seemed wrong I should have to give this man something to get him to give it. It hardly seemed like a fair trade. He wasn't as incorruptible as his reputation would have us believe.

I didn't trust him, but I was finally on the threshold of getting what I wanted. He wasn't my friend but he could be my ally. I leaned in to speak so as not to be overheard and he mirrored my movement to listen.

"There are silos of finely milled wheat at the palace for the pleasure of the King and Queen," I said. He gave me a look bordering on anger. I went on, quickly. "If the sans-culottes knew *how much* soft bread is readily and easily available to the royals while they stand in line for hours hoping to get a little rough rye to bake with and to sell —at exorbitant prices—they might be compelled to join the Jacobin cause."

"I don't think reminding the common people that their King eats well is enough to earn their favor."

"No, no, not on its face. But there's what you know and what you *feel*. It's one thing for a king to live in luxury but it's another to rub it in his subjects' faces. And still another for a king to actively engage in harming his own people."

"The average sans-culottes will tell you our King is a good man. They would never believe he's harming them on purpose."

"Well," I hesitated. "Perhaps they haven't made the connection between what he's doing and how they feel. First, Louis XV commissions the most expensive necklace in the world and the French people end up paying for it. Then, the Queen damages the French fabric industry by openly flaunting cotton textiles over French silk."

I knew from Madame that the Queen had posed for a portrait in her cotton undergarments like "a treasonous Austrian slut". Not only was the intimacy of the portrait a public disgrace, by forsaking French silk for cotton—the textile produced by France's mortal enemy, England—the Queen had further damaged the French economy. Of course, no one even mentioned the gross abuse and mistreatment of my fellow colonized Indians forced by England to create the beautiful cotton prints that were all the rage in England (that piece was of little consequence).

Madame had relayed news of Marie Antoinette's error with smugness masked by fake compassion as she pointed out that the Queen wasn't French and didn't know any better. And now, I saw Max's eyelids flutter as he made the connection.

"These are all things people know," he said, but not so surely this time.

"But are they looking at everything together?" I sipped my Chartreuse as the puzzle pieces started snapping into place in my own head.

"People could be easily persuaded to remember the cotton situation and connect it to the royal hoarding of grain. Another example of how the royals *don't care* about how their actions impact common folk. It's like a line I read about a princess who was told her people were starving and replied 'let them eat *brioche*' instead, as if being clever. I can't even remember who said such a vile thing but it seems the sentiment of our royals right now. That they intentionally misconstrue the situation so they can continue about their business and feign innocence. Just like when the King locked the Third Estate out of its meeting, claiming to have misread the date. '... Oh, did I miss a meeting? So sorry!' But he wasn't. The people know that now because the Third Estate representatives were there and felt the direct sting of being dismissed! Ignored! Hearing the excuse is one thing. Actually having a personal experience with the reality is another."

I took a sip, remembering that day when I led the Third Estate to the Tennis Court – how hurt and angry they felt at being made a fool of by the king they loved. Realizing they'd been had.

Robespierre's face showed dawning understanding and he nodded, as if thinking. I continued.

"So yes, the King pretends to understand when people are begging for food and he even sounds sympathetic. But the King and Queen go home to finely milled bread, overflowing. Morning, noon and night, there's always bread at the Palace of Versailles. Even I go into that kitchen and take what I want because there's so much, they don't even notice. They toss the left-over crusts of bread to the animals in the pens, did you know that? So does Madame du Barry. Sometimes the servants will smuggle food out to people on the outside who need it, but—as you know—taking from the Palace is considered theft and punishable." I could honestly say, I was likely the only person who could do it openly and get away with it.

I shook my head and mumbled my inner thoughts aloud. "Most commoners have never even seen the Palace—they can't even imagine the excess of the royal court." A thought came to me, quickly. "And we severely underestimate the impact our present situation has on women, in particular. Those mothers who can't feed their babies, they're most affected by this poor economy. If they saw what goes on at royal court on a daily basis with the steady supply of meat and several courses for *each* meal of the day...?" I snorted with a laugh at seeing that play out in my head.

"Where did these ideas come from? How long have you been thinking about this?"

"Ideas? No, it was just something that popped into my head just now." I shook my head. That was true, though I'd been inspired by the comment of a particular woman. Robespierre's face was impassive but then he leaned away, our quiet circle broken, nodded and stood up, putting his hat back on his head.

"This has been a pleasant meeting," he said. "You know what I want. I trust soon you will be a Jacobin, not just in name, but in spirit. And will do what's right."

My head snapped up as quickly as my annoyance. "I've just given you the good faith gesture you requested. I'm more than happy to continue to help you ... as a free citizen, Monsieur."

He spared me one last look and then walked out, his boots barely making noise on the stone floor. Valentin, who had been watching us, glanced at me and followed Robespierre out. Almost immediately, all eyes were on me.

8

————————

I decided to make a trip to the Palace to begin gathering information for future quid pro quo. I was walking through Versailles one day, scoping it out for information and gossip, when I passed the King's study, two guards outside the open door.

I avoided the King as best I could and usually when I passed his office the doors were closed. Outside his office, I often got the best gossip from the servants and guards, who had to remain close to him. But one day I wasn't paying attention and didn't notice his door was open until I heard his voice bellowing into the hall.

"Louis-Benoit!" he called to me. From within the room, I was surprised to see the King's face as he looked up at me from an odd position. In the middle of the room, he was lying on his stomach on an elevated platform with his neck resting in a curved wooden brace of some sort, which was sitting on a highchair in front of him.

It was an odd, undignified position to see him in but now I was caught.

"Come in, come in!" he demanded.

I nodded and walked into the room and was further surprised to find seven or eight men standing around, all of them with varying degrees of excitement on their faces as they watched the King where he lay, his coat taken off and his neck embraced in a satin-lined fitting. The King looked the most exuberant. I gave a quick bow to the room.

"Zamor used to join my grandfather to discuss science. Both of them spending hours looking at clocks and watches and talking about the stars."

"Is it possible that you joined them, as well, Your Majesty?" one of the men asked, causing gentle laughter that thrilled the king. He was always pleased when people around him laughed. "Clocks are amazing things but this may be even more so. It's the base of a machine we're making, Zamor. I tell you, gentlemen, this cradle is so comfortable I could fall asleep."

I still didn't understand what it was but then a man stepped to me from the side, gesturing toward a table. "This is the prototype of a new device for humane execution. The King has graciously allowed us to size the foundation of it based upon his neck but this is what it will look like when fully complete."

A little toy-like contraption sat on the table. I recognized the bottom part of it as a tiny version of the brace the king was lying in, however, with the toy, the sides of it were tall with a bracket that had a half-moon shape cut out that appeared to be the top half of what the King lounged in, keeping the neck in place, A second bracket was across the top, joining the two side beams like a frame, only it held a little straight blade that appeared suspended in place by a string secured on the side.

"Here is how it will work," the man said. He took a grape from a little dish of the fruit nearby and placed it in the rounded groove that simulated what the King's head lay in. "This is a little misleading because the head won't be in the brace, only the neck. And then this will be let go and..." he loosened the string and the blade came down quickly to slice through the grape after a little resistance.

"How did you get it to go so fast?" I asked.

"I added a little weight to the back of it, here, look." Behind it was affixed what looked like a piece of lead.

"What do you think, Zamor? Impressive, right?" The King had

exited the contraption and was standing next to me, looking at the little model. He tugged on the string a couple of times, enjoying the way the little blade moved. It was a cute toy. "I understand they've used a machine like this in other European countries but these two men here have made our French version even better. I hired them after I heard Doctor Guillotin report on the complaints in the National Assembly about executions. Apparently, people no longer enjoy watching criminals being broken on the wheel, anymore."

Another man spoke up. "And the decapitations are unpredictable. Sometimes Sanson can get them done with one swing of the axe but not always. Watching him have to hack away at someone's neck can be disconcerting. And the poor don't like the hangings or the quartering. They resent not being able to afford to buy a quick death."

"What do you mean, buy a quick death?" I asked.

"You know," the King said to me. "There's no incentive for it to go quickly unless one pays. It's like buying a cow. You pay little for a sick, spindly one and you get weak, rancid milk. If you're willing to pay for a prime one, you get excellent milk. I mean, I imagine it takes work to take a head off in one swing; no wonder it takes a couple of tries. If an executioner is expected to make death quick and painless then someone must pay for that service. It's only fair."

His face was a mask of innocence as he said it and I realized he truly saw nothing wrong in a person having to pay for a quick execution.

The King brightened, getting back to the subject at hand. "The doctor here invented this."

The man who'd demonstrated the contraption didn't seem to take much pride it this. "It's to be a quicker death. A more humane death, if death must be had. I would prefer we had no death decree—"

"—Ah," the King wagged his finger at the man. "We won't go over that point again. There must be the punishment of death for those tried and convicted, otherwise there would be pandemonium. No one would fear *anything*. Doctor Guillotin here and his friends in the Assembly demand humane deaths, and we will give it. I *listen* to my people!"

I tried the contraption myself, putting the grape in, pulling the blade up and letting go. There were little laughs as the blade came down, but I noticed just a bit of tension.

"Well, what do you think, Louis-Benoit? Tell me!"

I looked up and found their faces on me, a few expressions on those who clearly felt I had no business in the room. But since I was there...

"The blade—it is straight across."

"Yes," someone spoke up across the room. "This is modeled after a version used in another country. They have a curved blade but that didn't seem to provide a sharp enough edge so the King suggested making it a blade that extends straight across."

"Brilliant!" someone called out. The room exploded with applause as the King preened and blushed. But the King looked at me.

"Zamor, I can see on your face you have thoughts. Go on, then, out with it."

"Well, it is clever," I started. "I just noticed when the blade came down on the grape there is very, very slight resistance from the skin. It's not for long, but still..." I put a grape in place and gestured to the King's hand. He hesitated a moment and then gave it. I positioned it right in front of the contraption and let it fly. Again, it sliced the grape, but in doing so, a light spray went over his fingers. "Did you feel that? And did you hear that little pop? Just that slight little delay from the skin of the grape?"

"Ah, yes," he looked at it, speculatively. "But grape skin is tough. Human skin, not so much."

"Perhaps. But could it be pressure from all that is within us will cause very minute initial resistance?"

He tapped his lip. "I see. How can that be helped? Dr. Guillotin, you say we've improved things by moving from a curved to a straight edge, but what of the resistance he speaks of?"

"I have a thought," I said. "It's just that, when I'm in the kitchen watching Salanave cook..."

"Salanave used to be our cook, gentlemen. We speak of executions and he regales us with stories of the cook." Everyone laughed at his wittiness and I didn't bother to point out that I found them playing with the contraption like it was a toy.

"When Salanave prepares the chopped meat that she stuffs into the pig intestines, it is very delicate, that skin. Once she cooks the parcel the skin becomes a bit tougher so she doesn't cut them like this..." I used two fingers to pantomime a knife which I brought straight down on the table against a grape. "She cuts them like this." I angled my two fingers to the side and showed how her knife sliced through the, occasionally, tough skin.

The doctor stepped forward. "Ah, so the blade enters the skin at one edge to break it instead of the entire surface of the blade pressing on the resistance at once. That's what causes the tension, and the pop."

The King listened and looked at the contraption again. Then he said, loudly, "Dr. Guillotin, we will angle the blade. That way it will enter the body much more cleanly, don't you think?"

Dr. Guillotin nodded, "I think that's right. It'll be an easy adjustment to make, Your Majesty."

The room was quiet for a long moment and then someone called out, "Another brilliant idea, Your Majesty! I vote we call it the Louisette, named after our most gracious King." The room filled with applause and I looked at the King, who preened and blushed. "You will go down in history for putting this instrument to work for the good of the French people!"

I was dismissed seconds later. Once the doors shut behind me, I heard him say, "The page thinks he's a noble like one of us. We indulge him."

Fucking royals.

9

October 4, 1789

The banging on the front door shook the house. All of us servants came out of our rooms and listened as Gaspard went to open the door, followed by a few of his guards. We listened as best we could.

"What is this racket?" Gaspard said to two men in the uniforms of the royal guard.

"Please, help. Help!" the first man said, seeming to want to collapse, his face a mask of exhaustion, pouring sweat. "Please. They've overrun the Palace."

"What are you talking about? Who?"

"A mob from Paris! Let us in." The man, the larger of the two, pushed his way past Gaspard and stepped inside, but the expression on his face wasn't belligerence, it was fear. The second one could barely catch his breath and I realized they'd run all the way from the Palace. It wasn't a short walk. It was fifteen minutes by horse.

"They marched to Versailles on foot, they said." He sat heavily on a nearby chair, his forehead a mask of perspiration. "Said they wanted to meet with the King. It was the middle of the night and they wanted a meeting with the fucking King. Then, when we reminded them it was the middle of the night, they started telling us to send *her* out instead. 'Send out the Austrian bitch!', they said. 'Bring her out so we can rid our country of its curse! She's caused the famine!'" He rubbed his forehead. "There were more women than men. I've never seen so many women, and they looked angry enough to kill. They looked like they would tear her apart, and we couldn't do anything! We were overrun!"

"You mean, your team couldn't keep them out of the Palace?" Gaspard asked.

"Not the Palace, not even her bed chamber! She had to run through the tunnels to get to the King and I'm convinced only their love of him stopped them from ripping her to shreds. They had guns and knives and swords! They were on us before we even saw them coming. Thousands of them..." His voice hitched at that moment and before our eyes he dissolved into tears, wiping his face over his hand to hide them.

This is what we woke to, one man sitting in tears and the other comforting him like two lost puppies. Madame had come down while they were talking and now her face was pale, her movements shaky. She saw me in the other doorway."

"Louis, get them a drink," she said, and then bustled over to them. I went to the closest drink cart just off the hallway so I could still hear, but came back quickly with strong glasses of brandy for each of them. "Don't you worry, it's alright now. You're safe. Here, take a drink and you'll get fixed right up. Look at you, you're but little boys. A shame they should frighten you so."

"They did more than frighten, Madame, they killed some of our people! We were only trying to protect the Queen. They wanted to kill her on the spot. Over something to do with the people not being able to afford grain for bread. They said she told them to eat cake, instead, or some such nonsense. I never heard the Queen say any such thing, but they were livid. They went into the kitchen and tore it apart. They took the bread and everything else they could find in that kitchen. Then they scoured the outbuildings and stole barrels of milled grain. They didn't even have horses and carts to carry them, they were moving them out by hand out onto the road, I guess planning to carry them back to Paris. How are you going to carry those huge barrels all those miles back to Paris? But they were trying! Those women, especially, the ones not raiding the kitchen went room to room looking for her. Finally, when they caught up to her, the Queen asked them for mercy and they let her be."

"The Queen asked for mercy?" Madame remarked, as if that alone signified the seriousness of the situation. If possible, she went even paler.

"LaFayette was trying to ease the tension. He was loading the family into the carriage when we left," the man said. "The crowd was looking like they still had blood lust to satisfy. Almost immediately they started complaining about the dinner party at the Palace the other night. The guards get together sometimes—it's no big deal, really—and some cockades might have fallen on the floor. But it was no important thing, we were just blowing off steam! But the crowd starts complaining that we were trampling over the needs of the people by stepping on the cockades. It's only a piece of material, what does it matter if one or two got stepped on? But they started getting mad all over again about that and we were outnumbered, so we ran. It was a nightmare. I-I've never felt so helpless. Some of our guards tried to stop them. They killed them and put their heads on pikes."

"Oh, dear God," Salanave said from the doorway, making the sign of the cross on her chest. Salanave wasn't the religious sort but fear could drive people to God.

"Please don't make us go back. I think they want us all dead."

Then, there was more pounding on the door. The two men braced themselves until Gaspard opened the door to another guard, who arrived, ashen faced. "The royal family is on the road to Paris."

"Even the children?" Madame asked.

"Yes, Madame. The people who spoke out from the mob said they wanted the family in Paris where they belonged. They didn't explain why."

I knew why. In Paris, they could make it clear that he had no choice but to endorse a constitutional monarchy. They wanted him away from his officers and advisors – away from what they considered to be all the negative influences. I couldn't fault the goal, but the execution was a mess.

I handed out more drinks and slipped into the back of the crowd.

"Where is the Duc du Brissac?" Madame asked.

"He went with LaFayette and the King, Madame, to Paris. To calm everyone."

"Yes, he is a brave man, the Duc, he will make sure reason prevails. Come, have something to drink. Salanave, give the young men some food."

"No thank you, Madame," one of them said. "I can't eat, not after seeing that. What does it mean when they can take the King from his own bed? Threaten his wife's life in front of him and he can't do anything?"

"Where in Paris did they take them?" Gaspard asked. He, also, looked shaky. The royal guards were well-respected. He looked up to them. He used to be one of them and *knew* how well-organized they were. Seeing them so frightened seemed to frighten him.

The guard finished his drink as if it were water. "They're going the Tuilleries Palace until the King can calm the people. They'll return after that, likely in a day or so. The people said they wanted him to see more of what the regular people had to live with day in and day out. That he's too secluded at the Palace."

I absorbed the information while pretending to be as surprised as the others.

Where, with the Bastille I had just been happy to have my voice heard, with this I was annoyed and concerned. I was surprised that so much ire had been turned on the Queen, though I shouldn't have been. The women of France hated Marie Antoinette. The only person they hated as much as Marie Antoinette was Madame, though I wasn't sure she realized it. By throwing out a silly lie about cake I had tapped into something bigger; the reality that the Queen would be able to feed her children while the children of the common women would starve.

Of course, I wouldn't have even thought of it if I hadn't had a conversation with...

I glanced up and saw Véronique in the doorway behind the other servants. While they were watching and listening to the guards, she was watching *me*. I held her eyes for a moment, and I could tell she knew.

Véronique turned away and disappeared. I waited a moment and then slipped away to follow after her, catching up with her in the hallway to the servant's quarters. She was moving so fast I had to reach out for her arm.

"Véronique," I whispered. "Wait!"

She snatched her arm from me. "If I had known you'd take what I told you to use it for that..."

"You didn't tell me much of anything, and I didn't cause that. I only shared an idea."

"Don't come to me with that 'I'm *only*...' nonsense. You're a student of words and philosophy; you know better than anyone how dangerous an idea can be. People are *dead*. They were demanding the Queen's head! Something set them off. Mon Dieu, what did you tell them?"

I looked around and shuffled her into the closest closet. "All I did was suggest that the women of this country are fed up. And I might have mentioned some ridiculous quote I read, but only as a means to garner support, never as motivation for a mob. No one in their right mind..."

"When people are hungry and desperate they aren't in their right minds! You *were* in your right mind and look what you've done. Look what you involved me in. I don't trust you," she said. "I thought I could."

"That's not true, you *can* trust me." She was angrier than I'd ever seen her. "Véronique..."

"You used me. How dare you? You ... men! Always using us. Use our brains, our bodies, and then tell us to go stand in a corner and shut up. Manipulating us by playing on our fears, and then telling us we don't matter. You, with this new republic," she practically spit the word. "You want anyone to care about the oppression of the average man and yet you think nothing of stepping over others to get what you want. I spoke to you in confidence, and you twisted it."

"Don't you see, this is all for the greater good. When all men are equal, we can work to get women rights, too! Common men and men of color... the same as aristocrats – don't you see how we can change the world? We can become more like America."

"Land of the free? Working black people to the bone until they drop dead! Taking their children and selling them like chattel? Knowing nothing but abuse their whole lives? That's what France should emulate? They're no better than us!"

"But don't you see, the Declaration of Independence is the start. I tried to tell that American servant girl to stay here in France. She wouldn't speak of it. Maybe not everyone is ready for freedom." Véronique's hand moved like she was going to slap me, so I took a quick step back because I knew the feeling of her hand against my cheek. "Véronique, what did I say?"

"That young girl, Sally, the one you so blithely told that she could stay here in France and be free? Her brother is also in Paris, learning how to cook so he can take that skill back home and have a trade to survive on if ever he's allowed his freedom. Their master, the so-important Monsieur Jefferson, is paying for it. And her family—her siblings and her mother—is back home and would be lost if she didn't return. No telling what would happen to them if she stayed here, to free herself. And then there's the child in her belly."

At my look, she continued. "Oh, Monsieur Jefferson was short in his introduction. She's not just his daughters' maid, she is also the poor girl whose bed he crawls into at night. The girl he rapes time and again who can't do anything about it because she's a slave. Making that dirty old man happy directly affects the treatment of her loved ones. She's fourteen-years-old and already has the weight of the world on her shoulders, and more to come now that the babies have started. Freedom isn't freedom if it costs you everything, Zamor. You've been on your own too long, you don't remember what it means to love someone. If *your* parents were here with you in France, I'm sure you'd think twice about leaving them behind ... even if you were offered your own freedom."

I blanched. I don't know why I hadn't put the pieces together with the girl.

"I-I didn't know."

"Well, now you don't have to answer to me, either. I thought we'd gotten to a place of respect ... but you used me. I shouldn't be surprised but, foolishly, I am. And you did it to take information to those dangerous people you meet with. What are they giving you in exchange for betraying me? It's all about quid pro quo, isn't it?"

She knew me too well. Heat flowed through my cheeks at how well she figured me out.

"The *world* is dangerous. Véronique, the world outside these walls is a different place. I'm not *causing* danger, it's already in there. *I* didn't create the anger towards the King and Queen. *I'm* not the one hoarding grain while my people starve. If my one statement was enough to generate what happened last night maybe that should give you an idea of what's going on in the real world. But you heard them, yourself, the food was only part of it. Those royal guards and the Suisse guards and whoever else was at that party at the Palace were stomping all over the cockade! The people were mad about that, too. *You haven't been to Paris.* If you knew the conversations that are being had. If you knew..."

"When it's all said and done and things go badly *you're* the black man. It's *you* who will be sacrificed and crucified. They'll say you instigated it all! I want no part of any of it. You play a dangerous game and I'm just so ... disappointed. I had thought that deep down inside ... you were better."

She said those last words softly, avoiding my eyes. Then she opened the door, leaving me in the closet alone.

It hurt, her leaving that way and thinking those thoughts about me. It was unfair!

I would later learn more details. How the mob of women began as just a small group in Paris. After going to Parliament in the city, the Parisian politicians told them they didn't know how to help them. Disenchanted, the small group of frustrated women soon grew in size as they decided to go where they could *make* themselves heard, to someone with the power to do something. They marched from Paris, on foot, for two days to the Palace of Versailles. The mob grew like a snowball along the way, getting angrier as they went at the indignity of having to labor this hard to be listened to.

The women were followed by their husbands carrying weapons from the Bastille raid along with brooms, rakes, shovels, torches, knives and swords. There were a few revolutionaries thrown in for good measure, not by accident, I was sure. The royal army on guard wasn't large enough to counter the sudden appearance of upwards of 50,000 people on foot.

Later, when I was in my room, I thought about what this meant. Yes, how it had happened was ugly but at least now Louis XVI was in Paris where, perhaps, representatives of the National Assembly could explain the realities of the life of the common people to him. Maybe then he would understand why things could no longer go on as they had been. Maybe then he would understand that we all just wanted equality. We just wanted him to hear us.

And then, when the King was onboard, Véronique would understand that it was all for the greater good.

10

Madame asked me to go to the Palace early the next morning to pack some linens and stationery for the Queen. I was happy because it gave me an opportunity to check on the little boy, Jean. I found the manager and relayed the purpose of my visit, half expecting him to tell me to go away. Instead, he told me to wait a few minutes, and came out a bit later with a box.

"These things are to go straight to the Queen, her ladies packed it," he said, handing over a boxed bundle tied with ribbon. He was as haughty and unpleasant as always, but his red-rimmed eyes avoiding mine showed me he was shaken. The whole of the Palace was quieter than usual. "Don't bother going to the kitchen to steal croissants. It's a mess. They took everything, the savages. Even bigger thieves than you. Merci à Dieu, most of the food is locked up. They assumed what was out was all we had. They want us to starve."

I wanted to tell him it was the attitude of people like him that had caused them to raid the pantry at all.

It was the bubble. Nobles had no concept of suffering due to lack of physical necessities... that one could stand in front of me and say that, knowing what was happening in the country.

"Horrible," I said. "Monsieur, there's a little boy – the adopted child, Jean –"

He waved his hand. "The black one, you mean, that's the only one you care about. I know he liked to find you when you came to steal our pastries."

He had one more time to call me a thief.

"Haven't you noticed, he's been gone for weeks. The Queen already sent him away to boarding school before any of this. He's fine."

I was spending so much time in Paris these days I didn't often get to the kitchen at the Palace where I usually ran into the child. Or, rather, he ran into me. I was relieved to hear that he had missed yesterday's event, though no part of me imagined for even a second that he would be taken with the family to Paris. I wondered what happened to the other adopted children.

Back at the Chateau, the second I walked in the door with the box, Madame ran into the foyer and pointed to one of the sturdy tables.

"Set it down, there," she told me. She brushed by me and began rooting through it. Chon, her main lady, came after, with the other two ladies in tow. I stood back as Madame untied the ribbon and watched as the three grown women alternately squealed with glee and laughed at the contents. Madame held up a wig and plopped it onto her head.

"Look at me, I'm the Queen of the world!" she said, holding it atop her head with one hand while strutting in a circle. The ladies dissolved into laughter.

"Is the charcoal stick in there, Madame?" one of them asked, eyes big. She ran to the box again, searching until she found the stick that made Marie Antoinette's signature beauty mark. When the third lady found it, she pulled it out and held it up as the others chased her around the room, proceeding to draw a thick, wide circle on her own cheek. "What do you think? Too small?"

Their laughter rang through the house. When it was apparent

they planned to pull out and mock every item in the box I went to the kitchen for a break and had a cup of tea with Salanave.

A good forty minutes or so later, Madame came into the kitchen. It seemed her laughter was spent.

"Louis, I've made certain the King and Queen have everything they need. I re-folded everything and put it back. Are you going to Paris today?"

Absolutely!

"I thought I'd stay home but I suppose I can go and take that if you want me to."

"I'll add a few more things and have someone put it in the small carriage." The carriage came with a driver, which I didn't want or need.

"No need, I'll take the cart. I like to drive and it will leave the carriage free in case anyone needs it. I'll get you some chocolat confection while I'm in town."

"All right. I'd like some candy. Get the chocolat with the almonds and all the nuts and fruits. Merci, Louis-Benoit."

A few minutes later the box was in the back of the cart that was hooked up to Lightning, my horse. I looked around to see if anyone was watching and then began going through it to discover what else was in it, for my own protection. The last time I directly delivered something to the Queen from Madame I almost got hanged.

I unloaded things one at a time – the wig, some pillow coverings, delicate paper, some underclothing, some scarves, sachets, powder, charcoal pencil, and... nothing. Relieved, I repacked everything and was off to Paris.

I'd never been to the Tuileries Palace and didn't get far into it. My shoes sounded loud over the shiny marble floor and brought the attention of a servant who took the bundle from me and sent me away.

After taking a quick trip to the candy store, I was happy to get to the Club early to hear about yesterday's events. It looked like a party was already in progress. The events that were so traumatic to the guards signaled something else entirely to the Jacobins.

Some were calling it *The Women's March* and others were calling it the *October Days.* The march had re-lit the fire that started with the taking of the Bastille in July. Men who were normally dispirited and pessimistic came into the room with smiles on their faces. Men who used to disagree about everything now spoke to each other with respect and grace. We all felt we were on the precipice of a new world of our own. A new France that was stepping into the future. We were filled with hope.

"I was there!" said one man to others gathered around. "Those nobles looked at us like they'd never seen regular people before."

"Well, at least he's in Paris now," I said to Sebastien as we wove through the room to find a table.

"Salut," Sebastien nodded as we toasted. His eyes gleamed with uncharacteristic glee.

Applause broke out as Max Robespierre entered the room, followed by a man I didn't recognize.

"That's Georges Danton," Sebastien said, sitting down. "Voice of the people."

Max spotted me, tapped the other man, and pointed my way. They were headed in my direction when Valentin stepped into his path.

"Bonjour Max, Georges ... this is an amazing day. I'm excited to hear what this means for us."

"Yes, yes, it is. Excuse us," Max said, moving him aside with an arm to continue towards me.

"Georges Danton, this is Louis-Benoit Zamor."

"Du Barry's page?" the big man asked.

"Zamor is fine," I said.

"Zamor is the one who brought up the stresses that our sans-culottes women are experiencing."

"I just pointed out something I'd been told. I don't know who arranged the march."

"Well, Max did, of course," Georges said. "Put the right word into the right ear, it's what he does. But if it was your idea why aren't you shouting it from the rooftop? Claim your credit, Monsieur!"

Max leaned in to speak, discreetly. "Zamor is in somewhat of a difficult position. He can't make himself known, just yet. Living at Chateau du Barry, as he does."

"Ah, you work for us and you work for them, is that it?"

I didn't like the way that sounded. "I don't work for them. I mean, as a page, but I—"

"—I tried to convince Zamor to join the ranks and give us something we could use for fair trade in earning his freedom."

Georges smirked at me. "It sounds like he did, indeed, give you something you used very well."

"Unfortunately, not what I wanted," Max went on as if he couldn't hear Georges. "And now the window of opportunity has closed. We have the King in Paris and no longer need your help. All your leverage is now sitting in the Tuileries Palace. Pity you squandered your chance," Max said, giving a quick, smug smile before walking away to command attention from the group. "—Let's get this started, shall we?"

Georges looked at me. "Don't listen to him. When one window closes another opens. Life is all about finding the next open window and being spry enough to dive for it." He brought his hands together and pantomimed diving into water, then winked at me and moved away.

"Thank you, everyone!" Max called out. "I tried to guilt Georges to actually attend a meeting but could only convince him on the condition that he could tell us about his brand new wayward little Cordeliers Club." He reached up to clap his hand on the back of the large, gregarious man.

"I wouldn't have to tell you about what we're doing if you'd join us," said the big man. "But Max says he won't join it if he can't be in charge."

Everyone laughed and Max gave a small smile. "I'm happy with the Jacobins. Besides, I won't join your club because it's run by a drinking, smoking degenerate who manages to end every night in a room full of drunks."

"I'm a giver, Max," the big man bowed with a flourish to more laughter. "He's truly afraid if he spends time with me, he might learn how to loosen up and that scares him to death, the moral compass he thinks he is. Max, the Incorruptible! I'll bet I can corrupt him!" The crowd was giddy with amusement.

"They're old friends," whispered Sebastien from his seat behind me. I sat down at the table to watch the show.

Danton was personable and obviously well-liked. He held attention in the room like he was made for the light to shine on him and knew how to solicit laughter, easily. He did have a way about him, I admit.

Max proceeded to give us updates on proccedings of the National Convention until Brissot interrupted.

"Max, I'm as happy that the King is in Paris as anyone, but we are forgetting one important fact. We still have enemies planning to attack at any moment. We already know about Britain, but I tell you, Austria is our biggest threat. And Austria has troops here right now."

It was a common thing for countries to have small delegations in other countries. Especially with our queen being Austrian, it had made sense for years to have a small team of Austrian guards, as well as French, protecting the royal family. There was even a small Swiss unit.

"Despite the concessions made by deceased Louis the Well-Beloved, giving Austria back land we rightfully won from them, I imagine any positive will between us disappeared when Marie Antoinette was forced from her home to Paris. The Holy Roman Emperor can't be happy at how we've treated his sister. They'll want retribution. Our new republic won't be a republic if they attack us now. I know the King will sign off on the constitutional monarchy, but until then, we're vulnerable," Brissot continued, his face in a frown. "I don't think we should wait to be beset upon like foxes at a hunt."

"We went over this at the Convention, Brissot," Max said. "I don't want to re-hash it."

"But we *must* prepare our army for war against the Austrians and anyone else who dares to come into this country to undo what our Assembly is putting into place."

"Jacques," Georges Danton said, "We've only just gotten the King to Paris and now you want the first thing he does to be to declare war on his wife's home country? Let's slow down just a bit."

"With all due respect," Brissot said, wryly. "If it were up to you, Georges, we'd convey our wishes to the King on scented stationery. Perhaps from another province."

The room grew silent. Sebastien leaned in to speak low to me. "There's rumor that Georges is a secret royalist."

"Why not on stationery? We can always be civilized," Georges joked.

Robespierre and several people laughed, though Brissot wasn't amused. Danton continued, his confidence in correlation with the size of his giant frame. "Stationery or a scroll or carrier pigeon, from here in Paris or sent from the moon, Jacques, it doesn't matter to me how we communicate with the King so long as we do it. The sooner we help him see reason the sooner we can get things back to normal. After the constitutional monarchy is settled, then we declare war— when we are all of one accord."

"He's right," Max nodded, curtly.

Brissot's lips tensed. "Max, how can you say that? You've been at the King for a day. Haven't you won him over to our side yet?"

"You've been at him about abolition for years, Jacques, has that worked out for you yet? Or have you given up, entirely, and simply decided to fight a battle you can win—supporting gens du couleurs who want to continue to own slaves." Robespierre cocked his head. "You get something of substance done and you can lecture me about taking longer than a day to convince a king to transform his kingdom into a something it's never been," he snapped as we fell into short silence. "I know everyone is impatient. We all want this to happen quickly, but the King is besieged with new ideas and he's still very worried about this country's finances. Once he understands how this new type of government will take much of that stress and burden from his shoulders, he'll sing a different tune. It won't happen overnight but it's happening. And when we get him to agree to the constitutional monarchy, then he will lead the effort to fight off our enemies, with this republic firmly by his side. He is the King, after all."

Vive le Roi. Long live the King ... and all that.

But riding through Paris the next day I slowed Lightning down along the road as we passed the statue of Louis XV lying on its side on the ground. I wondered if it had been taken down to be patched up or polished. We kept trotting past the statue, and I was a short ways away when I turned around to look back. I saw a group of drunken revelers make their way to it, stumbling over their own feet, and then made a party of dousing the statue with alcohol, pissing, and defecating on it. It was such an amazing sight, Lightning and I watched it like it was theatre. I looked around for the secret police who, usually, had no problem dragging people off the road for minor infractions. This was more than that. This was a crime—and treason- -after all. But there were no secret police to be found and the statue was soon drowning in angst and wine-fueled urine. I was disappointed I couldn't partake of the revelry. Maybe once I got my freedom papers I'd circle back to add my bodily fluids to the collection.

11

I t felt like forever since I'd spoken to Salanave so I made a point of taking tea with her the next afternoon. "Hello, cook," I said, sitting down on a chair as she walked over to pour hot water into two cups. It was Gaspard's term for her but I knew she could take the teasing.

"You're lucky I like you, petit," she winked at me.

"Anything new happening with you?"

"I'm just so happy the noise has died down." Salanave stretched before sitting down opposite me at the kitchen table where she prepped. "What with all that trouble a couple of nights back."

I'd been in Paris most nights this week. "What trouble?"

"You haven't heard the noise from the troublemaker after what happened with Véronique...?"

"Véronique, what'd she have to do with it?"

"Well, she stabbed him, of course! Where have you been you don't know this? You know that evil boy who leads that pack with Chloe?"

Chloe was the curly-haired blonde apprentice who had arrived at the same time as Véronique. They were friends once. Chloe and I had been friendly, too. Now she just ran with the pack of servants who made it their mission to terrorize the strong workers and drink up all the alcohol in the house. The leader was a boy-child who was as lazy as he was spiteful.

"They were in the stairwell," Salanave said, sipping her tea. "And Véronique said he refused to let her pass and then got up too close and tried to trip her on the steps. You know how dangerous those steps are. She was livid so she pulled a little knife out of her head-wrap and stabbed him in the side. He got out of her way quick, then, stumbling through the house like he was dying. Been whining for two days about a flesh wound no bigger than a pinprick!"

My eyelids went into a blinking fit. "...tried to trip her on the stairs, you say?" I took a sip of tea.

"Oh, he claims he was just teasing, he didn't mean anything by it. But after that last incident she had every right to be suspicious."

"Last incident," I tore off a piece of baguette, hoping the chewing would stop my mad, uncontrollable blinking. "What was that?"

"You know, the laundry water! Didn't I ever tell you about that time when the whole gang of them lured her into the laundry and pushed over a full vat of filthy water onto her? Come to think of it, I don't think the two of you cared for each other much then. Well, Chloe lured her there, and the others were just laughing, but the troublemaker did the pushing of the vat. I had to hold her back that time. Our sweet Véronique was going to whip somebody's behind, and maybe I should have let her. So, she doesn't take anything he says as a joke, she knows he's evil as the day is long. Well, he's not laughing now. Whining about all the blood he lost. I feel worse for her! The poor girl did exactly the right thing. If it had been me I would have got to carving my name in him and he'd be howling for sure. But you know her... feeling guilty about it. Spending way too much time atoning at church. You ask me, she should be atoning for not jabbing him quick two or three more times."

The bread was like a wad of nothing in my mouth, just super hard to chew. Salanave glanced at me.

"I can feel the heat coming off you from over here. Now, don't you go making anything of this, she took care of it fine on her own."

"Of course not," I said.

"She doesn't like you in her business."

"No," I shrugged and laughed, weakly. I shrugged again. She was being silly. I swallowed twice to get the mass down. "It's fine, you said. No big thing..."

12

———

The wind whipped as my arms pumped faster. My legs have never been the strongest part of me but my arm action was picking up the slack, moving me through the wind. The boy ran in front of me, his pants and shirt billowing behind him.

"Leave me alone!"

I couldn't have said what happened. The conversation started simply enough. After dinner, I found him outside. He had a full bottle of wine that he'd stolen from the cellar and I'd simply asked him, "Hey, do you have a moment to chat, Monsieur?" and smiled.

He shrugged and I walked up to him.

"I heard..." I looked both ways and spoke under my breath. "I heard you tripped the woman from the east when she was coming down the stairs."

He smirked.

"I only give what's deserved. She walks around like she's better than everybody. Somebody's got to take her down a peg."

I gave a head jerk. "And I also heard you emptied a whole vat of filth onto her, that must have been hilarious!"

He giggled at the memory. "You should have seen her face." He stopped still, eyes wide, hands out and frozen as if acting out the scene. "I almost told her, 'Shut your mouth or you'll swallow even more, you sanctimonious pain in the ass!' It was just a joke, like the other day. I was just teasing, I didn't hurt her. But she cut me right here. Bitch."

As he was raising his shirt to look at the bandaged area, I was thinking what that must have been like for Véronique. I knew how big that vat was. Full of dirty, soiled water and lye? It was dirty, for sure, but the indignity of it must have been horrible for her.

"A whole vat, my..." I said. I was still smiling and nodding but something in my face caught his attention. It might have been the tic of my eyelid.

"Well, I've got to go. Meeting some friends in town." He turned and began to walk away.

"Oh, that sounds like fun. But, let me talk to you for just a minute more."

"What do you want, nègre?" he sighed, his arms rising and falling in exasperation.

"What did you call me?"

He realized a second too late he shouldn't have called me that. It set me off. I lunged and missed. He took off running. And like he was a fox and I was the hunter, I took chase because ... of course I did. Through the grounds, off the property, down the road headed toward town.

He was already half drunk and his body was failing him, his arms waving in wide circles instead of pumping like mine. He kept looking back over his shoulder.

"Leave me alone!"

But I was close now. I could smell his perspiration and the wine he'd already drank coming through his pores. He tossed the bottle onto the grass to use all his energy to get away but he was much too slow. He let out a high-pitched scream when I caught him by the collar and jerked him around.

"Leave me alone! What do you want?"

"Tell me again how funny it was, when you tried to trip her? Tell that story again, boy."

"What, is she yours or something?"

"Is she..." I slapped his stupid head. And then I did it again with the other hand and then again with the first while he cowered and whined.

"She stabbed me!"

"You listen here, boy," I said as I shook him by the scruff of his neck. He was taller than me but it didn't count because he was cowering so low we were on the same level. I could smell the alcohol on his breath as he took in deep gulps of air. "You will stay away from Véronique." Open-handed slap. "You go near her again, I can't even begin to describe to you the terrors I will unleash on you, you pathetic, mangy piece of merde." Back hand slap. "I will make you sorry you were ever born and that little puncture wound will be nothing compared to what I will do to you. I will come for you over and over and over again until you *wished* I'd just pick up a knife and stab you. I'll make you wish you were dead .You understand me?"

"Yes!"

"And you'll keep your mouth shut about this, hear me? No whining to anyone like you've been doing the last two days. You whine about this I'll visit you in your room when you're sleeping and give you something to really whine about. Do you hear me? Do you?"

"Yes! Yes!" he wailed.

I let go of his neck and he bounded away from me. I could see from the blossoming stain on his shirt that his side wound had opened.

I straightened, shook the fury off me. I had torn off my jacket off and thrown it on the road a while back—it was slowing me down—but I jerked my sweaty silk shirt straight and put my lace cravat in place and got control of my heavy breaths, wiping my brow of sweat. I cracked my neck to set me straight again.

"All right, Monsieur," I said, breath slowing. "I'm very glad we had this conversation. I do hope you enjoy your evening with your friends in town."

"You're mad," he said.

"Bonsoir, Monsieur," I said in my singsong way as I turned and began the walk back. I wondered along the way if I had gone too far. But on a glance back I saw him lean down to pick up the bottle of wine, to head into town, sniffling all the way.

—

Two days later I opened my bedroom door, after steady pounding, to see curly-haired Chloe. Chloe who had been my tumble-mate once upon a time, before Véronique caught my eye. When I ended our tumbling, she told me I was a fool and that Véronique would make me soft.

I didn't have anything against Chloe, but aside from intercourse we didn't have much to talk about. Apparently, we did now.

"My friend is gone. You made him leave, didn't you?" she asked, her face tight with anger. Without an answer she brushed past me to walk into my room.

"Sure, make yourself at home."

"He was my *best* friend. I hate it here. He's the only thing that made this place bearable and you chased him away."

"*He* made this place bearable for you? Really?"

"You did it for her, didn't you? Little Mother Mary, Saint Véronique, whined about the big bad man teasing her and you just jumped like a puppet on a string. She's making a mess and a laughingstock of you, you know. Trailing around after her like a little puppy dog. You used to be someone I half-way respected but now look at you." She gestured up and down the length of me. "It's pathetic."

I looked myself over. I didn't think I looked any different.

"Always the joker. Well, I'll tell you this, Governor..."

Having been termed the Governor of Louveciennes by dead King Louis XV as a joke, she very well knew the term would get under my skin. And it did. She continued.

"...here's the thing, *Governor,* if I'm going to be miserable I'm going to make things miserable for your precious Véronique, see if I don't."

"No, you won't."

"Why should you get a person here and I don't? It's not fair! She's going to pay for setting you on him."

"She didn't set me anywhere, Chloe. She didn't even tell me what the little ass-wipe did—I heard it through gossip—but once I knew, all I did was tell him to leave her alone. He decided to leave all on his own. So, you can stop with the threats..."

"Why are you fighting her battles?" She shook her head, like she felt sorry for me.

"She's the one who drew blood. I'd say she's fighting her own battles just fine."

"Then why did you get involved? It had nothing to do with you."

I shrugged. "I did it for me. The thing is, she doesn't have to fight her own battles because I'm here. You're right, she's too nice for her own good. She's deep down good. I don't have that problem, you know that. You and I are cut from the same cloth, after all."

"Well, 'deep down good' is about to get what's coming to her."

"Chloe, I like you but if you go after Véronique you're going after me. We're friends. I don't want to think about where that would end up."

"You're pathetic."

"Get out of my room."

I thought I'd set her straight but angry Chloe wasn't a pleasant thing so I decided to be proactive. That evening I was sitting in the parlor with Madame, her ladies strewn about the room—one embroidering, one reading, one dabbling on the piano—and I looked over at Madame. I had just closed the book of sonnets I was reading to her.

"That was lovely, Louis-Benoit. I love sonnets. And you read them so well."

"Thank you, Madame. By the way, you know the servant Chloe? She's unhappy here. A friend of hers left and now she's talking about leaving, too. Says she hates it here without him."

"Oh, that's a shame. Chloe is a lovely girl."

"Yes." I waited a beat. "If she's leaving, perhaps she can leave with something. All she ever truly wanted was to find a husband. All those meetings she had with you, you know her aspirations were to marry. She's not a romantic, just practical. Maybe you can make a match for her."

She looked at me. "That's not a bad idea, Louis-Benoit. Sometimes you are very thoughtful."

Two days later a couple and their grown son visited us. The son was in his twenties and looked like he'd rather be anywhere but there. He was arrogant and bored but handsome as far as that went. At dinner, Madame specifically asked Chloe to work the dining room. Since Chloe was a horrible server, I was immediately on alert.

There's something to be said for animal attraction.

The son was slouched in his chair in the room, ignoring small talk and his parents. Chloe slouched into the room—cranky at having to work dinner. The second their eyes met it was like a fire flamed to life. We all felt it. We all watched as he sat up straighter and she, suddenly, wanted to go around the table pouring wine. The roomful of us pretended not to notice their eyes on each other for the whole meal.

Just days after the family left, the son came back alone and within an hour Chloe's bags were packed. I only knew this because I was in my room when she opened the door without knocking, dropping her bag in the doorway, and walking in. Her color was high and her eyes sparkled.

"I'm leaving to get married. I wanted to say good-bye."

"Well, good riddance."

She nodded, looking like she wanted to say something equally combative and then stopped. She strode across the room to clutch me in a hug. "I know it was you who did this. I'm glad you're my friend. Thank you," she said.

I flushed, not knowing what to do with my arms. "I don't know what you're talking about."

"Sure." She reached up, kissed me on the cheek, and then she was gone in a flurry of skirt, bag flung over her shoulder, trilling laughter on her way out the door. I couldn't help but smile, after she'd gone. I was going to miss that reprobate. Good for her.

I was pleasantly surprised at how easily everything had rolled out. And I was surprised at Madame's kindness in making it happen.

"Chloe seemed very happy. You made a good match," I said to Madame that evening as we played chess by the fire.

"Oh, I know," she said, her eyes still on the board. "The boy was well known for his gambling and whoring and going through his family's wealth like it was an endless stream. I told them I was sure Chloe could get him in line but it wasn't until they saw them together that they believed me. That evening at dinner the two of them were on fire and everybody saw it."

"Still, I'm surprised they approved his marriage to a commoner," I said, moving a piece.

"They were desperate for a way to stop him from completely blowing the family fortune. I've taught Chloe everything I know about keeping a nobleman. The last question for them was answered when they saw how entranced he was by her. I explained to them, the benefit of a woman like Chloe is that she's smart and doesn't take nonsense. She will get that boy in check and make him feel like a king at the same time."

She moved her piece and I looked at the board planning my next move when she spoke again.

"They told him he could have Chloe's hand if he agreed to an allowance, in writing. It was a handsome allowance under anyone's standards, but significantly less than what he has been wasting. And I only asked for a nominal fee for making the match."

I looked up at her. "Fee? You were paid?"

"Of course. For my service in setting the match. I can feel your eyes on me but that's pretty hypocritical, don't you think? You were the one who brought the subject to me, after all."

She never bothered to look up from the board. My happiness for Chloe soured. We were quiet as we played.

"Don't sulk, Louis-Benoit, and don't pretend you don't know how it works. If it weren't for enterprising women like me and Chloe, you wouldn't have those fine clothes on your back. You shine because women like us are willing to sacrifice ourselves for you. The women who love you are happy to do it. You are worth so much more than money, chèr."

She called me *dear* while her words stung my soul. Being that she knew that Louis XV had told me my own mother sold me into slavery, her words were a well-placed dagger.

The indictment against the mother I couldn't remember, and against me, the man who flourished as a result of the indignities born by women—Madame, and now Chloe—resonated within me. This, on top of what Véronique had said about me using her, and using women. I never wanted to be a man who benefitted from the suffering of others.

Though my head knew Madame was manipulating the situation, I couldn't deny the silk on my body, the semi-precious stones on my cuffs, or the fine leather boots that molded themselves to my feet as if by magic.

If she was reprehensible, what was I?

13

———

I wandered into the Sainte-Chappelle Cathedrale one day, just hoping for a quiet spot to think about how terribly I'd messed things up with Véronique. I was certain she wouldn't be driving me to her church in Louveciennes to save my soul now that she felt I'd implicated her in my crime against humanity.

I was alternately angry towards her or myself, depending on the day. I knew that she was right about some things. I'd learned, and it was in my blood now, to expect that every communication, every conversation, and every transaction was up for sale, somehow. It was a sickness in me that I wasn't even aware of until she came along. And she wouldn't be able to cure me of it. I'd have to do that on my own.

But, perhaps, God could help.

Walking inside Sainte-Chappelle Cathedrale, I barely had time to catch a glimpse of the columns stamped with gilded images of castles and the fleur-de-lys symbol of the royal family on the ceilings of the main floor when a clergy member approached, stealthily.

"The pews are upstairs if you came to pray," he said.

I had only come to think, but since I was here I decided to go where he indicated I should proceed. He motioned towards a doorway that led into a narrow stairway. I fully expected to end up in some sort of attic but once on the landing, as my boots clicked on the buffed and gleaming floor past the pews and into the silent area, I looked up. The ceilings were impossibly tall, painted the same dark blue with the fleur-de-lys pattern as on the floor below. But on this level the outer walls were nothing more than thin strips of stone separating the tall stained-glass panels. The afternoon sun streamed through those windows: the colors lighting the place up like some shiny thing. The colors of all the jewels I had ever seen vivid and brilliant as though bursting with life. It was breathtaking.

I spun in a circle, looking up at those windows. It reminded me of a kaleidoscope in Louis XV's study. Held to the eye, the colors of the thing changed and switched with a turn of the dial. Here, I was the dial as I stood and turned in the center aisle. I felt bathed in those colors, lit up like a present, and I smiled, wondering if God above could see me better with this light shining on me.

A discreet cough and my light bath ended as I looked over to see the clergy member looking modestly away from me, hands clasped before him, as if he had not just interrupted one of God's children in worship.

"Thank you," I said, adjusting my coat and sitting down in a pew, quietly. He disappeared, as though now that he had sat me down his work was done. And then, I actually prayed, silently, for myself, my country, and my parents. I prayed for Sebastien and Instructor Barnier and Salanave, Henri, Fabien, and little Jean, the adopted child of the King and Queen who reminded me so much of myself. I prayed for Lightning, and even asked God to make Madame into a better person so she would be compelled to give me my freedom.

Then, after looking around to be certain I was alone, I put my hands together in front of me, leaning on the pew before me, as I'd seen others do.

"Dear God," I whispered aloud. "I know I don't deserve her. I know, for a long time I only wanted to bed her. But my feelings have grown for Véronique and I ..." I what? What could I possibly say to God to get him to give one of his most special flock to someone like me. "I-I will do anything to be good enough for her. If you would see fit to bless me with her love. I will try harder than I've tried at anything in my life to be worthy of her. Please make her forgive me and I'll show you. I'll prove to you I can be decent."

I mumbled the words, even as I heard the devil on my shoulder whispering in my ear that I'd never be good enough. I'd never be worthy. That I was damaged goods, sick with royal court rot.

"No," I whispered, squeezing my eyelids shut against that voice inside me. "I was a person, once, before I was a page. Before I was a slave. I was a person. I was good *once*. I can be good again. I will be, *for her*."

I left that glorious place feeling hopeful that the light streaming through those windows would bless me like holy water, and sad that the voice of God didn't come to me as readily or clearly as that devil that sat on my shoulder.

Still, I carried that feeling of wonder and hope back with me to the Chateau. That evening when I should have been sleeping I wrote a letter.

Dear Véronique,

I write this letter understanding it may be too little too late, but my conscience won't allow me to avoid this any longer.

I must apologize for the wrong I've done you. When you and I spoke I had no other motivation than to enjoy your company. Later, when having an unrelated conversation with someone, I unwittingly tapped into a subject on which we spoke. It truly wasn't intentional. But I understand how, from your perspective, it must have felt that I'd compromised your trust. Had I known how deeply it would offend you I never would have done it.

You are right that men are a selfish and self-centered lot. I don't want to blame my ignorance on my sex but as you so clearly stated we men, easily and conveniently, forget the source of brilliance when it comes from a woman's lips. As you pointed out, I should know better. Ignorance is no excuse.

But while the apology is owed, and has been given, I write because of another matter. You see, I was recently praying and asking God to help me to be what you want. As you might not find surprising, I sought to make a deal with Him. If He would make you forgive me, I would do anything, be anything you need me to be.

How you think of me has become very important to me. I don't particularly like the fact but it's true, none-the-less. It might also be worth mentioning, when I see you, my day grows brighter, inexplicably. When I hear your voice, warmth flows over me as if your voice were the sound of the sweetest music. Speaking to you and sharing thoughts with you have been the brightest spots of light that I've had since coming to this place so many years ago.

To me, you are Véronique of the East not because you come from the town of Burgundy but because you bring light to my dark places, and there are many. I like you as you are. If you were never to change a thing you would still be splendid to me.

But I wonder sometimes if you like me. I'm thread pure through with the royal rot of my upbringing, so much so I don't even know I'm wrong half the time. The poison of what I've learned flows through my veins easier than any good thing that seems to flow through yours. And yet, I don't believe I'm an evil man. At least, I don't want to be. I have good things in my heart, too. I never take pleasure in causing pain, though I'll cause it if I must.

Though I want to change to be someone you like and admire--because I want you—I can't promise that I ever will. I need to be honest with you on that.

All that said. I am not a sensitive man, nor do I care what most people think, but the thought of you staying angry distresses me. If we must be in this house together, it would be so much better as friends. Please forgive me.

Thank you for reading this if you've reached the end. I appreciate your time.

--Zamor

I slipped it under her door when no one was around and then worried all night that I'd made a fool of myself. The next day I passed her a couple of times and from under hooded lids, looked at her, but she didn't spare me a glance.

I was an idiot. Why would she forgive me when every day I did something stupid? I wouldn't suffer a fool like myself, why should I expect her to?

And then, two days later, I was walking through the hallway carrying a tray, my hands full. When I looked at her under hooded lids, again.

"Monsieur," she said softly, so I almost didn't hear, and I turned around, only to speak to her back.

"Mademoiselle," I breathed. She was gone. And that evening I heard the scratch of paper against the ground and bounded out of bed to snatch it up, unfolding it, quickly.

Dear Zamor,

I was very angry with you. But my anger wore off and became sadness. I worried that you didn't care how I felt. That you would never see how you hurt my feelings. Your letter shows me I was wrong, and I'm happy for that.

You're unlike anyone I've ever known and even when I'm angry, I like you. I like you as you are—que Dieu m'aide. {may God help me}. I only ask that you consider my feelings. If we're going to be true friends, you will never again use our conversations for evil. Or we won't be friends.

--Sincerely, Véronique

P.S. You write like a poet. I believe it's because you write from your heart. You should speak as you write and we would argue less.

I was smiling when I folded up the page and felt my heart blossom with all the colors of Sainte-Chappelle. I was starting to believe there was a God, after all.

14

December 1789

The retiring sun lit the sky in pink and orange over the nightline of Paris as Sebastien, Valentin, Marat, David and I walked the Pont Neuf Bridge. It was December and it was cold. But it was nice, feeling the biting air and feeling alive. We had stopped and were looking over the railing at the gently moving water of the Seine when Marat propelled forward, almost catapulting over the edge. We turned around quickly to see a group of men had come up behind us. One of them had a small drum strapped across his body and another held little sticks with streamers trailing the ground. Another one held a tambourine. The leader held his hands up in supplication.

"Truly sorry, messieurs, I didn't see you there."

All of the men wore ridiculously colorful outfits, and Sebastien immediately scoffed. "And yet we can't help but see you. Watch where you're going, idiots! All that drumming has made you daft in the head."

"I ask for the thousandth time," Valentin stepped up. "But maybe you can explain, why on earth this city needs troubadours?"

The leader tucked his chin up. "To make people smile, of course. This city needs joy, gentlemen. And our music brings that..." the word was some sort of prompt and the other men in his troupe straightened when he finished the sentence with "...regularly". All of them bowed low as if they were at court.

"What do you think of that, Page?" Valentin said with a head jerk my way. "He's the page. Page, jester, same thing, right? Like a son to our dear, deceased Well-Beloved and the lovely Madame du Barry."

"Is that right?" the leader asked, seriously. "Tell me, did I do it right?"

I wasn't keen with Valentin announcing me to just anybody on the street. We had an honor code in the Club, but I didn't know the people who were just walking around. Fortunately, it seemed unlikely this fellow would do me harm. "Your form was excellent, monsieur," I said, honestly. His eyes showed his appreciation.

"Do you think the King—the one who isn't dead, I mean—might need or like some m—"

"—you know, troubadour," Valentin interrupted, annoyed. "The King is just over there across the bridge at the Tuileries. You should go stand outside the windows facing the street, maybe he'll happen to be in the room and glance your way. Maybe he'll toss you a coin."

"Well, maybe," the troubadour said. "But that's a lot of maybes. You standing here in front of us is a sure thing. So how about it— would you gentlemen, perhaps, share some coins for a song?"

"No." Sebastien said it resolutely. He had a way of cutting to the chase and he'd been incredibly patient throughout our chatter. His patience had expired.

"Ah," the leader looked crestfallen. "No worries. This will do just fine."

Quicker than any of us could see, he had reached over and snatched David's bag off his arm.

"He stole my bag!" David yelled.

Before we even knew what had happened, the leader began to run, his troupe mates following behind. The last one in the pack turned around to laugh and sneer in our faces, as one began to bang his drum in song, all of them laughing along the way. And finally, our senses kicked in.

"Uh oh," Sebastien said. "They done it now." He took off running faster than his boxy form would suggest he could. Like a pistol shot, his movement was all it took for us to follow in chase. We must have all looked foolish, running and laughing as the troubadours managed to play, mock us, and run at the same time. It was obvious they'd done this before.

Valentin caught up with them first. Those grown men squealed like children as he pinned the first one down and Sebastien tackled the other one with the stolen bag. With two of them caught, the others stopped running from us, the leader throwing up his arms in surrender as Sebastien wrested David's bag from the thief.

"Fine!" the leader said. "We can be reasonable. How about we go back to our original negotiation? A few coins, then?"

I thought that was the highlight of my night but I didn't want to leave Paris just yet. Madame was staying with Brissot so the night was mine and I didn't want to go home.

"Well, Élise will have my head for spending all night out but you getting the night off is a special occasion," Sebastien said. We were on a street now that the sun had gone down.

"How do you get Élise let you go out as much as you do?"

"She knows I'm doing important things," Sebastien said.

"Is drinking important, friend?"

We turned to head toward the main drag to find a tavern but Valentin lagged behind. Then, he spoke, "You know, there's a new play over at the Comédie-Française, I hear. Written by a woman."

"A woman writer?" Marat said. "I won't pay good money to watch a woman's play."

"Are you intimidated?" I asked him as the others laughed at his frown.

"Women can't write anything of note and the world knows it." He doubled down.

"I know no such thing," I said. "But you're welcome to sit it out if you want. I hardly ever get a night out and I want to see the play."

Valentin nodded, giving me a glance under hooded lids, leading the way to the theater.

Valentin and I had a strained relationship. At times he seemed to like me well enough but other times I would taste a bit of his bad side. I looked over at Valentin's face as we walked, to see what mood he was in, but he kept his eyes to the ground.

Paul and David begged off so Sebastien, Valentin, and I headed to the theatre. I paid Sebastien's way to stop him from doing what he planned, which was to sneak in. The last thing I needed was to get arrested on my night out.

We sat at the back on the ground level and waited as people filed in the balconies above. Once again, I thought perhaps it wasn't the best idea to be in such a public place, but no one paid us much mind. Most of the people in this place were aristocrats with some bourgeois sprinkled here or there.

Sebastien, the official sans culotte of the three of us, was visibly uncomfortable, looking around at the fashionable clothing of the wealthy aristocrats and the tiny little binoculars they aimed at the stage, whispering to each other.

Only Valentin earned a lot of attention and that was from the women. He was handsome enough that even in this darkened space ladies were turning for second and third looks at him. Perhaps it was the insolence of his bearing they recognized.

Valentin was born a nobleman but his family—the Carnes—lost all their money, the family mansion, and their good name when his brother shot a police officer who was trying to evict them from the family castle. The brother had died in the Bastille and with him, had gone the Carne good name.

Valentin had become a Jacobin, living on the bit of family money left that awarded him an apartment and enough to eat. Even though this money was still more than many Parisians possessed, he was always resentful and carried his bad mood with him. Becoming a Jacobin hadn't taken the blue from his blood, nor had it alleviated his general resentment at being booted out of nobility. I thought it was due to his general bad mood that he didn't even notice all the attention from the women.

Though it was December, the throng of bodies in the theater generated sufficient body heat to keep the place warm enough, and soon, we quieted down once there was motion around the stage.

"You picked a perfect night to be at the theater," Valentin whispered next to me, slumped in his seat like he was settling in for a long haul. "It's called L'Esclavage des Noirs ou l'Heureux Naufrage." *The Slavery of Blacks or the Happy Shipwreck.*

"It's a play about slavery?" I asked him. His face shut down and he stared straight at the stage.

I started to press him further but the torchlights were blown out and I could no longer see his face. Torches lit the stage area as it started.

Two white people in dark makeup, meant to look like black people, I suppose, took the stage. It was the first time I'd ever seen blackface. It was a man and a man dressed like a woman on stage. I was paying so much attention to the ridiculousness of their makeup I almost missed the woman character's words a few lines in.

"Zamore, do you believe that the wicked Overseer was determined to ruin me?"

I LOOKED at Valentin's face in the low light and saw that it didn't move, though I know he felt my eyes. It didn't look like it was a surprise to him at all that the main character shared my name. Zamor wasn't terribly common. I sat back in my seat.

It was jarring hearing my name like that.

It was a story about renegade Indian slaves on a desert island who save a French couple from death. The enslaved couple have fled civilization after the man kills a white man in her honor, and now they find their hiding spot is visited by a couple after a shipwreck. Throughout, comments are made about the ills of slavery.

"A man debased by slavery loses all his energy; the most crushed among us are the least unhappy. I always showed such zeal to my Master and I was careful never to let my friend know what I was thinking."

IN REFERENCE to the man's master, he says:

"I was his son from the age of eight; he was pleased to educate me and loved me as though I were his son, for he never had one, or perhaps he was deprived of one."

BY THE TIME I heard that line I stopped telling myself it wasn't supposed to be me. It wasn't my story but there were enough pieces of my story to make everyone in the room, even those with little knowledge about court or Madame, clearly identify the man as me. Every time something was mentioned that could have been taken from my life story Valentin snorted under his breath. I wanted to punch him right there in the theatre.

"You do not know this accursed race; they would cut our throats without pity. This is what we must expect from Slaves that we educate; they are born to be savage and to be tamed like animals."

THERE WAS a negative response to that by another character but that barely took the sting away from the insult.

"...he has never found fault with him but all the colony demands their death, and he cannot refuse without compromising himself."

. . .

"Too much cruelty often leads to more disobedience than excessive kindness."

AND ON AND on and on...

At the end, the slave, Zamore, throws himself at the feet of the master who has forgiven him, even if he won't pardon him. He declares, so long as the master still loves him he will die happy.

The close of the play brought some applause but also a good bit of mumbling from people discussing what they'd seen. Discussing the notion that it was possible for slaves to be good and loyal and sacrificial. A few people stormed out, angrily.

I sat there, watching the stage as the actors continued to bow to the crowd.

Beside me, Valentin stood and leaned down to speak to me. "Who knows, it might *not* have been inspired by you." He walked out and I sat there.

I could feel Sebastien staring at the side of my face.

"Valentin's an asshole. Probably watched this play just imaging the moment he could get you back."

"For what?"

"For earning Robespierre's ear. *Twice.*"

"With no great results for me."

"It doesn't matter what Max said to you, the fact that he seeks you out to speak to you is enough. Most Jacobins are afraid of him and he's gone to you *twice*. Besides, tonight wasn't all bad. On the bright side, it seems Madame de Gouges is indeed trying to be an abolitionist. But I suspect she's never actually met a black person. Before I met you I would have thought that was a decent portrayal of black people. I know better now. Ready to go?"

Later that night in bed I thought about that play.

Is that what they want me to be, then? I wondered. *Is that what they* expected? A man who is only worthy of kindness after bowing and scraping and proving to them how good he is? Was my worth only counted if I was good to white people, to my own detriment? I was supposed to be kissing the king's feet? I was supposed to call him my god? Was that the only type of human I could be and still be considered human because my skin was black?

I couldn't be that, not even for a moment. Not even for a day. My name had become a character. My personage so well-known that no one for a moment doubted who this woman was writing about. They would take my very soul if I let them.

15

June 1790

It came to me that the only difference between Rousseau and myself was that he wrote his theories down. I could just as easily write mine. A philosopher was just a writer whose thoughts were discussed, after all. Why not me? Why not publish my own words and spread my ideas to the world?

I spoke to members of the Club, found out which of them were slaveholders and spoke to the others. I made sure they understood who I was and that technically I was still enslaved. I described some of the horrors of my childhood. Most of them didn't want to hear what I was saying and others thought I was exaggerating. Only a few listened as if they really cared. They'd never seen the brutalities of slavery, and they didn't want to know. All they cared about was whether they could enjoy their coffee, tea, sugar, and rum.

Writing my own words was at least better than spying. Knowing that I'd had a hand in the October march on the Palace had damaged my relationship with Véronique and I wasn't going through that again. If I could do what I needed to do without losing her respect, I'd try. She thought my words so powerful, I'd use them in another way.

I began with short one-page speeches because the Jacobins would only tolerate me speaking for brief periods. Max and Jacques Brissot weren't even showing up to most meetings. We could only hope they were off convincing the King of the virtues of our new republic. On the bright side, in their absence I had a chance to speak. Though no one seemed inclined to fight beside me, openly, a few listened. A few heard me.

Back at the Chateau it was an indisputable fact that Gaspard was getting old. His face was looking more haggard every day and he shuffled sometimes. He didn't shuffle as often as I did—old spinal injuries, I was sure—but he did occasionally. And he became forgetful, and when corrected, angry at the person who noticed.

I didn't know what he was going through and I didn't care but, alas, we still lived in the same house.

I had the misfortune of walking into him eating a knob of cheese in the kitchen. I had barrelled into the kitchen to collect the warmed chocolat Salanave left in a pan on the stove for me. Madame took her chocolat every morning but occasionally she wanted a cup at night. Seeing Gaspard, I almost turned the other way as soon as I saw him but knew if Madame didn't get her chocolat we'd all have hell to pay. I pretended like I didn't see him and headed to the cupboard to grab a bowl. His eyes followed me. Then he spied the pot of chocolat on the stove.

"I will get Madame her chocolat," he barked at me.

I cut my eyes at him, sideways. I had difficulty hiding my facial expression when I thought something was stupid. He caught the look, of course.

"Do you think delivering a drink is so complicated any dolt couldn't do it?"

"It's not the chocolat she wants, it's me. It's the conversation. Maybe she wants to discuss a poem with me. Maybe she'll show me a dress. Maybe she'll complain about the color of the sky. There's no way of knowing for sure until I get up there, but the one thing I'm absolutely certain of is that if I don't show up in the next five minutes, a task that normally takes a few minutes will take a few hours and she'll turn this whole house upside down. I'm no genius but even a dolt knows that much." I suppose I could have left that last part off but sometimes words escape before I can stop them.

He flushed red. I put the chocolat and bowl down quickly as he came across at me. Seconds later his beefy hand was around my neck and he carried me by the one hand to slam me against a wall. The bones in my back protested and my eyes shut for a millisecond at the streak of pain in my neck. I struggled for breath, trying with both hands to loosen his one.

A gasp sounded in the doorway and we both looked up to see Véronique, fumbling a basket of clothing in surprise on catching us. I was in quite an unflattering position with my feet dangling off the ground and this man's face close enough to kiss. It wasn't how you wanted to be seen by a love interest but there was nothing to be done about it at this point.

"One day, blackamoor, your mouth will get you hurt." His words came with spittle against my skin. He didn't need to tell me, I already knew he wanted to do me bodily harm. My face was swelling and my lips were likely turning blue when he let go. On dropping to my feet I coughed the air back into my throat as he shoved Véronique aside and rushed through the doorway.

She watched him leave, put her basket down, and then came over. "Zamor, are you mad? You can't speak to him that way. I heard you out in the hall and then it was so quiet I just thought that maybe you'd both left the room, only to find you up in the air like a shirt on a clothesline. What were you thinking?" She filled a small glass with water to hand to me. "Drink. Why use your words against him when you know he wants any excuse to hurt you?"

I swallowed the water. It seemed an obvious answer to me, in that my brain was the only weapon I had. "It's okay," I said through ragged breath to calm her down. "I've dealt with him this long, changing my behavior at this point would only make him suspicious."

She ran a hand over my cheek. I caught it and looked at her. Then I remembered the basket sitting by the doorway on the floor. "Are you doing laundry?"

She pulled her hand away, quickly, hiding it behind her back. "I know, they're hideous."

"No, I'm just worried because of all the lye. On top of the sewing..."

"It's fine, they're okay. I've got Madame's dress in the basket, to stitch a loose hem."

"You're supposed to be sewing your own things, not any little thing she asks for. She's got a tailor. She's taking advantage."

Véronique gave me a little smile. "And what is new about that, Zamor? Don't worry about me. I'm fine. And you'd better put that chocolat back on the fire and get it to her quickly before she screams this house down.

I had forgotten the chocolat!

Véronique left, and I did just that. Madame was sitting at her dressing table in her undergarments, her hair being tied up in torn rags that made the bountiful ringlets all over her head. She glanced at me in the mirror and her eyes glinted blue steel.

"I thought I was going to have to go get it myself. I don't ask for much. Now, I have to get my own chocolat? What are you here for, Louis-Benoit? Why do I do anything if the people in this household barely even respect me?" Her voice got louder with each word and by the end of her sentence her third lady had stopped fussing with her hair and stood, frozen, waiting to see which way the wind was about to blow.

"Take it up with your trusted guard, Madame, he insisted on bringing it himself and when I told him no, he assaulted me." I pulled my collar from my neck so she could see the handprint that was discoloring my skin. Lady number three gasped and Madame softened, her eyes moving back and forth from my neck to my face like she wasn't sure what to believe.

"By all means, ask *him* if he didn't just have my neck in his fist if you don't believe me? Ask the brute to deny being a brute. You know, I'm tired of this merde. It's not enough I have to deal with him, then I have to deal with you treating me like *I'm* in the wrong. Fine, see if I care. Here's your chocolat." I plopped the cup down on the dresser and turned to walk out, finally annoyed. I got halfway down the hall before her voice called out:

"Don't be angry, Louis-Benoit, *of course* I believe you. I'll see you at the party. Save a dance for me!"

Madame had decided to throw a party in light of the National Convention decree that noble titles be abolished. The guests were invited under the premise of using their official titles for one last time in public. And she wanted any excuse to appear to the world beside the Duc du Brissac.

I didn't mind. Whenever he was around she wasn't worried about me. I might not have to dance with her at all.

The famed Chateau du Barry Pavilion was opened for the occasion, with a formal dinner followed by dancing in the salon. Later, standing just outside the side door of the Grand Salon, I watched the string quartet play their instruments. They weren't as good as Josephe but, oh, how I loved the music.

With a wave of his hand, the conductor invited the people in the room to stand and come to the floor to begin to waltz. The room filled with whirling colors as skirts twirled over and around the floor. The candles lit the space so that every corner of the room sparked or gleamed from the lights and chandeliers and mirrors stretching to the sky-high ceilings.

The sound of the brush of material against itself caught my attention and I stepped outside to see Véronique leaving through one of the other doors, skirt swishing. She held a tray in one hand and a candlestick in the other, having left drinks or snacks, no doubt. I knew she'd been working all day, and was still busy. But still, she hesitated and glanced back into the Pavilion, not noticing me until I approached. She jumped a bit in surprise.

"Oh, Zamor, I didn't see you," she laughed a little, a hand to her chest. "I was just watching and thought I was caught. It's beautiful, not as beautiful as the last time when I was here with you, but still."

My heart fluttered.

It was dark outside, and in the moonlight we seemed to be the only two people there, though we could hear that music from inside.

"Let's dance," I said, pulling the tray out of her hand and putting it and the candle on the graveled ground. Then, I pulled her away from the building and farther into the green space just beyond the glow of the candles from the outdoor plaza. I bowed to her. She scoffed for a moment.

"I can't dance like them, Zamor," she laughed. I held out my other hand as well, and took her second hand.

"It's not difficult, you'll see."

She looked doubtful, but pleased. She took my hands and I pulled her back into the night, away from the open doors but still close enough to hear the music. She watched my feet carefully as I began the slow waltz.

"In a moment your legs will pick up the motion and you won't need to think about it," I said. I kept the same steps slowly, over and over again.

She smiled in the night and her eyes sparkled. "You're a good teacher."

"I have never taught anyone anything. I think you're just a good student. Now, let's go a little faster, shall we?" She was sure of foot, and when we picked up speed, her eyes widened for just a second as her body caught on quickly. Then we were whirling over the grass as though the ground was made for our feet ... until the music ended and we gasped for air.

Véronique wasn't one prone to laughter but she had caught the giggles, laughing with glee under the moonlight. We breathed out until we could catch our breaths, the cool air pleasant and the smell of the flowers filling our noses. Being as short as I am we were nose to nose, and because of it we could easily look into each other's eyes. I held her hands and spread her arms. She smiled and took a bold step closer to me so we could look each other dead in the eye. Her brown eyes were still sparking as if they had captured rays from the moon and they were stars, themselves.

"Want to go again?" I asked.

"No," she laughed, and stumbled a bit on the grass. "I'm lucky I didn't break my neck already on this uneven ground. Thank you for helping me stay on my feet."

"You're welcome, Véronique of the East."

"I have to get back or they'll come looking for me. Madame will wonder where you are, won't she?"

Our spell was broken. There was no point in denying it. Whether needed or not, on nights like this, Madame liked to see me there when she looked up from whatever she was doing. Even if she didn't need me beside her she wanted me there.

"Thank you for the dance, mademoiselle," I bowed again to Véronique. She blushed, went quickly to pick up her tray--her candlestick--and then walked down the path towards the Chateau, looking back at me once. I smiled. I wasn't known to be a flirtatious man but I was certain I had just done so, successfully.

I went back into the Pavilion and once lighting the doorway, looked around the room and did, indeed, see Madame looking for me, though she danced with Brissac. She seemed to relax upon seeing me over his shoulder. I was there. I was always there. I was always there.

16

———————

Dear Citizen,

*If I had to recount that moment with Véronique it would be the
feeling of the slightly cool night air on our fevered faces. I would
look up to the starless night sky and hold her in my arms and dance
forever. I would recount how it felt to hold her waist, how it felt to
be close to her sweetness, and how wonderful it felt to spin, spin,
spin in the night like sprites with all the world to play in.*

--Zamor, 1820

Though I wanted to see her every minute of every day, it felt as if the busier our lives became, the less I saw Véronique. I passed her in the hallways and caught glimpses of her working in the laundry, helping to milk the cows, raking leaves and pruning. One time, we were in the dining room and I saw her wince when picking up a saucer of dried fruits and nuts for a dinner guest. I looked down at her hands and noticed how she was slow to clench them and careful when holding anything.

It was obvious to me her hands were hurting, and that was bad for her. Madame loved the way she sewed and embroidered. Véronique was now doing all of the sewing work for Madame and her noble guests—not what she had wanted to do, originally. The detailed work was hard on the eyes and hard on the hands. Add to that, her work in the laundry, constantly having to plunge those hands into water filled with lye, and her blisters and calluses were damaged even more.

I made a trip to the Palace to visit the massive library. Louis the Well-Beloved had loved books on science and botany. His botanical gardens were long gone, courtesy of his grandson, Louis XVI, but the books were still there.

That night I knocked on Véronique's door.

"Zamor, it's late. Don't you ever sleep?"

"I know, I'll just take a moment. Please."

Her room was small and cozy, filled with scraps of material, bolts of fabric, and a small table just to hold an array of needles and threads. It was a hot night but the window was open. I'm sure it was open so she could catch whatever breeze there was. And though it was late, she was wide awake, in her dressing gown with a wrap over it. Her eyes were red-rimmed. I noticed a piece of fabric on the second small table with a needle threaded with silk atop it and knew I'd interrupted her sewing.

"What is it?" Her hand fluttered up to her hair. She wasn't wearing her normal headwrap, but had a bonnet over her hair and seemed suddenly self-conscious. I reached out for that fluttering hand and she immediately snatched it back and put both hands behind her back.

"Let me see, Véronique?"

"What? No. What is this foolishness, Zamor?"

"I could tell earlier that your hands were hurting you. Tell the truth. They hurt. Let me see."

"No, go away. Go to bed."

"Véronique..."

Her eyes welled with tears and her lips bunched. "I don't want you to see them! They're hideous. Yes, they hurt a little, but I can deal with it." A tear fell down her cheek and she brushed it away with her shoulder, as if angry to reveal it. Her chin came up and her lips were firmly closed against argument.

Of course, she wasn't going to easily admit to pain. Or fear. Or weakness of any kind. She was Véronique of the East, whose fierce determination was the first thing I discovered about her. I was going to need to be pragmatic to move her.

"So what if they are? Did you come all the way across the country to show us how lovely you are? Is that why you're here? Or did you come here to work your fingers to the bone to do the work you want to do for yourself? If it's the latter, what does it matter how your hands look to me, or anybody? I only want to see if they're injured, that's all."

My words took some of her defensiveness away and she thought it over just a moment longer before putting both hands forward and turning them over so I could see.

Her hands were small and angry. Incredibly small, considering how mighty they were. The calluses, cuts, and reddened pinpricks were no surprise. But I could tell the worst were the areas between her fingers, especially the tender flesh between thumbs and index fingers, that was causing the pain. The skin in those places was very hard; likely caused by the almost scalding lye-infused water of the laundry. I could see cracks in the hard parts revealing pink flesh underneath that threatened to bleed, and probably already had. Without a chance to heal they would crack and bleed over and over.

I nodded, looking back up into her face. "They're taking advantage of you. You have to say something."

"No! I can handle the work, Zamor, it's just slowing me down a little."

"But—"

"This is what I always wanted to do!" she said, desperately. "My whole life, this has been what I wanted to do. I'm not going to stop because my hands hurt a little bit. I'm not going to go whining to Madame telling her I can't handle it. I won't do anything to stop me becoming known as an excellent seamstress. Look," she walked over to one of the little tables, pulling a sheet of paper to bring over to me.

"Look," she wiped her tears away and pointed to the names on the page. "All these people I've done work for. These are *customers*, Zamor. They've given me their addresses for after I've gone. I'm making real progress. Someday those women on this list will fund my life." The page trembled in her fingers, as if the pain gave them a life of their own. "I gave up too much to be here. I can't now tell her that I can't sew. I gave up everything... I can't go back. Not like this."

I understood. Some things were worth the pain.

"Oh, but I might have something to help," I said. I'd been so busy enjoying being her support I almost forgot why I was there. I took the page from her and lay it back on the table. "That's what I meant to tell you. Come sit, I brought something." We sat on the edge of her bed and I reached into the satchel over my arm, pulling out a small clay pot with a lid, opening it to the ugly goo inside. "I asked around. Did you know there are recipes for things to put on your skin?"

She pulled back a bit. "I can't put that on my hands, I have to work."

"What's the point of doing all that fine work only to stain the fabric with your own blood? You need to heal. I mixed up some wax and almond oil and a little water. Then I found this book at the Palace—more of a ledger, really—did you know the ancestors of the black people in the colonies brought all their knowledge of plants and botany from Africa? I even saw some notes about remedies from the Malagasy people. That's ironic because I might be Malagasy, or Siddi—I don't know for sure—but I know those were black people from India like me. I found some papers about a man named Charles Rama, a black man from my very own birth country of Bengal. He was a master gardener. I think the kings have been stealing ancient African recipes from him for their own. I added some peony petals and ground them down with a mortar and pestle. The books say the peony is good for the skin. And some other things that the books said were healing to cuts and burns. I wasn't sure what all to add, so I added a little of everything. I didn't just find notes of black people from India, I found notes on things like how to grow different plants and fruits and how to harvest different grains and crops. All this information written down and taken from enslaved people! I find it incredible that not only are they forcing our people to toil, but they're also taking our very knowledge. That has to be a sin, don't you think?"

While I was talking endlessly to put her at ease, I was smearing the goo over her hands. At this moment I was beginning to feel foolish and worried I was making the situation worse. But no going back now.

"It feels funny, sure, but I'm sure by tomorrow it will be different." I rubbed the uncomfortably sticky potion into the skin of her hands with my fingers and palms. "You'll see. A night of rest and they'll be as good as new."

When I finished, she looked at her glistening hands as if they were foreign instruments. I wiped my palms on my clothes and reached into my bag.

"Now, I'll just put these on you." I carefully began putting short white gloves on her hands.

"Where did you get those? Those belong to Madame! Oh, Zamor, I can't wear Madame's clothes!"

"You won't wear them *outside* of this room. You'll only wear them at night after you put this on your hands. Madame puts almond oil on her hands when they're dry and then she sleeps in gloves. She's got at least thirty pair; she'll never notice one missing. You keep these gloves on all night and then hide them away during the day. Here." I pulled a sheet of paper out of my coat pocket. "I wrote down all the ingredients and now we both know what's in it in case I can't make you more when you need it. But when you need it just tell me and I'm happy to do it."

She flexed her gloved hands and looked up at me.

"You did this for me? Why?"

I snorted, "That's a silly question, Véronique. You know why. Because ... your hands hurt."

Before I knew it, she was in my arms, clutching me. "Thank you, Zamor."

It was such a strange thing, to be turned to for comfort. I felt a wash of emotion that she would turn to me. That she felt comfortable enough to let me this close to her, again.

"It's nothing, really. All right," I said, pulling away because I was beginning to get warm and I didn't want to embarrass myself. "I'm going to leave you now. Get some sleep."

I didn't know if the goo would do anything for her at all but I had hope.

The next morning, when I was setting places at the table for breakfast, I saw her across the room. The tightness was gone from her features and she looked at me and smiled. Then she picked up the pitcher without even a small sign of pain, lifting it as if to show me her hands were fine. She winked and I smiled, the flush going through my whole body. Our friendship was sealed.

We took to stealing moments together as if, by unspoken agreement, we wanted to keep our growing friendship to ourselves. We often met behind my tree because, unless one were to squint really hard from the house, we weren't noticeable at all.

On one such occasion, we were sitting side by side with half a baguette on a napkin sitting between us along with a couple of pears. I was reading Rousseau and she was stitching her signature colorful flower bouquet on a patch of cloth. Her lips were moving silently as though she was memorizing the numbers.

"Are you self-taught?"

She glanced up. "Yes. It's no big thing. You taught yourself the violin."

"Yes, but I've been around musicians my whole life. I had people to emulate. You do what you do all on your own. It was brave of you to come all the way out here like you did."

"Brave or stupid. I still haven't decided which."

"Do you ever think of going home?" I snuck a glance her way.

"My little breakdown the other day didn't show you how I feel about that?" she smiled. "I love my parents, but I left home because an unmarried woman at my age is considered an old maid. In my town, I'm known as a disgrace and burden to my family."

"What a peculiar term. You're not that old. And lots of men come through here who have *never* married."

"Men are allowed to live their lives, women are not."

"Why didn't you marry? I mean, I remember you said that one man who came here to the Chateau looking for you was your intended. The one you ran from."

"I didn't run from Hubert. I walked fast. But yes, there were other attempts. My father tried hard to find me a black husband."

"Why only black men? Were there a good supply of them where you come from?"

"There were *none*. He would travel out into the vast unknown to search for them, claiming to be out fishing." She smiled at that. "Many came and went because—their words—I'm too soft to be the wife of a sans culotte laborer. At the time, it seemed the pampered state of my hands doomed me. Maybe they were right because look at me now. Knowing what hard-working hands *truly* look like, I can't argue with their logic."

"Well, that just means you need a man whose hands are at least as soft and pampered as yours, and then he can't rightly complain about you. And, what do you know..." I held my hands out, looking them over, speculatively. "... will you look at that? Soft as a baby's behind."

Véronique laughed and pulled down one of my hands, holding it in hers as if it were special, clasping fingers and dropping her head on my shoulder. Her laughter sounded pretty in the late spring open air, especially nice because she hardly ever laughed out loud.

"I told you my papa was probably about to marry me off to my friend Guy."

"The friend who died?" It was her friend who had taken his own life. Véronique's face no longer crumpled with pain when he was mentioned.

"Yes. Papa was that desperate. I didn't want to. I just didn't love Guy that way. And then, Papa thought Hubert was perfect for me – a black man who was finishing his law exams and preparing to open his own practice."

My eyebrows went up in surprise. It was no little thing for her father to have found any man of the bourgeois class interested in marrying his poor, common daughter—the daughter of a formerly enslaved man. It was quite an accomplishment.

"That would have elevated your social standing." It would have taken her from the category of working-class peasant to the highest level that anyone without noble blood could reach. Mixing among the classes was still virtually unheard of – one of the reasons why Madame's ability to snag a king had been such a scandal. Though she hadn't been the first common woman to snag the Well-Beloved, she was the first *working* woman.

She shuffled in discomfort. "Hubert made it clear he expected his wife to live the life of an aristocrat."

"How dare he?" I scoffed. A bit of sarcasm that she caught.

"I like a bit of comfort as much as the next person but he wasn't going to let me sew my dresses. He wanted me to start having babies, immediately. He wanted to put me up in a fancy house where I'd have nothing to do all day but read poetry, listen to music and pick flowers."

"But you like music and flowers. You danced with me."

"Yes, but I didn't like *him*."

We were going in circles. I stopped asking questions because I could see the little wrinkle between her eyebrows coming in strong. We were silent for a long moment and then she spoke softly.

"He treated me like I was a piece of trash picked up off the road. He made it clear he only wanted me to be pretty and shut up or he would treat me like the trash I was – a woman with a reputation for having been sullied by a man who took his own life. I never sullied with Guy. But Hubert shamed me and made it clear I would never be anything more than an incubator for his children."

Anger flowed through me at the sadness that was palpable on her. That anyone should make this woman feel less than the wonderful woman she was, it was a crime.

"So, the one man who knew your worth is dead and the only man to ask for your hand vastly undervalued it. And you took the first carriage ride out of there."

She nodded. "I had to try to make a life for myself that wasn't waiting for a man to choose me. At my age and circumstance, I would only ever have the very worst of men looking for me. But I knew that some women lived alone and worked for themselves. To me, that was better than living with a man who repulsed me. I had to try to give myself better than Hubert. So yes, I ran, and broke my papa's heart."

"I'm sure he's already forgiven you, if he loves you half as much as you love him. I'm certain if you decide to return it will be to open arms."

"I'm afraid to go back. I'm fine here until the moon leads me somewhere else. Besides," she looked over at me. "Here is where you are. Where will I learn to dance if you're not around to teach me?"

Her brown eyes were like a feather on my face and I smiled, slowly, like a fool. Never did I ever feel wanted in the way I felt at that moment. And though she claimed it was the dance that enchanted her, when I stroked her cheek with my finger, for a moment I thought, hoped, dreamt ... it was more.

17

J*uly 1790*

THE NEXT TIME I met with my new friends, Josephe Bologne and Thomas Dumas, it was at the Palais Royal, home of the cousin of Louis XVI, the Duc d'Orléans. Like everything else in Paris, it was a stone's throw from the Tuileries Palace.

I'd never been to the Palais Royal but soon learned it was a combination home and local haunt for political activists. In record time it would become one of my favorite spots in Paris. But on this day I was directed to the gardens in the central courtyard where Josephe and Thomas were already laughing and drinking, a little table with glasses of drink and three chairs awaiting me.

Josephe stepped forward with a smile, no doubt to alleviate the mild alarm that must have been evident on my face. "Don't worry, Zamor, the Duc is a supporter of the new republic. This palace is friendly to the republic. You won't find any of the King's associates here."

"Will we be raided, do you think?"

"No, this is private royal property. Anything that happens at the Palais Royal *stays* at the Palais Royal."

My shoulders relaxed as Thomas waved me over. "Come on in, friend, we've been waiting. There's much learning to be done!"

At the Chateau and the Palace, even with my somewhat twisted physique I was never the worst looking man in the space. But approaching Josephe and Thomas, I suddenly felt wildly inadequate. Both men had taken off their jackets and stood in breeched pants with vests, Josephe with his cravat hanging casually loose. Without overcoats, their muscles rippled through their pants and their shirts strained at their broad chests and wide shoulders. Their dress made it easy to see they were both ridiculously fit from the top to the bottom, and both easily stood a head taller than me, on top of it. My hopes began to fall about serving in an army alongside them.

However, I had agreed to come and, truthfully, after ten minutes I was enjoying myself so much I forgot I was the ugly duckling of the group.

We began talking about Josephe's introduction to the republican army and why he'd been chosen.

"They said because I'm a master fencer and swordsman I would, surely, be great on the battlefield."

"Of course!" Thomas boomed. "Why else would they ask a man to lead an army if not for his ability to wield a weapon used in battle a century before? A master fencer *has* to be great in battle, says no one who knows anything about fencing. Sending a man into battle with a sword when all the world is using guns is suicide."

"Ah, but they meant well," Josephe said, pulling up a pistol to line it up with a target at the far side of the garden. "Fortunately, I also know how to shoot, but I took it as a compliment, besides. And, frankly, the diversion from anything related to music is a good thing for me. Take away my life's work? – I'm happy to pick up a gun to shoot somebody. It feels so much better than constant rejection."

"What they don't realize is that some of us are of the personality that feeds off rejection. Tell us *no* and we'll find another way," I said.

"They won't let me be a delegate at the National Convention. Won't give me my freedom. And yet they want me to turn spy for them."

"Is it Max Robespierre?" Thomas asked.

"How did you know?"

"Well, no one else would dare make those kinds of decisions for the Convention."

"Don't feel too badly," Thomas said. "I know a man from Saint-Domingue named Vincent Ogé who's has been at Max for the same reason. He and Julien Raimond want to represent gens du couleurs on the Convention floor. I hear now he's meeting with LaFayette. He's a member of your Friends of the Blacks, Josephe."

"Ah, Vincent," Josephe nodded. "We've crossed paths but I don't know him well."

"Here you go, Zamor," Thomas said, handing me a pistol.

I turned it over and around in my hand, trying to memorize all the pieces. Then, doing as I'd seen Josephe do, I picked it up to line with the target.

"This leg back to ground you," Thomas said beside me, kicking at my back foot, which I moved as instructed. "The sound of it is atrocious. Don't let the sound cause your hand to waiver. Look, like this." He took it from my hand, raised, pointed, and went completely still. Nothing moved on him until the second his finger pulled the trigger. I winced at the crack and the sight of what appeared to be a tiny explosion from his weapon. Still, his arm was in the exact same position. "Now you try."

I, immediately, reached out to take it, but Thomas pulled it away from me, both of them yelling like there was a fire.

"What?"

"The barrel is burning hot, man, I meant for you to take it by the handle." Thomas shook his head. "Here, put your hand where mine is. Never take a pistol by the barrel with your bare hand after it's been shot. Never point it at anyone you don't intend to shoot. Never wave it around or toy with it. That goes for any weapon."

I flushed. I was new to it but I wasn't an idiot. "Yes, yes. Give it to me."

He handed it over and put his hands up in supplication, backing away. "If you tell me you've got it I'm going to believe you do, page. Go ahead, shoot."

Now that I had it in my hand, with the two of them staring at me, I was nervous. My hand shook a little. I aimed, but damn that tiny shake. And when I pulled the trigger the power of the thing went all the way up my arm to my shoulder and my arm jerked up all on its own as the bullet rocketed out of the gun, across the yard, and into a tree about two feet higher, to the right of the target. A covey of birds screeched and scattered.

"Sure, you've got it," Thomas said, clapping me on the back. "No worries. Try it again but this time do as I said."

I tried it at least ten times. My arm didn't like any of my shots. Finally, tired of watching me, Thomas took his gun back. "Don't' worry, friend, it takes a little time and practice." Then he and Josephe competed with each other for the bullseye in the center of the target. I couldn't tell you which was closer because they both hit precisely in the center.

"Obviously, I win," Josephe said, finally lowering his shooting arm.

"Keep telling yourself that," Thomas said with devious a smile. "Tell the leader whatever he needs to stay happy, Zamor."

"I don't think I could ever shoot someone," I admitted.

Thomas said, sarcasm all on him, "I don't think that's a problem, page, unless you *want* to shoot up a bunch of birds."

"No, I mean I don't think I could kill someone." The comment slipped out of me, before thinking. Probably not the best thing to say to two men on their way to battle, willing to have me join them. "I mean, I wanted to, once. I tried, but the circumstances didn't let it happen. But to stand in front of someone and shoot them, I don't know if I could."

"No one knows if they can until they do it. You can do anything you have to," Josephe said, frowning. "If it comes down to your life or theirs, the instinct to survive kicks in." He put his gun back down.

"Josephe and I are teaching this to our troops right now,"

Thomas said it, his eyes steady on me. "A good soldier doesn't enjoy killing, but sometimes a soldier must kill. You have to know that once you do and that door is open you can never shut it, again. You will never forget it when you take someone's life. And you shouldn't."

Josephe was sitting now, leaning back in his chair, drinking something amber in his glass. "Consider that well, Zamor. If you decide to join our army you want to do so for the right reasons, so that all is right in your heart."

I hadn't thought about that aspect of being in their army. But I was still very interested. Surely, I could learn to be as assured as the two of them.

"Can we try the swords?" I asked. "I think I would prefer to learn that, to be honest."

They looked at each other, then Josephe had us wait while he went inside. As he walked away, Thomas called to him, "I think we lost this recruit, Josephe!"

The man in question came back with his arms full of several encased items I assumed to be swords. He tossed one to Thomas and managed to do it in a way that the handle remained upright. Thomas caught it just as easily mid-shaft, immediately putting the other hand on the handle and pulling the sword out of its jacket. Sunlight glinted off its sharp edge.

"Here, this one is for you to practice with, courtesy of the Duc d'Orléans. Okay, first thing is stance. You have to stand tall and straight, but once again, the back leg positioned to steady you. This is the same in both swordplay and fencing."

I stood between the two of them as they demonstrated pulling the sword from its holder. Then I tried myself and they both yelled, "Whoa!" with Josephe moving quickly out of my way.

"Mon Dieu, man, you'll kill the man beside you!" Thomas yelled. "Keep the sword pointed toward your sheath and raise your arm like this."

It took several tries, and much space between us, until I was able to pull the weapon out, smoothly.

"Now, take a look at each of these, all methods of a duel. You know what a pistol and a sword looks like. This one here is a rapier."

The item he pulled out was long like a sword but it was very small in comparison.

"In a duel, opponents may fight till first blood is drawn, if it is agreed upon, or until death. A dueler may bring a second if he chooses, but that gets messy. Once blood is drawn, emotions run high and a friend might step in to save another, which goes against all the rules. It used to be that you could challenge someone to a duel if they insulted you. If they lied about you. If they disrespected you. That used to be the case until somebody decided to outlaw them. Now we have to do them in secret, like animals. Once the rules are set, the game starts."

They spent the next few minutes showing me how to properly hold and use a sword. At one point, the three of us moved in a circle as the both of them instructed me on how to walk, how to move with it, how to avoid it.

"The number one mistake people make in a swordfight is they assume gentlemanly fair play. Listen to this, friend. If you ever find yourself in a duel and think it's over, it's not. Until both weapons are out of hand and you are out of danger, the game is always on. You understand? Never relax with a man when a weapon is near. Or a woman, for that matter. There are plenty strong swordswomen only too happy to draw the blood of a man."

"En garde!" Thomas yelled, sword at the ready. Josephe turned to him, quickly, sword up. I stepped out of the way as they circled each other, fighting with their swords in what could only be described as a type of ballet.

"Duels are illegal," Josephe swiped.

"But they will always exist because men have huge egos," Thomas said, his eyes on Josephe.

"Why are you watching him and not the weapon," I asked.

"His eyes will tell you what he plans to do with the weapon, friend," Thomas replied. Just at that moment, Josephe moved to jab the sword and Thomas countered, as if expecting it. I was starting to get nervous.

"I understand," I said. "You can stop now."

Josephe gave a fierce smile. "We stop when we're done." Swipe. "Thomas has been getting on my nerves lately, whining about being my second in command."

"And Josephe has always been on my nerves, thinking he's France's greatest gift. Let me tell you, if his courage is as big as his ego we'll win in battle on day one." Jab!

I stepped away as they continued to lob insults at each other. I didn't know either of them well. Could it be I was about to witness a murder?

Suddenly, Thomas lunged, and I thought I saw him plant the rapier into Josephe's chest. My eyes grew wide and I wondered how quickly I could run before the police arrived. My panic must have shown on my face as, instead of seeing red blossom across Josephe's chest, he lifted his arm and I could see the weapon had gone just under it. From my vantage point it had only appeared to enter his chest.

"Mon Dieu, will you look at his face," Josephe said. "We're only teasing you."

Thomas burst into laughter at my expression and came over to slap me on the back. "We're sorry, Zamor, we have a sick humor between us. Are you all right?"

Now that I could breathe, I laughed, awkwardly. "I thought you'd gone insane. I was about to pick up that pistol and shoot you both."

"You would have tried!" Thomas laughed. They relaxed and proceeded to put their weapons away. Josephe cocked a sideways glance at me. "By the way, it kept nagging at me that I'd seen you someplace else and then I remembered a black man at the tennis court at Versailles. Were you there when they signed the oath?"

"Ah, early in the day, yes, but not at the signing."

"How did you manage to position yourself at the Estates-General?" Thomas asked.

I shrugged. "You know, the royal court is its own beast. You learn how to tame it and survive. For me, it helps to be a servant."

"Are you a puppet master, little man?" Thomas asked, looking at me, shrewdly. "Everywhere but nowhere. Pulling strings, yet power-less. *And* you know the court inside and out."

"He's smart. A survivor. That's why you should join my Légion," Josephe said. "I hope you're considering it. We *can* teach you to shoot, eventually."

"Oh, the damage the three of us could do," Thomas smiled. "I can already hear the stories of our prowess."

"Well, you both should know something," I said. "I don't know what my rights are if I'm not free. I don't even know if I could join the army. That's why I'm a Jacobin. It's my only way out."

They looked at me, soberly. Then Josephe said, "I can't give you freedom. But no one would stop you if you chose to join the army. We have many immigrants who fight for France because they love this country. With our army you'll be among brothers and you'll at least, be away from your current circumstance. With God's grace, our success on the battlefield will cause Max to look at your situation with new eyes. Think about it."

I smiled, too. These men were starting to make me believe I really could fight in their army. They were starting to make me really want to.

18

———————

"Is that your page, Madame?"

The man was sitting in our dining room grinning at me as I stood behind Madame. He was a new one and it appeared he was going to be a pain.

"He most certainly is," Madame said, sipping soup. "Louis, introduce yourself to the man."

"I'm Louis," I said, without a smile. It didn't matter, the man started giggling.

"Aren't you the lucky noir. Look at you, standing so close to the lovely Madame du Barry. It must be wonderful for a nègre such as yourself to be near this splendid woman every day. How did you get so lucky?" His cheeks were red and shiny like an apple.

"I must have pleased the gods, Monsieur," I said.

"You certainly must have been a good boy!"

Anger spiked in me but he wasn't the first ignorant guest we'd ever had. I ignored similar comments throughout the meal until finally, over Tart Tatin, I snapped after the zillionth comment about how lucky I was.

"Mon Dieu, Monsieur," I drawled, perhaps louder than I needed.

"Can you shut up about my luck. Frankly, I think Madame is lucky to have me – a man willing to deal with countless asinine guests and their stupid innuendos. I work here, Monsieur, I'm not in love with her."

"Well," Madame toyed with her dessert, pouting. "Now you've gone and hurt my feelings, Louis-Benoit. Are you saying you don't love me."

"Not right now, I don't," I snapped.

"Nonsense. We always love each other. But he's right, Monsieur, I'm lucky to have Louis-Benoit. He's the son I never had with my dear Louis the Well-Beloved—"

"—When is du Brissac coming back?" I interrupted, earning an annoyed glance from her. "I can't wait until he comes back so you have something to do besides get on my nerves."

"That's it!" Gaspard headed across the room toward me. I wasn't done.

"And please stop inviting ignorant guests. This country might be going through a difficult time but Chateau du Barry can still afford to be judicious about who we invite. We have a reputation to uphold!"

The guest's smile finally disappeared and he turned to Madame and said, "That nègre is being rude to me Madame..."

"I'm so sorry, Monsieur, he has a mind of his own..."

By that time Gaspard had pushed me out of the room and shut the door in my face. I thought no more about it until the man returned some weeks later with a smile on his face, like he had a secret. I decided to disarm him immediately before the meal even started, hoping to shut him down so I didn't have to deal with his comments all day.

"Oh look, it's our brilliant guest again. Have you come to regale us with more insights ... like the sky is blue and the grass is green? Or will I be left alone in peace today?"

Unfortunately, I didn't derail him at all. He smiled brightly.

"I'm happy to see you, Governor."

No good ever happened when people called me that.

"Madame, I come bearing a gift to the residents of the Chateau du Barry."

Her eyes brightened and she sat up straight. She loved gifts. I couldn't help but notice he kept looking at *me*. My warning hackles rose.

He stood and proceeded to unfold a large stand that had been hidden behind a curtain. Then, he pulled a canvas from under the table. Madame leaned forward, excited, as did the others at the table, mumbling about what it might be. He cleared his throat.

"I told my son what a wonderful time I had here at my last visit and about how impressed I was at the respect and adoration of your lowly nègre servant here and he insisted on drawing a portrait. I had to describe you, of course, but I think he did a very good job."

He flipped the sheet over the back to reveal a charcoal drawing of Madame, looking beautiful, gazing down and over her shoulder at a buffoonish black man with exaggerated wide nose and cartoonish lips pressed firmly to her backside.

Jeanne du Barry and the room exploded with laughter as they alternately looked at the drawing and looked at me. Looked at the drawing and looked at me. I tried to calm my breathing and felt, rather than saw, Véronique trying to send calming waves my way but, alas, it was too late. Fury blossomed in me.

I stalked over to the easel and snatched the drawing off the stand. "Ha, ha! Ha, ha, ha!" I faked-laughed, loudly. I began walking with the canvas as Madame slapped the table in hysterics and the guest ran to me, trying to clutch my arm. I slapped his hand away every time he reached for it, marching past him out the door and down the hall.

"That's mine! That's mine, give it back!" He yelled.

"No, Monsieur," I shrugged him off. "You clearly told the entire room that this was a gift to the residents of the Chateau du Barry"—shrug!—"And as a member of this household any one of us can do whatever we want with it!"

I had marched out of the house to the graveled front drive, where I threw the drawing onto the ground.

"Stop, that's mine! Madame du Barry, stop him!"

I grabbed a lit torch from a wall sconce.

Madame's laughter had calmed a little, but her eyes were sparkling with mirth as she lounged against the doorframe, watching the scene. "That isn't nice, Louis-Benoit, it was such a thoughtful gift."

"Yes, it was, dearest Madame," I said, taking care to catch the corner of it on fire. "So thoughtful to give us kindling for an outdoor fire this chilling October evening. Lovely, lovely gift. So lovely it's too special for the human gaze, it will burn our eyes with its beauty. I do this for the safety of our simple human eyes."

It was going up in flames surprisingly quickly. The man ran back to whine to Madame about me. I heard her pretend concern as I watched the drawing burn, the smell of the smoke finally calming me down a bit; smoke as hot as my angry breaths disappearing into the chilly air.

Later after the nobles had retired on finishing dinner, I was sitting against the outer wall of the servants' quarters outside the kitchen with Henri on one side of me and Véronique on the other. Véronique didn't bother to talk to me about dinner, she knew how I felt.

"I went outside for some air last night and came upon Madame again. Digging. She didn't see me. It was well past midnight so everyone must have been in bed," Véronique whispered to me.

Only a few of us were aware of Madame's nighttime excursions. On any given day she would slip out of the house, take a shovel from the gardener's shed, and dig up the earth in the ragged area just beyond the manicured grounds. Being placed so made it seem as though an animal might have been digging so no one noticed.

But many years ago, when I was out having brandy on a breezy spring evening I watched from the shadows where I sat as she took a shovel to dig a hole, dropped something inside, and used the back of the shovel to pat the earth back over the spot.

Of course, when she went back inside I dug it up myself, and found a small cloth bag full of emeralds. I put it back, making a mental note of the spot.

The first time Veronique told me she had seen Madame digging I shrugged. "Rich people are strange," I told her. "She's hoarding jewels like a squirrel hoards nuts for the winter."

Henri began talking about his own problems.

"Did you see that man who came this morning?" Henri asked with a frown. "Did you see his boots? Gold on his boots. Looked at me like I wasn't worthy to even see the glimmer from them."

Henri's sadness was palpable. He was a sensitive man, for all his worldliness. And I still felt slightly protective of him.

"I hate to say it, Henri, but you aren't worthy to look at those boots," I told him. When his eyes swung my way, I continued. "Neither am I and neither is Véronique. Haven't you learned that yet? The sooner you learn, the less difficult life will be. We are riffraff to them but that doesn't mean we are riffraff *to us.* In fact, the less they think of me the more I think of myself. From my perspective, by treating me like the least, they have practically ensured I will always believe that I'm the greatest thing God put on this earth. Because we're polar opposites, you see. And if they are the merde they prove themselves to be everyday and I am opposite, then I must be the greatest thing, right? So, I will gladly be riffraff to them. I will gladly be the man they think the least deserving of human decency in all the world. You understand?"

Véronique picked up on my facetiousness, immediately.

"We are the dregs of society," she said. "Not worth the thread we use to mend their clothes."

"I mean, look at those horses you tend," I continued as Henri's face lost his sadness and began to pick up the game. "Hundreds of livres for my horse Lightning. Our good man Gaspard told me to my face when I was very young and at the height of my popularity at court--"

"—What did good Manager Gaspard tell you?" Véronique listened with mock intensity.

"—When I made the error of trying to escape on horseback, upon dragging me back he made sure I knew I should be whipped, not for leaving but because of the value of the horse that was carrying me.

He was right! I didn't even realize that horse was worth ten of me until he told me."

By this time, Henri was watching our verbal volley with amusement.

"You dared to take the King's, property, Monsieur?" Véronique looked scandalized. "Well then, you deserved a sure beating."

"Mademoiselle, they should beat me three times daily for what I think of them. If only they knew the thoughts that go through this depraved mind of mine."

"Blasphemy!" she called.

"Blasphemy!" Henri repeated. We all fell into laughter, which caused Salanave to poke her head out the door.

"What on earth is going on out here with you all making a nuisance of yourselves?"

"Salanave, have you heard the news," Henri said. "We're riffraff!"

"Salanve already knows, she told me when I was a child. I must be small, small, small. We are the worst of the worst!" I said. The three of us continued to pelt her with proclamations of our worthlessness until, finally, her face lost its sternness and she gave us a sly look.

"You're all wrong," she said, wiping her hands on her apron. "You're not worthless, entirely. You're more like the horse dung that Henri shovels every day. Useless to good people, directly, but more than helpful to make important things grow to keep those good people alive. You know. Among the lot of you, you are not worth one coin. But together, you all—plus me—make one healthy pile of merde."

We hooted in a cacophony of celebration. Her lips wiggled in a smile. "Oh, you are crazy children." She went inside and left us to our ruminations, but we were out of self-criticisms.

Since most of our day was done, we secured a bottle of wine and shared it, passing it along, us three. It was a nice red; rich and deep. The wine cellar was overflowing, and it wouldn't be missed. Again, Salanave came to the doorway, having finished in the kitchen and preparing to go to bed. Usually, she slipped away quietly because she had to rise so early to have breakfast prepared before the household woke. Today she leaned in the doorway, and when I handed the bottle up to her, she wiped it with her apron and took a long drink.

We joked a bit more and laughed. It grew a bit chilly but the wine kept us warm.

After the sun went down, even though a few candles burned outside, the night was so dark we could only hear the trees swaying.

19

———

Véronique had never been to Paris, but she agreed to come with me one night.

I took her with me to my good friend's house. I knocked on Sebastien's door and snuck a look at her. I didn't know why I was nervous, but I smiled at her and she returned one almost as shy as mine.

So, of course I would choose this time to start an uncomfortable conversation as we stood there looking at the wooden door.

Then, the door opened as quickly and forcefully as always, causing Véronique's eyes to widen at the sudden appearance of Sebastien, in all his gruffness and high volume.

"You must be Véronique! You are much too pretty to be with this old man masquerading as a nobleman. Ma chère, they're here!"

Of course, his wife didn't have far to walk in their tiny house but she moved forward to give a kind smile to Véronique. "Pardon him, he forgot he's supposed to actually allow his guests through the door."

"I just bull my way right past him," I told Véronique, whose eyes had lost some of their fear. She was smiling genuinely now.

"I could try," she said. "But something tells me I wouldn't be successful."

"You'd be surprised." Sebastien's wife moved him out of the way with one hip, leading Véronique inside. "I'm Élise." His face had gone red.

"It's been so long since we had a woman visitor who wasn't known to me," he whispered to me. "I don't know what I expected but the two of you look good together."

"Sebastien! Get inside and close that door. The draft! You think we have so much heating oil we can afford to waste it?" his wife called. It was late fall and though it rarely snowed, it was pretty chilly.

Once inside, we gave them gifts. I had taken Salanave up on her offer to bring along a small package of cured meat. The whole family gasped at that, it being so long since they'd had meat.

"You will spoil us, Zamor," Sebastien said, pleased but embarrassed to be seen feeling quite so pleased.

"I can do so much with that," Élise said, having a hard time looking away from that package, which she immediately walked over and put in a high cupboard.

Véronique had brought her own gift for Sebastien's wife; an embroidered handkerchief holding a few lovely, dried stems of lavender. Sebastien's wife's eyes lit up and she immediately held it to her nose.

"Real lavender? I didn't even know it could grow so far north. This will go right in my drawer, thank you."

"You're very welcome," Véronique said. "They're not my flowers even, but it seemed to me if someone puts them in refuse, they give up the right to determine what's to be done with them."

"Refuse? Why? They're perfect!"

"Madame doesn't like flowers around that are past their prime," I said. "You'd be surprised what gets thrown away."

"Criminal," Sebastien said, frowning.

"My family is of modest means," Véronique told her. "We don't particularly understand how wealthy people think. To us, a flower is a beautiful thing and if we can keep it longer we will."

Sebastien's wife nodded eagerly. "I feel the same way. It's a shame flowers are so expensive here in the city—"

"The flowers are beautiful but there's more." I looked at Véronique, who was already so pleased at the reception her gift had received I knew she would say nothing else. But I was also sure neither Sebastien nor his wife had noticed the handkerchief.

"If you turn that bit of material over you'll see a pattern. See that stitching?"

They did, and oohed in response.

"Véronique did that herself."

"This is a true talent you, have," Sebastien said. "You can sell these to all the fine ladies."

She blushed. "I do. But I can also do what I enjoy best, and give them *as gifts* to fine ladies, instead." The two women shared a look as if they were already friends for life.

"Come, sit down," Élise said, picking up her skirts to make her way into the little cooking area where she was stirring soup.

The children had been quiet until then, but the second they'd seen their mother welcome the new lady into her kitchen, they came to life, sticking close to the mother while asking Véronique all sorts of questions: where she was from, why was she here, why was she wearing a headwrap.

One child came running to me and nearly knocked me over after grabbing hold of my legs in a hug. Not much of a child person, I was stiff with discomfort and Sebastien had a good laugh while I struggled to regain my balance. It was a noisy, happy din until one of the children wailed.

"The water, again, papa!"

We looked up to where he pointed and Sebastien cursed as a wash of bubbly water gushed in under the front door from the gap between the door and the ground.

"I've told that bastard to empty his dirty wash water in the middle of the street. He knows there's a slope and he does it anyway. I should go there and turn him upside down."

"Sebastien, hush," his wife caused. "It's an inconvenience but it's nice living near a washerman. Don't forget."

He busied himself mopping up the water with rags and then we were soon eating.

"Tell us about your home in Burgundy, Véronique," Élise said. "Did it prepare you at all for life in Louveciennes?"

Véronique smiled, discreetly. "Madame Élise has a sense of humor."

We laughed and she went on, describing her little town and the farm she grew up on. Élise seemed to come alive the more she spoke and before long, we were chatting as if we'd known each other forever. We talked about the city life compared to the country and all agreed the air in the country was better. We laughed about the differences in clothes and hair and social expectations in the country vs the city. She and I were so obviously opposites, but we enjoyed each other anyway.

Inevitably, Sebastien turned to political matters as he and I tended to do.

"How do you feel about all the time Zamor spends in Paris now that he's a Jacobin?"

She looked at me. "Well, now, I wasn't aware he was a Jacobin, Sebastien. You didn't tell me that, Zamor."

No, I'd never said it out loud. I glared at Sebastien, who shrugged, like there was nothing to be done about it now.

"I didn't want to involve you in anything you might not want to be involved in," I said by way of explanation. "And I wanted you to have deniability, if anyone should ask."

"Deniability?" Sebastien asked.

Élise explained. "He doesn't want to give her information she might feel the need to lie about. If she doesn't know, she can easily say she doesn't know."

"I see, I'm sorry I let the cat out of the bag. But now that you do know, what do you think of this all, Véronique? Is there madness like this in Burgundy?"

Véronique measured her words. "My mother tells me a Jacobin Club has sprouted in our hometown. And even more amazing, my very own mother has joined a group of women in the town to discuss the issues central to our well-being."

"Your mother's a Jacobin?" I asked.

"Not officially.

"Well, officially, us women can't be Jacobins, isn't that right, Sebastien?" Élise said with a frown.

Sebastien held up his hands.

"It's not my choice. Besides, you know the women meet anyway. I mean ... they use the club when we're not in session and they call themselves Jacobins."

"Call themselves—we should all be calling them Jacobins if they are, no matter their sex." Élise was indignant. "They have to sneak in whenever the men aren't using it, like children. They should be an official part of the movement!"

"I agree with you."

"We both agree," I said.

"Official or not, women will gather," Véronique said. "I sometimes meet with women at my local church."

I looked at her. "On Jacobin matters? I didn't know that."

"You call it Jacobin matters, but I call it our country's matters. Like I said, women will gather, permission or not. I sent my mother a copy of the *Declaration of the Rights of Man and the Citizen*. She immediately complained to me about the lack of mention of women or black people."

Sebastien looked back and forth between us, and then gestured toward me with his spoon. "Did Zamor tell you he wrote it?"

Both Élise and Véronique looked at me, surprised. Before I could explain, Sebastien did.

"I mean, the final version was Gilbert's, but Zamor is the one who went to him first. He gave him all his notes on what it should say. He's the reason it happened, just like he's the reason for the storming of the Bastille."

Véronique's eyes were boring into the side of my face. "Is that so? If you wrote it why did you leave out any reference to slavery or women?"

"I included plenty about slavery. He took it out."

"Of course, he did," she said. "My father is finally a free man after having been enslaved all his life at Saint Domingue. Maman was born in France but as a woman with black skin, it's almost certain that things as they are, she'll never be a citizen in her lifetime. So some French people will never be citizens due to their skin color or their sex or their religion. And if a person born on their own country's soil is not a free citizen, what value is there in citizenship?"

"The value is in the fact that we all want it," Sebastien groused.

Véronique looked at me. "So, if that's why you're coming here to Paris all the time, I finally understand. You're going to change things."

I shrugged. "I want to try."

"My mother never imagined her daughter might live a different existence but now, she says she has hope. Her group is demanding rights for women. She does this for me, even knowing that there are many who want her silent. For me, she's become radicalized. Every time I read of what this new government might be I think of my mother and her safety. As she's back home thinking of mine."

"But it is improbable, isn't it?" Sebastien asked. "That you, as a black woman, will ever have citizenship if this republic can't even get it for the poorest white men. I'm sorry, I don't mean to offend, I just don't understand. How is it your mother has hope? Her women's group is undoubtedly focused on the needs of women, but black women? What need might they have that's not addressed, either through abolition of slavery or the women's movement?"

Véronique gave a small, sad smile. "No offense taken, Monsieur Sebastien. We black women might overlap several populations but together we are another thing, entirely. Any rights we might earn in time as black people are negated by the fact that we are women. Or any advances made by a woman are cancelled out by our blackness if this country refuses to see black people as equal. You see, unless rights are had by all of us, black women will never be whole."

"I never considered that," Sebastien said, sipping his soup. "I don't know why I never thought of that."

"Why would you, Sebastien," Véronique asked, gently. "I'd

venture to guess until you met Zamor you never considered the rights of black men, either."

She was so good at explaining. She should be in the Jacobin Club instead of me.

"I hear Olympe de Gouges is fighting for the rights of women and trying, in her way, to be an abolitionist," Élise said.

"Olympe de Gouges?" Sebastien perked up. "We just saw a play she wrote, didn't we? Don't worry, chère, I didn't pay to get in. It was called 'L'Esclavage des Noirs ou L'Heureux Naufrage" featuring a character—get this..." he leaned over and nudged his wife, pointing his spoon at me. "...a character named Zamore, an Indian slave who kills a man for trying to hurt the woman he loves. The character refers to his master as *Governor*. And he says he's like a son to him. Sound familiar?"

Sebastien laughed at me, but either didn't notice or didn't care about the discomfort suddenly in the room or that no one else was laughing.

"How is that possible?" Véronique looked at me.

"Zamor is well-known," Élise said. "Even people who don't know him, know of him, isn't that right, Sebastien?"

"It's true. He was a legend; the young slave who kept trying to escape but became the closest confidant of the King's mistress? I knew about him long before he walked into that tavern the first time," Sebastien said. "Of course, he's known better in his circles. Madame de Gouges is a noblewoman, after all. She would certainly be familiar with his story."

"That must have been strange," Véronique said to me. "How did that make you feel? Why didn't you say something?" She looked at me now, concerned.

"Say what? The woman wrote a play calling me ... what was that term, Sebastien?"

"Noble savage?" He drank his wine, eyes wide in innocence. Élise elbowed him as discreetly as she knew how. "Zamore's character goes on and on about how the Governor is so good and kind-hearted. And that he murdered the man as a result of his nature."

Véronique frowned. "That sounds horrible, sitting there hearing your name through the whole thing?"

I shrugged. "I'm certain she never expected me to be in the audience. Besides, I imagine a lot of people know my story. It's not a secret."

"You should be proud to have survived what you have," she said. "I admire the person you are, after all you've endured."

It was at that moment, watching Véronique sip soup that I realized how little I had thought about what this new republic had in store for *her*. France would be bankrupt were it not for women like Véronique. And here she was, comforting me, when she had so much more at stake.

It made sense why she was so angry at me regarding the Women's March. All of France was so used to taking from women like her we barely even noticed when we trampled over them. I was ashamed it took me this long to even consider what change meant through her eyes. But now that I was looking, I wouldn't look away again. Véronique glanced up at me and gave me the tiniest, most lovely look. My heart took flight.

20

Dear Citizen,

Lest you get caught up in the growing love between Véronique and I, I remind you there were other things happening.

I was used to being privy to the machinations of devious people but I was rarely on the receiving end of a master plan. Gaspard wasn't smart enough on his own to plan against me and Madame never had a reason until 1791. That year I discovered what it was like to be on the receiving end of her master plan.

My "personal page and servant" duties expanded to include being a scapegoat, whether voluntary or not. It wasn't voluntary.

--Zamor, 1820

January 1791

One day, Madame decided to spend the evening with du Brissac in Paris, to return the next day. I was happy to have been able to sleep in that morning—no need to get the morning chocolat—only to be interrupted just before lunch.

"Monsieur Zamor," said the boy who had knocked on my bedroom door. He was the son of one of the cleaning servants I happened to like. He and his little sister took care of many of the little jobs no one else liked to do like milking the cows, gathering eggs in the morning, and interrupting me in my room. Fortunately, I liked the whole family of three.

"Yes, what do you want, child?" I asked him.

"Madame says to come to the parlor immediately." He bowed quickly and walked away. I didn't know she had returned.

"Come in, Zamor," Madame said when I entered the room. I stopped short, noticing she was sitting on a chair opposite two officers who were sitting on a chaise. The sun streamed through the window and struck them, so they were lit up like shiny new presents, their white faces a mask of discomfort. Gaspard stood closest to the window on the other side of her, his eyes swinging to me when I entered.

Madame continued. "I was just telling our fine officers from the villages of Versailles and Louveciennes that we've been robbed," Madame said, extreme dismay showing on her features.

I looked around at the other faces. "We've been robbed?"

"Yes, thank you for joining us," one of the officers said. He turned to Madame. "You say you discovered the theft from your guard?"

"Yes," Gaspard spoke up, trying to sound very important. "Madame had gone to visit with the Duc du Brissac in Paris yesterday."

"Did you go with her?"

"I did. But I rode alone and returned here before her this morning. That's when I passed her bedchamber and noticed the door slightly ajar. On entering, I saw many of her things thrown about as if having been rifled through. Then I noticed the ladder perched outside her open bedroom window. I told her as much when she returned."

"I immediately looked for my jewels when Gaspard told me."

"That would mean it was a planned attack," one of the officials said. "It would mean someone would have known you were gone ... to know when to attempt this."

Madame dabbed her forehead. "It disturbs me greatly to think that anyone from my own household would have been involved. I can't imagine anyone here would betray me."

"But you say you asked a servant to sleep in your room to protect your jewels while you were gone?"

"Yes, I did. I asked my trusted Governor, Louis-Benoit Zamor, to sleep in my room. You remember, Louis?"

I almost got whiplash from the jerk of my head, looking at her. Never had she ever asked me to sleep in her room to protect her jewels while she was out. My name coming from her mouth at this moment sent more than alarm bells ringing in my head.

"I believe you are mistaken, Madame," I said. "Perhaps it was Gaspard, your guard, who was to watch over your jewels while you were gone. I know it's easy to mistake the two of us."

Gaspard glared at me from across the room. Madame brushed off my words with a wave of her hand as if they were as insignificant as I was.

"My Louis-Benoit fancies himself to be amusing but this is not the time, Louis. You know Gaspard goes with me to Paris. I definitely asked you. You are my closest confidant and the only one I trust with my jewels. Everyone knows that."

"Yes, Madame," one of the officers said. "All of France knows of the closeness of the relationship between you and your trusted page. It is truly inspiring."

"With all due respect," I interrupted. "Lesser known—but no less inspiring—is Madame's relationship with her manager and head guard, Gaspard. Surely you posted one of your hand-chosen guards to watch the room, knowing you were both going to Paris? Officers, it is Madame's guard who was comfortable inspecting her bedchamber before even our esteemed law enforcement had a chance to look at the scene. I've never been instructed to sleep in her bedchamber. I'm sure Madame only dreamed she asked me to do it. Perhaps too much wine for dinner put that thought into her head."

At their expressions, I allowed my lips to quirk just a bit to take the bite out of my words because contrary to what she had said, I didn't have much of a sense of humor. I meant everything I said and intended no amusement in them.

But I had everyone's attention, so decided to do a little sleuthing since I could.

"Though it's curious ... I'd think a person who worked here and stole from under the nose of your trusted Gaspard would have left the premises. Are any staff missing, Madame?"

"I was going to ask you that also, Madame," said the officer.

She shuffled with discomfort. "I don't know. Gaspard, is anyone missing?"

"No, Madame, but that means nothing. Perhaps they knew that leaving would cast suspicion on them. Maybe the worker isn't the only culprit and he had friends commit the actual theft."

He was about to point to my trips to Paris, I knew it!

"If it's an inside job," I interrupted to stop that path. "Why would a ladder be necessary at all? If someone from this household betrayed you, they would only have to walk down the hall to take what they wanted since, apparently, your guards are worthless. That would be much simpler than taking the chance and the time to set up an elaborate ruse with a two-story ladder openly propped outside your window."

Unless, of course, someone wanted to set it up to look that way.

Madame looked at me a long moment and then continued to instruct the officers to do all they could to find her jewels, and she would contact her jeweler for an accounting of everything that was missing. Then she excused me.

I left the room seething, convinced my benefactress, the so-called honorable Madame du Barry, was attempting to set me up to take the blame for the theft of her jewels. With the help of Gaspard. Why would she do such a thing unless she was guilty of coordinating the theft herself? A theft that wasn't really a theft. Why?

I had perhaps five minutes before the officers came out of the parlor. I left the room and headed straight to her study to look through her papers while she and Gaspard were still with the officers. I opened and shut the first drawer and found nothing out of the ordinary. I moved to the other side of the desk and jerked open another drawer. On the third drawer I hit pay dirt with paperwork of bank accounts she had set up in England, along with property descriptions.

The answer was clear: she was trying to set me up for the same reason she was setting up banking accounts in England and looking at real estate outside of France. She was building a nest for her escape and she needed a way to get her wealth out of the country without the government noticing. What better way than to fake a theft?

Two days later, when Sebastien and I sat on stools at the bar of the tavern drinking cheap ale, I told Sebastien what had happened.

"That's brazen," he said. "But nobles are creative when it comes to getting what they want and saving their own skin. And they listened to her and didn't raise objections? If your name comes up further you'll want to let Jacques or Max know you're being framed; they both know the law, maybe they can help. It seems like Jeanne du Barry has more power and influence now than she did when Louis XV was alive."

And more money. Sebastien didn't know the half of it. She had influence because, when the King returned all of her property and the Chateau to her, the King had given tacit approval of her affiliation to the crown. No one would harass her unless they knew they wouldn't suffer repercussion from the crown.

"More influence and entirely no oversight," someone said.

We looked up and found ourselves being watched by a man with red hair and green eyes who'd slipped so easily into eavesdropping it was obvious it wasn't his first time. I didn't much care for my personal space or conversation being invaded.

"And who are you?" I asked, sharply.

Sebastian answered. "Zamor, this is George Grieve. He's new to France, from the Americas. He's a friend of Paul's. And Max."

"I've spent time in America" Grieve said. "But, technically, I'm a Brit."

"He knows what it means to change a country, isn't that right?" Sebastien said. "Paul says he's here to help us change ours."

"And why does Monsieur Grieve want to help change ours?" I asked.

"Why?" Sebastien laughed, slapping me on the back. "Because he believes in our cause. Excuse him, Monsieur Grieve, he's a skeptic by nature, as I told you."

I wondered how much Sebastien or Paul or anyone had told him about me, but I found out moments later, as Grieve chimed in, a look of smug superiority on his face.

"It's alright, Sebastien, I know all about Louis-Benoit Zamor. You are the black page given to Jeanne du Barry as a child. Enslaved from the age of seven. Led around on a leash as a boy, no better than one of their dogs. Dressed up like a toy and forced to tumble and twirl on the floor like a dancing clown for the court's amusement. Set up for a lifetime of mockery and ridicule, prepared for little other than being the plaything of nobles and kings."

I kept my expression as flat as my words. "Why, such glowing things you've been saying about me, Sebastien."

"He didn't need to say anything, your reputation has traveled across the channel. As an example of the debauchery of the royals. Louis-Benoit Zamor, godson of a weak fool who hit the lottery of bloodlines and his scheming streetwalking whore lover. They say the three of you routinely had relations together in the King's bed. They say you brought with you perversions of sexuality of your race and she is still your willing student. They say you are little more than an animal. All these years they have been saying this and she does nothing to disabuse the rumors. This is the woman you serve."

I could see clearly he hoped to get a rise out of me. Some of what he said was new to my ears, but not all. At this point in my life, I wouldn't have been surprised to hear that I was the devil himself. But I was not foolish enough to take the bait. Not with this man. I didn't like his eyes.

"As though it's possible to disabuse filth and lies from ears eager to hear them and mouths more than willing to spread them. By your own account the Madame is just as much a victim of those lies as I am. You seem overly concerned with my benefactress. There are bigger issues than Madame du Barry, don't you think?"

"The royal rot must be dealt with – it festers from the inside out. But it would not fester so deeply and widely were there not the support system of the nobles; both those of birth and those bought, like your Madame. That necklace debacle set France back millions. Millions for a necklace that never should have been made, all for a woman who bought nobility on her back. Now, for the past year and a half, nobles have been scurrying like rats, taking their money and wealth with them for fear of being taxed. The French people have suffered under the unfair laws and practices for over a thousand years and yet now, you ask the King to tax the nobles and they clear out their bank accounts and flee the country. That will end. The purchase of privilege will end and women like Jeanne du Barry will no longer be able to take advantage of foolish men."

"She couldn't have bought privilege had the Well-Loved not offered it to her on a platter," I said. He was starting to annoy me. The last thing I wanted to do was defend the Madame—I came to the tavern to complain about what she was doing to *me*, after all--but it seemed odd the way he fixated on her, alone, as if the fall of France was on her shoulders and not on the men who ran the country. "It seems to me your anger is misplaced, Monsieur Grieve. It seems to me the one who did the true harm is lying in a crypt and his grandson has picked up the reins. And with all your talk, you still haven't answered the question: Why do you care about France and its political state, or will you keep trying to distract me with insults designed to make me dissolve into a puddle of tears?"

Grieve looked at me for a long moment. "I might have underestimated you, Monsieur. You are small, and no one could ever take you for handsome, but you are intelligent. You're lucky to be here and not in the colonies or the Americas where they punish people like you to stop them from learning. Is that why you're beholden to her? Gratitude?"

"Beholden?" I said. "I'm beholden to eating nice food and sleeping in a warm bed at night. And I've developed a strong liking for champagne and prefer to be in spaces with walls adorned with fine art. I like to be surrounded by lush trees and manicured gardens and a pavilion that overlooks the Seine. If that makes me beholden, so be it. Until the republic accomplishes its goals I plan to pass the time in the state to which I've become accustomed. Unless, of course, you offer me comparable shelter and an invitation to live with you?"

He gave a mirthless smile. "I do not believe my abode would be anything you are used to. I can barely afford bread to sustain me so another mouth to feed is out of the question. Justice is my comfort. Fairness, my food. That's why Max asked for my help and why I'm here. Well, gentlemen, I'll hold you up no longer. I bid you good evening."

Sebastien and I watched him walk away and my friend immediately turned to me, "Okay, so he's not pleasant but he's an important friend to have. It's obvious Max sent him to get you to help implicate du Barry, and after what she did, maybe you should. Tell him what he wants to know and you'll become a respected leader in this cause. And stop pretending the money is so important to you, people will begin to think you're a royalist, like when you first came here. You fought hard to be respected by this community, don't throw it away to put Grieve in his place. We both know you'd give up your way of living in a second for the right reasons."

"Well, he doesn't need to know that. I don't like his eyes. He's shifty. I don't trust him," I said.

Sebastien nodded. "Who said anything about trusting him? You shouldn't trust *anyone*, my friend."

The promise of power was never something to be taken lightly but I wasn't ready to hitch myself to a man I barely knew who had offered me nothing in return for my information.

On the way out of the café I was handed a pamphlet and as I read it I couldn't believe what I was seeing.

21

Dear Citizen,

I remind you there were other things on my mind. Nothing meant anything without my freedom. That was why I went to Paris in the first place, searching for one of those windows Georges Danton spoke of. Any window to provide a sliver of hope.

So, as I was living my life, the time was ticking away with little progress.

It was the kaleidoscope.

The members of the Jacobin Club were like those disparate pieces of glass; each beautiful on its own but coming together to make something different. We were about to experience a kaleidoscope come to life. We would begin to feel the pains of that dial being turned. Unlike the toy, the pieces didn't fit smoothly. When our republic began to turn, the pieces of colored glass rubbed and splintered. Those dangerous, jagged edges rubbing against each other and causing damage.

Looking back, I can now clearly see the first time I felt approaching doom. I sensed the fractures on the horizon.

--Zamor, 1820

I found Sebastien and Valentin at a table in the Club. The latter did little more than raise his cup in acknowledgment when I arrived, slumped in his chair in his very Valentin way. In the year since he'd blindsided me with the theatre performance of the distorted version of my life, we'd had a chance to clear the air between us. I told him he was an asshole to his face and he had, amazingly, apologized. Now, we were civil even if we weren't friends.

"Hey," Sebastien greeted me with a quick, brusque hug. "Georges Danton is here tonight. It's always a circus when he comes. Sometimes I wish he'd just stay away."

Across the room, the man in question was surrounded by people hanging on his words, laughing and drinking. "Look at them. Just look at all of them. It's starting to look like the National Convention in here. That's the last thing we need."

"It doesn't matter," Valentin said. "There's one leader here and everybody knows it."

The National Assembly now called themselves the National *Convention*. It was still mostly former Third Estate representatives with a few nobles and clergy for good measure. One would think that a governing body mainly composed of people of similar class would be in agreement. That wasn't the case. The National Convention, and the Jacobin Club, had sub-segmented itself into factions.

"Look at them," Sebastien said, pointing to a man with his drinking hand. "Look at them drift. It's like they're pulled to their beehive by a magnet."

We watched as people came in, spoke to others, and then crossed the room to join their clusters.

"It doesn't matter," Valentin said. "We can split into a thousand groups, the only group that matters is the one on top. Danton can come and go and bring all his little friends if he wants. He talks to hear his own voice, he doesn't ever have anything significant to say anymore."

But the factions did matter. Just like the country had been divided by class before, now we were dividing ourselves. And where there was division there was weakness.

I looked over at Georges and his boisterous crowd of drinking Cordeliers. In a far corner, the much more subdued Robespierre was sitting with members of his Mountain, as they were nicknamed because they liked to sit in the top seats at the National Convention; a strategic move, I was sure. Would-be abolitionist and founder of the Society of the Friends of the Blacks, Brissot, was there with his followers, the Brissotins. The Brissotins were increasingly becoming known as the Girondins.

The Cordeliers, the Mountain and the Brissotins/Girondes were the most powerful of all the groups. I was encouraged by the fact that the leaders of all three were staunchly against slavery. But I couldn't say that everyone in their factions felt the same and I couldn't see that it was a priority for any of them.

"Snake," Valentin sneered under his breath, his eyes following a man who did seem to be slithering his way through the room, a drink in one hand, his eyes shifting back and forth over the crowd.

He was a stray, a wild card, with no determined division or loyalty. But he, and others like him, spoke up sometimes and proved themselves to be irrational. We began calling them slithering snakes because whenever they did speak it would be to say something evil. At odd times one or another of them would call out for someone's murder, with no provocation. Someone would declare that we should burn down a city block or a whole town for no valid reason.

Most of us had a natural aversion to the snakes. We could feel them every time they entered the space and, collectively and without discussion, tried to make them feel as uncomfortable as possible. We pretended not to notice when they wanted to speak. We pretended not to hear them when they managed to gain voice. We looked over and around them instead of directly in their eyes. We did everything we could, but the bastards kept coming back, spouting nonsense about murdering en masse, or being cursed by the devil or the evil in the blood of an entire class of people.

The extremists always looked sneaky, like they knew they weren't supposed to be there and were getting away with something, eyes darting every which way.

"Why won't they *leave*?" Sebastien hissed as more of them came through.

"They're hoping to wear us down," Valentin replied. "It was no big deal when it was only one or two, but there seem to be more of them every day."

"Why do you recruit them, Sebastien?"

"Me? I didn't recruit them. They're getting in, somehow, but it's not by my word. I wonder if anyone let them in at all or if they just slithered on in while we weren't looking."

There were a few tables of mixed blood, so-to-speak. Our table. Valentin was a Mountain, though he was more like a powerless hill in that organizational chart. Sebastien was a Brissotin/Gironde. Paul Marat, a Cordelier, was headed to our table. I was a free agent but I never called for murder or carnage so I wasn't considered a snake. Though I'd met with Max Robespierre, he hadn't given me what I asked for yet so—to me—that wasn't a solid relationship.

"Is it just going to be a free-for-all, then?" Paul sat. He wore a cloak with a hood, as I did, but I dropped mine as soon as I came indoors. He still wore his, and under that a wrap around the top of his head and a scarf over his face. I noticed whenever the rash and itching on his skin was particularly bad he tried to hide it with a scarf, which only managed to draw more attention to it. The spots of skin that showed were red and angry, like he'd been scratching.

"Is David here, yet? If we're not going to have a useful discussion I'd rather go home. There's writing to be done."

"Ah, come on, Paul." Sebastien reached over across the table with both hands and grasped Paul by the sides of his neck, giving him a good shake. "You need to get out more! Lively discussion and body odor are good for the sinuses and the brain!"

We chuckled as Paul blanched and gave Sebastien his dirty look. One thing that always happened when Sebastien and Paul Marat were in the room was that Marat would give Sebastien a dirty look over *something*.

"Let's get started!" someone called out.

I pulled out a sheet of paper and my quill, prepared to take my own notes. "Who's first? What news from the Convention, Max?"

The room quieted down to hear Max speak since he never raised his voice, unlike Georges who didn't know how to speak without blowing out an eardrum.

"We're still in discussions with the King. At least, we're *attempting* to have more discussion. Since he arrived in Paris it seems he's busier than ever with steady meetings with parliament and members of the Convention. And to be frank, we're in no rush to push him. We want to be sure how this new government will work in concert with the monarchy. The worst we can do is pressure him. We brought him from Versailles—"

"—*We* didn't bring him anywhere, Max," Georges said. "The women brought him from Versailles. It's the working people and peasants who got the King and Queen out of their glass house and put them right here for us to finally talk to them. So, while we're trying to decide how to make things work in concert let's try to make sure the people are part of that equation."

The Cordeliers clapped and Max sat silent, his hands folded in front of him, looking down at the table, patiently. Once the applause died down he spoke again, careful and measured.

"I'm very happy you brought your little group to clap for you, but I was speaking. Theatrics mean nothing, Georges. You can take them back to your own club." There was bite in his simple words and I felt the tension between the two of them.

"Did something I say get under your skin, Max?" Georges asked.

"All you do is get under the skin, it's the entirety of your personality. It would be nice if there was some substance underneath all that talk."

I mumbled under my breath, "They're missing the point." I was getting antsy at the direction of the conversation and it was making me twitchy. With everything happening, time was of the essence.

"Hush," Valentin whispered. "This isn't the place."

If this wasn't the place, what was? I wasn't allowed to speak to the Convention. With half of the Convention in this room it seemed the *only* place.

Brissot broke in. "Messieurs, all we need is an audience with the King and he'll see what we're all about. Let us in. We know you're the most level-headed among us, Max, and so we've been happy to defer to your recommendations on how to approach him, but perhaps you aren't explaining things to him as you should if he still hasn't full-heartedly agreed to a constitutional monarchy. We'll tell him what we're thinking and let him decide how to proceed. Has anyone considered that perhaps he has some good advice?"

"No," I called out before I realized I was going to. But I couldn't take it anymore. All eyes swung my way. "If you haven't convinced the King to approve a constitutional monarchy by now, you won't. He understands you fine, he just hasn't said no, directly. *We* need to decide what we want to do, *do it,* and then tell the King. We need to do what we feel is best and then inform him after it's done. Not before."

"Are we letting just anybody talk tonight?" a voice rang out. It was an annoyed-looking man with a receding hairline and a lace cravat over his portly stomach.

"That's Antoine Fouquier-Tinville," Valentin whispered to Sebastien and me. "Pompous ass." The pompous ass continued, glaring at me.

"What do you know? Sit down and be quiet."

Sebastien spoke up. "Give him a chance to speak his mind! All of you speak your mind all the time, let's hear from someone else for a change. It's like Georges just said, we need the voice of the people."

"And who are you?" Antoine asked Sebastien, turning to Max before he even got an answer. "Max, this is ridiculous. All these commoners interrupting--" Fouquier-Tinville said.

"Hey, I'm a member of this Jacobin Club, and have been since the beginning," Sebastien responded. "These commoners are why we even have a National Convention. Any one of us should be allowed to speak."

I jumped in, immediately. "I'm saying we can't rely on the King to make this decision about adopting a new constitution. I was as hopeful as all of you at first but it's been almost a year. If he hasn't agreed by now he never will. I know the man, all he's doing is stalling until he can figure out how to avoid doing what you ask. *We* need to create the constitutional procedures, put them in place and then let him know how things will work."

"I understand your passion, Zamor," Georges started. "But what you say is..." he stopped and shrugged, his hands out to me. "It's mean-spirited at the very least and disrespectful at best. He deserves the respect of his station."

"Thank you, finally someone speaking reason," said Antoine.

"Has everyone in this room forgotten the Estates General?" I asked. "He locked the whole of the Third Estate out of the meeting rooms so he wouldn't have to hear you. This is a man who is almost afraid to speak with anyone who doesn't have a title with blue blood running through his veins. He looks over regular people like we are a sickness he doesn't want to catch. What has all of it been for? What is this republic all about? If you only wanted to preserve the monarchy why in hell did we do all this? If we're too scattered to make a decision, do we even deserve a republic? Finally, the King is in Paris, where everyone has been saying they want him–brought here by force, a crime punishable by death—and now you all want to wait for *him* to tell *us* what to do? I'll let you in on a secret – he's not going to cooperate. He's not thinking about it. And if I know him like I think I do I can tell you it's the exact opposite. He's pissed! He's putting on an act and waiting you out until he can figure out how to throw the lot of us in prison or worse. And what are we doing? We're sitting here arguing about how we can't move a muscle without his permission. God forbid we're disrespectful about it."

"Will you sit down!" the Antoine man said, standing up and slapping his hands on a table in a display of over-reaction. "And shut up!"

"Now, Antoine," someone tried to calm him down.

"No, this is ridiculous. We're in a room with the most brilliant minds, philosophers, lawyers, and politicians this country has to offer and we're listening to a courtesan's blackamoor who spent half his life serving coffee and the other half on a leash. What do you know of making important decisions or even being a respectable human being?"

"I'm sorry," I said in fake deference. "I must be in the wrong. Is this not the group that claims to ascribe to the Declarations of the Rights of Man and Citizen or did I accidentally end up in the hypocrites' club? Yes, I'm a courtesan's page, say it louder so everyone can hear you. You're absolutely right. So I'm well and truly aware of when somebody's getting screwed, and right now it's us!"

"This is too serious a subject for jokes," he said, turning red as laughter sounded in the room. "The King is a reasonable, good man, we all know this. And, frankly, I think he'd be horrified to know someone who was like a son to the Well-Beloved has this opinion of the monarchy. Someone should tell him—"

"—You won't," Max said softly but firmly enough that the room looked his way. "We will not tolerate a violation of the honor system of the Jacobin Club, Antoine. You can tell anyone you want that you are part of this club but you will not expose this man out of petty malice. You understand?"

Antoine sniffed but relented. "I would never violate the code. I didn't mean that. But some members of the Convention have already spoken to the King, and he is more than amenable to our ideas. He is excited and anxious to get to work setting this country right. It would be asinine to ignore him at this point. We all know the only problem with the King is the ministers surrounding him who have lied to him time and again. He is out of the bubble, we let him know all sides of the situation and we will see our King shine like the natural leader he is."

Someone started clapping, and though there were some who were slow, they joined eventually. Max looked my way and shortly later they adjourned the meeting. I stood from the table to push my papers into my satchel, maybe a little more forcefully than I needed.

"Don't worry about Antoine," Sebastien said. "He's a prick and everyone knows it."

"I don't care what he said about me, Sebastien, I care that they aren't listening. None of them are listening. They're wrong!" A couple of people looked at me, so I tried to lower my voice, but instead we headed out of the room where my opinion mattered so little. Outside, Sebastien tried to keep up with me.

"Maybe there is some reason to hope they're right, Zamor" he said.

"There's absolutely no reason. They're wrong!"

"Why are you so upset?"

I stopped in my tracks and turned to him to express my fear. I almost didn't want to say it out loud. "When I came here tonight I realized the Jabobin Club is double the size as when I joined, not even including the guests. With more clubs all across the country. What's going to happen when they find out who the King really is?"

"He seems an affable man. Kind..."

"He can be kind to his friends. He's not the worst man in the world, that's not what I'm saying."

"Then what's the problem?"

"He's got no spine! He can't make a damn decision to save his life. Everyone's pissed at the Queen because she makes decisions. She makes decisions because somebody's got to do it, he *won't*. He's a liar! He will smile to the face of anyone. Everyone in that room going on and on about how wonderful and rational he is doesn't know him. He has no intention of giving up the monarchy. He will never willingly give up his power. He will never betray the nobles because the nobles are his friends. He's not going to tax them. He's not going to remove their privileges," I was counting with my fingers as I spelled it out. "He's not going to abolish slavery. He's never going to agree that we should all be equal. That man who sits in the Tuileries has no concept of a life without people at his feet and he's not made for it. And our whole plan is to rely on him and trust in him? He'll tell us what we want to hear and do everything to save his own skin."

I pulled my bag up on my shoulder and my hood over my head. "They'll never listen to me. For all their talk I'm still only a black-amoor servant to them but they ignore me at their own peril. At *our* peril. What's going to happen to all those factions in that room; those factions that only agree on one thing, that the king is truly listening to us? What happens to us when they realize it's all a lie? And we have nothing holding us together? What then? Get him out of the bubble of his ministers, huhn?" I parroted Antoine. "*He* is the bubble."

Sebastien was my friend but he looked confused and worried for my sanity. He didn't believe me any more than they had. But I wasn't confused. I was like a fish wife who could feel trouble in her bones. It was like I was holding a broken kaleidoscope in my hand and all the beautiful pieces of jagged glass were falling onto the floor.

I was crossing the Pont Saint-Michelle on the way home. Glancing over in the distance towards the front of the Tuileries Palace I could clearly see that on the Place Louis XV plaza, the statue of said King that had previously been lying on the ground was no longer there. I wondered if the King was situated at a window in the Palace where he could watch as they removed the statue of his grandfather. God help us.

22

———

Dear Citizen,

*Those roving gangs were increasingly becoming a problem.
Violence was becoming a problem everywhere. LaFayette
complained to the Convention that his guards were overwhelmed
by the volume of street-fighting, riots, and mob activity. Unorga-
nized and without political purpose, the activity of roving gangs
was almost impossible to stop before damage was done.*

*And then in February 1791, a group of noblemen tried to whisk the
King away. How to accomplish this with all the guards in place?
Why, knives, of course. All armed with knives.*

*Fortunately, LaFayette and his guards were close enough to prevent
what would surely have been an all-out brawl.*

*Now we call it the Day of Daggers. It's a catchy name, don't you
think? At that point there seemed no end to the number of incidents
that precipitated the need for guards.*

--Zamor, 1820

Madame had been distant from me since the visit from the police and always, suspiciously, preoccupied. She even had Chon block me from delivering her chocolat in the morning, her main lady taking the bowl of chocolat from me herself. Or she was missing from the room when I dropped it off. Or, she was off with du Brissac at his home in Paris.

Finally, I caught her alone one evening in her study, sipping tea by the fire. I slipped in quickly before anyone tried to keep me from her, plunging straight into conversation.

"First you blame me for your lost jewelry and now you publish a pamphlet telling the world about them? I saw it in Paris. You've even listed each piece and its value for all the world to see. A 2000-livres reward for the return?"

"Bonsoir, Louis. As a matter of fact, I slept very well, thank you for asking."

I perched on the edge of the chair on the other side of the fire, anxiously leaning towards her as she sipped her tea. "Why would you do such a thing?"

She tossed me a glance over her teacup. "How else will I get my jewelry back without people out looking for the thieves? At the very least, if a local jeweler is presented with my stolen jewels they'll know they are mine and give them back or turn them in to the police for reward."

"You never asked me to sleep in your room," I seethed. She wouldn't look at me. She was doing that thing she did, distancing herself from me. When she treated me like I was insignificant it made me feel like a child all over again. "Had I known that you felt your jewels might be stolen I would have gone into your room, pulled them all out of your drawers, set them in a pile on the bedroom floor and sat on them like a mother bird protecting her eggs!"

"What on earth are you going on about, Louis?" she laughed. "You're like a quacking duck. Of course, I told you to sleep in my room. You forgot."

"No, I didn't."

"*I'm* not a liar," she snapped. "Do you want me to call the law officers back here and ask them whose word should be believed between the two of us?"

There was no point in responding, her point was clear. She softened her tone and put a soft smile on her face. "Don't look like that, you know I love you. You're in no trouble. I know you're just as upset about all this as I am. It's just a miscommunication. You must have forgotten I asked you, but I did, indeed, ask you. All that matters is the officers get my jewels back. That's what we both want."

She was framing me right in my face. And there wasn't a thing I could do about it.

"This was Gaspard's idea, wasn't it?" I asked. "There's a lot of talk throughout the country of how reckless the royals were with the country's money, so on Gaspard's advice you just gave them even more reason to hate you."

"Gaspard knows my greatest strength is that I'm one of the people and they will want to help me."

"It's not a good idea to…"

"Did I ask for your advice? When I want to know what you think I'll ask you."

My temper flared. "Oh, by all means, listen to the idiot dog, Gaspard. Between the two of you there's not a single brain. Because you blamed me once, now I'll be blamed for everything that goes missing at Louveciennes. And because of his stupid advice now all of France knows how reckless you've been. Gaspard has seen to that. You're both pathetic. When it comes back to bite you see if I care. Just keep me out of your schemes. I won't let you throw me to the wolves. This fox will survive its hunt, you hear me? I'll protect myself!" I stood up and stormed out of the room.

Her amused voice followed me with, "Bonsoir, Louis-Benoit!" in a singsong tone.

I knew the framing was a way to keep me as an option to be used if she found herself in hot water. If she had pressed the point with the police, they would have already arrested me. A noble woman didn't need evidence to convict a black man. I was merely a potential alibi to back up her story if it came down to it.

It was a dangerous game, encouraged by an irrational man trying to show off. Gaspard was driven by emotion and now influenced by alcohol almost constantly. I had no idea why she didn't see that.

But it no longer mattered to me what she told me or what stories she was weaving. I didn't like being in the dark and my investigations into what was going on in the Chateau had been too circumstantial. She made the first strike by framing me—I meant it when I told her I'd protect myself, starting with gathering any information I could find.

The next time she left to visit du Brissac in Paris, I slipped into her study, closing and locking the door behind me.

The room was filled with exquisitely carved wood pieces of furniture and every flat surface had a vase full of roses or peonies but none of that caught my eye. I headed straight to her desk. I sat down on the delicate chair and pulled open the drawer. On top, a love letter from Brissac. I took it out and tossed it onto the table. Then, a letter of gratitude from a local charity for the money she'd sent over. But that was it. I put them back and sat back in the chair, looking around the room.

"Where would you be?" I muttered to the items I knew were hidden. I knew in my bones there was more in this space.

She knew better than to handle important papers in my presence. It was almost as if she felt she couldn't trust me.

My eyes lit on the paintings on the walls. I stood, and one by one, pulled them away to see if they hid any openings for safe keeping, but only smooth wallpaper was behind them. I crossed the room and the expensive imported rug to the fireplace, where I stuck my hand inside to check the flue. Not the most practical place for important papers, but a great hiding place in summer when the fireplace wasn't needed. Apparently, not the right hiding place.

I straightened up and clapped the soot off my hands, when my eye caught the bust of Madame that sat on a pedestal along the wall beside her desk. It was a bust of Madame that had been commissioned by Louis XV before he died. The artist, Augustin Pajou, had turned Madame into a goddess, complete with the curls the king loved and the cleavage he appreciated. It was Madame's favorite piece of art with her likening, having been sent over with every other item with her likeness from Versailles. It stood on a pedestal with a firm, wide base.

I went over to it and found it was too heavy to lift. I walked around it and then I saw it. The placard hanging on the front with the artist's name hid a tiny gap. I could now see it hung on with only one screw in the top left corner. I moved it with my finger up and it slid, revealing a hidden cubby behind it.

I felt the way you feel when you win a bet or come across a coin on the street. Reaching in, I pulled out the stack of papers and sat at her desk to look through them.

A deed to property in Great Britain. The list of the jewelry that she had reported missing. Another inventory list of jewelry I didn't know about. A list of nobles with notations of countries beside them. An accounting of funds.

It was the deed that stuck in my mind as I put everything back. It was the deed that made me most concerned. It was the deed that made me wonder about myself and my future and my fate. I thought about what Max said. It was clear now that she planned to go to England. I knew I didn't want to go to England now that I finally had friends in France. I had no idea if she planned to take me or what she planned to do with me.

I was going to have to be more proactive to protect myself.

THE PALAIS ROYAL was fast becoming one of my favorite places in Paris. Not only was it a haven of Jacobins, republicans, and revolutionaries, its arcades were full of shops and food sellers, musicians, artists, and writers. And there was always a card or chess game in progress. It was a place for Jacobins but not heavy with politics like the Club. Because I loved the place, Sebastien and Valentin started to spend more time there, as well. I was with them at a table playing cards when we were interrupted.

"You see this list," the man named Grieve said as he slapped the list of paper down on the table when I went to lay down a five of clubs.

"George, how nice to see you, my friend." Marat smiled up at Grieve, who didn't seem to see him at all, his face was steady on me.

"This is the list of nobles who have taken their money and left France. Look at it."

I looked at it grudgingly and my heart sank when I saw a quarter of the names of people who had visited Louveciennes in the past few months.

"What, nothing to say? We could have stopped them from leaving the country if we knew. You're a fool. I hear you have a lot to say about the King but the easiest way to get him to do what we want is to leverage information on his support system of noble flunkies."

His eyes had trouble focusing, he had the fever of obsession.

"Grieve," I acknowledged him. I hadn't seen him since our introduction, and I didn't particularly want to. I also didn't like to have sensitive conversations in such an open place. "They're gone, what difference does it make now?"

"It's her money that saves them!" he said, tapping the paper pointedly with his index finger. "She opens her purse and gives them the means to take their property and leave this country, without a moment of punishment for taking all the best things that this country has to offer and leaving the dregs! Do I have to explain to you what the movement is about?"

"Of course not."

"'*Of course not*'," he sneered, repeating my words with angry sarcasm. "People like du Barry will always find a way to cheat and lie and steal. It's time for that to stop. You see how this looks, don't you? The rats are fleeing and she's giving them the boat."

"Please, Zamor," someone called from the back of the room from a group that had been watching Grieve make his appeal. "Put this poor man out of his misery. We're tired of hearing him!"

"Shut up!" Grieve yelled to laughter. "This isn't a joke!"

No, it wasn't a joke. None of it was even a little bit funny.

Indignant, and more than a little on edge, Grieve finally grabbed his papers and left the room without even shoving them into his bag.

His fever-pitch paranoia troubled me. I didn't like people who were out of control around me, and he seemed more obsessed than the last time, and that wasn't long ago. I didn't know how long I'd be able to keep putting him off if Max was behind him.

It wasn't that I owed her anything. It was more that I didn't know if I was prepared for the consequences if I handed her over to them now. I didn't want to make a move without knowing what that move would cause.

23

May, 1791

Madame had continued to send linens, books and stationery to the Queen at the Tuileries Palace. Still, it was a surprise when, one day, she was summoned to visit the Queen. Her face lit up when she read the letter from the sentry. Finally, Madame's efforts had paid off. Finally, she'd be accepted by her nemesis.

I recognized the sentry in his slouchy hat and formal attire and britches. We'd passed each other once or twice. Normally, his face held a perpetual sarcastic smirk. He wore that smirk while walking through the hallways at Versailles, heightened by the prestige of his position. He might look ridiculous in his red and purple outfit with tassels and a slouchy hat like a court jester, but his proximity to the royal family elevated him above his clownish look.

Today, he stared off over my shoulder, his face aloof and without even a hint of smirk. That told me he was here on official business.

"We've been called to the Palace," Madame told me, her cheeks pinking with excitement. She picked up her skirts and headed to the stairs. "I need to change. You, too. Hurry, we can't keep the Queen waiting!"

An hour and a half later we arrived at the Queen's rooms at the Palace of Tuileries in the heart of Paris. The Palace, connected to the Louvre, was only five minutes away from the Jacobin Club on foot but this was the first time I'd been to this Palace, which had been the family's primary residence until the Sun King moved his kingdom to Versailles. It had also been where Louis XV lived for a time as a child after the Sun King's death before taking permanent residence at Versailles.

After the Queen's maid gestured that we should sit, Madame picked up her skirts and moved forward, taking one of two ornately padded velvet upholstered seats. I stepped back to linger near the doorway, but moments later when the Queen swept in, head and hair high, she barely looked my way, but said, as she passed, "You too, Zamor. I asked you both here. Have a seat."

I could feel Madame grow stiff, her head swinging to me in surprise, but she said nothing as I straightened my lapels and sat next to her.

So this is what it's like to be a guest, I thought. I'd sat in seats like this plenty when I was in the rooms alone. I'd even sat on the King's throne before when I was alone. But never, until that moment had I sat as a guest. It felt strange.

The Queen sat in an ornate chair across from us. Her face was impassive and pale but without the white powder. Powdered Madame caught the difference, and I saw her eyes sweep over the Queen as if taking a mental list of what she wore, how she sat, how her hair was styled. Though some aristocrats still wore powder, it had been long going out of style.

It had been almost two years since I'd seen the Queen. Her signature black dot was just as pronounced against her white skin and blood red lips. Her wig was more than two head-lengths tall on top of her head.

"Thank you for making the trip to town, Madame. Are you quite well? You look pale."

Madame blanched. Decades ago, Louis XV had told her she looked good in yellow, so she still wore it now even though it did make her look pale. Add to that, that powder on her face and she practically looked like a corpse opposite the stylish Queen. The dig was well-placed but Madame managed to hide her dismay.

"I'm very well. It is the sincerest honor for me to come, Your Majesty." Overwhelmed at finally being forgiven, she had barely sat still during the ride from Louveciennes. Instead she had peppered me with countless questions along the ride. I couldn't answer any of them, as I had no idea why we'd been called. As I sat, I was wondering if the Queen had heard I was cavorting with revolutionaries. Perhaps I should be running out the door.

Jittery, as if she'd been drinking coffee all morning, nervousness was causing the words to spill from Madame's mouth and making her shake and quiver. "Just to be in your presence is the greatest gift. It has been so long since I've seen you and you are still as lovely as if time stood still."

It was almost embarrassing to watch how she groveled. She didn't sound like the Madame I knew. In her voice I heard all the breathless hopefulness of a person in the presence of someone they admired and wanted, beyond anything, to be admired as well. Their rivalry was famous but I always knew Madame hated the Queen, mostly because she so wanted to be accepted by her. I heard that hope in her voice now, and I knew the Queen did, as well.

"You have always been so magnanimous and gracious," she continued, sounding like a twelve-year-old. "I should not be surprised that you could find it in your heart to accept me and show me this kindness. But still, you are the most important Queen with many important things to do. And so kind to call me--"

Marie Antoinette put up one hand and the gibberish stopped, to everyone's relief. Then, her Majesty spoke.

"I appreciate the things you arranged to have sent to me from my home. Leaving the Palace so quickly was unexpected. Of course, I wouldn't have left if LaFayette hadn't riled the crowd so much. Asking his Queen to bow to the people." She sniffed her disapproval. "In the heat of the moment, I would have done anything to get rid of them but no one but that impudent traitor would have suggest such impropriety. And once he did, and the people heard him suggest it, I really had no choice. When this is over he'll pay for pandering to that crowd at my expense. But I'm here now. And I'm given to acknowledge it was very enterprising of you to send Zamor to gather items you know I like. In retrospect, I wish I had done the same for you when you were away for those many years."

Madame didn't say anything but her chin quivered, slightly, and her eyes grew shiny. It was as close to an apology as she was ever going to get but it was enough, and more than expected.

"But that's water under the bridge. It's a new day," said the Queen. "I have called you here for a matter that's small, but important to me. I know you're aware I adopted three children. The King's blood children are here with us, of course, but the others were left behind. The oldest two are plenty old enough to fend for themselves."

I was told the oldest two had joined the revolutionary army. I didn't blame her for not admitting it out loud.

"They say no good deed goes unpunished. The oldest two are sore disappointments. Of the three, the only one that has truly shown himself to be a blessing is the youngest, Jean Amilcar. You've met Jean." She looked at me.

"Yes, I've met him. The child has the disposition of an endlessly happy babe and the eyes of an angel. I could barely tolerate his presence."

She smiled a bit at that. "No, I imagine it would smart a bit, being in the presence of your opposite."

"His gaze on me burned like holy water on a sinner, Your Majesty."

"I'm sure you know the sensation well."

"Well, Jean was an unexpected spot of goodness but the rest of Versailles, sinners all. Barring you and the King, Your Majesty, it's a cesspool of evil and corruption. Which made it all the more amazing the child was so sweet."

"You make a fair point. Perhaps we should have allowed you to stay at the Palace in your natural habitat."

But then, how would you have punished me? I thought.

"I'm sorry, I never met the child," Madame said, trying to make her way back into the conversation, looking back and forth between us to keep up. "He sounds charming."

"Yes," the Queen continued. "He's been away at school for some two years, with occasional visits here. And now this business is taking a bit longer than we planned and the King and I feel it might be best for him to return. The only problem is the school has been unresponsive. We understand from our manager that they have been negligent in providing updates on Jean's welfare. It seems our financial accounts have been temporarily frozen and the school has not been paid. You would think they would have the wherewithal to reach out to us with an arrangement until things are back to normal but they did not."

"Why, that is a travesty," Madame exclaimed.

"Their behavior is unconscionable. They will pay for this when all this confusion is over; they have forgotten to whom they serve. Someone will hang in the gallows for this." She said it quickly with lowered lids as if the fate of the offenders was already sealed. I wouldn't want to be the headmaster at that school when the Queen returned to Versailles.

"They told me they sent Jean to live with one of his instructors who was kind enough to give him temporary shelter." She looked at me. "I'd like you to find him and bring him home. I believe with your–resourcefulness—you would have an easier time of it. Our guards are so busy, besides. Surely it would be easier for you to handle it." Her eyes shifted from me.

I knew they had no guards to send looking for the boy. The royal guards were at Versailles and the ones in this place were solely here to keep them in Paris. The King and Queen had little authority right now.

Madame saw an opportunity to contribute, "I can send my man, Gaspard…"

"Under no circumstances is that man to come anywhere near Jean, do you understand me?" the Queen snapped. "He is not fit to be near children, nor most adults. If I were to find Jean has been left with that man, someone will earn the same fate as the headmistress of Jean's school. No, Louis-Benoit—Zamor—you will find him for me, won't you?"

I nodded.

"You, Madame, I ask for you to keep him clothed and fed in the manner befitting the child of the King. And when all this is over we will pay you handsomely for your loyalty."

"You have no need to pay me, Your Majesty, to be able to do this for you is my honor. To be trusted with your sweet child is the biggest compliment. I will love him as if he were my own child! You don't know how you've lifted my heart this day. I might almost believe we'd finally become friends."

Madame could no longer contain herself. She pitched herself forward from her chair to the ground at the Queen's feet, taking the queen's hands in hers and kissing them, profusely. The Queen winced slightly, though her lips tried to smile.

"Please, rise, Madame. This is a happy time. Yes, we are friends. Now, my maid will show you out. I have a few words of instruction for your page."

Madame stood, flushed, tucked a lock of hair behind her ear, looked at me, and then did as she was told.

"Now," the Queen said as the door shut. "Just so we understand each other. I will need you to do whatever you have to, to find Jean, and once you have, do whatever you must to keep him safe from *her*."

"Your Majesty?"

Her mouth worked a bit as if trying to bite her words. "He needs a place to live and someone to look after him. He can't stay here, I've already asked—we have decided that only the King and his heirs should be here at the Palace. Just the blood relatives. So Jean needs a place to live and ... someone to look out for him. I'm not blind nor dumb. You and the Madame, you are both cut from the same cloth. The only difference is, she has no capacity to love, selflessly."

"I think you are confused about me, Your Majesty."

"I'm rarely confused about anything, page. My adopted son is a nuisance to you and probably you've got no desire to have anything to do with him, but he loves you and you are readily willing to come to his aid. I suspected but now I can see in your eyes that you care for him. That's more than she can ever feel. She's not an evil woman. She's not even as calculating as I once thought. She's just selfish and self-centered and feels no one's pain but her own. She left the one child who came to her as an innocent little boy to Gaspard. That's all I need to know about her capacity to care for anyone beyond herself."

Far be it from me to defend Madame but the irony was too strong for it not to show on my face.

"You have something to say, by all means, say it."

"Only that, she's not the only one who left me with Gaspard. Two kings, a queen and a maîtresse-en-titre and not one of you ever lifted a hand to protect me. But you expect me to protect your child."

"Well, then I suppose you have a reason to hate us all. But you don't hate little Jean. Now, I trust you will do as you're asked." She stood and swiped her hands down her skirt in the universal sign that she was done with me.

I stood in response and bowed.

"I promise you, as I did her, that you will be paid handsomely when all this is over."

I wasn't interested in payment. When all this was over, none of us knew what things would look like.

She began to stride past me but then stopped beside me. "I know you only ever asked for one thing. It wasn't in my power to give it to you. Despite what the world thinks, the King makes his own decisions on some affairs. Personal affairs. He never quite forgave the way you and your Madame made a mockery of his grandfather. He had made up his mind."

I wanted to remind her that that the King had forgiven Madame. To the point of giving her back all her wealth and assets. What she didn't bother to say was that it was me—at the time a black boy—

disrespecting the King that had been unforgiveable. She glossed right over that and continued.

"But Jean, he is a free citizen of France. You inspired me to do that for him. But I will keep speaking to the King about your status. Perhaps he can be persuaded to change his mind when all this unpleasantness is over. Especially if you do this thing for us. He's quite fond of the boy."

"Yes, Your Majesty," I bowed again.

I asked Madame to send the carriage back for me later and I stayed in Paris to begin my search for the baby-faced nuisance.

24

―――――――

I visited the school first, where I found the name and address of the instructor. Once there, the man told me he couldn't afford to feed the child and had put him out.

"On the street?" I asked, anger flaring at the cavalier way he said it. His hair was in tufts of gray on his head and his face, sallow. He peered at me from a crack in his open front door. "If the King or Queen had been bothered to pay me something I might have been able to keep him, but I got nothing!"

"They didn't know, you idiot. Why didn't you tell the Palace?"

"It's not my responsibility! It's not my fault! Besides, he's not even their real child. What does it matter?"

I moved toward him, and he shut the door in my face, quickly, as if knowing I was about to hit him.

"When did you put him out?" I called through the door.

"Just a couple of days ago. Leave me alone!"

A couple days ago? I couldn't imagine where an eight-year-old child might go. I went to Sebastien because he knew everything. Indeed, he spent the evening asking around and the next day he told me he had a lead on a man in town who helped children in trouble and had set up a meeting.

He was a thin man in a dusty loose vest and pants that almost covered his second-hand, but functional, shoes. We met on a street corner in town.

"Bonjour, I'm Tate," he said, thrusting a hand my way. "Sebastien told me you were looking for a young black boy named Jean.'

"Yes. Who are you? How do you know Jean?"

"I'm no one, I just know a lot of young people. I have a house and I take in young people who have no place to go."

"You do that, why?"

He gave me a sad look. "Because I know what it feels like to be alone in the world. Paris is in dire straits but the kids always get the worst of it. Are you up for a walk?"

We began a walk through Paris. I'd never been far from the main drags in town but that day I got a crash course in streets and alleys I'd never seen. I saw people huddled, gathered socially, and a lot of people walking, going about their day. My legs began to tire. The entire time Tate continued to talk about his life growing up without a father, how he'd had to steal to survive. He talked about the times he'd been locked away for petty crimes and his determination to help others like him. At one point I looked around and saw nothing I knew and wondered how well Sebastien had checked on this man.

Finally, we stopped on a corner, and he gestured across the street to a gated area. "Over here."

I headed across, happy to finally be done with his yammering. There were tall walls that converged in a gate at the corner where an old man sat on a stool just inside. I walked up to him. "Hey there, I'm looking for a boy."

He smiled, a crooked smile of decay and liquor. That, and his tufted hair made me doubt this was a place for any child. But he said, "I got plenty boys," and stood to open the gate for me.

"I told him you were looking for a young black boy, possibly with a royal crest on his clothes," Tate called.

"His name is Jean," I said as the gate swung open. I stepped inside to see a large, muddy open area enclosed by the walls, with what appeared to be mounds of dirt against the walls covered by tarps. But no kids. I turned to the man and Tate.

"I don't understand, I don't s---" The smell caught me at that moment. I looked past the smiling man, past Tate who stood just inside the gate like he didn't want to be there. My nose was full of the sickly, rotten smell now. I looked around the space and saw, on the farthest side, against the wall, the material over a mound had been uncovered, and I saw a flap of cloth.

"Tate," I asked, my lips growing cold. "What is this place?"

He looked at me, confused. And then his face changed, softened, crumpled a little, though he hung back.

"I-I-m so sorry, I thought you understood. I—"

The old man broke into cackles of laughter at my distress. I ran forward. The mud was soft, not from rain. It hadn't rained in days. But the mud was soft. I ran over it quickly so as not to get stuck. I ran to the far wall, all along telling myself it wasn't so. All along, reminding myself that the two men at the gate were insane. But when I got to the pile, and kneeled beside it, pulling that cover off, the sweet smell of decay blew up my consciousness and my eyes began to water from being so close to it. Still, I told myself they could be wrong, as my eyes adjusted and I uncovered the mound a little more.

"They told me you'd be coming for him. I pulled him out and put him on top, for you! Blackamoor boy, he said ... not many of those," the laughing man said. "Put his clothes on him and everything. 'Cept for his shoes. Didn't have no shoes. Didn't have none of those fancy cuffs like you got on but with that shirt he would've needed them, right? Like you?"

I looked down at Jean. The man had pulled the child's body on top of the pile of dead, decaying bodies. Many of them were slim-boned and short, like children, but it was impossible to tell from the shape of them. But Jean, apparently, was most recently deceased because I could still recognize his face. His baby face had slimmed some with his age, but the skin was now slack. His eyes, those strikingly innocent, sweet eyes – were still open but frozen in death.

Those eyes looked into me and a flash of the white, dead eyes of a stone-cold fox statue blinked before me.

No! I couldn't escape this. As a child, whenever I was afraid or feared for my mortal soul, the sight of that stone fox statue from the Labyrinth of the Palace of Versailles would preclude my escape from consciousness. That fox would pull my mind from this world when I was in mortal fear. It was trying to pull me there, now. But I couldn't go. I was a grown man. But if I stayed, if I stayed…

I fell to my knees and a cry broke from me as the pain welled inside me. Behind me I heard the old man begin to howl like a dog, his howl breaking into laughter. I barely noticed him now that I felt my heart trying to crawl out of my chest.

I reached out and pulled his limp body, took him into my arms. He was so light, small, even for a child his age. I cradled him for a moment, my eyes still looking into his, willing them to clear and blink, willing it to be a mistake. But there was something inside me wracking my body that told me it wasn't.

"Jean," I whispered. "Little boy," I shook him, gently. "Wake up! Wake up!"

God performed miracles, didn't He? Brought back Lazarus from the dead? *Please God, bring him back. Please!*

I cradled his head with its gentle short black kinky curls. I felt those curls in my hand, soft and spongy. I stroked his face with my hand. Held him to my chest--

--the crazed man was laughing and spouting gibberish—

--and the world seemed to whirl about me.

Tate yelled for the maniac to shut up as the child in my arms stared at me with eyes that couldn't see. Stared into my soul. He didn't wake up.

I closed his eyes with my fingers. I held him closer to me. Then, I took off my cloak and wrapped him with it.

"What are you doing?" Tate had come over and I could hear his voice close.

I wiped my dripping nose with the back of my sleeve and stood in a half crouch. My back screamed when I picked up his body and threw it over my shoulder.

"What are you doing?" Tate tried to keep up as I stood and walked through the den of hell. The old man cackled as I walked away, trying to keep from getting stuck in the mud, trying not to think about why this ground was so soft when there had been no rain. The old man laughed, mad or cruel, I couldn't tell which.

"I'm taking him home. I'm not leaving him here in this place."

I WALKED through Paris with the child over my shoulder. I was stopped once by a policeman who insisted I let him see what I carried. When I flipped the cloak up and showed him what I had, his antagonistic attitude disappeared. If it had been a white boy, I knew I'd have gone to prison then and there. It was a black boy.

"He fell, hit the back of his head and died. I'm going to bury him." That's all I said. He let me go because he didn't care. No one cared about a little black boy in Paris. If he had noticed the royal crest, he might have.

By the time I reached Lightning, it was late afternoon. My horse stayed still while I laid Jean across her back, like she knew. I thought about riding the body to the Tuileries Palace to hand over to the Queen, but knew she couldn't do anything there. So, Lightning and I rode away from Paris, back to the Palace of Versailles, the only home he knew.

The Palace was still staffed even though many of the nobles had left for their country homes or left the country, entirely. No one cared when my old wrestling instructor and friend, Fabien, and I found a quiet spot in the back of what used to be the botanical gardens to begin digging with shovels. Fabien managed to find a large crate they used to deliver trees to the Palace. We emptied it and I raided one of the empty bedrooms to line the box with silk sheets and pillows so Jean had something soft beneath him and pleasant over his face.

We buried Jean in a spot perfumed from the flowers of the

gardens, secluded and peaceful; a place befitting the remains of pure innocence and love. When we were done, I wiped my brow and Fabien took our shovels in his hand.

"I'm glad you came back now. This is where we say good-bye, friend," Fabien said, clapping me on the shoulder as we left the garden. "We're no longer being paid and it's dangerous here at night with marauders and drunkards coming through when the mood strikes them—the royal guards too confused and half the time drunk, to protect things as they should. So, I'll be on my way."

"Where will you go?"

"I'm thinking about going to the new Americas."

"But will they let you leave?" I asked, thinking about all the restrictions on travel these days.

"Brother, nobody cares if us peasants leave France. They want us to go! They only care to keep the wealth. They might roll out a red carpet for me to walk right on out. Maybe America, but I'll see what I can afford when I get to the docks at Marseilles. I'll take any place but France right now."

"But things will get better soon, when the constitutional monarchy goes into effect."

"What is that? I don't know anything about politics, friend, but I won't dash your hope if you want to believe things will get better. All I know is when the wealthy, educated men decide to make changes it's always us poor people who get screwed. I sense things here are about to get a whole lot worse and I don't want to be here when it all goes to merde. Good luck to you. It was a pleasure beating your ass."

I didn't bother reminding him that the last time we wrestled I'd put into practice all the lessons he gave me and beat *him*. Instead, I clasped his hand and we shook, firmly. I would miss his smart mouth and crooked nose. "Happy voyages, friend. Stay safe."

Fabien turned and headed back to the servant's quarters, looking like a bull pushing its way through the world as the sun began to set.

Returning to the Chateau I wrote a letter to the Queen informing her of the fate of little Jean. I wrote clearly at the bottom:

I have buried him at home in your gardens so he may be surrounded by the beauty he deserved in life. I will find someone to speak last rites over him.

AND THEN I TOLD VÉRONIQUE, who promptly arranged for the pastor from the tiny church in Louveciennes to come to the Palace. Two days later on a chilly, gray day—the rain had finally decided to visit us--the pastor said the words over the new grave, causing the frown of concern to leave Véronique's face. With each word, her forehead became smoother and by the end of the ritual her face was peaceful. I wondered what thoughts plagued her so that this final resting should put her at such ease. I wished a few words could put me at peace.

The man from the church was sandy-haired and soft-spoken. He didn't seem put off by the circumstances or by the fact that we were in the gardens of the Palace. He didn't ask questions, so I imagined Véronique must have told him about the situation.

All along, I watched him as he spoke, searching for a sign of insincerity in him. Searching for a moment of condemnation or dehumanization towards the little black boy so I could pounce on him. But his words were kind, telling the child to go home to his Father's arms. By the time he finished and looked up to find me watching him, I'd still found no fault in anything he said. I relaxed.

"It was good of you to make sure he was laid to rest in peace," he told me as I walked him to his horse. Normally, horses didn't come to the gardens behind the Palace but we were in different times. The royal guards wouldn't stop anything so trivial.

"That was Véronique's doing," I told him.

"Véronique tells me you are a new believer."

"Véronique told you wrong," I replied, knowing she was looking at me. "I don't believe in a god that allows this."

"Our heavenly Father loves us all. Little Jean knows no more pain. He holds this child in His safe, heavenly care, now. We are all His children, even when we are angry with him. Even you."

"No, Monsieur. I'm a child of the revolution."

"Even still." He didn't argue with me further, and after he left on his horse, Véronique and I climbed into our carriage for the quiet ride to the Chateau. She stared out into the chilly air and finally her eyes sparkled with unshed tears.

"You've told the Queen?"

"Yes," I said, full of words yet none could come out.

"This is truly a tragedy for both the King and Queen. I pray for them, also," Véronique said, swiping the moisture from her cheeks. "Even the most corrupt among us love our children."

An unpleasant noise erupted from me at that, against my control.

"Why do you make that sound?" she asked. "Zamor, you know the Queen loved him. She sent you to look for him, after all."

"Don't talk to me about what the King and Queen loved. If they had an ounce of humanity between the two of them that child would be at home with his parents, alive and well. Instead, he died in the street, as helpless as a babe in a city full of vipers. Murdered for the shoes on his feet." I had bathed the body, just so he could go into the grave, clean. I saw the handprints around his neck. The bruises on his torso. "Someone beat and choked the life out of him as he stared into their eyes. A child. That's what *they* did to him. That's their love." My face twisted with fury and something else putrid that lived deep within me. "They take and they destroy and they pervert everything!"

I kept my gaze to the road so I couldn't see the worry in Véronique's eyes.

"But at least he had you," she said, softly and kindly, stroking my face. "Your presence was a comfort to him and I know he felt that love very much."

"Me? He felt my love? I didn't love him. Listen to yourself, Véronique. You were there, you saw . . . I was horrible to that child! You saw me with him!" It was long ago, but she was there with me when I snapped at the child about referring to the Queen as his mother when he was five or so. "I was cruel and dismissive. I told him to leave me alone every time I saw him!"

"And yet he came back over and over with a smile on his face because he knew you didn't mean it. He could sense that you cared for him. *I* could sense it."

"I was envious of him!" I spit out, my eyes watering. "Envious of the fact that he had his freedom. He didn't even know what that meant, but he had it because the Queen looked at me and thought to herself, 'look at that waste of a man, Zamor! I will adopt this enslaved child but I won't allow *this* child to end up like Louis-Benoit!' And she plucked him out of the home of heathens to bring him here and make him a better version of me. If I hadn't been here, and those women had not been obsessed with besting each other, the King never would have brought another black child into that place. You said it yourself, I started a trend—"

"—No, Zamor, you know better than that. I didn't understand the situation."

"I know that no matter how he came here and no matter that I knew the hell he was likely going through in that place, every time I looked at him I saw the free man he would grow up to be and it made me angry. I saw a man who would never have to fight to prove he belonged. A man who would have the title of the monarchy behind him and the free will and money to do as he pleased, and I was jealous of that child. Love was not in my eyes when I looked at him."

Shame filled me like a well that threatened to drown me. I couldn't look at Véronique, and instead I stared at the road. My outburst left an awkward, gaping pause in our conversation and I knew Véronique was thinking what I terrible man I was. Better she knew the kind of man she was spending her time with.

"And yet, still . . ." she continued, her voice firm. "You sit here on the verge of tears not due to shame. Your envy makes you human, Zamor. But that child, he didn't feel your envy. He only felt the love tucked away behind it; that love made him light up with joy every time you were near. That love made you kind to him even though you hated to show him any kindness. You were envious of him and now you're angry with yourself for loving him all the same. Love may not have been in your eyes, but it was in your heart and he felt it."

Emotion welled up in me quickly and unbidden and my voice came out in a croak. "Please stop, Véronique," I said.

She took her hand and cupped it over mine, on the reins, before nodding and looking away discretely off to the other side of the road. Thankfully, perfectly in time to miss the tears that escaped my eyes and rolled down my cheeks; her ears deaf to the sound of the sobs I tried to strangle within myself as the road blurred before me.

PART II

THE GROWING SEASON

25

———————

Dear Citizen,

Thus, in May 1791, I had buried half of my moral compass with a little boy named Jean.

Making sure Jean Almicar was sent to heaven also meant being truly understanding of the juxtaposition of my sinning soul set against his pure one. That I was still here and he was gone taught me much about life's reward for the good people of the world.

I didn't know I had begun a new phase in my life. In farming it might be called the growing season, when the planted seeds take nourishment underground, away from view, and begin to sprout.

Have you ever known someone to plant something, not quite sure what it was until it sprouts and blossoms? At the Chateau, shoots were coming up from the ground based on the seeds we'd already planted and we just weren't quite sure what we'd get.

In Paris, quietly, the new republic began to question the role of the church and religion in the lives of its people. Individuals at the highest level of the clergy were seen as corrupt, having the benefits and advantages of the highest nobility. It made some sense that corruption would need to be weeded out just as in the second estate.

In the nearly two years since the King and Queen had been displaced from the Palace of Versailles, the new republican government was seizing properties previously owned by the Catholic Church. Rent paid by tenants to the church could now be funneled directly to the new government.

And the republic began looking at individual clergy members. As one man put it: "We do not need to be led by corrupt church leaders teaching us about a god they don't believe in. Unmarried men living lavish lifestyles while the country starves need to be removed."

There would soon be a drastically expansive effort to undo the people's reliance on the church. And then it became an effort to shift the people's reliance on God in favor of reliance on the republic.

It was science, after all. The Enlightenment was an educated man's game and the most educated were often the ones most resistant to the idea of an all-seeing, all-knowing god. For some, the two things couldn't exist at the same time.

So, a contract was drafted whereby priests and leaders in the church were asked to declare their oath to the Constitutional Church.

"Asked" is the wrong word. To ask suggests the recipient has a right of refusal. Compelled *might be a better term. For the purpose of furthering the republican goal of strong families, unwed leaders in the church were compelled to marry. Priests who obeyed were able to keep their station, lifestyle and salary.*

Priests who could not be compelled to do the right thing were labeled "refractory" and punished with significant reductions of salaries. This would progress into the possibility of jail time. This would progress to...
I'm getting ahead of myself.

What was done with the church would later be called De-Christianization. Such a simple term to describe the complex and painful act of extricating religion from a country of faithful believers. It snuck up on us, beginning right around the time when the people needed religion the most.

At the time of writing these journals, we still have not fully recovered from it. Now, we have atheists who don't believe in God at all, and never have. But back then, we were a society still strongly tied to religion. Not me, but most.
So, when we buried Jean, we didn't realize it was the end of an era. Soon, the act of openly praying and grieving for the loss of a loved one would be outlawed. Soon, the very concept of God, heaven and hell would be up for debate.
But I say this all in hindsight. At the time, we were preoccupied with other things.

We buried Jean in May 1791; it was almost as if the murder of that pure soul caused unexpected events that would change our country.

The summer of 1791 changed everything.

--Zamor, 1820

26

"I don't understand, what do you mean you need to question me? I told you everything I know," Madame said to the police. The police had returned with questions about the jewelry theft, to Madame's surprise, and were sitting with her in the study. She sat on a chair while they stood, looking surprised and worried all at once. Notably, she did not offer them a seat. She was so angry she was having trouble keeping her mask—an expression of pleasantness that she'd practiced on me when I was a child—on her face. Her lips quivered and jerked as her fury threatened to boil over.

"And we truly appreciate your cooperation, Madame. It's just that we're making every effort to be thorough in our investigations. As you know the new government takes the theft of the country's wealth serious. The theft and the publishing of the inventory has brought many questions our way."

"What's the country got to do with it, they're my jewels. They were given to me, so they're mine. What kind of questions?" she asked, confused. "I published the list because I want my things back. What's wrong with that?"

"Just that people don't understand how it is that you were away on the very night of the theft. There have been no such events at the

Chateau before. It just seems convenient that the very night you are gone to Paris, all our most valuable jewels are stolen."

"...*our*?"

"Excuse me, *your*..."

"...damn right. *My* jewels." She pointed at herself.

Any second now she was going to blow and it wouldn't be pretty. I could see the struggle to keep control on her face.

"Who says it was convenient? It wasn't convenient for me. And I never said they were my *most* valuable jewels," she said. "I told you, someone knew I was gone. Tell them, Gaspard."

"Yes, I'm certain someone must have gotten wind that the Madame would be out. Have you questioned the house staff?"

Son of a bitch. He was at it, again.

"We have questioned your staff, of course. No one roused suspicion. You must understand, after the business with the necklace, there are many in the country and in the government who wonder if the jewels might have been stolen in some sort of manufactured event, like the other time," said the first officer.

"They remember what happened with the necklace and the Queen, you see," the second followed.

It was clear now they thought she was lying. Perhaps now, thinking she had been involved in the scheme of the *first* necklace, along with the Queen.

Madame's head swiveled back and forth between the two men as they spoke, eyes large. I could see her taking in what they were saying and running it through her head. Her eyes suddenly filled with tears and her lips began to quiver and her voice came out barely a breathless whisper.

"How dare you? How dare you come into my home and accuse me of horrible, horrible things? Suggesting I had something to do with stealing my own things?"

"They're not suggesting that, I'm sure," Gaspard blustered, stepping forward to face them, his face in warning.

"I would never do something so horrible," she continued. "How could you compare me to that ugly affair and that ... *Austrian woman*."

"Well, Madame, it's just that the necklace was made for *you*, wasn't it? By Louis the Well-Beloved? It's just the chance of two jewelry incidents connected to you seems an unlikely coincidence."

"The necklace situation wasn't connected to *me*, it was connected to the *Queen*. It was the *Queen's* sordid affair, not mine. I never even *saw* the necklace, you can hardly blame me for what took place without my knowing. This is an unconscionable accusation!"

"Madame, I'm not accusing you of anything. But both you and the Queen—"

"—Stop speaking of me and the Queen in the same sentence! I am not the Queen. I am a Frenchwoman, damn you. I am loyal to this country!" She stood up and actually stamped her foot.

Since our visit to the Queen at the Tuileries Palace, her feelings for the Queen had changed again. Excited at first that they would be friends, she didn't understand why the Queen had dismissed her to speak with me. I had lied and told her it was to do with her needing to give me information on Jean's possible whereabouts. That had mollified her for a short while, but then the Queen had failed to respond to any follow-up letters from her. Madame, rightly, assumed that Marie Antoinette no longer had use for her now that Jean was dead, and she was right back to where she started. And thus, she lapsed back into what she was most familiar with – hatred of her nemesis.

The tears finally spilled over the rims of her large blue eyes and her face crumpled.

"That's enough," Gaspard said to the officers, angry. "You will leave this house."

"We didn't mean to upset you, Madame. We only—"

"—you called me a traitor to France! This is my country. My home. I would never cheat the French people!"

One of the officers looked like he regretted having come. The other looked like he'd never seen a woman cry before. Both received a stare-down from Gaspard.

"My apologies, Madame," the lead one said. "We will take our leave."

They turned and walked out. But I knew this was only a temporary reprieve. Gaspard followed and waited until they were out of sight and clear of hearing before he closed the door behind him to walk over to Madame.

"They won't be back. They know better than to show up here with that nonsense, don't worry."

"Don't worry?" Madame said, the quiver gone from her voice. Her tears had stopped flowing as if they never had flowed, and she wiped the remnants away with the backs of her hands, her face losing its softness, lips thinning and white with fury. "You told me you had everything in hand. You told me you would take care of everything."

"I-I have. I will. This is nothing..."

The sound of her hand cracking against his face filled the room and I blinked in surprise. In all our years I'd never seen her hit Gaspard. She had to reach way up to do it. His eyes were wide as he reared back.

"Nothing?" she continued. "They think I was involved. They think I'm no better than the Queen!" She picked up a glass from the bar and threw it across the room where it hit the stone fireplace and shattered.

He winced.

"It's just due diligence," he mumbled. "I looked that man in the eye, he knows better than to come back here."

"Oh, you think you frightened him away with your loud voice and dirty look? They aren't afraid of you. Oh, mon Dieu, I was a fool to trust you." She brought both hands to clutch them, the backs against her forehead as she paced. "Oh, I was such a fool. Louis-Benoit told me I couldn't trust you and I told him he was wrong. Now, look."

"You," Gaspard suddenly turned to me, murder in his eyes. "Get out. Now!"

When she didn't object, I turned and left the room, but once outside I listened at the door, of course.

"I trusted you. All these years I trusted that you knew what you were doing. You said we only needed an excuse for me to be able to go back and forth to England and this would work. You said this would be a simple thing. You said publishing that list would make me look transparent and honest, those were your words!"

"And I still believe it does. They just want to say it's a fair investigation."

"The first time, maybe. Two visits from the police means they don't believe me."

"I tell you, it means nothing."

"You think I will ever listen to anything else you say? You're a fool! I was a fool to listen to you!"

I wanted to stay but I knew how Madame's blow ups tended to end as quickly as they started and I didn't want to be caught listening.

27

____

June 1791

I was carrying a bucket of water from the well when I passed two guards talking, picking up their conversation mid-stream.

"...they took him right from under their noses," one of them said as he lounged against a wall, eating an apple.

"Who?" I asked. They both looked up, not sure if they should speak to me. They knew how much Gaspard hated me, after all. But one must have decided he didn't care enough about either of us to have an allegiance.

"The royal family's been kidnapped from the Tuileries Palace. They think the Prussians took them. They've gone too far, this time, there's going to be hell to pay."

"The brazenness," the other one said, grouchy.

The blood ran cold in me.

They continued talking while I walked away, thinking. How could this happen and what did it mean?

I was anxious to skip dinner, recalling that I might have mentioned to Véronique that I needed to get to Paris to find out what was happening, so I would have to do something to one of the guests to get Madame to order me to leave. I was trying to decide between starting an argument or dropping a bowl of soup on someone, when out of the blue Véronique walked over to Madame. Just as calmly as you please, she suggested that Madame and her ladies might want matching handkerchiefs and that the little shop in town that sold satin should be receiving a new shipment of brilliant colors. Her ladies could barely sit still at the excitement of wearing something that matched their Madame.

"Of course, let's go!" Madame said, bounding from the table. The four of them giggled as they left the room. "Give our guests my apologies," she said to me on her way out.

I smiled and mouthed a "thank you" to Véronique . Ten minutes later, after the guests had sat down I told them, "Madame sends her apologies. Tonight's meal is buffet. Please, serve yourselves." And then I was gone, changing, and jumping on Lightning, headed for Paris.

The Club was abuzz, and not in a good way. This time, instead of happiness, voices were raised in argument, excitement, and anger. The room hadn't been this full since that night in October two years previously when the King arrived in Paris.

I took off my satchel and cloak, and spied Valentin in a far corner, pacing and alternately yelling a response to whatever snippet of conversation reached his ears. I headed over to him.

"Hey," I said as I reached him, "what is this? What's happened? The family's been kidnapped?"

His eyes were red. "The whole family is gone. They say it must have happened in the night. Right from under us."

"They've kidnapped him, the bastards!" someone yelled. "It's England, I tell you!"

"Is there a plan?" I asked. Valentin didn't have much power but he did at least have access to Max. Surely, he knew something.

"We don't even know for sure exactly how long he's been gone," he said. "The Convention is in an emergency session right now."

"Was there a note from the kidnappers, then?"

"I don't know. Stop asking me questions. *I don't know.*"

I could see from his eyes he was telling the truth. He didn't even know if there *was* a kidnapping. Discomfort roiled in my gut.

Sebastien arrived, skirting the crowds at the door, his face grim. He and I were joined by Valentin, Paul Marat and David at one of the tables. I leaned next to me to mumble under my breath to Sebastien.

"All these people think he's been kidnapped. But..."

"You think otherwise?"

I gestured him closer. "Their adopted son, Jean, was murdered in Paris just a few weeks ago. The child was wearing royal insignia and they strangled him and took the shoes off his feet. I think they got scared and ran."

He looked at me sharply. "That would mean..."

I nodded. "Yes, I think that's what he did. Probably felt like he was no longer feared... and all that."

He shook his head as if shaking off the thought. "No, that would be the worst. That would be the worst possible thing. He wouldn't. If he did, God help him." He took a long swallow of beer. "God help us."

We waited with the gravity of a loved one on the deathbed of the loved. We waited.

"Maybe Brissot was right," somebody said loudly, breaking the unease calm. "He said they would attack. We should have done it first. We left them vulnerable for too long."

"They'll be sorry. If it's time to go to war, we'll teach them they can't attack France and get away with it. We'll teach them!"

Valentin stood and jumped up onto the table causing the rest of us to grab it from wobbling our drinks onto the ground. "Jacobins, this is no time to jump to conclusions. Max will be here as soon as the Convention adjourns and he'll tell us everything."

"What's he going to tell us, Valentin? That's it's time to go to war? We know that."

"Hell, yeah!" Someone slapped a table in agreement, standing up, putting a revolutionary cap on his head. Along with the cockade, revolutionaries had begun to wear the odd-looking red cap. Designed to model a similar cap from ancient times, it had, along with the cockade, become a symbol of the new republic. This man wore it now and pounded the tricolor cockade he wore on his chest. "France will fight!"

Soon, the Convention representatives began to filter into the room. I spied Brissot and, later, Georges Danton, who was immediately swamped by men volleying for his attention. His face was pale. When Maximilien Robespierre entered the room he looked tired and serious. We quieted immediately once Robespierre noticed Brissot and Danton were both there. Then he raised his hand and all remaining chatter ceased.

"In the early hours of the morning of this June 21, 1791, near the midnight hour, our King and Queen, their children and nannies, disguised themselves as common people and left the Palace of Tuileries in a disguised royal carriage. The royal family purposefully and willingly left the royal abode in an attempt to flee France."

"No, they didn't. They were kidnapped!" said a man, stubbornly, looking around as if to get confirmation from others.

"Did you hear what I just said? I will repeat it so there's no question," Max said, looking as though he was torn between crying and tearing someone apart. "Our royal family, purposefully and willingly, attempted to flee the country." *By disguising themselves as commoners.*

A low murmur of disbelief buzzed through the room as people couldn't decide whether to believe Max or not. They stopped short of calling him a liar, but the buzz of disbelief was in the air.

My head was buzzing, too, as I remembered a conversation I had with the King when I was about fourteen and he was new to the throne. Stung at not being allowed to leave the Palace upon the death of Louis XV, I had flippantly told the brand-new King Louis XVI that if *I* were king, and didn't want to be, I'd disguise myself and sneak out of the country. He had declared to do so would be to betray himself, his ancestors, and his people. I never would have imagined the King would remember it or think to do it, but he had.

"Why do you tell us that, Max? You're wrong!" someone called, almost angrily. "We've all heard the King was kidnapped!"

"Rumors and gossip. You heard wrong." Robespierre glanced to Brissot. The other man picked up the report.

"That is what we thought, initially," Brissot called out. "We saw no reason to believe otherwise, we assumed our enemies had come and taken them by force."

"We assumed it partly because we've been listening to your nonsense about every country declaring war on us for the better part of two years," Max all but spat at Brissot. "And the narrative of a kidnapping suits your purposes since all you care about is going to war."

"That's unnecessary and uncalled for," Brissot said, red-faced. "It's not I who twists the facts to suit my purpose. We all thought it was a kidnapping until a short while ago, no longer than an hour."

"Please tell us what's happening!" Valentin called out, worry on his face. "Tell us, how do you know?"

For all his criticism of Brissot, it seemed like Robespierre had something on his mind he was almost afraid to say. That was when I knew.

Robespierre said, his face a mask of fury, "The royal family attempted to escape France! Fortunately, sharp-eyed and conscientious republicans recognized them and the family was turned back almost at the border in Varennes. We caught them. Oh yes, we caught them. They will stay there tonight and then be directed back here to Paris tomorrow."

"But how do you know?" someone asked. "How can you be certain they weren't forced to leave."

"We know because the King left us a letter. Like a scorned lover, he left behind a letter making it clear exactly how he feels about this republic!"

28

Dear Citizen,

Sometimes you're not happy to be right.
I would always wonder if the murder of the sweet soul named Jean
might have triggered the latent survival instinct among the King
and Queen. Up until Jean's death they'd operated as if they were on
vacation. Surrounded by the luxuries of the Tuileries Palace, it must
have been easy for them to imagine their lodging as a temporary
thing until the republic came to its senses and begged his
forgiveness.

But then, little Jean was murdered.

Five years prior, no one would have dared harm any person with
even a remote connection to the royal family. Now, the adopted son
of the King was openly targeted and set upon by no less than three
people: The school master who discarded him like nothing, the
instructor who took him away and also discarded him, and the
person who had actually strangled and taken the shoes off the feet

of a child with a fleur-de-lys emblem in the lining of his coat. That fleur-de-lys might well be what had gotten him killed.

The disrespect, displacement, neglect, and murder of Jean was more than a homicide. It was a message that the reach and influence of the monarchy was gone, and the royals were no longer safe.

To flee was a selfish move, but to be honest, it was understandable. It was the most human and the most relatable I'd ever found the King. I knew better than anyone how it felt to be trapped in an untenable situation. I didn't fault them for running.

But what angered me to the point that I still shake with the violence of it while sitting and writing this today, is the arrogance and ineptitude of the attempt. He had everything he needed to escape! But, instead, Louis XVI bungled it.

To those who would argue that I'm wrong, I ask to look at the facts.

He had only to stay in disguise. If he had stayed in the carriage and stayed in disguise, they would have easily made it across the border without notice. But he'd gotten comfortable and gotten out of the carriage, deciding to talk and laugh and socialize with strangers in towns along the way.

It was the curse of the King to have a face known by all, it being printed on our currency, as it was. It only took one person to recognize him, which they might not have if he hadn't gotten out of the carriage and proceeded to address the townspeople as if he were their king, and not simply a traveler on the road. But in true XVI arrogant fashion, he bungled it as if he would have another chance to get it right.

When one's life is on the line, you respect each and every chance you have to escape. But for the privileged among us, even that

*reality is sacrificed to their overriding belief that someone, some-
where, is obliged to save them, even from themselves.*

*And then, by some misbegotten belief that anyone would care about
whatever excuse he would provide, he left that letter behind. If he
had left well enough alone and just made his escape, even if caught,
he might have been able to talk his way out of it. And if successful,
he could have written that damning letter from Austria, once safely
in their care. But no, our Louis XVI left that letter behind him--
detailing his part in the crime—so that it was found before he was
safely gone. That letter, blaming the French people for* his
cowardice. His *duplicity.* His *abandonment.*

*Even the sans-culottes who wanted to follow him couldn't after his
blatant display of disdain towards them.*

*To my way of thinking, duplicity isn't a crime if it is done in the act
of saving oneself. Any other belief would be hypocritical of me; we
owe nothing to anyone more than we owe to ourselves, after all. But
at least claim it for what it is and move on. Don't blame your
mostly poor, starving, desperate subjects; many of whom still love
and adore you and pray for you every night before they sleep.*

*He had everything he needed to escape. He should have done it! Yes,
we would have hated him, but time would have lessened that anger.
Hindsight would have bred compassion, eventually. And he would
have escaped what was to come!*

*All he had to do was cross the border. Oh, what I wouldn't have
given to be able to cross a border into freedom and safety. His
squander of his chance infuriated me, especially since it was his
fault I had no chance. But he was soon going to truly understand
how it felt to be captive. He was going to understand how cruel
your captors could be.*
We would later learn there were Prussian and Austrian guards

waiting for them on the other side. More loyal guards had been prepared to escort them--flanking him the entire ride—and would have been, had he not been more than an hour late leaving the Tuileries Palace. Because of their lateness, some of the envoys expecting to meet them left, thinking the plan had gone awry. (A quick aside – many of those who tried to help them were later captured and put to death for treason.)

Still, even without that extra protection the envoy managed to travel three-quarters of the way to the border at Varennes. That was when the King decided to get out of the carriage, stretch his legs, and greet his subjects.

Imagine, walking around a town, smiling and preening, lounging and nibbling on snacks – so close to freedom you could taste it. I would have hopped up to sit next to the driver and cracked the whip on those horses, running down anyone on my way through that town. Or, I might even have grabbed my children in my arms and run. Run like the wind. Run to safety as if my life was on the line! He did none of those things. Of course, he realized he was supposed to be incognito, but his arrogance wouldn't allow him to be ignored. Such is the way of royals.

It was the curse of one who believes they are the greatest thing God put on earth when they are not. It is near impossible for weak men to make themselves small, small, small because in the effort they simply disappear. It takes no strength at all to believe you are great if you are small. A small man will tell himself that greatness is his due without any effort at all.

It takes incredible strength to make yourself small when you are great. It is how I finally understood the greatness inside of me, that I had spent so much of my life making myself tiny and yet ... here I was. Still alive and kicking. Still trying, despite the odds. I had no sympathy for a person who didn't even try.

With his actions he condemned everyone--his wife, his children, and everyone who had once felt something akin to friendship toward him—to hell. His escape, taken less seriously by him than the eating of his evening meal. As if the fate of his family, all those envoys, and his country didn't rest upon whether he succeeded or failed.

Most of France would soon hate him with passion. We French people felt like Louis's scorned lover—humiliated and abused—only to find our beloved stuck in a locked closet with us.

He wasn't a friend to me but I had never been emotionally invested in him as a person until it became clear that he had never loved, cared for, nor respected his people. At least not enough to keep the fucking disguise on his arrogant royal head. Apparently, concern for anyone else wasn't a trait of Bourbon blood. He didn't deserve our love.
And now, I hated him. Even more than I hated his grandfather, for the gift of freedom that he threw away.

--Zamor, 1820

29

———————

A more damning letter had never been drafted.

The Convention had already pored over the original letter and were holding it as evidence. Robespierre regaled us with bits of it that stuck out in his memory or had jotted down to re-tell the Club members, his lips quivering with fury as he repeated them.

"He writes...

'How could you do this to me, your King?
How could you treat me this way?
I've given my all to this country as a father to his children.
The disloyalty hurts me to my heart.

It went on and on. While we thought the King was considering how we should work together he was, in fact, writing letters encouraging other countries to attack us and restore the monarchy."

Robespierre's face grew tighter with each piece he paraphrased. He folded the paper with his notes on it with trembling fingers and a white face.

We sat there, uselessly.

After a long silence, where only the sound of muffled tears filled the space, Max gathered himself to speak again. "That is the situation we are in. That is all I have to say." He stood and left, soon followed by the other leaders. The rest of us stayed a bit longer but then we began to drift out, as well. Stunned faces turned angrier with every passing second. Hurt dissolved under fury. Louis XVI had been loved. He had clearly betrayed the entire country in word and deed.

Everyone was visibly heartbroken, except for one man, whose eyes skittered to and fro, taking in all the pain like he was drinking champagne. I tapped Sebastien and pointed, discreetly. It was one of the slimy, slithering snakes. They had organized into the Enragés and the Hébertists subgroups but still hadn't gotten much attention. But something like this would be exactly what they were looking for. We watched as one of those snakes locked eyes with another. A little smile between them came and went, quickly.

"I've never seen anything so frightening in my entire life," Sebastien whispered.

"It was what they wanted. All they needed was the tiniest thing to grasp onto." I could see in their eyes they would do damage with this. I didn't know how, but I knew it would happen. We were broken, and snakes prey on the weak. It was all they could do not to dance happily in the middle of the room, thrilled to have justification to burn everything to the ground.

That night, pounding on my bedroom door brought Henri into my chambers, flushed with excitement and animation.

"What is it, Henri?" I was in my dressing gown, reading by candlelight when he interrupted. "You should be home by now."

"I was, I came back to tell you the King and Queen weren't kidnapped, they were trying to escape! All of Paris is in an uproar. They were deserting us, Zamor. After everything, they would leave us high and dry. To save their own skin."

I put my book down and sat on the edge of my bed. I wanted to tell Henri that saving one's own skin was quite possibly the best reason to attempt anything.

"They're under guard by the army of the republic," he went on, and then looked at my face. "But you know this already, don't you? You always know everything. How do you always know everything? It's those back rooms, isn't it?"

"It's late. Go home, Henri," I said.

"Can I go to town with you tomorrow? I want to hear what's happen..."

"I'm probably staying here, nothing for me to see in town."

He looked at me like he was disappointed I didn't want to go on with the conversation. I was tired. *Soul* tired. On my way home from Paris earlier, the looting had already begun. I didn't have the patience to deal with his questions.

I knew that, now, pressure would be put on everyone around the King, including his closest in command. Including his friends and nobles. Including clergy. Maybe even Madame. Soon, his most trusted agents would turn on him, if compelled enough. There was no good solution that I could see. Everyone would be under suspicion now.

My feelings for Véronique were getting stronger every day, but I'd been trying not to let anyone see how I felt. Now, as things became tense in Paris and at the Chateau, with me being accused of crimes, I didn't want her to be caught up in anything because of me.

The next day, I tracked Véronique down and pulled her into a quiet storage room. "Bonjour," I said.

"Bonjour," she smiled up into my face.

My lips echoed hers, curving into a smile. It was thrilling being in this space with her. "And, why are we in a closet?" she asked.

"Yes, you've heard what happened with the King? And about the theft here?"

"Yes, to both. Is it true they tried to leave?"

"It is. And Madame tried to frame me for a jewelry theft, but that's neither here nor there. It just occurred to me ... with all that's going on, it might be best if no one knew how close our friendship is. I don't want you to be caught up in my mess."

She looked disappointed. "I doubt anyone will care about you and I being friends."

"Just for a little while."

"If that's what you want, of course."

"It's not what I want." She turned to leave and I took her arm. "Véronique , it's *not* what I want. I just want you to be safe."

"I don't know why you think I can't keep myself safe, but I heard you. I'll keep a wide berth, Monsieur Zamor." She turned to leave again, and I took her arm. "What, there's more?"

"It's just that, I think maybe you should write to your parents. I think there's about to be some blowback because of what the King did. Everyone he knows is going to be under suspicion, and even people he doesn't know, if there's reason to suspect they might be royalists. And ... you may want to consider telling your parents ... it may not be a bad idea for them to start 'confessing'—if you will—to their neighbors that they kicked you out because you wanted to work for the Comtesse."

"What madness is this?"

"Have them explain that they simply didn't want to admit to having a disobedient child. They should tell people they disowned you."

She shook her head, "They'll never say that. They never will."

"*Convince* them, Véronique. They won't be doing it for real. Send them a letter now, tell them why. You don't want them to be accused of being royalists by association to you. You and I at least have Madame's guards but your parents have no protection. Everyone in your town needs to know they don't approve of you working for Madame. You can always say you came to your senses if you want to go back home but in the meantime at least they won't be questioned for having a daughter who works for the royal court. If they're not monitoring the mail now, they will be soon. Contact them as soon as you can. Your parents are smart people, find a way to speak to them in code. You understand?"

She nodded, her eyes wide and scared. She didn't have to ask me if she should be worried. She could see it in my eyes.

I probably scared her more than I needed to but I'd rather have her be more cautious than less.

I WAS READING a paper while walking down a street in Paris when sudden activity of passersby caught my attention. At first I didn't notice much because it was so quiet, but when I saw people jogging by me, all headed down the street to an intersection I followed behind. Pulling the hood of my cloak over my head, I walked behind and noticed, in the hush of the crowd, the sound of hooves on the road followed by the slowly, lumbering rolling of wheels.

LaFayette came into view first, back firm and head high as he sat on his horse leading the way. He was followed by members of his National Guard both on horse and on foot. They surrounded two carriages being dragged by horses. Those horses walked as if spent, with their heads hanging as if they felt the mood that descended on all of us at that moment.

The vehicles had been painted black so you could just barely see the shadow of the fleur-de-lys symbols on the sides. Though the scene was crowded, the crowds were eerily silent as we watched that somber scene of our royal family being escorted back into Paris.

But the silence didn't mean there was no violence. The drivers of the carriages looked to have taken the brunt of the crowd's fury along the trip from Varennes. Even now, someone threw a rock at the man where he sat, already covered in rotten fruit and trash. He was bleeding from cuts on his head, a swollen black eye; barely conscious as he held the reins of the horses, trying to lead behind LaFayette. And then, through the window, I saw the side of the King's face.

"Fat pig," came a voice from beside me. I looked at the speaker whose face was twisted in anger, but whose lips were down-turned and wiggling, his eyes full of standing water. "Greedy pig and his greedier wife." He spat onto the ground and turned, walking away.

During the last few days, the King, formerly known for his appreciation of food, had become the punchline of jokes about his weight. Affection for his body type had been twisted into mockery of him. He was no longer on a pedestal and "fat pig" was the gentlest thing they could call him.

Marie Antoinette did not get off so easily. Under their breaths, the people lining the streets to watch abused their former queen with names and terms that shocked me. As their carriage passed, the King's face resolutely faced forward, as if refusing to look at any of us. I couldn't see the two children, but at one point, the Queen leaned forward to peer around her husband, looking out the window, her gaze moving over the crowd and taking in the furious faces. And then, I could swear she looked my way and saw me. I was in shadow, but in my gut, it felt like she saw me. And she kept her eyes trained in my direction until the advancing carriage took her out of sight.

30

July 1791

A few weeks after the King and Queen were escorted back into town, Sebastien and I decided to go to a happy event. Sebastien squinted in the afternoon sun and looked over the crowd. "You have to give it to him, Georges knows how to pull a crowd. I suppose if you give people enough beer and a good time they'll forget our own king tried to run away from us. I suppose you think we're fools, believing he would come around. You never did."

We were at an event organized by Georges Danton and Camille Desmoulins in an open park area called Champs de Mars, for the purpose of signing a petition to depose the King. But unlike our normal Jacobin events, this one had included families. The Jacobin Club was primarily the domain of men so it was nice to see women and children. Though I also heard there were clubs for teenage Jacobins, and groups of them gathered today in the green space, laughing and greeting each other. Sebastien and I came, curious to know how Georges would speak now that things had changed.

"No one's a fool, everyone had hope. Even me. I just knew him better, that's all."

Sebastien hit my arm and gestured to the edge of the field. "I see beer. You want one?"

"Of course."

Georges was across the lawn in the midst of a crowd, drawing people in like a magnet. As usual, his clothes were sitting on him, frumpy, almost as if he were a sans culotte and not a bourgeois who could afford to have them tailored to his frame. I couldn't very well feel he was being duplicitous when every time I came to Paris I took off my fine shoes and put on the cheap ones I had bought off a beggar in the street. Some things were necessary when you were in a different environment.

"And isn't it a fine day for a party!" he yelled. Though he was a good bit away, I had no problem hearing him.

His proclamation and smile spurred others to applaud him while pointing him out to others. To this crowd, Georges was a hero, speaking up for their rights among the nobles. On that account, he deserved respect no matter how he got things done. He went on about the promise of our new republic for several minutes while I watched the performance, trying to figure out the magic of his appeal so I could steal it for my own. To be able to keep them hungry for one's words was a gift I hoped to capture.

"They should bottle that zeal," Sebastian said, coming up beside me, handing me a cup of beer that sloshed. "These people would do anything for him. Maybe I should ask him to remind them to be civil."

"They look civil, to me."

"Here, yes, but over there, beyond the beer vendor, they found something or other," he took a big swallow of the lukewarm amber drink. "Back there," he pointed, again.

I glanced over, but at that moment Georges kicked into a new level of excitement. If he was a horse, he was a horse that had been slapped with a whip, gesturing wildly with his arms and hands to get people laughing and smiling. Camille, beside him, did the same.

"...And we'll *always* speak for you, the people of Paris! No one will silence us!"

Georges raised his hands and then stepped away, his speech, apparently done. Sebastien finished off his beer in two huge swallows. "Well, this was pointless, then. On that note, I'm going to take my leave. Élise says if I stay here all day drinking again while she's juggling kids she will have something unpleasant waiting on my dinner plate tonight."

"She should, you take advantage of that woman. And you drink an awful lot…"

"Mind your business, page," he raised a hand in acknowledgement as he walked away. I laughed as he left, turning back.

It would have been nice to have brought Véronique, and we could have just shared some time together. But as always, I came out on a mission. I didn't come for pleasure. A few more minutes under the beating sun and I decided, as Sebastien had before me, that this wasn't worth the time being there.

I tossed my cup into a garbage bin and was turning to leave when someone brushed by me, almost knocking me over, followed by an equally brusque figure who, at least, avoided knocking people down. I turned around to see them striding off towards a group of people by the tree line. A growing number of men were headed in that direction, so I followed, walking over to a man who was on the tips of his feet, straining to see something. Short as I was, there was no way I was going to see over the crowd. I tapped him on the arm.

"What's happening?"

He turned to me, and then looked back at the scene. "I don't know. Someone passed by and told me somebody's dead."

"Dead? Is it from the heat?"

"That's all I know."

I turned and headed in the opposite direction, milling about to see if Georges was around.

Everyone seemed to do the same as me; walking, aimlessly, wondering if the event was over? If Georges was done? If they could stay for more free beer?

I heard unexpected claps of a horse's hooves, and when people in front me began moving to the right and left, the parting of the crowd revealed a man approaching on horseback. LaFayette? I recognized him, immediately, but his eyes were roaming the crowd, unfocused on any one person. And he wasn't alone. Other men on horses soon followed. He cantered in a small circle, yelling to the crowd:

"Good people of Paris, this gathering is no longer a friendly one. There's been a murder. You are all to disperse."

Murder?

I looked up as his horse passed. Even from the ground I could see the frown on his face as he continued further along, spreading the same message as he galloped the length of the park. I gave a wide berth as some of the other guards followed, some looking around the main area, searching for the criminals, I suppose.

I didn't need more prompting. I turned to leave and ran straight into Georges and Camille, speaking to each other while trying to get people to stay. "Friends, we have nothing to do with whatever is going on over there. Don't leave. Zamor!" He came over to me with his hands, imploring. "Help me to calm things down. We want to finish our event, help me tell the people."

"But LaFayette and the National Guard..."

"Gilbert is as useless here as he was in keeping an eye on the king. I have absolutely no confidence that man knows how to put on his pants in the morning. All the crime in town and he comes here—long after a murder has already happened—to ruin our event."

"But someone died?" Apparently, he knew more than I did.

"Zamor, he's making a mountain out of a molehill. Are we to be blamed for every crime that takes place in this city? There's a man a street over picking someone's pocket. There's another one publicly showing his privates right over there. What has that to do with us? The guards will handle whatever is going on over there, but that doesn't mean the festivities have to end. Help me to push everyone this way. That's all," he laughed as if the affair was preposterous. But I was no longer in the mood for any revelry.

"That's crazy, Georges, I'm leaving, and I..."

"He's scared," Georges motioned towards me, speaking to Camille. "He's afraid of crowds."

I started to deny that but the two of them had already walked past me while in discussion, stopping people from going along the way. I saw people who had been headed to the exit as I had been, turn back when Georges reached him. He was nothing if not convincing.

"Disperse! Disperse!" LaFayette yelled from the other side of the park.

"Never!" came an errant response, with laughter following.

I lost sight of Georges. The beer was flowing again. The sound of the clap of horse hooves started again, but this time it was clear there were several horses, and they weren't walking slowly. A scream rent the air and, suddenly, the horses hooves sounded more like ten or twenty. The bodies were milling about, moving faster now. A woman wandered in front of me, calling… "Gerard? Gerard?" A man picked up a child, putting her up on his shoulders, turning to and fro, seemingly wondering which direction was less hectic than another. And then, a loud scream erupted up ahead of me, followed by two or three more. People parted left and right, quickly, and I barely had seconds before a massive horse charged into the opening in front of me, coming at full speed.

Jumping quickly to the side to avoid being trounced, I felt my knee wrench in protest, but looked up in time to see three or four horses fly by at full speed. I watched a horse step on the leg of a man and heard the loud, ugly snap of the bone. And then, I couldn't believe my eyes when a man on a horse slowed his steed down, reached to his side, pulled up a gun and put it onto his shoulder at the ready.

I didn't know what was happening, but in a split second everything changed. For a moment time stood still as my eyes widened, focused on that gun on his shoulder.

"Disperse! Disperse!" Gilbert's voice in the distance was the last thing I heard before the sound of the first shot.

They were shooting at us. A collective scream went up, and we turned and ran.

. . .

THE CRACK of the shot and the acrid smoke from the barrel propelled movement like nothing else could. Even as the screaming caught on like sickenss, another crack sounded. More smoke filled the air.

Then it was pandemonium. The sound of the screams fought with the heavy gallop of horses moving over grass, thick and plodding, as though people were being chased. It was no longer an issue of single shots; those men on horses had turned into hunters and we were the prey. I was the fox, once again!

Another crack, too close, had me ducking, but I didn't know where it was coming from. There were so many guards on horses now, so many people running, so many screams and so much smoke! And so, I just ran. I ran the best I could over grass, with a knee that was throbbing with sharp pain. We all ran, stepping over and onto each other, trying to get away. People on the ground screamed from being stepped on. I saw someone lying, trying to protect their head as I passed, and I reached down—my upper body is the strongest thing on me—and pulled the stranger to his knees by his collar. Able to get his feet under him, he ran. I wasn't far behind.

The gunshots were coming faster now and the man running on the other side of me, suddenly collapsed, stopping me in my tracks.

Run, run! my head told me.

I started again and saw a woman up ahead of me come to a sudden stop, her elbows bending behind her as if she'd been pushed. The blossom of red that spread across her back said otherwise when she fell forward.

Run, run! my head screamed.

I was right in the path of a shooter that had already, barely, missed me twice. I didn't have the speed to outrun a horse. I veered right and tried to move forward again. Seeing an opening in the trees, I headed toward the clearing, with plenty of people running before me. But when we thought we'd gotten clear, a horse and rider moved into the space in front of me. I skidded to a stop and pivoted, almost slipping, my fingertips brushing the ground. I knew I couldn't fall. To fall would be to be trampled under foot. I managed to stay on my feet and went in another direction, crashing straight into a table holding cups of beer, which collapsed under the weight of me.

On the far side of the broken table a woman in motion with a toddler boy in her arms fell hard, dropping him. He screamed in terror, his face cherry red and wet with tears or sweat or both. She managed to get up to her feet again, snatched the child and ran, one hand holding up the long skirt that had tripped her before.

I rolled off the table and scrambled, once again trying to get my legs under me, and heard more hooves coming my way. But my legs never were my strongest trait. The next time I tried to run my knee buckled sideways and down I went. My heart beat in my chest as I managed to turn over in time to see a horse skid to a stop in front of me. Its rider raised his rifle and aimed it at my head. Uselessly, I put my hands up in front of me as if to ward off the bullet. "No, no, no...!"

This was it. I would die on the ground in the middle of a park on a beautiful sunny day, the smell of smoke filling my lungs. I turned my face so I couldn't see the bullet coming.

Suddenly, the ground underneath me was dark in shadow. Looking up, I saw another horse and rider had crossed directly in front of the first, moving between me and the man with the gun.

The second rider seemed to have used his arm to knock the other man's gun up and away. "Stand down!" he yelled.

As I squinted into the sun to see the silhouette, the horses moved with each other and I watched my rescuer's horse rear up onto its hind legs. He was using his horse to protect me. The horse landed as I was lifting my arm over my brow to counter the glare of the sun. I couldn't believe it.

"Thomas!"

"You're all right?" he called down to me. The other rider had moved on and Thomas reached an arm down, which I grasped, pulling me onto my feet.

"Yes, yes!" I nodded. He nodded in acknowledgement before riding away.

I wanted to leave. I wanted to run. But all my knee would allow was an awkward walk. By the time I stumbled over to the entrance of the park, the gunfire had died down. My eyes watered from the smoke, but I could see Thomas with LaFayette. Gilbert looked confused and overwhelmed, turning his horse in a circle, as if he didn't know what to do. Thomas was yelling at the remaining guards to stand down.

Finally, LaFayette yelled at the last man who still held a gun on his shoulder. I wobbled over to an overturned bucket and sat down, wiping my brow and sucking in the air I could get. My knee forced me to sit there, at least for a few minutes. And so, I was there when the smoke began to clear and the shock began to dissipate. I was there when the cease of activity gave way to the stillness of death. And the carnage.

31

"I'm happy they shot them down. I'm just disappointed they didn't manage to shoot more," said a woman sitting at our dining table.

It was the morning after the event at the park. No one at the Chateau knew I'd been there, my only evidence being my throbbing knee. The woman was drinking Chardonnay from Madame's crystal, the brunette wig on her head wobbling as she spoke, vibrating with indignancy. Beside her, her husband was holding a print paper in his shaky hands. I longed to pick it up and read it.

"More than forty people dead, it says…" he continued. "It doesn't say they were all shot, though."

No, they weren't all shot. Some were trampled. At least one had a heart attack on the spot; the second a gun was pointed at him.

"It doesn't matter, they deserved it," she said. "The nerve of the lot of them, gathering like a mob of ruffians to protest our King."

The smell of gunpowder was still in my nose hairs.

"There were women and children, too," I said, softly, but loudly enough that all of their heads popped up. They looked at me as if surprised to hear the potted plant speak. Then, they went back to eating and reading like before.

"It's their own fault," the woman continued. "How dare they protest against dear Louis? He's just the *sweetest* king. That's his problem, he's too sweet. Could take a lesson from his great grandfather. The Sun King never would have tolerated this. He would have put every single one of them on the rack."

"Yes, from what I hear the Sun King did keep that rack busy," her husband smiled. "Kept them in line, too." His wife continued.

"Sans-culottes might as well call themselves vermin for the nuisance they are to this kingdom. Angry at us because of their pathetic existence, resentful that we're a better class of human. We didn't make the rules! I say the Queen was right. Let them eat cake and shut up!"

Madame was spooning some sort of sweet pudding into her mouth.

"But you think otherwise, Louis-Benoit?" she asked without looking at me. The others stopped again and glanced at the potted plant, annoyed with me for being asked a question by her.

"Like I said, there were women and children."

"They killed two men and two guards," the man said, laying the paper on the table beside him, eyes beginning to blink quickly. It was his sign of fury.

"Still," I said. "You don't kill everyone because of the crimes of one or two. Guards are trained to aim and shoot."

"Well," the woman sniffed. "They didn't kill *everyone*. Only forty or fifty. Maybe that will teach them to know their place. This new revolutionary body will never survive because they don't seem to understand this society only functions because we all know our place! Sans-culottes are like poison, killing us a little at a time. They're like that plant ... what was it called—the plant that poisoned all those people at the Palace?"

"Belladonna," her husband supplied.

"That's right. Belladonna growing around the edges of the garden. Those beautiful dark berries that looked so tempting, but touch one and you're dead. That's sans-culottes. Everyone of those people is like one of those devil's berries. Put a bunch together and they will rot out this country from the inside, isn't that right, Madame?"

The wig wobbled, wanting to topple to the floor. Her face was white with a heavy dose of powder that, still, somehow managed not to hide her blemishes. Her husband nodded, reaching out to take a knife and fork in his trembling hands, anxious to cut more of the soft, braised chicken meat still on his plate. The room sounded with the tinkle of silver against china, followed by the grating, scratching sound of him, indelicately, pulling the knife across the surface. They were a relic sitting there, but then so were we all.

Madame tilted her head and nodded, serenely.

32

____

Dear Citizen,

*News of what happened at the park spread all over the country. In
the following days we would learn that it all began before the event
even started. Early arrivals found two men under a table, likely
drunk. That led to accusations that the drunkards were counter-
revolutionary spies for the King. They were dragged out, beaten,
and decapitated.*
Decapitation was becoming a thing.

*By the time the rest of us arrived they were already dead. Someone
went into town to alert the authorities and when LaFayette and his
National Guards showed up, someone threw a rock. The guards
opened fire.*

*Speak to a noble person and they would say no more than ten died.
I say it was more like one hundred. The papers split the difference
and suggested around fifty sans-culottes were killed in that pretty
park with its glorious green grass. The papers called it the* Champs
de Mars Massacre.

Afterwards, Thomas and Josephe were more than a little angry at LaFayette. To their way of thinking, a general should be able to take a pebble to the head without responding by shooting indiscriminately into the crowd. Because, after my knee had settled down, I had helped Thomas walk some people out of the park to the closest hospital, Thomas declared I had bravery three times the size of me. They both declared they'd take one of me over two of LaFayette, any day.

I admit, their praise still warms me.

LaFayette was forced to step down as leader of the National Guard. Madame's lover, the Duc de Brissac—and his new Constitutional Guard—replaced LaFayette's National Guard. Georges and Camille dropped out of sight for a time.

European papers were writing that France was broken. Even the United States, previously supportive of our revolutionary efforts, was now saying that we had failed our attempt to become a constitutional monarchy and should stop trying. Oh, the irony of the quickness with which the new country turned on us after we'd gone bankrupt helping them earn their freedom.

Of course, I had never deluded myself that we could count on the King's help. I had been afraid of what would happen when the others realized, but at this point things hadn't completely broken down so I was optimistic. We could now move on with something entirely new! I reasoned.

One month later, on August 27, 1791, the Queen's brother, the Holy Roman Emperor Leopold II, and Frederick William II of Prussia, issued the Declaration of Pillnitz. In short, it called all other European countries to be on stand-by to wage war against our new republic to restore the monarchy. Later, they claimed it wasn't a direct threat, but our new government took it as one.

And I'd like to mention another item of note:

On September 15, 1791, Olympe de Gouges, the woman who had written the play about me, released her Declaration of the Rights of Woman and of the Female Citizen, *to address the half of the population left out of LaFayette's document. She dedicated the work to imprisoned Queen Marie Antoinette. Even though she embodied Jacobin ideals, she was a woman. The Jacobins who hated Marie Antoinette joined with Jacobins who hated the thought of women having a voice. They both agreed Madame de Gouges's actions constituted treason.*

But there were good things, too.

The black people of Saint-Domingue had launched a revolt. They were writing about it in the papers, expressing all sorts of shock and dismay that people enslaved against their will would murder for their own freedom. The revolt gave me hope and turned a difficult summer into a promising autumn.

Then, we celebrated Christmas in 1791 at the Chateau, and the Duc du Brissac spent it with us, bringing his adult daughter along. The woman got along swimmingly well with Madame. Madame was so happy she even allowed us servants to join the dining room, at du Brissac's request, and asked me to play my violin. All the servants had meat that day. It was the happiest I'd ever seen her.

But, still, there was something in the air that I can't even define today. I don't know why worry began to settle on me. By all accounts, things were going well. But the seeds were already sown. By mutual agreement of the King and the Convention, death by La Louisette officially became the only legal method of execution. That fact hungover me like a pall, though at the time I had no idea why it should worry me.

Oh my, to see the real Louisette – the experience was beyond words. They perched it where Louis XV's statue once was. After having played with the harmless, tiny replica... seeing the actual thing was frightening. I suppose that's why they uncovered it, to scare Parisians into good behavior. People drifted by to look at the strange beast, wondering how it worked. We'd find out soon enough.

The former royal executioner, Charles-Henri Sanson, became the republic's executioner. The job having been in the family for generations, everyone knew the Sansons. But very soon, Charles-Henri would rise in fame and become known as "The Great Sanson"— reaper of justice for the new republic.

In April 1792, we declared war against Marie Antoinette's home country of Austria.

--Zamor, 1820

33

April, 1792

There was a crowd for the first kill.

The man was dragged onto the stage-like platform, eyes wide staring up at the blade like the machine was a rabid animal anxious to get a taste of him. The guards pulled him towards it, and Sanson, the executioner, pointed to a platform that tilted.

"On your stomach, your neck in there."

The man complied, eyes looking around, feverishly, once he was in. For one so afraid of the machine, I couldn't imagine why he walked to it in such a docile manner when ordered to do so, except for shock. He was the first to be taken by the machine and maybe he thought if he was cooperative someone might change their mind. He did his best to angle his head up to look at Sanson in a panic.

"Will it hurt, Monsieur?" he asked, lips trembling. "Will it hurt?"

His words and the softness with which he said them sobered me and I looked at him. I didn't know this man or what he'd done, but I felt compelled to see him, now. Felt compelled to have some gravitas for this, the end of his life by such terrifying means.

A few people laughed at him and spit in his direction. I felt his fear seeping into my bones.

"This is Nicolas Jacques Pelletier," called the executioner. "He is a thief and murderer," the executioner read.

"Sanson," Sebastien mumbled, equally dazed by the sight. "Been killing people since he was born. A most lucrative family business," he said with scorn.

"It's honest work," I said. I figured, someone had to do it. I wouldn't want to be in his place.

The crowd was heavy, now, because so many people wanted to see the new contraption.

"Nicolas Jacques Pelletier, you have been sentenced to die."

Sanson stepped over to the side, took a moment to unravel and release the chain, and as the crowd watched the blade was released. The sound of the blade moving through the air came over us like a breeze; the *hush ... swish...* smooth and surprisingly gentle. I liken it to the sound the sword had made when Joseph cut it across the sky. The cutting of air made a low-grade wobble in the frame of the thing, but when the blade picked up speed the sound was smooth and seething. A swish ... and then the sudden bang of a knife blade into wood, jarring and shaking the whole contraption.

A spray of blood covered the few people closest to it. By the time we realized the flesh spurting blood was his headless neck, the head had landed with a dull thud. All in all, I felt I was right, there was little blood compared to how it might have been had the blade come straight down.

The crowd looked around in confusion. A few people in the front laughed nervously at the splatter on their clothes. Then the booing began. That booing confused me. Had they wanted him to live?

"What is this nonsense?" I asked, still shaky from the sight.

"Bastards are angry it happened so quick. They wanted a show. Decapitation by ax or sword takes three times as long. Sick. They're all sick."

I was sick, too. So, they would have been happier with a bloodier affair, after all. I didn't want to see any more of those deaths after that. I was told Sanson later changed things up, put on a bit of a show to draw out the ordeal and make the crowd happy. It was all macabre to me, but more and more people began to attend. *For the entertainment.*

Back at the Chateau, Madame received word the jewel thieves had been captured in England, beginning a series of trips to Britain to assist the investigators in the case. It was as good an excuse as a person could find to make trips out of the country without having the government on your tail.

Madame hired new bankers--a father and son—who were now handling all of her financial affairs. And she kept throwing those parties and inviting nobles from all over France. They were desperate for fun, after all.

One day, Madame was excited, in the way she was when someone important was coming to visit. We already had five guests in the house but a letter had just arrived informing us we were to expect another guest for dinner and an overnight stay.

"We're having a special visitor, a friend of the King," Madame said to Salanave. The cook was in the kitchen, her giant spoon dripping with the soup that she'd been stirring when Madame came and stopped her. Salanave looked pained as she listened to the detailed instructions Madame gave her.

"Two each? But Madame, we don't have enough pheasants in the pen for everyone to get two birds. I can only work with what we have."

"We can't tell a guest they can only have one bird, Salanave. I'd be the laughingstock of the kingdom!" She put up a hand, as if to stave off a headache and took some deep breaths. "Kill some chickens and dress them to look like pheasants."

"Why not pork?" I asked. Both of them looked up at me, Madame's annoyance swinging my way, now.

"Because pork is not as impressive as perfect pheasants on a plate, Louis-Benoit, that's why. Do I keep you around to ask foolish questions like that?"

"You keep me around to remind you that not serving pork, which we have plenty of, because you'd rather impress our guests with tiny little unfulfilling birds we're likely to run out of is asinine. And I daresay, anyone should be more than satisfied with any type of animal on the plate."

"I didn't ask for your opinion!"

"But Madame," Salanave started...

"No more argument!" She swiped her hands across the air, a blond ringlet jiggling over her forehead. "Cut the birds in half and ..." She paused as a child sprinted through the kitchen. She looked at him like he was a roach that had gotten into the meal. Soon enough another one streaked by, giggling to chase the other. "...mon Dieu, where do these uncouth ragamuffins come from? Where are their parents? What kind of household do I have that children interrupt adults and almost knock them down in their own kitchens? Gaspard! He'll find the parents of those two."

"They mean no harm, Madame," Salanave said, quickly, dropping the spoon to wipe her hands on her apron. "You are right, I'll cut the pheasants to make one half-bird look like more. I'll cut them so no one would ever know."

Salanave, making nice to throw Madame off from going after the mother of those two children. For all her gruffness, Salanave was always trying to protect children.

The frown was still on Madame's face—I knew she was suspicious at Salanave's sudden agreeability—but what choice did she have? She looked at me out of the corner of her eye.

"All right, then. Make it look like they're supposed to be that way. Arrange them on top of that stuffing you make like, like..."

"Like they exploded with goodness," I helped.

A teenage servant across the room caught a laugh behind her hand, which she turned into a cough when Madame looked her way.

"I'll not stand for obstinate staff. Set the table!" The last command, she yelled at me and walked out, already thinking about the next thing on her list.

"Oh, I'd give anything to be able to speak to her like that." Salanave headed to the sideboard where nine sad little bird bodies were naked of feathers and ready to be carved in the name of impressing a friend of the King.

We all had our roles to play and sacrifices to make in the name of impressing someone important.

By the time we were lined up in front of the house I was dress in lace and bows. My own sacrifice to Madame's reputation. Salanave had created a masterpiece display at the dining table. Madame had decided we would eat country-style so all of the dishes were laid out on the table. The cleverly-butchered birds looked as though each was the very best portion, sat atop torn bits of baguettes mixed with cauliflower and broccoli sprouts cooked in the bird stock. Adorning the edges of the platters; glazed carrots, roasted onions, vivid emerald green pea puree seasoned with more bird fat and little pots of gravies made of fresh cream, butter, a little flour ... and more fat. Sparkling grapes and candied fruits were piled high on the sideboards by the windows so the light reflected off the sugared bits, leaving them glistening like jewels. Little cakes were soaked in a syrup of orange liquor or rum imported from the colonies. Baskets of baguettes and brioche sat beside boards covered with brie and camembert cheese. And glasses of fruity chardonnay, sparking champagne, and deep red cabernet were at each place. Each place laid out by me, the many silver pieces laid out just so, managing to bring order to chaos, as was the art of the royal table.

The table was a bounty.

"My," said a woman who came into the room on the arm of her lover, looking over the table, eyes lit up. "This is even more stunning than last night's dinner, Madame. To what do we owe this?"

I could feel her flush of pleasure from across the room, though her face barely changed as she tipped her chin, demurely.

"It's nothing, really. Just the best a poor, simple woman can do for her truly beloved friends and guests."

Madame allowed herself to be helped to her own seat by Gaspard. Four couples and the new guest came in last. He was a thin man with a beard shaped like an arrow, with its point elongating his chin. His eyes were coldly amused as he looked at the table.

He was average sized with a look on his face that was a smirk and a frown at once. He was dressed in silk, and under his coat I saw the gleam of a coat of arms on something sticking from within his vest. Men who battled often liked to carry their swords. This man carried a knife, likely because of that crest. Nobles and their family symbols weren't easily parted.

That look of his—calmly dismissive—I had noticed from the second he stepped from the carriage.

He stepped over to Madame, leaned down to take her hand, pressing his lips to it, then he immediately let go, looking up and beyond her in the dismissive way people normally looked at me. He peered over her shoulder, like he didn't care to look at her. I saw her eyelids flutter from the slight, but she was nothing if not able to keep her chin up.

"Please, Monsieur, please sit and meet my other guests. They'll be delighted to dine with someone of such esteem."

He straightened.

"Actually, Madame, might you and I have a quick word before dinner?"

She looked surprised, a quick frown at the thought of the food growing cold, but recovered quickly enough. "Of course. Louis-Benoit, please help everyone get situated and top off their wine... we will be in momentarily. Gaspard, will you join us, please? You understand, monsieur, how people like to talk when a man and woman are alone together."

The Duc looked annoyed but nodded in ascent.

I did my job and kept everyone in wine, circling the table as they grew even more impatient at the smell of the succulent meat they couldn't touch. Finally, about fifteen minutes had passed when the three of them returned, Gaspard walking around to hold her chair as she sat, back stiff and face tight. Gaspard, also, looked tense. Only the stranger looked relaxed, sitting down to tuck a napkin into his cravat and giving a smile to the table.

She introduced the Duc to the other diners and they all looked suitably impressed but my eyes were on Madame, who had difficulty looking up. Once we began to eat I could tell from the way she cut her meat that she was not feeling right, the sound of the silver on the porcelain hard and sharp.

She cleared her throat of some of the meat.

"I hope everyone is enjoying the hen."

"Oh, it's delicious, Madame," someone said. Another person agreed. Madame put her fingers to her lips and coughed, delicately.

"You're all so kind to ignore my cook's overly generous use of peppercorn. The commoners don't quite know how to season – they tend to overcompensate from lack of discernment."

I bristled at that, knowing how delicious the meat was.

"Really," I said from where I stood in the doorway. "It must be my imagination but I distinctly remember a particular woman in this room who shall not be named saying, ' for Goodness's sake, Salanave, season it like you mean it!' But that must be my imagination."

The table laughed and Madame's quick annoyance melted away at the sound of it. The laughter seemed to bring her back to herself. She took a sip of wine.

"Perhaps I did say such a thing, but I didn't expect her to take me quite so seriously."

"But if she didn't, you would be there saying what you said last night," I continued. "Does anyone in this room care to remind her?"

A woman called out, "You said ... 'my goodness, how much money do I have to pay to hire a cook that will give me food that tastes like *something!*'"

Laughter exploded again and I gave a gesture with my hands tantamount to resting my case. By this time, Madame was smiling for real.

"Oh, stop," she said, patting her updo. "Always trying to show me up."

"He could never do that," said another guest.

The stranger cleared his throat, and her smile faded as she put the water glass to her lips.

"Why, I've been introduced to everyone at the table but no one's introduced me to this man," he said, his voice soft and sharp. "The infamous Louis-Benoit Zamor deserves a direct introduction, don't you think? I must admit, when I sent my letter requesting an audience with Madame I half did so because I wanted to meet you."

He winked at me from across the table. I looked around to see if anyone else found it as creepy as I did. "And the two of you back and forth like an old married couple. It's charming."

"Nonsense," Madame said, cutting into her bird. "Louis-Benoit is like a son to me. If you know so much about us then you should know that."

"A son, a husband, a pet ... what's the difference, really?"

The table had quieted down again as if everyone was sensing discomfort. The rest of the meal was equally uncomfortable and I found the stranger's eyes on me more times than I should have, a smirk on his features.

I'D NEVER BEEN SO happy to be done with dinner, but a short time after things had been cleared and people had gone to their rooms, a knock at my door brought me looking down at one of the little boys who was always underfoot. He was a nuisance who always managed to disappear when work was involved, but apparently he hadn't been fast enough to escape a chore.

"Monsieur Zamor, the Duc asked me to find you. He says you are to meet with him in the study."

"Madame's study? Is she in there with him?"

"No, sir, he's alone. He's sitting in the big chair, Sir. He says you're to come now and be quick about it."

The boy turned and ran off. I thought about the situation. The big chair was the one that only Louis XV would sit in. Now, Madame occasionally sat in it when she wanted to feel closer to him. But no one else, ever. I felt some trepidation but I wasn't afraid of the Duc. I soon made my way out of my room and through the house to the study. The hallways were quiet at this time of night and I had to take a candelabra to light my way.

Opening the door, I saw a fire had been lit in the fireplace. The Duc was laid back in the chair that Louis XV used to lean back in, his stockinged legs pasty and round. This man also laid back as if it were his place.

"Monsieur, I understand you've asked for me? Is there something you need? Linens or towels for your room?"

"Close the door behind you," he said. He was puffing on a cigar and didn't bother to look up at me as he smoked. He must have felt my hesitation because he followed with... "You don't want anyone hearing this. Do as I say and be quick about it."

A prick of anger kicked up in me but now I was curious. I shut the door and came into the room.

"Sit down," he ordered. He had a drink in one hand and that cigar in the other, puffing on it like it was a sport.

"Okay, I've sat... what do you need, Monsieur?" I kept my tone jovial because I hoped it would rub off on him. And because joviality masked my discomfort. "I see you've made yourself comfortable. Does Madame know you're in this room?"

He looked at me through eyes slitted from the smoke. "Absolutely. She gave me permission to use the room for the night. Rolled out the red carpet for me, in fact. Told me I could have whatever I want."

"She did?" I looked at him closer. "That was very ... accommodating of her."

"Yes, she can be very accommodating when she wants to. But I fear I've run into a wall on one point, which is why I asked you here. I need you to get your Madame to help me get out of the country."

"I'm sorry, I don't know what you mean," I said, though I had an idea.

"I mean, I want her to use her connections in England to receive me on the other end and I need her to open up a bank account for me there and put money into it. So, I can leave this Godforsaken country."

"Monsieur, what you're suggesting is a crime. We are at war. You can't leave without the permission of the government."

"Ah, yes, so it is. But she's helping others, isn't she? The only reason she won't do it for me is because I can't pay her. Unfortunately, due to a circumstance of bad investments, I find myself without funds to pay for her services. But I want out. I told her so. Right here in this room, I told her she was going to get me out of here or I would go to the King and pull on every friendship heartstring he had to punish her. She sat right where you're sitting now and told me no. Can you imagine? I'm noble born since France became a country and that woman sat where you're sitting now and told me no. So, I called her a slut to her face."

He took a draw on his cigarette and laughed at my silence. I was wondering what made him think the King could do anything about it now. Perhaps, once things blew over, *if* they blew over, but he seemed to be gambling on the King coming out of his present situation with his power restored.

"You don't believe me, do you? I did. She looked over to that dog of hers, that Gaspard fellow. And you know what he did? Nothing. His face went red but he's not that stupid. He knows his place. But she wouldn't agree, so now I'm here talking to you, the Governor of Louveciennes," he laughed, coughing on the term. "Governor! What a ridiculous laughingstock the two of you made of the good Louis the Well-Beloved, so desperate for attention and adoration he would turn to a whore and a male nègre whore. But I'm not one to account for another man's proclivities, all I care about is me. I read about how you could get that woman to do *anything* and I saw with my own eyes today that the rumors are true. You manipulate her like you've been doing it all your life. She'll do it if you tell her to."

"But monsieur, why would I tell her to?"

He smiled a slimy, smarmy smile, relishing what came out next.

"Because I saw you in Paris, coming out of a print shop talking to Paul Marat, publisher of the paper that puts out treasonous bile against the King. I saw you, blackamoor, with my own eyes. I saw you."

"I speak to all manner of people," I said, as my heart began to beat harder. "I'm just a page, I don't even know who's who. I'm just happy to be in Paris saying hello to so many cosmopolitan people."

"Oh," he nodded like he was listening intently, his mouth turning quickly into a grin. "And ... after that, I decided to look for you whenever I was in town. Looked into the window of a place where the Jacobins go and who did I see? I saw," he leaned in toward me and whispered. "I saw the page in the same room as the *Incorruptible.*"

It was the nickname for Max Robespierre. If this man saw me with Max there was no lying about what I was doing. Max wasn't a man for idle chatter with strangers. Max wasn't idle at all.

"Ah, I see *you* see now. I've got you, page. I've got you in the palm of my hand." He sat back and took a sip, which he savored. "Your Madame agreed to allow me to stay for dinner tonight—gave me the use of this room, even--but she told me I have to leave in the morning. She thinks she had the final word but I won't leave until you've convinced her to put that money into an account for me. I'll get out on my own, but I expect her full cooperation. And you will get it for me. She will sign over funds for me before I leave this place, I guarantee, or you will be sorry. The King will pull you apart piece by piece. Or her dog Gaspard will, once he finds out."

He puffed on his cigar, no longer looking at me now that he'd made his point. People like him, the wealthiest people, show you what they think of you by how they dismiss your very being. I'd been around long enough to know how they worked.

My mind was working furiously. If he told the King, he would be right about my fate. Louis XVI had put up with me when I was just a nuisance but to give him a reason to mistrust me again would be the end of me. Even if he couldn't have me killed directly, he had friends and loyal subjects. And it would most certainly be the end of what I'd begun in Paris. Gone, would be my freedom. Gone would be any chance I had of making a life for myself or ever obtaining freedom. My stomach roiled inside me, my hands began to shake and my jaw clenched. But I'd been around nobles threatening me long enough to cover how I felt. I leaned into what I knew.

"May I get you another?" I gestured to his empty glass.

"Yes! Another!"

I stood and took his glass as he chattered on about where he thought he'd settle in England. He wanted a townhouse and membership in a fancy club to re-build the networks to gain wealth again.

I didn't plan to get him a drink but it gave me an excuse to stand up and walk behind him. I put the empty glass down on the bar and flexed my hands as my mind screamed in horror. This man would take everything. My hands shook but I stepped behind him.

"You should have seen her face when I told her to shut up." He went on, reliving his moment of de-basing Madame du Barry. "'Shut up you street whore,' I told her! And that thing called a man beside her stood there with his balls in his hands like the sorry piece of merde he is, scared and pissing his own...."

What came next came without thought or plan.

I stepped forward and put one hand across his mouth from behind, quickly pinning him back against the high-backed chair. I remembered that glint in his vest and reached quickly down to grab the handle of the knife from within his jacket, brought it back up, and before he realized what was happening, jabbed the tip of it into his chest where his heart should be.

My hands were shaking but it happened so quickly he was still raising his arms to pull my hand from his mouth when the blade went in. From behind and above him I saw his eyes grow wide, felt the tension in his body, the buck of his body's natural response to the blow. And then, suddenly ... slowly ... his eyes lost their focus on me. They stared, without seeing, at my face.

I took my hand away from his mouth and a strange sound like a squeak came from between his open lips before he sagged, as if someone had reached down into his body and pulled his soul from him, leaving the husk of body behind. My heart beat so loudly I heard it in my ears, along with the sound of my own panting.

Panic began to set in. I wasn't a killer! A lot had changed since the death of Louis XV. I was a child when I'd set out to do him in, but as a grown up I had a deeper understanding both of death and the amount of trouble I could be in for causing it, directly. It was the "directly" part that was shaking me. This man had died by my hand.

Not a bit of poison in chocolat or chance opportunity to steer him toward the danger. This was something different. I was the danger. I shook with fear of what I'd just done and fear of myself.

How was I going to get out of this?

I looked down the front of him and then reached down to take his hands and bring them up to cup the blade as if they had been holding the handle. Then I let them fall down before him. I reached down and used my hand to push his eyelids down over his sightless eyes and finally, blessedly, stepped back.

"Why did you make me do this?" I whispered, my voice shaky with the erratic beating of my heart. My heart wanted to come out my chest. Then I tilted him forward in a more natural pose so his chin rested on his chest.

The room was silent but it struck me that anyone could walk in at any moment. Suddenly the door seemed miles away from me.

Calm down, Zamor! Scolding myself brought me a little levity. *One step at a time. Make it to the door, Zamor. Hurry up!*

I quickly sprinted to the door, put my ear to the wood and tried to sense vibration on the other side—reduced to the actions of an insect in the ground trying to sense danger. The only thing I felt was the beat of my own erratic heart and the puffs of my fast breathing bouncing back at me from the wood.

Slowly, I opened it. Slowly ... slowly ... I peered outside, a bead of sweat dropping into my eye. The hallway was empty but dark. I forgot light.

Stupid, stupid!

I ran back to grab the candelabra and left. Every step was a mile--my room a trek across unknown territory rife with danger and interruption. It felt so far away.

But God was looking out for me, again.

You've gotten this far. He will take you the rest of the way! I assured myself, desperation convincing me that God would somehow be on my side when I'd just committed the greatest of sins.

Finally, once inside my bedroom with the door closed behind me, I sagged with my back against the door. I was gasping and holding my own heart from outside my chest as if I had damaged it, too.

I looked across my room, which suddenly seemed like a foreign space and saw the bowl of the water basin across sitting on a small table. I got there as if by magic and plunged my hands into the water, rubbing them, vigorously, until the blood was gone. Then, I ventured out of the room again, taking the bowl out the hallway of the servant's quarters to the back of the house and then emptying it outside onto the soil. Fresh water from the well obliterated the evidence and I took it back to my room.

"I want to stay here," I whispered to myself, taking a few minutes to pace out my lingering anxiety. I was wringing my hands and my eyes were filling with water but I knew what I wanted more was to protect myself. I *had* to protect myself.

Every second felt like a million and I couldn't seem to breathe right but I kept going, shaky hands and all. I went to the kitchen and stirred up a brew. A few minutes later I had calmed my breath and slowed my shaking.

I knocked on Madame's door. Opening the door she looked surprised to see me.

"Chocolat, Madame?" I lifted the cup on its little saucer. I said this with my jovial smile.

"Chocolat?" Her face was pale but her eyes were red. She hadn't been sleeping, that was sure. The man had dismayed her, too.

"Yes, I know you didn't ask for it, but you didn't seem yourself at dinner and I thought perhaps you might appreciate a cup. And a chat, if you'd like?"

Her suspicious face relaxed and her lips quirked a bit in an almost-smile. "That's very sweet. We haven't talked in a long while. It's like we've been growing apart. Yes, a little chocolat and a chat would be nice."

I wouldn't call it a chat. I listened while she talked. She complained. She gossiped. I relished every passing second. Sometime deep into the next morning she went to bed and I went back to my room.

34

———

I didn't sleep. I stayed up all night perched ramrod straight, on the edge of my bed. Around sunup when the rooster crowed, I dressed myself in clean clothes and sat down again on the edge of my bed, waiting. Waiting. And when the scream rang out through the house, setting off a cacophony of sounds--bumping furniture, slamming doors, running steps and shouts—I stood up, jerked my vest into place and opened the door to start the performance of my life.

The woman who milked the cows was coming down the hall, fast, her face pinched.

"What's happening?" I asked.

"Oh, Monsieur Zamor, it's horrible. That Duc that came in last night is dead. A dagger to his heart! The Manager has sent for the police."

"Oh, no!" I said, but she'd already passed by me so I dropped the act and wondered if I should wander out into the fray. Ultimately, I knew every ounce of my energy would be needed for the time when the police arrived, so I went back into my room and sat on my bed again and waited. Waited.

It must have been an hour before the knock came to my door. It was the boy again from last night. His eyes were wide on me when he looked up at me.

"They say you are to come to the parlor at once, Monsieur Zamor."

"Who says?"

"The Madame and the manager, Monsieur Gaspard. And the police."

The boy ran off. I adjusted my clothes again and took the path through the house.

"Did you hear, the Duc is dead," Salanave whispered to me as I walked through the kitchen.

"I know. I've been summoned," I told her.

"It wasn't the birds, if that's the smart mouth thing you're about to say. They're saying he killed himself," she hissed as I left the room. Killed himself. This was a new, and unexpected turn.

In the parlor, Madame stood close by the door with Gaspard on the other side of her. Across the room, two police officers wearing insignia of the town of Versailles were sitting, looking ill at ease and uncomfortable, on the delicate furniture. The young one sipped coffee out of our tiny porcelain cups, with hands as shaky as mine had been last night. The older one sat stiff and straight, his face showing he was only concerned with his job, not the niceties of modern nobility. He nodded at me as I came in and looked them all over, giving a nod to the guests.

"You are the servant, Louis-Benoit Zamor?"

"I am."

"Louis-Benoit, it's terrible. The Duc was found dead this morning by his own hand," Madame said, her face a mask of sadness and horror, eyes looking like they could sprout tears at any moment. She quivered with fear, and the sight of her trembling lips made the police officers panic. The older one looked away from her.

"That's what we're trying to determine, Madame. We do not know how the Duc died. It might have been murder."

"Murder!" Madame's face flushed white and she threw a hand up over her forehead. Gaspard reached over to put a hand under her arm to steady her.

I had to hand it to her. She was good.

"These things happen," the officer continued, looking at me. "What do you know about all this?"

"Me? Why, I don't know anything."

"That's not true," Gaspard spoke up, gruffly and eagerly. "We know the Duc called for you in the study—that you were with him. I told the officers."

Fucking Gaspard.

"Oh, that, yes. The Duc had a desire for a good, strong drink and sent for me because he was somewhat fascinated by me. People come to the chateau sometimes expecting me to be the character everyone reads about and are instead to find I'm simply a humble servant. I fixed the man a drink just like one I might have served our good King the Well-Beloved, allowed him to look me over and then I left."

"Prove it, page!" Gaspard was red-faced with excitement. He looked at me with something akin to glee. I could see he finally planned to be rid of me, certain this debacle would expunge me from his life. If I wasn't careful he would be right.

"But he's correct," Madame said, lightly. Her face had lightened and brightened and she stood firm. "Louis-Benoit might have given the Duc a drink but he spent most of the evening with me."

The young officer sputtered his coffee. "Madame...?"

"We were talking all night. He made us chocolat, isn't that right?"

"That is correct."

"You never make chocolat in the evening," Gaspard declared, growing ill-tempered.

"You're wrong. Occasionally Zamor and I take an evening drink together to catch up. I don't feel the need to notify you, Gaspard, because you know how close I am with Zamor. He's like a son to me. And last night we took chocolat together." There was admonishment and firmness in her tone and I knew she knew.

"And nothing seemed off about his demeanor, Madame?"

"Not at all. We had a lovely evening talking about our day and our upcoming plans for the chateau. He is my social director also, you understand. We talked and were in good spirits. And it was a pleasant thing. As you know from our other dinner guests, the Duc was somewhat depressed and it seriously ruined the mood for everyone. Salanave had made such a lovely meal and the Duc was so ill-spirited everyone wanted to retire early. He had told Gaspard and me, prior to dinner, that his family finances were slim and that a visit to Chateau du Barry was almost like the heydays of his youth when his family was swimming in bounty. It's why I allowed him the use of my study to, perhaps, elevate his mood and give him encouragement for a new day. Had I known he was so depressed I never would have left him alone. I daresay, that drink might have bought him more time in enjoying it."

The older officer looked at me. "Is that what you found? Was he depressed?"

I sighed. "After I gave him his drink I asked if he needed anything. He said he had a good drink and a warm fire and everything he needed. That things were perfect. I wish now I had pressed him on what that meant but at the time it simply felt like he was finally in good spirits He was so quiet and introspective, I left to give him the solitude he wanted."

Madame shuddered at the thought.

"Might I ask how the nobleman died?" I played.

"Dagger to the heart," the officer said. "It appears to have been a knife he brought with him – a family heirloom. Perhaps that was why he brought it to begin with. Well," he stood up and his partner fumbled his china cup and saucer. He put them down on the little table beside him and stood, as well. "We've taken up enough of your time. The body is well ensconced with the undertaker by now and the family will be informed. I see nothing suspicious here. But we will return if more is needed or questions should arise. Thank you, Madame."

He half nodded and half bowed at her before heading to the door. Once they'd cleared the room and were halfway down the hall, Gaspard could no longer contain himself.

"Madame, he's lyi---!"

She made a quick sound and a gesture for him to shut up, poked her head out the door. When she had apparently discerned they were gone and we heard the distant sound of the front door opening and closing she stepped into the room and shut the door.

"Madame," Gaspard practically whined. "If he came to you last night it's because he did it. He murdered that man and uses you to cover himself."

Her face had lost all semblance of frailty or weakness as she glared at him. "And what of it if he did?"

"Madame?" Confusion marred his features. "It would mean he's a murderer."

"And thank the Lord someone in this house had the good sense to eliminate our problem. That Duc sat in my study--the *King's* study— and dared to insult and disrespect me. My King would have had him drawn and quartered for the things he said to me and the threats he made but you... you... his trusted, brave guard, what did you do? You stood there while he rained insults upon me like it wasn't your job to protect my honor."

Gaspard ducked his head in embarrassment. "They are only words, Comtesse, and he's a powerful man even without his wealth."

"Only words?" She cocked her head at him, pointing to her ear like she couldn't believe what she was hearing. "Are you an idiot? Is that what you are? Because let me know if all these years I've put my trust into an idiot. That man—I will not honor him by referring to him by a title he shamed—attempted to blackmail me and threatened to end my existence as the Comtesse if I did not do his bidding. I haven't come all this way to allow a man to put me to work for *him*. I came to the King willingly and I'll roll in my grave before I live that life again. And hear me well, the suicide of the Duc is the best possible outcome of a horrible situation. Only you and I know how he threatened me yesterday. If the police get wind of it, it isn't my servant the police will suspect wanted him dead, it is me. They'll think I put him up to do it. If you indict him you indict me, so keep your mouth shut about the fucking chocolat, you idiot!"

He flushed red and seemed to be having difficulty raising his head.

"And you," she whirled on me. "Evening chocolat with your Madame was a stroke of brilliance. You are very lucky that what you did served me. You have always been resourceful. Your instinct, impeccable. I don't know what happened or what was said to you, and I don't want to know. I only appreciate any person who rouses themself to defend my honor, like a true protector should. That said, if you ever in your life attempt to use me for your own advantage without warning me again, I will make you sorry. I will cut you loose like a cur. Now, you are dismissed."

I pinched my lips, did a quick bow, and left the room. Once the door closed behind me I heard something close to the sound of tears and wondered if it was Madame or Gaspard.

35

Dear Citizen,

Maybe it was the introduction of the guillotine that changed the dynamics. Maybe it was me having killed someone. No matter the audience, the group or the people — every place outside of the castle people seemed to be unified in the feeling that blood needed to be let. It was a sentiment that hung heavy in the air like a storm cloud brewing. I smelled the blood as strongly as if I'd doused a handkerchief in it and held it to my nose.

The Comtesse was happily sweeping in and out of Louveciennes, going to England or Paris, visiting her attorney or some generals or other people, I don't even know who all.

All the while I smelled it. Lord how I smelled it. And I was afraid.

--Zamor, 1820

May, 1792

All this time I'd been pestering Valentin hoping to get an invitation to speak to the National Convention but decided it was now time to give that hope up. Max Robespierre was, by this time, the most powerful member of the Convention. Valentin arranged a meeting for me with Max at the Café Procope. I was unpleasantly surprised when George Grieve walked in and sat across from me at my little table. My delicious coffee suddenly lost its flavor.

"So, you want favors from Max," he said without preamble, snapping his fingers to a server across the room for a coffee. "What are you willing to give?"

I was annoyed. I knew Robespierre was a busy man but I expected at least the courtesy of his presence to turn me down.

"I gave him a favor the last time I saw him," I said.

"And he wants another," Grieve's eyes were hard on me. "When are you going to learn, page, that you don't set the terms for a negotiation with Max Robespierre? He tells you what he needs and you give it. Without hesitation. Without quest—"

I began shuffling my papers back into my satchel.

"--He never gave *anything* for my good faith effort. At the very least I would think he could give me one small thing to make up for the deal he never satisfied."

He watched my movements—eyed my many, many pages of words. "Whatever you gave him wasn't what he wanted."

"Not what *you* wanted, you mean."

"Max and I are of one accord. The republic demands satisfaction. You only have one thing we want, Zamor, and every time you deny us you anger us a little more. You do not want to be on Max's bad side. Do you want to be considered an enemy of the republic?"

"You mean, an enemy of you? I don't for a second believe Max cares anymore about the mistress of a dead king, he's got a living king right in his grasp. If he cared at all it would be *him* sitting across from me, not you." I closed the flap of my satchel, tossed a coin down and got up. He stood quickly to block me.

"You want your citizenship, and you want to speak before the

Convention, don't you?" He glanced at my satchel. "That's what all those words are for, am I right? I can convince Max to let you in. You can say whatever you want to the most powerful political body in the world." He waved his hand when he said it, like someone promising a pipe dream to a fool.

"Forget it. People have been holding citizenship over my head like a carrot all my life, I no longer believe in pretty words or shiny things. I don't believe you and I don't need your help."

I walked around him and headed to the door.

"You're a fool! I can get you in front of the entire Convention!" he called to my back.

I decided to scrap the idea. Maybe the Convention wasn't for me, after all.

Outside, I began walking, head down, only to brush by a passerby.

"Zamor…"

I looked up into the face of Georges Danton, who looked at me and then peered inside the window of the café, spying. "Ah, the Englishman. I was going to ask why you have that frown on your face but now I see."

"I was expecting to meet with Max."

"Max is difficult to speak with these days. But, would you like to come in for coffee? I live just a couple of doors down."

I didn't know how I felt about Georges Danton. He certainly held some responsibility for the Champs de Mars Massacre, but LaFayette bore most of the blame for that. And, maybe, he could help me if Max wouldn't.

We walked just up the street to his townhome. Once inside, his serving staff gave us coffee in little cups, just as fancy as the ones at the café. His home was modest, but the few figurines and bobbles on the tables were of high quality. The pillows on his settee were covered in silk. His casual, informal style masked the signs of his upper-class bourgeois status.

He avoided my eyes while settling into his seat and carrying his cup to his lips. "My wife is out of town visiting friends. So, go ahead and say how you feel. I can tell you were conflicted on whether to take up my invitation for coffee."

I hesitated. Then, "Fine. I'm having a difficult time getting over how you abandoned those people at the Champs de Mars when they needed you. And then you disappeared, entirely. Now you're back in town and no one's heard a word from you. Not even an apology in print."

He winced with each point. His face, normally so exuberant, was slack and pale. His voice, when he spoke, subdued.

"Yes. I did all those things, and then ran like a coward." He put his cup down. "But despite what you think of me, one thing I've never been is so wedded to my ego as to trample over a tragedy to clear my own name. There's nothing I can say or put into print to bring back the lives that were lost that day. Had I known LaFayette would come in, guns blazing, of course I never would have held the event in the first place. The bastard may be a hero to the Americans but they can have him."

"But we're talking about you," I reminded him.

"Yes. Well, have you never made such a terrible error in judgement it made you question your own mortality, Zamor?"

His question shook me and I looked away. He didn't know I was a murderer and I wasn't doing any confessing today.

"I tell you on my life, I care for the sans-culottes. And I respect them too much to make this tragedy about healing my ego. I made an error and I will work to atone for it. I'll earn back their trust if it's the last thing I do."

He looked on the verge of blinking back tears but then sat up, shaking himself to, calling on the servant just outside the doorway for a refill of coffee.

I wondered if the interrupted onslaught of tears was real or just an act. If he was sincere, or just as convincing a speaker in private as in public.

"You want...?" he gestured to my cup.

"No, thank you."

His cup re-filled, he sat back again, his hand steady as he brought it to his lips.

"I thank you for coming, Zamor. Everyone else is avoiding me these days. Thank you for at least hearing me out."

"You don't need to thank me," I looked him over and said, honestly. "I'm no one to judge."

He nodded. "Were you planning to go to the Convention to convince them to free the slaves? Is that why you want to see Max?"

"Of course."

"We have representatives from Saint Domingue at the Convention but they haven't made much fuss about slavery and it's their home."

"Are they black slaves?"

"Of course not. They're white landowners speaking on the general needs of the island. Maybe they own slaves, I don't know."

"How can you have slavers speaking on behalf of the enslaved of Saint Domingue? That doesn't even make any sense."

"They're the voting representatives. You sound like you believe black people from the colonies should speak at the Convention."

"Who better to speak on the rights of the enslaved than the people who've lived in chains? What about you? You can speak before the Convention. Can't you do more?"

"At this moment I can't help anyone, not even myself."

"Well, after today ... I'm thinking, maybe I should focus on the club anyway. Maybe that will move the needle."

Georges took a long sip, his face thoughtful. "Honestly, the bourgeois is showing itself to be more in line with Max and the Mountain, and they are the ones who decide this issue. Some of them hold slaves and they're afraid. They've heard of the revolts, people massacred in their beds."

"There would be no revolts if people weren't held against their will. Have they also heard of the atrocities done to those people that would prompt such violence? Do they know what's happening? Do *your* followers know?"

"My followers are more concerned with themselves right now."

"Then *make* them concerned. Slavery will destroy our entire republic if allowed to continue. Who's to say if France gets desperate enough for money it won't be poor white people in chains?" I didn't believe that, but I wanted to put any bug in his ear that he might use for his argument. "I'm going to try to speak at the Club. I invite you and your club members. They'll come if you ask. And, maybe, you can tell me how you get people to listen to you?"

"Well, it might take a bit before they listen to me again, but you are a different story. One thing I've learned, you can speak to a crowd and hope a few of them care about what you have to say. Or, you can speak to your friends—people who already like you even a little—and speak to their concerns. You know what they care about and you know why they hesitate. Speak to them and overcome their hurdles, because once they're on your side they'll become your voice. And they'll care about what you care about even more than you do. You tell me when you're set to speak to the Jacobins and I'll get my Cordeliers there."

—

THE CARRIAGE ROLLED over roads worn and pockmarked so that the ride was neither smooth nor pleasant. We were returning from an out-of-town visit to one of Madame's friends in our somewhat modest gilded carriage. It was the two of us, along with Gaspard and Chon, Madame's lead lady.

It should have been an uneventful trip but the carriage slowed. Gaspard pulled the curtain back and we saw what appeared to be a crowd of people swarming another carriage.

"What's happening to them?" Madame asked, straining to see.

"It looks like they are pulling the people out of the carriage through the window."

Gaspard stood and banged on the frame of our carriage, yelling to our driver, "Go. Go!" The driver whipped at the horses, and we picked up speed quickly to pass.

"No, we must help them!" Madame cried, pressing to see as a well-dressed man who'd been fully extricated was being pummeled on the ground. As we flew by, we could see the face of a woman in the carriage, screaming in terror as they proceeded to go after her.

"We can't," Gaspard told her. She had managed to grab the handle and had opened the door, which Gaspard jerked closed quickly. "No! Faster, damn you!"

The horses picked up even greater speed to put distance between us and the mob.

"I don't understand, what was happening, what were they doing to those poor people?" Madame's eyes welled with tears so Chon reached over to hold and comfort her.

"Must have been a robbery," Gaspard said, an unsettled express on his face. "I'm sure they'll get help soon. We are only two women, a man, and a blackamoor – little help for them, I'm afraid." He settled back in his seat, looking as if he was spooked and eager for a drink. He caught me staring at him.

That sort of violence had been popping up all over. It occurred to me it might be a good cover for me to convince her to leave.

When we got back to the Chateau I followed her upstairs with her bags, dropping them in her room. She sat at the dressing table to begin unsnapping her hat from her head.

"That wasn't an isolated event, attacks are happening all through Paris. Random groups of people swarming both nobles and sans-culottes, for seemingly no reason other than the thrill of it. The next time you go England, perhaps you should stay for a little while. You know, until all the confusion is over."

If she was gone I wouldn't have to keep avoiding Grieve. I'd have some time to focus on what I could do in Paris and not worry about when and how to turn over du Barry and, more importantly, how to survive after I did. With her gone, I could actively focus on my free-dom, and maybe earn it before she came home. That would take some time.

"I appreciate your concern, but Gaspard and I think I'm fine here." She turned back to look at herself in her mirror.

My hope fell. As she put the hat on the table, a servant came in and laid a cup of tea on the dressing table. She took it to her lips to take a sip, continuing.

"You know those people we passed on the road? I recognized them. Not at first. But it nagged at me. And now I remember her. She was a friend of the Queen. She spread terrible rumors about me. That's water under the bridge, of course. When we see our fellow man suffering, we help them. I'm so angry at Gaspard for not stopping to help but in hindsight, it wouldn't have done anyone any good to have *all of us* mobbed on the road. Shame, I might have helped her. No matter how badly she hurt me. Just like I still help our dear Queen, who treats me abhorrently. I might have helped her. Perhaps. Or, it may have been God's will, what happened. After all, we turn the other cheek so God can take his vengeance. Perhaps what was happening was God's work. What do you think became of them?"

I thought it would be a miracle if that couple lived ten minutes after we passed them by. More likely, the woman was lying dead in the road, feed for the wolves in the area. Maybe five minutes longer than her husband.

Every fox must survive its own hunt ... and all that.

And here was Jeanne du Barry, the unmistakable glint of satisfied retribution in her eyes. Her cheeks pinked up as her little feeders fed on the notion of that woman's suffering.

Yes, this was the woman I knew. This was who she was deep down. I had to remember this when I weakened and felt sorry for her. I needed to remember this if it ever came time for me to do something I didn't really want to do.

"I'm sure she's fine," I lied. Her eyes met mine in the mirror. For barely a tenth of a second I saw the slight tic of a smile and then it was gone in an instant, her blue eyes wide and innocent again. Almost as if I had imagined it.

36

Dear Citizen,

Fear moves people in strange ways.

Among the Jacobins, those slithering snakes who we barely wanted to acknowledge, the Hébertists and the Enragés, grew in number, bolstered by the anger and growing hatred towards the King and all nobles. They claimed to want to make France a better place but we knew they simply wanted to destroy the world in varying degrees. But now, some members of the Mountain were beginning to listen to them.

And panic was running rampant. Now, I'll list the next things that happened in rapid succession so you can understand how fast things were changing:

- *In June 1792, sans-culottes invaded the Tuileries Palace to persuade the King to agree to the constitutional monarchy. The royal guards were quickly overcome and the protestors made it to the King's suite, forcing him to wear the liberty cap of the republic. Surrounded by men who had overcome all his protectors, of course the King put the liberty cap on his own head. But once they left, he still refused to sign over power to the new constitutional government; neither jointly nor completely.*

- *LaFayette spoke to his colleagues at the National Convention to complain about the radical sections of the Jacobins. He was right on that front, but by doing this he made a powerful enemy of Max Robespierre. Any remaining sans-culottes supporters turned against him. I was walking through the Palais Royal one day and saw LaFayette's likeness being burned in effigy outside in the courtyard. France's hero was no more.*
- *In July 1792, on behalf of Austria and Prussia, a document called The Brunswick Manifesto was sent to the National Convention warning France that if any harm came to the French royal family, Austria and Prussia would rain hell upon the French people.*

You might recall at the beginning of my story I told you the French Revolution was about transformation, and that at some point it was too late to go back to what we once were? We were now at that point.

The Brunswick Manifesto might have stopped the progression in 1789 or even 1790. By 1792 we were a different country. No longer a kingdom, without a king willing to cooperate, we wouldn't be a constitutional monarchy, either. We later learned that the manifesto was approved by the King and Queen before it was even sent to the National Convention. Louis XVI was now, clearly, an adversary. From here on, the man formerly known as Louis XVI would be referred to as the Citizen Louis Capet.

- *In August, 1792 the new Constitutional Guard stormed the Tuileries Palace and chased the royal family into hiding in the legislative offices. In the process, they killed many of the royal family's guards, as well as Swiss guards on duty helping to protect the French Royal family. Today they refer to it as an insurrection. Back them we just called it another massacre.*

The royal family was then moved out of the Tuileries Palace to the Temple Prison for their safety. Louis Capet was no longer involved in any way with the new republic and the absolute monarchy rule was abolished. But at least the family was still together, taking meals and walks, at will.

- *In September, 1792, Prussia pushed its troops further into France. Fearing that prisoners—including those many imprisoned refractory priests—might rise up and side with Prussian troops against their captors, prison guards turned against the prisoners. During a horrifying three-day span, over a thousand prisoners throughout Paris were dragged out of their cells and butchered. It would come to be called the September Days.*

Perhaps because the prison massacres happened just after Georges Danton gave one of his rousing speeches, some people blamed him. And yet, even with these missteps he was becoming more powerful in the new government. Perhaps it was his guilt, but Georges became overly concerned that people were using this time of transition as an excuse for abhorrent behavior. No better time to strike than when a society was most vulnerable. Georges drove the creation of an entity called the Revolutionary Tribunal, and headed up the Committee for Public Safety.

So much was happening in Paris I failed to notice what was happening at the Chateau.

--Zamor, 1820

37

September, 1792

I walked into the kitchen and went straight to the sideboard to grab a brioche and smear it with crème fraiche. I glanced at Salanave, standing at the oven, stirring cereal to add to the breakfast buffet. She had been missing a lot lately—her backup cook taking over the kitchen in her absence--and when she was around, she seemed quieter than normal. Add to that, Gaspard was also in bad spirits these days. The Chateau was an uncomfortable place.

"If you cause me to be short for breakfast I will make you sorry," she said. Her back was turned to me but she sensed me all the same.

I finished chewing and swallowed the sweet bread and cream. "You make that same threat every time. I have never been sorry to steal your food, Salanave."

"You are the devil's own child, Zamor. Be off with you." The smile in her voice told me she took my teasing for what it was. It was nice to hear the humor in her voice. I walked over to kiss her cheek as she reddened, swatting me off with a smile. I didn't realize we weren't alone until I turned to leave, almost running into Gaspard.

"Madame wants you," he said. "Go now."

"Oui, Monsieur."

I sat with Madame, reading aloud. Then, I went about my daily chores. Later, once I was finally finished with the things I had to do, I got to do the things I wanted to do. It was lunchtime so I walked outside to my tree and found Véronique already there. The smile popped up on my face all by itself.

"Bonjour, Véronique of the East," I said, sitting down beside her. She gave a brief smile. She held a bit of baguette in her lap, a half-eaten pear was in her hand.

"I didn't think I'd see you," she said. "I've barely seen you at all, lately."

"I know, I'm sorry. Things are so crazy in Paris these days."

"You're not a politician or a member of the government so I have no idea why what's happening in Paris should take you away from me so often. I mean, the Chateau."

I liked what she said the first time. I told her about my talk with Georges and my upcoming speech to the Jacobins. To my surprise, she asked if she could come to see it.

The thought was exciting to me, but it was also frightening. I didn't mind failing, but I didn't want to fail with her watching. This would be my one chance to make an impact with my own voice and words. I'd been working up to this for years. I didn't know how I'd do it with her there. And, with things being more tense at the Chateau, I didn't know if it was good for both of us to be gone at the same time. I told her, perhaps, the next time.

"I don't understand. Why can't I go with you?"

"It's not that I don't want you to come ... but there are rarely women at the Club, you'll be noticed. There are some unsavory people in the Club, I don't know if I want you exposed to all that. And I don't want people to know that you're a friend of mine."

"Why do we have to hide that we like each other? Chloe used to bed whoever she wanted, and that slimy boy who used to work here had a different woman every two days, and everyone knew it. He even snuck into the nobles' wing at night to pleasure some of the women over there. So why can't we be open that we care about each other?"

I was flushing with pleasure over her confession to liking me but I ducked my head so she wouldn't see my quick, unbidden smile. I hadn't even dared to hope the feeling was mutual, and here she was saying it out loud as if she meant it.

"Well," I continued. "We did get caught speaking last week and were asked by that Duc if we were planning a coup d'etat because we were speaking so intently. The last thing I need is anyone around here being suspicious of me, or you. One day I'd love to have you at all of my speeches. One day."

"I want to go," she said.

I wanted her to go, too. "I can't walk in there with you on my arm without taking a real risk that it will get back to people it doesn't need to. I don't have to remind you that my words might be considered incendiary, depending on who hears them. You being with me only puts you in harm's way. One day..."

"...Are you ashamed to be seen with me because I'm a peasant?"

I almost choked on my apple. "The fact that you would even say those words show how innocent you truly are. If you had even an ounce of life experience you would know it's you who should be worried to be seen with *me*."

"Then, if I'm willing to take the chance why are you fighting with me?"

"There is no fight, it can't happen, that's all. I'm sorry. It's just not safe."

"*I'm* sans-culotte," she said, reminding me of her peasant status. "*You* are the aristocrat. I'm not afraid of sans-culottes, I'm one of them. Perhaps you need me there to protect *you*."

But it wasn't the sans-culottes of Paris I was worried about.

"I'll let you read it afterwards," I offered.

"No, you won't. You'll burn it when it's done, just like you burn all of your papers."

"Not this time. I'll save it long enough to let you read it."

"It's not the same as seeing you say the words in public."

I looked her over, and saw her face held such disappointment that

I felt a softening in my heart. She cared about my speech. She cared that much.

"I'm sorry, Véronique. I'll make it up to you..." I said, softly. I was sorry for us both. This was the biggest thing I'd ever done in my life and it would be a dream to have the most important person in my life there. But my fear, perhaps doubling down on itself, told me to keep her from me, at least for now.

Véronique's expression had shut down. She stood up, brushing her hands down her skirt.

"Well, if you've decided..." she didn't look at me, walking away, firmly and resolutely.

"Véronique..." I called after her but her stride was steady.

Later in the day I passed through the kitchen on my way to the servants' quarters and stopped when I saw Salanave's face, with one eye swollen shut. The purpling around it told me it had happened some time ago.

"What happened to you?" I stepped forward.

"Nothing," she looked away, quickly trying to hide her face. "Go and let me finish dinner."

"But what happened?"

"Gaspard says I'm too friendly with you. He didn't like the kiss on the cheek. It doesn't matter. Manager says I am not to befriend or banter with you anymore."

"That's ridiculous, we've been friends for years. We'll be more careful when we speak."

"We won't speak, Louis-Benoit."

I was taken aback by her use of my Christian name and heartbroken she had been hurt because of me. But also, desperate not to lose her friendship.

It didn't make sense. Salanave and I had been friends since I first arrived in France at ten years old. Everyone knew it and no one cared.

"I don't care about the back-hand," she whispered fervently, as if afraid Gaspard might overhear her from wherever he was. "I don't know why he hates you so, but he's drinking a lot now and he seems ... scared. All I know is, I'm the only one with a job in my home. My parents, my husband, children, and grandchildren all rely on me." She wiped her eyes, brusquely. "If I lose this job we'll all be in the soup line, starving with the rest of this country. I can barely pay the heating oil for them as it is, I can't doom them because of you. Go away, petit. Just go away."

"It's not right. He can take everything from me, then? Even your friendship?"

"What else do you have for him to take, Zamor?" she said, wiping the table harshly. "He takes what he can. That is the way of men. Show him that he's broken you so he can stop looking for more to take. And leave me be. I'm old and tired, Zamor, leave me be."

When put that way, there was no response and nothing to be done.

I would be lying if I said I truly listened to Salanave's words. Showing Gaspard I was broken was impossible because I wasn't. I'd already made myself small, small, small. But I was nowhere close to broken.

38

I was sitting beside Madame at dinner one evening. Though I hadn't yet made an excuse to leave, I was already finished. My impatience must have flowed over to her because she spoke without looking at me, after bringing a fork full of steak to her mouth to chew. The steak was so tender it barely took any effort.

"Look at Louis-Benoit," she said to the table, drawing attention. "He's practically jumping out of his seat. Louis has been spending all his time in Paris these days. Haven't you? It's starting to hurt my feelings. What's so exciting about that filthy city, mon cher?"

"Why nothing, Madame," I said. "But in Paris there are plenty of spots to gamble."

"Gamble away the allowance I give you?"

"What else could I possibly spend it on, Madame? I'm barely allowed to leave here."

"Oh, here we go," she rolled her eyes and patted the back of her hair. "My Louis-Benoit is about to start whining about his difficult life of being kept. I ask, who among you wouldn't love to be kept like he is?"

"I would love it, Madame," smirked a man across the table. "Just put me on a silk pillow beside your feet and I'll purr like a cat and lap up any attention you choose to give me."

"Yes, he would love that," someone else said to the table of people laughing.

I started to rise.

"I didn't say you could leave," Madame said, quickly, her voice cutting as her eyes avoided me. It was never good when Madame didn't look at me.

"My apologies, Madame," I sat down. "I thought since the meal was mostly done—"

"Gaspard," she called. "Can you come over here and stand beside Louis-Benoit."

I looked up to see the manager walking over, a satisfied smirk on his face.

"Uh oh, you're in trouble now, Monsieur Zamor," one of the guests said, to laughter.

I took my napkin from my neck, put it on the table and started to get up, only to feel Gaspard's hands on my shoulders pushing me back down.

"Uhn uhn uhn," she said with a smile, wagging her finger in my face. "I didn't give you permission to leave. Did I give him permission?"

"No, you didn't, Madame!" someone yelled, thrilled.

It was to be a game now. I didn't have the stomach for it.

"Fine, no Paris for me, tonight. I'll just go to my room, then..." I went to stand, but Gaspard pushed me back again.

"Did I say he could go?" Madame asked the group, her eyes beginning to sparkle.

"No!" they yelled. She giggled.

I have never liked to be laughed at. I went to stand up to be pushed back down.

"I want to leave," I told her. I stood all the way up, only to have Gaspard push me back, hard, as laughter rocketed through the room.

Blood rushed through my cheeks. Gaspard kept his hands on my shoulders now, so his laughter was the loudest thing in my ears.

"This isn't funny," I said.

Madame was almost on the table as she leaned towards me, squinting with eyes sparkling and her smile wide. The glint of those eyes echoed in the shine of each pearly tooth in her mouth as the ..." No, no, no!" from the guests rang out, in time with their fists banging on the table. She twisted with glee at seeing my anger and discomfort.

She was in her feeding zone. It was what I'd learned to call it long ago when the evil in her needed to be fed. The more pain she caused, the higher the color on her cheeks, the brighter her blue eyes, and the sweeter her smile and raucous laughter. It was never good to be on the receiving end of the feeding frenzy. They were a mob now, ravenous with the need for something on which to feed.

"This is merde...!" I said. Gaspard pushed me back.

"—It doesn't matter, Louis-Benoit!" she yelled over the pounding. "The meal can be done, the plates clean, and the wine drunk to the last drop. We might stay here all night, you and I, until you learn that *I'm* in charge. What do my guests say? Can he go?"

"No, no, no..." they chanted, their fists pounding on the table.

The chanting brought me back to childhood. Years ago, when a roomful of people chanted and cheered like that when I was violated. It brought back the panic and threatened to send me to the icy place in the Labyrinth where I went when I was desperate – to gaze in the stone-cold eyes of the dead marble fox. Impending panic made my heart start to beat fast and my palms grow sticky with sweat.

"Okay, everyone's had their fun," I said through numbing lips. I started to rise again and the hands let me rise high enough that when he slammed me back down with excessive force on my tailbone I saw stars. My vision blurred with the pain, eyes watering.

"He goes *up* ... he comes down!" Gaspard played, laughing. And then to my ears alone, "Get up again, blackamoor, so I can really show you who's in charge."

It wasn't going to get any better. They all had the frenzy now. Mobs never stopped on their own steam. My eyelid ticked.

I scoped the table and saw the tip of a steak knife peaking from under my dinner plate. Gaspard was laughing hard, joined by Madame, who leaned towards him as though they were sharing a private joke. I stretched my hand forward, slipped my fingertips towards the tip of that knife.

So this would be the day, I thought. I'd either wound him or kill him. From his vantage point, I could either wound his hands or plunge the knife under my arm and into his belly. I'd go to prison, for sure, but maybe one of my friends would help me. Max? Brissot? But at least I'd be free of him. I'd figure out the rest later.

All these things went through my head as my fingers met the tip of that knife. When my skin touched the edge, I used the pad of one finger to slide the knife toward me. No one was noticing my hand under the plate, all so focused on laughing with each other and pounding on the table like a malicious gang of hyenas.

The government wanted to get rid of the roving gangs in the street but what about gangs indoors? Gangs in the pristine, wealthy salons of castles, where nobles hunted and preyed on the weak? Where was the law enforcing the fact that with no more kingdom, no one had a right to treat another human being this way?

The knife slid my way. Madame pounded the table in hysterical laughter. I pulled the knife to me and clutched it, feeling the serrated blade bite into the skin of my palm before I flipped it, quickly, unobtrusively, catching the handle, preparing to jab it into one of the hands holding me. *Now, Zamor, now...*

"Madame!"

All sound stopped as the gang of nobles ceased pounding, eyes drawn towards the voice that had interrupted the frenzy. In the doorway stood the Duc du Brissac, an expression of surprised confusion on his face.

Madame sat up straight. It took only a second for her to come to herself, allowing that mask of innocent, wide-eyed sweetness to drop over her face; her voice going gentle and soft.

"My love! You're here! I thought you were in town tonight."

"It's been days since we've been together and I didn't want to miss another dinner. This... what is this?" His worried gaze moved to Gaspard's hands still sitting on my shoulders. The sound of my heaving breath was the only sound in the room. "Might you instruct your man to take his hands from Monsieur Zamor's shoulders, my love?"

Her eyes skittered over, quickly, and she nodded like it was given. "Of course, of course! Gaspard, you've had your fun. Now let him be."

Gaspard's hands lingered longingly, on me like he wanted to keep them there. Then he released me and stepped back.

Face burning, I pushed the knife back onto the table, stood. The sound of my chair skittering back was loud. I walked out, passing the Duc on the way.

This was my own fault. I'd gotten complacent, like I had all the time in the world. The scene I just left—the humiliation of it—made me seethe with anger to the point of numbness. The stone fox called out to me and I felt myself trying to escape reality as I walked. Half-way down the hall I heard someone call my name and stopped, back on earth again. Seconds later, the Duc had caught up to me.

"Zamor, what I walked in on, I'm sorry about that. Madame sometimes acts out when she's feeling vulnerable, but I know she loves you. It's, just that sometimes when she's around some of those people they influence her to behave not like herself. Why, if she was in her right mind, that never would have happened. She's so stressed with everything going on in the world, she just wasn't in her right mind, I'm sure. She tells me all the time abou—"

I interrupted with one hand up.

"—Monsieur le Duc, with all due respect, I've known Jeanne du Barry since I was an innocent child. I'm thirty years-old. Don't come into this house and presume to tell me who she as though I can't figure it out on my own. You're a nice man and I like you. I won't if you proceed to speak to me like I'm a man who can't make his own determination of these things. I'm many things but I've never been stupid."

"But she ..." he stopped himself at my expression. "I'm very sorry.

I will try to take her into town with me more often. I think if she spends less time with Gaspard she would be a better person. He's a bad influence."

"Bonsoir, Monsieur le Duc," I said with a quick nod, continuing to my room.

Later that night, a knock sounded at my door. Ignoring it, after the third time, I finally stood and opened it to Madame, looking shame-faced and innocent. And condescending.

"Hello, Louis-Benoit," she simpered. "The Duc suggested I should come and see if you're all right after our little teasing earlier, since we hadn't seen you since. I explained to him that you and I tease each other all the time and that you're fine, but he said your feelings might have been hurt. You are fine, aren't you, cher?"

I was too angry to play the game. I would leave this place if it was the last thing I did.

"I don't have feelings. I'm fine," I said.

"That's exactly what I told him. That no matter how much we tease each other, we love each other. And you know I love you, don't you?" She stepped closer to bring her two palms up to my cheeks, moving my head so I was gazing directly into her eyes. It was what she used to do to me when I was a child, force me to stare into her eyes while she practiced facial expressions—and lies—on me, like I was a mirror instead of a person. This evening's expression was *love*. Her large blue eyes were as cold as ice.

"You're the most important thing in the world to me, Louis-Benoit. Why—"

"—I am like your very own son. We belong to each other, you and I. You love me more than life."

I said it with such falseness her eyes hardened. She hated it when I said her words back to her.

"That's right." Taking her hands from me, she stepped away, looked at me dubiously, and stepped back into the hall.

"Bonsoir, Madame," I said, shutting the door.

I waited for her to start yelling that she wasn't done, or to open the door herself to start yelling. Or for her to call Gaspard. But as the seconds ticked by, it was obvious she didn't know what to do and I imagined her on the other side of the door thinking, planning, stewing...

I heard her soft muffled footsteps as she walked away.

39

___

And then it was the day. I walked into the Club, nervously checking that my red cockade was firmly on my chest underneath my coat. It was finally my day to give my first significant speech.

It promised to be a decent turn out, and as I entered I saw there were enough people that they spilled out the door. I slipped inside, my two bags on my shoulder and scoped the crowd. I saw Georges Danton at the far side of the room with some unfamiliar faces, likely his Cordeliers. Sebastien and Valentin were making the rounds. When they saw me, Valentin jumped onto a table.

"Jacobins! Tonight's speaker has arrived. I can't imagine what he wants to speak about."

I made myself comfortable amid the laughter. They all knew what I wanted to talk about.

Pulling my notes from my bag I was surprised to see Josephe, Thomas, and Jacques Brissot walk in. Though I invited them I had doubts they would come but seeing them warmed my heart. Tables had been moved out of the way to make room for more people to sit and some people even put risers around the edge of the room so that everyone could see me.

Fear began to creep up on me like an insect crawling on my scalp. Looking out at all the faces, I could feel their questions, as if they'd asked them aloud. Who was I to be worthy of gathering a crowd? Why had I taken their meeting time which, let's face it, was sometimes no more than a social get-together. My heart beat like a drum.

"Please, gentlemen, please sit," I said to quiet the talking. I cleared my throat.

"We don't have all day, page!" someone called. But they were still talking.

"I think he's waiting for the sound of Madame snapping her fingers..." someone else said. They broke out in laughter. I forced myself to relax my features and gave an awkward small laugh to show them I wasn't humorless, but my nerves threatened to overtake me.

Valentin had advised me to find a way to take control early. "Jumping onto the nearest table works for me," he advised me. "Others jump onto chairs but me, I jump onto *tables*. You'll need to find your own thing." His serious face told me he wasn't teasing me.

I wasn't going to jump onto anything, but I did what I could. From my bag, I pulled out my violin, put it to my shoulder. Seeing it, the crowd quieted down and I saw Valentin's small nod of approval. I began pulling my bow across the strings, playing the Marseillaise—the song of the Revolution that was being sung in the streets. At the end, the room was silent and I put my instrument down.

"Liberté, Égalité, Fraternité," I said, loudly to the quiet crowd. I pulled out my papers.

"I have these notes that clearly spell out what I'm supposed to say..." I looked down at the papers that were rustling in my shaky fingers. "But this is more than a speech to me. I stand before you, an enslaved man asking for those of you who claim to believe in freedom not just to hear me, but *to care*. To care about me and others like me. Care that we are human beings with the rights of nature, as defined by our own illustrious Jean-Jacques Rousseau. I wrote three pages to convince you and now I look at them and I ask myself what I'm doing? Convince you of what? That I'm a man? That I'm a thinking, breathing, sentient being? That I'm human? Is that what's stopping you from caring about enslaved people? Because if you know that I am all those things then why is my freedom even a question? Why aren't you running to our Convention delegates, reminding them that if this republic is to be successful it can't be hypocritical. It can't be a lie.

"I asked myself, why would anyone listen tonight? I've been a member of this Club for years. Spoken to many of you, directly. Annoyed plenty of you to the point where when you see me coming you look the other way."

Some faces did that right now.

"But I remind you, how do *you* feel when the nobles in this country look at you and see nothing worth considering? Some of you know what it feels like to have a noble look at you like you're dirt. And you new bourgeois, you're paying your taxes to support this country—taxes the nobles don't have to pay—and you bring wealth to rival some nobles themselves, and yet they still look down on you. You know how it feels to be treated as less than a man. Now, imagine if they could also put you in chains and force you to work all your life for no money. They can take the woman you love, your children—or *you*, for that matter—do what they want with them and you have no say. They can beat you, starve you, tell you that God permits them to do it to you because you deserve it. They can force you to pray to the God they just told you hates you, and your own country agrees and approves of the treatment.

"Now, you Jacobins come here to discuss your woes and I hear bits of conversations about how you want fair pay for your work. You want affordable food. You want fairness in law and equal punishment. It's reasonable for you to expect those things from your home. Because whether or not you are a legal citizen, at least you are free Frenchmen. You feel the right to demand proper treatment. So why wouldn't you care that your fellow men and women are treated little better than animals? Why aren't you just as outraged?"

"I ask you here today, not to convince you to end slavery. I already know for some of you, refusing that request comes to your lips easily, without even thinking. So, instead, I ask if you truly believe in this new republic and what it can be? You are Jacobins! I know in your heart you say, *yes*. *Yes!* In your heart, you are believers of liberty, equality, and fraternity or you wouldn't be here. In this new republic there's no room for hypocrites. We either believe in liberty for all or we might as well put Louis Capet back on the throne. You can't decry our brutal class system when you are at the bottom and then say it is fair when you are at the top.

"When I was a child I spent time with other enslaved children. I won't split myself open to show you the wounds that still live in me from being stolen from everything I knew. I won't continue to describe the atrocities because I know many of you can turn off concern for people with black skin as easily as you shed your clothes at the end of the day. Instead, I ask you to think of your own children; the son or daughter at home that you love. And imagine someone comes along and steals that child from you and sells them like cattle. See it in your mind's eye: that person who buys your child harming them. Starving them. Abusing them with words and actions; destroying any chance your child has for a future. Forcing them to work from sunup to sundown with barely a moment's rest before doing it again in the new day.

"I want you to see that in your mind's eye. The thought that when your loved one cries, you will not be there to hear it. Never again able to give that child comfort. Never again able to even hold them. Do you see it, friends? Do you *feel* it in your heart? Does it hit you another way when the person enslaved is someone *with your face*?

"We sit on the precipice of a new world. Even now, the Convention is putting radical changes in place. Public education for all children, not just the wealthy ones. A standard weights and measures system so fishermen and farmers will no longer be robbed of their hard-earned work. Even the possibility for married couples to dissolve untenable marital unions. These things were unimaginable just five years ago. But today, with this new republic, we can make this country what we *want* it to be. These are amazing times! Don't disappoint me by saying in the midst of all this, you still want to live in the backward ways of the age of kings? Holding onto the mistakes of the monarchy; staying silent when men who aren't white, aren't Christian, aren't lovers of women, are castigated or abused or enslaved.

"I no longer want to be a hypocrite, either. When I came to France, I was cared for by women, and yet I look around this room and there are only a few because we Jacobins have chosen to leave women out of this new republic in the ways that truly matter. Forced them to gather on their own by barring them from these meetings.

"And yet, just this month, the National Convention adopted a symbol—Marianne—as the face of our new republic and no one bats an eye at the blatant irony. We say one thing and do another. We rely on women and they give without question. It is the goodness of our women that strengthens us. It is the warmth of their wombs that brings life into the world. It is the steadiness and dedication of their spirits that give us all a safe place to come home to. It is the women who raise us to be the revolutionaries in this room. And yet we don't allow them to join our meetings?

"Liberty, equality, and fraternity! we shout. I ask, can there even be fraternity without sorority? Or are we so insistent on a class system that we create them where there needs to be none?

"I know an amazing black Frenchwoman. She carries herself with this quiet dignity and a spirit strong in faith, even though our society tells her she is worth little. Being just shy of the devil myself, every instance of grace she shows me is a lesson in this notion of brotherhood. She thinks about the welfare of people. While I espouse republican values, I'll admit, there's a part of me that couldn't care less what happens to you or you or you."

Gentle laughter rumbled through the room.

"She cares about *everyone*. But this country doesn't care about her because she has black skin and she is a woman. I have friends whose mothers are enslaved black women whom society tells them they are little. And these black women carry life that sometimes they are not allowed to keep. They work as hard as any man and are not acknowledged even for that. They suffer with us, for us, and *because* of us. And still, they survive. Still, they love us.

"I knew an enslaved black woman—a girl, really—who, despite

her dire circumstance, took it upon herself to help me. She taught me what I needed to survive. She cared for me when she had no reason to. She understood how my success would impact our shared condition as two enslaved people, so she helped me. No one had to teach her that, she knew it on her own. She also knew that her enslavement was simply a condition under which she was forced to live, not her identity. She had hopes and dreams for her life, just like every human being does. Just like you do.

"I don't tell you these things to display how saintly black women are because they are no more saints than you or I. I know them to be pragmatic, logical thinkers who see the situation and understand how to face it. Change it if they can. Prevent it if possible. Embrace it if the opportunity arises. Able to rein in their emotion better than any man I've ever known. Better than me.

"Because of these women, I tell you today, freedom for enslaved people will impact the shared condition of France. For equality to mean something it has to work for everyone or it means nothing. We want a France that shows the world what equality truly means. We are *Marianne*; fierce, strong, intelligent, and brave. We are a country of fighters. A country of survivors. A country that loves so much we will re-make ourselves from the bottom up. I love the promise of this new republic with everything in me. My fellow Jacobins, I implore you: Allow this republic to love all its people by freeing those among us who have given the most so we may spread the good news of freedom. To do so is essential. *Marianne demands nothing less!*"

I was out of breath by the end of it, gasping out my words and feeling like I was gasping out my heart. Finally, the sound of one person clapping sounded in the room. My eyes swung to the movement when the man stood up and continued his slow clap, picking up in speed. And then, without provocation, more applause came slowly, but quickly it picked up steam. Then, the room was loud with applause, paired with smiling faces and eyes filled with respect.

My heart swelled.

I was right. This was my purpose. In this new world, my name would go down as one of the world's great philosophers, alongside

Voltaire and Rousseau. I would write books and spread my philosophy to educated men and women. I would tour the world. I would go down in history as a national treasure! I would be buried in the Panthéon along with Rousseau and Voltaire!

I was suddenly shy as the clapping continued. My eyes watered and I smiled at these men who loved and accepted me. Upon swinging my gaze up to salute the people standing on risers around the perimeter, my scanning was halted by a familiar figure. There, beside Sebastien and his wife, Élise, stood Véronique. My sweet Véronique. She was beautiful standing there like a woman who might have been the model for strength and hope. Her eyes were steady on me, but I was certain I saw a tear on her cheek as her smile shone on me.

I had told her not to come but I was glad she didn't listen. I was happy she could see me; see that I was someone after all. *This is me, Véronique*, I tried to convey through my eyes. *I am a man. I am someone you can be proud of.*

40

One rain-soaked afternoon, Henri and I were tending the horses when the fast clap of hooves riding toward the house drew our attention. It alerted Gaspard and two of his guards, who also came out of the house to see what was causing such commotion. When the horses and riders skidded to a stop in front of the house, Henri and I looked on from the side. I recognized one of the riders who worked for the Duc de Brissac. The other followed at a fast pace, and Gaspard reached up to grab the reins of the first horse.

"What is happening?" Gaspard asked.

"It's the Duc. They've arrested him because he wouldn't turn against the King. They say he's a traitor to the republic. They've taken in everyone who works for him and they're ransacking his home now. They said we're complicit. The Duc wanted us to warn the Madame but they may have followed us. Can you hide us?"

"Hide you? Are you mad, leading them here?"

"We're only following orders. And Madame has always been so kind..."

"Madame, nothing! Turn around and go before I shoot you myself!"

But Madame had heard the commotion and the last part of the conversation and had run out into the rain, arms reaching for the guards.

"Let them in, Gaspard! Now!"

Gaspard's face was awash in rainwater, stunned and de-fanged once again.

Henri took the reins of the two horses. We held them steady as the men climbed down and ran into the house. Gaspard and his guards followed. By the time we had turned the horses into the stables, more horses rode up, only this time there were about ten of them with armed men. They were a rag tag party of sans-culottes without uniforms, but they carried rifles and swords.

"Where are they?" the front man asked us.

I said nothing. Henri shook, his face white in the rain. They scowled, thinking there was no point in speaking to the stable hand and the idiot blackamoor. They must have been low-level revolutionaries not to know who I was or they might have asked me twice. They were soon pounding on the door, and then they kicked it in.

"I'm going to take care of the horses," Henri yelled.

I knew he would hide. He was petrified. Alone, I listened as the house shook with the boots of the soldiers pounding through it.

"Zamor!"

Véronique had come out through the side door. Her face was shocked and afraid, likely matching mine. I reached out for her hand and she came to me. We stood together in the doorway so we could see without being seen.

It didn't take long for Brissac's men to be found. We knew it when the screaming and yelling started. Those grown men screamed like children as they were dragged out of the house. When pulled far enough away from the front door--closer to the horses of the sans-culottes—we could see them, fighting their captors, being hit with the back end of rifles, told to shut up. And Madame, chasing behind with Gaspard holding her back, as she pled for them not to be hurt.

It was difficult to watch these men, their fear seemed disproportionate to the simple act of being taken in and arrested. But their sense of normalcy had been upended. If the King, himself, was imprisoned, what did that mean for those who worked beneath him and done his bidding? Everyone in this house could be considered complicit as an extension of the royal court.

All of us were standing in the rain, shaking from the violence of it all. I looked at Véronique's large eyes, and for a long moment we could only watch each other. Something of the mortality of the situation brought to light something else. We watched as the army threw the men on horses and took them away.

"The world is going mad," she said. Gaspard was helping a deflated Madame back into the house as she cried and called out to me.

"No, the world is only righting itself," I said softly. "Like shoving an arm back into its shoulder socket, there's pain to put things back into place." I heard my name being called. "I have to go to her."

"I know," she said. "She seems to have a deep need for you, that one. Claims to be tired of you but then can't let you go. What's going to right that?"

I looked at her. It was the first time since I'd come to this place that anyone had seen the Madame's dependency on me in that way.

"But then, so do I," she said, sheepishly.

I stepped forward and kissed her, at that moment. In the cold rain, all I could feel was Véronique. When the kiss ended she touched my cheek with her hand. "I have to go, too. We'll talk soon."

41

____

Véronique and I had already been keeping our closeness secret, but with tension rising everywhere, it occurred to me to hide our relationship even more.

Dear Véronique,

It has been three days since we've been able to speak yet I have thought of you every minute of each one of those days. I know you have heard rumors of what is happening in Paris and I tell you upon good authority that the rumors are true. Every week a new attempt is discovered, exposing people who are trying to break the King and Queen free. They are failing. They end up feeding that beast, the guillotine, that never seems too full to eat another soul. And Prussia is pushing farther into our borders. But Madame insists on proceeding as if nothing is happening and Gaspard is more erratic every day. I know she feels it, even if she doesn't say it. Now that du Brissac is gone, her patience will be short.
Stay away from Gaspard as much as possible. The more tense she gets the more she'll take it out on him. He'll take it out on anyone he can find. He's already lashed out at Salanave.

Take care, my sweet. My thoughts are with you and I will see you, soon.

Love,
Zamor

I slipped it under her door and the next day found one in return at the end of a busy day. I eagerly opened it.

Dear Zamor,

How strange it is to be so close and have such a difficult time finding moments alone with you. I share your concern. My maman tells me things are tense in Burgundy. I feel here at the Chateau, we're in the eye of the storm.

I'm confused. If the King and Queen can no longer reign, will they be released to one of their homes soon? It is not that I knew them at all, but what is to replace them, that I truly fear. Are we ready to replace them?

I must go. You must sense my nerves--Gaspard has been watching me, lately. Sometimes he watches the candlelight under my chamber door from the hallway and yells at me, asking what I am doing at night. I don't understand him. All these years and he's left me alone but now he seems to be watching me all the time. Since we can't see each other as often as we'd like, I'm lighting a candle to put in the window. It will be my message to you, I am thinking of you.

I will see you soon.
Try not to get in trouble in the meantime.

Véronique

And so we communicated. And when I was sorely missing her, I would walk by her window and see a single candle burning in the window. It calmed me as if it was a stroke of her hand on my cheek.

42

———————

Dear Citizen,

Beautiful feelings aren't enough to sustain us. When a woman like Véronique has to work her fingers to the bone to survive, and an orator like myself was relegated to getting a wealthy woman's chocolat every morning, it can cause doubt even to the loftiest of dreamers.

In September 1792, in keeping with our severed relationship with the monarchy and the church, the First Republic was born. And just like the year of the birth of Jésus-Christ, our faithless new republic decided its birth warranted at least as much gravitas as the birth of the son of God; especially since believing in God was no longer a priority.

September 22, 1792, became the first day of the first year of the First Republic. The names of the months and seasons were changed according to the official Republican Calendar.

- *An hour was now 144 minutes*

- *A day was now ten hours*
- *A week was now ten days*

Months and seasons were named according to planting.

You might be asking what Parisians knew about planting that they would base the whole new Republican Calendar on aspects of rural life? Absolutely nothing. But the Parisians in power were followers of Rousseau for whom nature-above-all became a literal consideration.

We even developed a brand-new method by which to measure numbers called a "decimal system". The Decimal system would very shortly lead to the Metric system that, today, is the standard system of measurement throughout Europe.

Though the Republican Calendar was the rule of the land, I won't bother to explain further since, as of the writing of these journals, everything has been put back to the Gregorian Calendar. I never knew I could be happier about anything. I only mention it here as an example of how great and small were the changes that formed our new republic.

--Zamor, 1820

Listening to Madame complain about not receiving an invitation to a soiree, and her ladies going on about how the hostess of said soiree should be drummed out of society for snubbing her, I managed to escape her notice and slipped out of the room. They would be preparing for *our* soiree very soon, as tonight we were having guests. In an hour, the house would be a flurry of activity. But now, all the activity seemed to be in the hallway of the servants' quarters where a crowd gathered in one of the back rooms.

"What's going on?" I asked a passing servant woman who was the last in the pack of women peering into one of the rooms, standing on her tip-toes to see.

"The servant girl finished Madame's dress and she's trying it on before it's sent up to Madame. It's stunning."

That was Véronique. She had been working on the most important thing Madame had ever asked her to sew—a custom gown for tonight's ball. I moved my way up to the front of the crowd and peered into the room, listening to the women gasping and smiling with delight. And then I saw Véronique and time stopped.

She was wearing brilliant violet blue of the purest French silk. The fabric was so fine and delicate it lay against her, yet picked up the slightest movement of air, like a gossamer wing. It draped her skin, skin that looked blooming with reds and golds highlighted and enhanced by the color of the dress and the bodice, a panel of all the flowers that grew in our gardens. She had removed her headwrap and her hair was dark with tight curls that mirrored mine, only longer, gathered at the nape of her neck, also tied with a silk ribbon.

She was the most beautiful woman I'd ever seen.

She spun in a single spin. The gown billowed and shimmered in the gloom of the servant's room, causing everyone to make noises of appreciation.

"What do you think she'll wear around her neck?" someone asked.

"It would have to be her finest jewels to compete with that!"

Véronique blushed and couldn't stop her lips from curling.

"Mon Dieu," said Salanave. "I didn't even know quite how lovely you are, chère. Let's get you out of that dress before it decides to mold itself to you."

If only I could afford to put her in gowns like that, I thought. If I could earn enough, she could sew like she wanted but I could also buy her jewels and a fancy dress every now and again so that she wouldn't have to sew on her own.

I wanted to give her anything and everything she wanted. I wanted her to dream, to sit by a fire in that little house overlooking the river. Quiet nights reading together. Both of us doing the work we loved. I wanted *her* most of all.

I didn't say anything, and tried to slip away. I moved away just as her face turned towards me. I didn't have the words for her and didn't trust what might come out of my mouth in front of all those people.

Later, I was in the parlor dusting when I saw one of the servants pass by in the hallway, headed to Madame's room, and curiosity propelled me to drop my duster and follow so I could be there to see her reaction. The servant had deposited the dress to excited exclamations. I poked my head in to see Madame pick it up from the bed.

This gown could be Véronique's ticket to the life she wanted. It could open her up to be a woman of her own means. She could actually do it!

"Oh, my, it is lovely. Help me put it on."

"Do you have news on the Duc de Brissac, Madame?" one of her maids asked.

Brissac was a decent man as far as nobles and generals, went but he held steadfast loyalty to the King. He firmly believed in the monarchy. When Madame received his letter yesterday, telling her he would be going to trial, she clutched at it desperately and lost color in her face slowly as she read, her fingers trembling.

"He says he's being transported to Versailles," she responded, sounding more hopeful today. "If there's anything positive in this it's that maybe I'll be able to visit him. But it's difficult to ... to...."

I was smiling when I looked in again, to see what had stopped her speaking. Madame had the gown on and was looking at herself in the mirror, her smile dying.

Immediately, I saw the problem. Madame had chosen the fabric and the brilliant blue color herself, no doubt influenced by how striking bright colors looked on Véronique. But the color wasn't as complimentary to Madame. Against the bold hues, her skin looked sallow, the hollows under her eyes too deep. She looked a shell of herself.

"You'll be the prettiest woman tonight, Madame," one of her ladies said.

"Yes ... yes..." she said. She saw me looking in and her face hardened. "Zamor. Look at what your friend made me to wear tonight. What do you think?"

Her eyes were sharp on me. Now I knew that she knew Véronique was my friend. "No one will outshine you tonight. No one ever does," I said, hoping the flattery would appease her.

"Hmm. I suppose we'll see. Thank you, Louis."

I took her cue to leave. I hoped I was being paranoid and that the look she gave me wasn't what I thought; suspicion.

But we had a party to prepare for and I had to help set up the Pavilion. Putting out the linens and candles and helping the musicians set up took the rest of the night until it was time. I put on my noble dress and perched in a doorway to watch as people entered. In my side vision, I saw Véronique and Salanave across the room. Some other servants found things to busy themselves so they could be close by for Madame's big entrance, wearing Véronique's dress.

I realized it was a big thing for all the servants. Even the servants who didn't like Véronique were eager to see the success of this gown. It was beyond personal feelings. A common working class woman dressing nobles would be something that would give all of us hope for anything.

The guests were plentiful and wine was already flowing when Madame made her entrance on Gaspard's arm ... in a white gown. I looked over to Véronique, her face once so excited now frozen in surprise.

"Is this the new gown from the dressmaker you were raving about, Comtesse?" one of her guests asked.

"No," she blustered. "I thought to give her a chance but you really can't trust the lower classes to make anything of value. It's beyond their understanding. Why, they would have us all looking like court jesters if left to them. No, I will stick with designers who know what they're doing and know how to dress the upper class. You can't teach good taste, ma chère."

It was cruel. All the work Véronique had put into making a beautiful dress and to throw it in her face like that – to try to humiliate her like that – was cruel. And worse of all was the fact that I was certain Madame did it as much to spite me as to take the blame for the debacle from herself. Véronique was my friend, and that was enough to earn her Madame's wrath.

All the servants looked at Véronique, who quietly picked up her skirts and left quickly from the room. I knew she was a strong woman and she could deal with this on her own, but I didn't want her to. I turned to follow her out.

"Zamor!" Madame called, stopping me.

I turned around to find her eyes sharp on me. Holding out her glass, she spoke firmly. "I need more champagne and you're the only one who knows how to pour it just right. Will you?"

I hesitated. I was angrier than I should be to serve but I took a bottle from a nearby table and brought it to her. As she tipped her glass for me, she goaded, as she did so well.

"It seems pouring my wine is the only thing I can trust you with. That's a sore disappointment."

"And what have I done? Do I not run to you fast enough? Fetch your chocolat quickly enough? Tell you how beautiful you are one hundred times fewer than I should have?" I asked as I finished the pour.

"Such innocence in your voice when you very clearly plotted with your lady friend on a dress I can't wear ... to make me look a fool in my own home in front of all my friends!"

"The style was as current as the dress you're wearing right now. If it's the color that bothers you, then you should be angry with yourself since you chose it."

"I'm no dressmaker!" she hissed under her breath. "She *knew* the color wouldn't favor me and she didn't say a word, just like you. She knew what she was doing. I saw your face earlier when you looked at me. You could clearly see it didn't suit and yet you stood there, laughing at me."

"No, I stood there hoping you would for once be gracious enough to make the best of your mistake and use the jewels and scarves in your wardrobe to make it work. I've seen you do more with much less. You could have worn one of your other wigs."

"The only one that would have worked was the brunette one and that would have made me look even more sallow. I haven't worn it in years! Enough with you, it's obvious you don't care about me or how I look to my friends. You are a pathetic ingrate and I'll not allow you to make a fool of me."

She stepped away and soon enough she was busy with her guests. Fine. I put the bottle down and went looking for Véronique in the house, but she was nowhere to be found. I went back to the Pavilion but my mind wasn't on the music. I performed my duties, distracted.

After an hour or so, the champagne was working on the guests. Everyone was happy. I noticed three young female servants in the doorway, huddled, but fiddling as though they didn't know what to do with themselves. One of them spotted me and headed over, only to be intercepted by Gaspard.

"What is it?" he barked.

She curtsied quickly and spoke, worriedly. "There is news that there's a gang on the road headed towards the Chateau. They are making quite the racket."

"It's no matter," he said. "We have guards. Those gangs are nothing more than kids drinking too much and making a nuisance. Pay them no mind and they'll move along."

Madame and some of the guests had overheard this. They talked among themselves, expressing gratitude to Madame's security team as even at that moment we heard the sound of the gang approaching. They came singing with drunken song, and as we looked out the windows we saw the light from torches in the dark night.

"Madame du Barry...!" one of them shouted, gaily, from outside.

"Oh, they're saying hello," said a noblewoman. "Everyone loves you, my dear. Why, you're more popular than the Queen ever was."

Madame smiled, showing her teeth, her previous anger melted by her favorite compliment. Her cheeks went pink with pleasure.

"Madame du Barry!"

"Oh my," another woman said as they looked at each other.

"Beautiful, Jeanne – we hope you're having a lovely evening!" they called, happily.

"I *am*," she whispered, conspiratorially to her friends as they laughed. She cocked her head, playing the coquette, to listen for their next flirtation. "And to what do we owe this pleasure?" she called.

"Away from the windows," Gaspard said to a couple that was peering out. As they moved deeper into the room, some laughed nervously about the increase in voices of the group outside as they laughed and sang drunken songs.

Gaspard peered out and when he turned back, his face showed no concern. "It's only maybe ten or twelve, not likely to be a bother..." he was saying when something came flying through the open window, bounced once and landed on the floor ... to laughter from outside.

"What is it? It can't be flowers..." someone laughed.

It was a brown potato sack with dark brown spots. Gaspard stepped forward and jabbed at it before lifting it by a corner to empty the contents. My body went cold.

The head of Louis Hercule Timoleon de Cosse-Brissac rolled to a stop, face up; his eyes staring at us in horror.

43

The first scream unleashed cries from the rest of the people, and soon the screams filling the room were drowning out the laughter from outside, which rose in a wave on the sound of the screams. Then, everyone started to run.

"No, stay here!" Gaspard yelled, but the panic had taken over. Madame, eyes stuck on the gift on the floor, stood up and began a slow slide into unconsciousness.

"Get *her* back to the house!" Gaspard said.

But I was busy looking for Véronique, peering over the heads and around the bodies of people running, screaming, and walking in a daze not sure where to go. I didn't see her anywhere.

"Did you hear me?"

"You take her!"

"I have to secure the property. Don't argue with me, get her out of here before she's trampled!"

Madame was half on, half off the sofa. People were stepping on each other to leave, stopped only by the guard.

"Open the door," Gaspard called to the man blocking it. "Back to the house, everyone!"

Once the outer doors were flung open guests began to run out into the night. It was a mad dash into darkness. I crossed the room to grab Madame, picking her up and hefting her over my shoulder. I ran out of the room and outside.

It wasn't until that moment, surrounded by the dark, that I realized it could be a trap. They could be waiting for us to run from the Pavilion to ambush us. That made me run even faster. There had been torches and lamps lit, but people must have grabbed them because it was pitch black, now.

The night was a vast soup of nothingness and only instinct and a thousand times walking to the path led my way. Some people up ahead were way off track, running in a direction closer toward the street. I could barely see them but a woman's pink dress picked up some light from the moon. I yelled at them to come back, they were going the wrong way, and saw the cloud of dress stop, and then they were heading in my direction.

For a moment it seemed like we were humans lost in the vast dark night sky, various pale-colored skirts picking up the light of the moon as we flittered, aimlessly ... fireflies in the night unsure of where to land.

"This way!" I yelled, trying to lead them with my voice through the dark night.

And like that, we ran through the grounds to the house. Once there, I burst inside and carried Madame up the stairs to her room, putting her down on the bed.

"Chon! Chon!" I yelled. The woman came running in.

"Oh, thank God," she said. "I lost sight of Madame and they said to run. "

"Come help her. She needs help!"

One of the other ladies stumbled into the doorway, face pale with hair dangling in her face, panic in her eyes. "Madame!"

"Help her."

By that time, she was starting to wake up. I heard her garbled cries to the ladies begging them to tell her it was a bad dream. This was a bad dream.

I ran down the stairs and through the house to the servants' quarters. I burst into Véronique's room and my heart sank to see she wasn't there. Where could she be? Were they in the house? Could they have taken her?

I went through the hall, asking people as they passed if they'd seen her and with every person who said no, I grew more afraid.

If they'd taken her, if they hurt her…

I ran into the kitchen, looked around, and then headed towards the front of the house when I heard her voice.

"Zamor?"

I turned to see her standing there with a cup of tea.

"The ladies told me to make a cup of tea for Madame. Is it true that someone is dead? What happ—"

I ran across the room and grabbed her in my arms, causing the cup to jiggle in the saucer.

"You're all right. Oh, Dieu merci"—*thank God*—"you're all right. I thought, I thought…"

I couldn't say what I thought. I buried my face in her neck and held her tight. She must have put the cup down on a table because her arms came around me to hold me back.

"Oh, my love, I'm fine. I'm fine."

"Véronique, Madame needs her tea." Salanave's voice made us spring apart and I used a sleeve to quickly swipe at my eyes.

"Yes, Madame Salanave," she said with a quick curtsy, picking up the cup and leaving.

Salanave was quiet for a moment, and then she said, without looking at me, "That might have been anyone walking in and seeing you holding her like that. Seeing how much you care. I might have been anyone, Zamor."

"Yes," I nodded. I didn't need her to remind me what that meant.

44

———

"You," Gaspard barked to me as I was putting away glasses later that night. "Come with us."

I followed him and one of his guards outside. He handed me a shovel and thrust the stained burlap sack at me. Even in the dark I could tell that what appeared to be black under the moonlight was the stain of blood. "Bury it. Bury it so it's never found again."

"Why me?"

"Because we're busy securing the house. Don't argue with me, nègre!"

I took a lamp and walked the length of the property into the surrounding trees, found a remote spot and began digging. As I did so, the night felt like it was closing in on me. I dug and felt foreboding and fear.

Gaspard and his guard abandoned me to this gruesome work. When I had a hole good and deep I picked up the sack, accidentally at the wrong end, and in the darkness, the sudden whiteness of Brissac's face stared up from the ground where he'd dropped. His eyes were still open. In them was fear that mirrored what I felt in my soul. I leaned down and looked into those sightless eyes. For a horrifying, brief moment, the head was mine. Cold washed through me as I realized how easily that could be the case.

This was not something I was meant to see, this bodyless head.

Back at the chateau, the guests staying at the house were too shaken to sleep, so they gathered in the parlor, passing around bottles of cognac to drink by the fire. Most of them went to their rooms to pack to leave at first light—no one wanted to venture out at night with that gang on the road.

Later when I checked on her, Madame was sitting in her room while a maid pressed a cool, wet cloth to her brow. She took gulps of cognac.

"Oh, my Duc," she gasped on a cry as fresh tears erupted. "Am I cursed? To never have a man I love by my side? Other women can have love but mine are taken from me, always." She looked young in tears, and a part of me felt for her as her ladies encircled her with their arms, crying for the seemingly perpetual misfortune of their mistress.

I had spent the night sitting outside her bedroom door as her ladies came and went, hiding yawns under their hands. Madame was supposed to be sleeping, so every few minutes she would lie back on the bed, closing her eyes, her hand being held by one of her ladies until she drifted off. The second the lady removed her hand, so she might leave to go to bed, Madame would pop up, sitting straight up, eyes, wide, searching the room. If one of her ladies was there, she would begin crying again. If she was alone, she would begin wailing about her lot in life that after loving so many people she was always abandoned. And sometimes she would roll over, open her eyes and, no matter who was in the room, call out, "Where's Louis-Benoit?"

Twice I tried to go to my room, and twice, as if she were mentally connected to me, she would call for me and one of the child servants would come on emergency orders to get me. Then, I'd go to her room, tell her I was there—"Hush, go to sleep. Everything is fine. Fine, fine, fine...--" and she would close her eyes while staring at me.

And one time she woke up as if in a trance, climbed out of bed, and walked of the room.

"Madame?" I called as she stepped over me in the hall, one of her ladies following and looking at me in question. I shrugged, but got up. By the time we reached her she was in the study shoving papers into the dying fire of the fireplace.

"Madame," I asked again. She whirled at the sound of my voice, her face looking like a captured animal. She was clutching even more paper, tossing it into the fire before rushing back to her desk to grab more.

"Madame?" came the voice of a guest from behind me, the man looking inside the room."

"Leave!" She yelled.

I backed away, forcing the man back into the hall if he didn't want to get run into. Then I closed the door. "Go to bed, Monsieur, leave her be." I said to him. The second he turned to take the stairs I headed to the servants' quarters, hoping to finally get some sleep. Twenty minutes later one of her ladies was pounding on my door. Exhausted, I jerked awake and opened the door to the woman's blotchy, tear-stained face.

"She told me if I didn't get you and bring you back she'd kick me out forever. Why are you down here?" she wailed.

I went back up the stairs and stepped into the room. Madame was sitting in bed, wild-eyed, scoping the space as if it was foreign to her. The second she saw me she stopped.

"Why do I have to go looking for you, Louis-Benoit? Why can't you be loyal to me? Why are you always leaving me?" Her yell dissolved into tears.

"What do you need, Madame?"

"You stay close by!" She pointed, gesturing to the floor. "You better stay close, you hear me? If I have to call you twice ... oh why am I being punished?"

The tears started again.

"I'll be right here, on the other side," I said. I gave up thinking I'd be able to sleep and just sat outside the door.

I knew it was morning when I jerked awake to the sound of a man and woman jostling their bags in the hallway. They stepped over me as they passed, anxious to get out. And then I stood up, while my bones groaned, and went down to the kitchen for the morning chocolat. By the time I entered her room, one of her ladies was there, eyes red, and hair messy all over her head.

"Ah, see, there he is, Madame, just like I told you," she smiled, tremulously, with tight lips. Madame was sitting up in bed, one hand folded over the other, eyes red but sharp and focused.

"Where were you? I go through the most horrible experience of my life. Is it too much to ask my ladies and my closest confidant to be by my side?" she said. There was no bit of the mask on her face this morning and not an ounce of fake sweetness. It was going to be one of those days.

"Now, you were going through a very difficult time or you might have noticed me and your ladies were with you all night." I stepped forward and placed the chocolat on the table beside her. "There was barely a second when you were alone."

The lady nodded vigorously. "That's what I told her. See, Madame, it's just like I said. We were all with you..."

Our benefactress picked up a pillow and threw it at the girl, who burst into tears and ran crying from the room.

Madame glared at me. "If you were with me all night, Louis-Benoit, why was I alone when I opened my eyes?"

Who knew? Maybe her lady stepped out for a moment just to stretch her legs. Maybe she was on the side of the room opposite Madame's face. Maybe the lady was there, and Madame was lying. It might have been any of those things.

But she wanted to rail this morning, and rail she would. Her ladies wouldn't come back, not when the first one told the others how Madame was this morning. Everybody knew, this mood was for me, alone, as her closest confidant.

"Haven't I been a good enough person?" Her eyes squinted with the onslaught of fresh tears? "Why am I plagued by sadness and, and..." she looked around the room, searching for the right word. And then her eyes landed on the discarded blue silk dress from last night, draped over a chair. "...evil. I'm plagued by evil! Take that dress outside and you burn it, Louis. You burn that piece of filth."

It was the dress Véronique had made. Véronique's hands had bled from making that dress. She'd gone nights without sleeping to make that dress. Now Madame wanted me to burn it?

My hesitation made her both angry and gleeful that she had hit the mark with something to cause me pain. Her face twisted into a mirthless smile as she nodded, frantically.

"That's right! You'll take that thing from this room and you'll burn it. Or, I'll make you sorry."

I wasn't going to do it. She picked up her cognac glass and lobbed it across the room at me. I ducked and it shattered into the wall.

"Do it, now, Louis! Or you'll be sorry!"

A muscle in my jaw flexed but I marched across the room and grabbed it, leaving the room on a fast stride. I moved as fast as I could through the house, almost running into the kitchen.

"Salanave, I need something to burn like a towel or a sheet."

Seeing my face, she didn't ask questions, reaching into a cupboard to pull out an old, stained tablecloth. I took it and then ran to the servant's quarters to Véronique 's room. I opened the door to find her curled on the bed, her back to the door. She sat up, eyes red.

"What's happening?"

"I don't have time to explain. Do you have scraps from this dress?"

She saw her blue gown balled up in my arms and then nodded, bounding out of bed. Crossing the room, she rifled through a bag and pulled out the scraps of material, handing them to me. I traded her the dress. "Hide it so it's never seen again. And don't go near Madame today."

I left the room and, quickly, went through the kitchen again, out the back door just as Madame was coming through. Wearing her dressing gown, eyes wild, hair unkempt she burst through the door.

"What's taking so long? Do what I say, Louis. Burn it!"

The servant children's eyes were wide as, in the process of their morning chores, they saw me burst out the back door and throw the old cloths to the ground, tossing the blue scraps on top to mimic a pile of blue silk. I, hurriedly, grabbed a torch from the wall to set the whole of it on fire from below.

"Burn it! Burn it!" Madame screamed from the doorway. The children scattered. "Burn it to hell!"

The pile made a healthy fire on the graveled ground and as all the remnants were rendered unrecognizable but a flash of blue here or there, she collapsed against the doorframe, spent.

"That's right," she pointed to the pile, with lackluster energy now. "Burn it all."

Behind me, I heard her shuffling, and when I looked back she had gone back into the kitchen and into the house. Moments later Salanave stood in the doorway. She didn't speak, but she nodded.

I breathed in relief as my shoulders sagged, hands on my hips. I stayed until the smell of burnt fabric had filled the air and the pile turned to ash before returning the torch and going to my room to try to get a little sleep.

I'd barely had a moment to digest all that had happened. But the second I undressed and sponged off, sitting on the edge of my bed, I realized there was a sickness in the air, I could feel. And I knew we'd just entered a time when what I felt was more important than what I knew. We were entering the desperate season. God only knew what new fruit would blossom next.

DEAR VÉRONIQUE,

I WILL KEEP this message short. Madame has a sense that you and I are close and I believe that's why she ordered me to burn your dress. I had hoped we would be safe, but the bloodshed is now at our door. Though it hurts to even think about it, it would be best if you ask your employer, the Noblewoman Martin, to send for you. Go back to Burgundy with her, it must be safer than here. I will find you someday, somehow. But you must go.

. . .

Love, Zamor

It was difficult to put that in writing as I wanted anything but for her to leave. But I wanted her to be safe, and nothing about Louveciennes was safe anymore.

The next morning I found her letter around lunchtime.

Dear Zamor,

Only this morning I received a letter from Madame Martin. She apologized with great emotion but told me she and her husband left the country several weeks ago. They thought it prudent to ride out the situation with friends in Spain and had been afraid to travel so close to the Palace to retrieve me. The writing was smeared with her tears but, it seems when a situation like this happens you find out that even those who call you family do not truly understand the meaning of the term.

The good news in all of this is that I can still be close to you. I can think of nothing worse than to be without you at this time.

Véronique

I wanted to cry. Véronique was a free woman but she was stuck in this place just as I was. I couldn't keep her safe and I couldn't send her away. I'd never felt so helpless.

PART III

THE DEVIL AND HER POISONOUS FRUIT

45

———

Dear Citizen,

Way back after the Champs de Mars Massacre, that guest at the chateau had likened the sans-culottes people to the poisonous belladonna plant.

I saw it differently.

Way back when I was a boy I had learned that the people in the royal court grew in power in correlation to how much pain they were willing to give. Feeding on the pain they caused seemed to grow their own esteem. I learned how to feed off their pain, also.

In all the time since, I had forgotten that in order to feed on pain you had to cause pain, first. No one was better at causing it than Madame. She knew how to give little bits of it with a smile. She knew how to make it seem palatable. She knew how to plant herself just exactly where she could cause the most of it.

Yes, the Belladonna plant was beautiful. Its flowers pleasant. Its berries, temptingly dark and lovely. They called them les cerises du diable — the devils' berries. Eat just one of those berries and you'd be dead.

Madame was a belladonna, meting out little bits of evil like she was handing out those berries, smiling while you bit into the tempting fruit. At least that's how I began to see it.

She got over the Duc very quickly. It was the most peculiar thing, how quickly she got over the Duc's death. I knew for a fact she loved him. At least, I thought I knew. But maybe love had become something else to her that she could forget him so quickly. We fell back into our way of living as if nothing was different.

But there were cracks in her persona which showed up in her errors in judgement.

--Zamor, 1820

I walked into the salon and came upon Gaspard standing just behind and to the side of Madame as she sat. He was looking down at her and something about the position of his hand suggested it had just been close to her face, as her cheek was turned up, as if recently stroked.

On seeing me, he sprung from her and she straightened right away, the color high on her cheeks. He was suddenly fidgeting as if he didn't know what to do with his limbs. My eyes quickly went back and forth between the two.

"Bonjour, Madame," I said. My eyelids fluttered as I walked across the room to take the chair on the opposite side of the fireplace.

"That'll be all, Gaspard," she said, her words releasing him as he nodded and walked out, stiffly. The door closed behind him.

I crossed my legs and opened my book to begin reading, though my eyes weren't taking in the words. They were simply frozen on the page as discomfort hung in the air. I know what I saw but it couldn't be, I told myself. Such a thing would be horrible for everyone in this household. The two most volatile and mentally unstable people in the house, together? I couldn't even fathom the endless number of ways that could go wrong.

We sat in silence for a long time while my stomach tried to come up out of my body. Finally, the silence was too much.

"Do you want to say something?" came her clipped voice.

"Mon Dieu, you have *got* to be joking!" exploded from me. "Gaspard? Gaspard?" I felt my throat closing in and allowed the retching sound to erupt from my throat.

"I'm lonely! And I have needs! What am I supposed to do now my Duc is gone?"

"Anybody!" I spread my arms. "Do anybody! All the noblemen who traipse through this place every day, *any one* of them better than Gaspard! You could have any of them!"

"Keep your voice down! Gaspard understands me and he's easy. Why am I explaining this to you? I don't have to answer to you, it's none of your business who I bed. This is exactly why he constantly tells me I've given you entirely too much freedom, to think you can speak to me like this."

"Did you ask me, or didn't you? I don't care who you sleep with, I just always thought even *you* were smart enough to choose a man, and not a slimy slithering dog-snake like Gaspard! How could you tolerate the stench of alcohol that's become his own personal scent? Alcohol mixed with sweat mixed with putrid musk."

"He loves me and it feels wonderful to be adored, not that it's something you will ever know."

"You don't love him, do you?"

"Of course, I don't *love* him. I like him. He's convenient. I already told you, I have needs, Louis-Benoit. I'm a vibrant woman. I'm not going to jump into another relationship just yet. A relationship has to be cultivated. But in the meantime, who will take care of my needs if not the man who protects my person? Why am I explaining myself to you? It's none of your business!"

"The Well-Beloved would roll over in his grave."

"Oh, now you worry about disturbing my Louis, after all the hell you put him through? I'll remind you, when I came back from the convent there were no less than ten people telling me all about how you spread yourself around the Palace like a two-livre whore—"

"I was fourteen, of course I bedded whoever would let me."

"I didn't judge you..."

"Yes, you did! You judged me and punished me, too!"

"A body is a body!"

"How do you go from a Duc's body to Gaspard body? That doesn't even make sense—!"

"Will you shut up and stop going on—"

"—You can find anyone, anywhere for a roll in the hay. But you choose to roll in the mud with filth—!"

"—shut up, shut up, shut up!"

We were yelling by this time, our faces twisted.

This was exactly what Salanave had said all those years ago. Madame liked to pit Gaspard and me against each other. No good could come of that union but there was no point in continuing the argument, what was done was done. If she didn't see the wrong in the situation, I wasn't going to convince her. Gaspard was clearly having his season in the sun while I was in a season of disfavor.

Almost as if the moment or two of silence had cleared the air, we each straightened away from each other, she patting her hair and me giving the lapels of my jacket a shake as I stood. I gave a brief nod.

"Bon après-midi, Madame."

"Oui," she said, curtly, picking up her embroidery.

I opened the door to nearly run smack into Chon. Her face was pinched and tight, eyes slivered on me. When she didn't pass into the room behind me, but kept looking at me, I closed the door behind me. "Something you want to say, Madame Chon?"

"I don't know why she puts up with you," she seethed on a wet, angry whisper. "All these years and you're still the arrogant, presumptuous little merde you always were. How dare you question Madame? She's a saint for putting up with you."

I blinked as if waiting for her to say more and when she didn't, I said, "I'm sorry, Chon, I thought you might have something to say other than the same drivel I've heard all my life. 'Madame's a saint' ... blah. 'I don't know why she keeps you' ... blah, blah, blah... All these years and you can't come up with something original?"

"*I detest you! You are a curse on this house.*"

"Once again, I crave something fresh and new. Put a blight on me. Something—*anything*—different! Do you even have the imagination to say something that hasn't been said a thousand times before, or have you exhausted your capacity to curse me out? This is your chance to get it off your chest..."

She had already walked past me, opened the door and was headed into the room; skirt swishing with each movement of her angry hips.

"Bon après-midi, Madame Chon," I said in a sing-song as I turned and headed down the hall. I didn't care for Chon any more than she cared for me. I found it odd that she transferred all her anger to me, when Gaspard was the one who deserved it.

46

———

Dear Citizen,

It's pointless to make plans in the middle of a revolution. I imagine God looked down upon us like we'd once looked down on the animals in the menagerie at the palace, watching them all living their little penned-in lives, running back and forth in circles, going nowhere.

I had my thoughts of what I wanted for my future but it wasn't until I heard someone's concrete plans that I realized how weak my thoughts were.

Envy comes quickly and unbidden. I'm not proud of how prickly I was when it came to the happiness of others. Even people I liked weren't immune to my moments of sharp response to their good news.

I'm human.

By the way, they took most of those animals from the menagerie away and put them in an enclosure in Paris. They are calling it a "zoo". But we people were still running in circles in our personal enclosures and we didn't even know it.

--Zamor, 1820

November 1792

"Congratulations, Thomas," Josephe said, raising his wine glass. Since the last time we'd seen each other, Thomas had gotten himself married. As Josephe teased him and Thomas laughed and blushed, I raised my glass and toasted, feeling a lick of unexpected bitter envy.

"Yes, congratulations, Thomas," I said, working up a small smile. "I didn't know you were in the market for marriage."

"Neither did I," he said, leaning in, conspiratorially. "But the thing with love, once you finally feel it, nothing in the world will keep you from it."

My eyes caught the quick wince on Josephe's face. It seemed I wasn't the only one prickly about this particular subject. I looked down at my Chartreuse, my favorite brilliant green liqueur.

"She knows you'll be leaving soon?" Josephe asked. The Legion St. Georges, the first regiment of men of color in all of Europe, was now populated with volunteers and preparing to fight for the new republic.

"Of course. It wouldn't have been fair to marry her before telling her that I don't know when I'll be home again. Turns out Marie loves me enough to wait for me. And as my wife, if anything happens, she'll have my pension."

"Nothing will happen," Josephe said, with certainty. "Other than us trouncing our enemies and bringing home victory to the republic, that is."

"When are you marching out?" I asked.

"In January we're marching to Laon," Thomas said.

Josephe motioned to the server to top us all off. We fell into quiet. The unknowns loomed over us like a cloud in that tavern.

We'd become good friends, the three of us, despite the difference in my station. In another world and another time we might never have socialized. But in this new world our shared skin color provided commonalities beyond the differences of social class; commonalities most of France would never understand. This, even though I was a black peasant and they were both aristocratic gens du couleurs.

"Any news on the King and Queen, Zamor?" Josephe asked.

I knew he had been friends with the Queen, serving as her musical instructor. Rumors had spread through the palace that he'd been more, but I didn't have evidence of that and I knew how easily untrue rumors spread when it came to anyone with black skin related to what they might or might not be doing with their bodies.

"You mean Citizen Capet and his wife," I corrected. "Not recently. I've heard the family is fine, though they're in the Temple since the insurgency, for their own safety."

Though Josephe was in the Society of the Friends of the Blacks, neither he nor Thomas were Jacobins. They wouldn't have heard the stern reproach from Robespierre at the last Jacobin meet when someone suggested mercy for the King.

"Mercy?" Max had repeated, his face pained and angry at the same time. "How much mercy did Louis Capet show when poor, sorry souls came to him, begging. Those reporters he locked up in the Bastille with no trial and no charges—with only having said an ill word about him as their crime—left to rot in cold, wet cells for years until death. People rounded up by his secret police, swiped off the street based on little more than a rumor. A word. A look, that someone in the King's circle didn't like; disappeared from this earth as if they'd never been. And when the families went to him, *begging*, did he give them mercy? According to the monarchy, people who committed crimes had to pay for those crimes, it was only right. No mercy! Men and women torn apart on the wheel, hung from their necks, tortured, brutalized by his guards ... we have always been reminded that any talk against the King was treason and punishable by death.

"Now, we are a republic. We are the chosen and elected representatives of the people of France, and we have the same law against treason; if found guilty, the punishment is death. No more or less than before. Citizen Louis Capet instructed France's enemies to declare war on *this* country. Trying to subvert *this* government. None of us like what is about to happen, but happen, it must. Unlike the monarchy, we make no allowances for friends over foes. This is either a country that *lives* the equality it preaches, or it's not. This is either a country that is just or it is not! This is either a country that is incorruptible, or it is not!"

He left early and I hadn't seen Max in the club since. I didn't want to share this with Josephe and Thomas. If Josephe was even a little friendly with the Queen it would hurt him. They'd find out soon enough. I diverted.

"The Palace, on the other hand, is an empty shell, full of servants who don't have any place to go, confused nobles, and thieves. Most of the guards are gone and no one will lift a finger to stop the thieving. The last time I visited I saw two fellows walk right in like they'd been there a thousand times before, straight to begin pulling the gold fixtures off the wall. I called out to one and said, 'Hey, should you be doing that?' and he said to me, 'Do you care enough to make me stop?'" I took a sip of my drink and admitted, "I did not."

"Can't say I blame them," Josephe said. "They need money and the Palace is a giant jewelry box. I imagine they're not still serving nine-course meals and entertaining musicians anymore."

"Troubadours," I said, recalling the last time I'd seen the troupe that Sebastien, Paul, Valentin, David and I had run off on Pont Neuf. They finally had their day and time to shine at the Palace, playing their music for visitors who took a break from stripping the silk off the walls in the parlors to take a snack and listen to their wild tambourine play.

"No, you can't blame them, under the circumstances. If they can find something to sell so they can eat, God bless them," Thomas said.

"What are you hearing at the Club about what they plan to do with the family?"

"Well, you know Brissot wants us to fight Austria before we deal with the King. He approves of having the King abdicate from the throne and pass the torch to his son, the Dauphin. As does Danton."

Josephe leaned back in his chair and looked at me long and steadily.

"You just conveniently skipped right over what it is that Max wants. Will he be satisfied with abdication?"

"I don't know. I hardly see him."

He polished off his drink, quickly, and motioned to the server to bring the whole bottle he held. Taking it, he uncorked it like a pro and immediately began to pour. "Sometimes I feel old. Maybe I should have run like the nobles. Funny how it's only when it comes to advantages that France decides I am not of noble blood," he said into his wine. "It has no problem allowing me to fight or shed blood for the revolutionary army. I might as well join the army because I have no life or hope for the future. Fighting is a balm to my soul if I can't have a family like every man deserves."

"Mon Dieu," Thomas interrupted. "You do get maudlin when you're drunk. The best-looking man in all of France with women doing just about anything to get into your bed and you're complaining about one woman who's still happily married to another man. *That's* why you're blocked from getting your due, Josephe. You chose the wrong one." Dumas looked at me again and took another swallow. "Josephe is afflicted with the illness of being fundamentally plagued by the "should have" way of thinking. Yes, we should have every advantage of our family status but the reality of it is that it is impossible for society to look at you and me and see nobility. Especially me, with the darkness of my skin. When my father looks at me he sees his son *and* his property. He knew that as a man with African blood I wouldn't be able to enlist in a higher rank due to no fault of my own, yet he still took my family name from me as though it was only his and not also mine. His title was more important than my identity. I say *no* to that. My identity, my personhood, is more important than any name. I am now Thomas-Alexandre Dumas, and his shame, be damned. You are too gifted, Josephe, to let this society's backward ways make you think less of yourself."

Thomas clasped Josephe's shoulder and the musician seemed to shake himself out of the moment of morose.

I had a name once, I almost told them. But I was too embarrassed to admit I'd forgotten it.

"Speaking of names," I said, instead. "did you know I was baptized Louis-Benoit Zamor as if I were a brand-new babe, at ten years old."

"Of course, because you *were* new to *them*, and that's all that matters to the wealthy," Josephe said, wryly. "Sprung from a clamshell and delivered to them with no attachments worth speaking of."

Thomas smiled. "Just like every new piece of land we come upon on—claim it as ours as soon as we find it. Nevermind those people that live there and what they call it. It's ours, now! God knows the natives of the new United States are getting that same treatment now."

"Yes," I mumbled. "Well, the name Zamor was swiped from a bad story by a white man."

"But it's a memorable name, at least," Thomas said with a kind smile. "You could go down in history with that name. Do you know how many Thomas's there are in France? Or Josephes. Or Louis's?"

"You need more than a name to be remembered. You two will definitely go down in history. You're both courageous and will do this country proud. Me, I'm starting to worry that despite everything I've been trying to do, I'll never make a name for myself."

"Your fake humility is boring," Josephe said. "A man who doesn't believe in himself doesn't write a speech like the one you wrote. You have a way with words as good as Danton. Better."

I shrugged. "I can only dream I'll get an opportunity to raise my voice again, for myself. As it is, I write in ways that aren't entirely appropriate."

The General looked at me with a keen eye. "You write those trashy rags." Both sets of eyes seemed to bore into me.

"Don't judge me. I have to make money. But I write other things, too." I leaned in and lowered my voice. "I write some words for a well-known, popular revolutionary."

"That's dangerous business, Zamor," the General said.

"I know. I didn't have a problem with it until someone I know found out and scolded me on the responsibility of my words. She thinks I'll be used and thrown out – blamed for the trouble that results. But like I told her, I couldn't sell my words if there weren't people eager to buy them, correct? I don't feel like I can be held accountable for what other people do."

"But you can. And you should," Thomas said. "I'm sorry, I agree with this woman. Josephe and I, we'll soon be leading troops. We both know how words can compel people to do just about anything for you. We rely on it. Look at that mess with Danton and LaFayette. All that bloodshed. If you rile people up, you have a responsibility to calm them down again. But if you leave them in that state and point them in the wrong direction you hold some responsibility when all hell breaks loose."

"What about the responsibility of the people, themselves? Certainly, Georges Danton lost control, but he didn't cause what happened."

"What he did is worse," Josephe jumped in at this point. "He goes out to the streets and speaks to people who are in the most desperate and dire straits. They were already frightened because our own king had just tried to leave us high and dry. Most of them financially dependent on the same nobles who've taken advantage of them for years. It's those people he preys on. Of course, if a man comes along to speak for them, they will be grateful and happy. An educated man. A moderately wealthy man—speaking for them. He made them feel cared for. But people like Danton, and even Brissot – they don't feel the desperation in the same way as commoners. They will always have food to eat. These people he brought to the Champs de Mars, likely didn't know where their next meal would come from. He offered a lovely day and all the free beer they could drink. Now half of them are dead but he's still having steak for dinner. Don't be as removed from reality as he is. Think about the words you're putting into the world and where they might lead."

It was clear to me there was no love lost between Josephe and Georges but I didn't feel quite the same about the man.

Georges had invited me to be on the Committee of Public Safety. I was pleased to be on it because he presented it as the body that would re-establish calm and peace in the country. Stop the roving bandits and gangs. And, he suggested that perhaps my service would impress Max enough to give me my freedom.

"Danton and others like him are very quick to tell people what to do," Josephe continued. "Not so quick to actually pick up arms and fight," Josephe said, earning a glass clink from Thomas.

"No matter. The brave among us will do that, non?" Thomas said. Then he looked at me. "But our friend here is from a different world. Raised at court and of a mind for change. Use what you know to make a change in this country but use it responsibly."

"I'm trying."

Josephe nodded. "This revolution is ugly but there's good to some of the changes. And this Légion of ours, if we can represent the republic well, who knows where it will lead... perhaps towards the emancipation of our people. And with our success, earn the respect of our countrymen."

"We walk in January, Zamor, and you know where we'll be. The invitation stands."

"We'd be honored to have you," Josephe said.

At my hesitation, Thomas piped in, again. "Is there someone keeping you here? This woman you mention in passing—the one you wrote that music for? The woman who gives you such good advice? Is she special to you?"

"All I want in the world is to make her my wife. She's free but I'm not. I can't marry her, legally." *And the thought of leaving her...*

Josephe smiled and signaled to the waitress for more wine. "Now I understand. Well, whatever your decision, cherish the love you have for that woman."

"Yes," Thomas said. "We welcome you to come with us but don't begrudge you if you decide to stay here and influence this republic of ours from the inside. No matter what, can the three of us agree to meet here again after our enemies are defeated and the revolution is won? Each one of us for all, right brothers?"

The sentiment warmed me. Being considered a brother to these men was an honor.

We toasted again and I went home lighter that evening, knowing I had two options in front of me and both of them were things I truly wanted. To fight for this republic could fast-track my freedom and earn me respect—if we were successful. I had to weigh the possibility of death on the battlefield with the accolades I might earn if I managed to survive. And my survival in true battle was a longshot.

Or, I might stay and continue to pressure the Jacobins to abolish slavery completely. Because I did, indeed, have someone worth staying for. Until the moment I said it out loud I had never dared to think of marriage in a real way. I thought all day about whether I truly felt I could leave without Véronique.

I wanted both. I would give anything to have them both. But I wanted one just a tiny bit more.

47

____

Véronique's room was one of the servant's rooms along the lowest level in back of the house. I waited until the Chateau was still and padded down in stocking'd feet to her door in the servants' quarters.

After meeting with Josephe and Thomas, during the entire ride I could think of nothing but Véronique. Picturing our life together, imagining how it might be just as soon as I was free. Wondering if her feelings for me were as strong.

I put the horse away and went to my room, fully preparing to retire. Sponging the road grime off my body and changing into my bedclothes, I lay down for all of ten minutes until I was up again. A few minutes later, I was outside her door, as if transported by magic, knocking softly, just once. If she didn't answer it would be a sign. I'd go back to my room and...

She opened the door wearing a simple white shift. Her headwrap was gone and her dark hair was picking up highlights from the small fire in the fireplace, sparkling with gold and red. Her eyes were so dark I felt she would scope my soul. That tiny line between her brows was evident and I worried about what was worrying her.

"My apologies for disturbing you, Véronique, it's just ... I haven't seen you in several days and though the letters are fine, I wanted to see your face," I said.

Her brow smoothed out. "I was worried seeing me less might make you forget about me. But my heart told me, after that last letter, I was wrong. But I haven't seen you and I thought you might have changed your mind. After that last letter," she whispered.

The last letter, where I had poured my heart out to her on paper. Her eyes were focused seriously on me.

"For days I've been walking around fidgeting like a little girl, wondering how I'll know if anything you say is true, and how to ask. And now you show up here at my door. I still have that letter."

"You should burn it. You never know who will read your letters," I said.

"Later, maybe. After you read it to me. You'll come in and read it to me, now."

It wasn't a question. That little frown told me it also wasn't a joke. "All right," I said, stepping inside.

Her room was cozy. A crucifix sat on her tiny table along with a Bible and some sheets of paper with a quill. On a second little table, embroidery in progress with a needle sitting on top. A small glass with red poppies sat on a windowsill next to the lit candle. In one corner of the room there was a pile of pieces of cloth and a large bag with more spilling out of it. At the foot of her bed was a trunk. She leaned down to open the trunk, took out a folded letter that lay on top, and closed the lid again. She sat down on it.

"Please sit," she said, motioning beside her.

I hesitated. She was wearing a simple, plain white gown but the light from the fire had already given me a glimpse of the outline of her body, the curves immediately stirring reaction in mine. Sitting that close to her would make it worse. I was having a hard time not looking at those curves.

"I didn't mean to disturb you, we'll do it another time," I repeated. "I should leave and come back at a more appropriate time of day when we're both proper. I don't want to be disrespectful or embarrass myself. I truly didn't mean to come for any reason other than to see your face."

"I don't care about that, you're a grown man and I'm certain you can control yourself long enough to do what I ask. Sit beside me, Zamor. Read me this letter out loud. Read it to me so I can see your face when you say these words. So I can know what's in your heart."

"I write because it's too difficult to say, Véronique. I never meant to say those words out loud," I scoffed, on a bit of a laugh.

She didn't smile, looking up at me, flatly. "I'm just a woman from a small farm and a small town and I barely know my way around a place like this. I know, it's funny to tease me. But I won't be toyed with. I've come a long way and changed my whole life to be here. I didn't do that to be anybody's fool. I'm not a game to be played. My feelings are not sport. Before I allow them to grow any further, I need to know who you are and how you truly feel about me. I don't care how uncomfortable you are. Sit down."

"Vér—"

"—Sit down and read it now or leave and don't ever say pretty words to me again. And we will go back to being civil, but I won't go one more day wondering. Not one more minute."

I had looked away from her but snuck a glance at her sitting so resolutely on that trunk, her emotions betrayed only by a slight quaver in her voice.

This was frightening. I said those things on paper because paper was always safer than speaking out loud. That was why I liked to write at all. The quill summoned things deep from me, things I sometimes didn't even know about myself. I could hardly even remember what I wrote; once I folded that letter up and gave it to her it was purged from me. Maybe I intentionally forgot, I felt so exposed in writing it. But now, she was going to make me say it and I didn't know if she—or anyone— was worth me laying my soul bare. But I... I meant those words.

I sat down, hesitantly, leaving a space between us.

"Véronique—"

"Read it," she said, her eyes on my face, thrusting it at me.

I took the page with my fingers and opened it, cleared my voice, and began to read, my voice shaky.

"*Dear Véronique,*

It has been three days since I spoke to you with any meaning and I feel like a starving man, or one in the desert dying from thirst. I rely on you and our conversations to stay sane.

The other day in the dining room, I stood there for two hours across from you, struggling not to look at you for fear someone would notice. And then I worried they would notice how hard I was avoiding looking at you. Your beauty is undeniable but it is your soul I crave.

I told you that when I was young, my mother created a lullaby for me, which I remembered long after I forgot her face. I remembered that song even after I forgot my own name. I'm embarrassed and ashamed by both those things, but still, for many years my body knew that song like it was an extension of me.

You have become my lullaby. I no longer think of myself without thinking of us. When I think of my future, it's always "we" and no longer me. When I think of happiness and what it will look like, you pop first into my head like the sun pops up in the sky every morning.

It frightens me how deeply you have planted yourself into my heart. For that split second when I thought you might have been hurt or in danger, my world was suddenly re-defined with shocking clarity. You are my heart. You are the blood that beats in my veins. I dream of holding you and know without a doubt that I can never again be without you.

I'm a selfish man. You already know this. I know I should leave you alone because I'm not free. Legally, I can't marry you unless I'm free.

I was in a chapel in Paris and the lights from the stained-glass windows bathed me in colors. For that moment I felt I was loved by God. The only other time in my life I feel that is when I'm bathed in your light. I risk sacrilege by comparing the two, knowing that my sweetness of feeling for you fights with the heat of passion that rages within me for you, as well. I've tried to place what I feel for you in a category but I cannot. All I can say is the entirety of you is all-encompassing.

I love you, Véronique. I love you like the dawn. I love you like the sky. I love you more than I love myself.

Sometimes I wish I could go back to loving no one, rather than feel like a fledgling babe experiencing the world for the first time. I am a seed waiting to bathe in your light to blossom. I am helpless to what is happening to my heart and it angers me. I do not like to be out of control. But it's too late. I've lost all control. You have it now, my love. You have my heart to do with as you please. I beg of you, don't crush it. To do so would surely kill me.

Yours..."

I stopped. I stopped because there, in ink, I had signed the name I had just said was forgotten. The name I hadn't said aloud in decades. I looked at that paper, crinkling in my hands and brushed a fingertip over that name. It was as if someone had come along and written it in for me.

And yet, when I looked up at her, she was watching my face, with her little frown, searching me for what, I didn't know. Her eyes bore into mine.

"These words weren't meant to be said out loud," I whispered, again. Her hands came up to cup my face. "You must burn this letter. You can't leave me bare and exposed like this, Véronique, you—"

"—Shh... I know," she stopped me, leaning forward to rest her forehead against my chin. I took the fingers of one hand and kissed them, leaning in to press my lips against her palm.

We sat like that, as I waited for her to speak. Then, she raised her head and the little frown was gone. Pulling my head towards her until our lips met, I breathed her in and breathed out the last of my fear. Her lips tasted of red wine and were as soft as the silk of the royal bed pillows. She laid a hand on my chest. Just it being there set me aflame.

I didn't want to leave but when she ended the kiss I stood up, ready to bolt. I had made my decision but she still had hers to make. And I didn't know how to be there and not reveal my level of desire for her. As it was, I clasped my hands before me to hide my body's response.

The air that entered my lungs smelled all of her. I breathed her in like she was the air keeping me alive. My heart beat like a galloping stallion.

"Y-you have changed everything for me," I said, my voice shaky, as if I were learning to speak for the first time. She stood up. "You have made me happy in a way I never knew I needed. Véronique…"

My eyes watered a bit as I spoke. I thought it might be irritation from the fire. Seeing her face soften even further, her lips tilt just a bit like she was happy and in wonder all at the same time, filled my heart.

She pressed her soft lips to mine, again. Her kiss was soft and insistent all at once, the intimacy of it, reeling my senses. I don't think either of us expected what came next. But we clutched each other at the same time as if trying to absorb each other. And then we gave in.

Though I wanted to be patient and gentle I had never been with a woman I truly wanted. I didn't want to tumble like I did in the past with other women, some whose names I never even knew. I wanted it to be special with Véronique but I didn't know how. Instead, I fumbled to remove the shift from her shoulders. She stopped me gently, with her hands on mine.

"I want you, too. But slowly, Zamor. We'll take our time, my love. People go slowly so they may enjoy each other, when they want to make love."

My hands trembled. I didn't know how to take things slowly. All I had known in my life was how to copulate; there had never been any feelings to it. I almost didn't know how to feel with my body responding so strongly to a woman I had such deep feeling for.

So, I followed her lead. We undressed each other and threw the blankets back to nestle under the bedcovers. I watched as she climbed in, taking in all I could see of her in the room, darkening with the waning fire. Once we were both covered, I followed her lead. I let her tell me where to touch, how to stroke, when to kiss, when to enter her. And when it was over and we were sated, I held her, tightly.

"I love you, Véronique," I said, earnestly, embarrassed that my eyes filled with tears. "I love you more than I love myself."

She looked at me in the low light and smiled, sweetly. "I love you, too."

Until her, I didn't know what making love was. I never imagined what we shared was possible. That small hovel of a room opened up. I felt as if we were sitting atop a mountain, just she and I in the crisp, open sky. I felt the air of worlds and the sun blossoming all around us. I left my body and ascended to the heavens. And while I floated above, I realized there was no set of icy cold eyes of a fox frozen in captivity. This wasn't the escape of pain. This wasn't escape at all. This had to have been a touch of heaven on earth.

It came to me then, an understanding of the ceiling of the cathedral under which I had been baptized. I thought of its height. The height was to make us remember the soul was meant to soar above the earth-bound pettiness of man. The stained-glass windows that flooded the space with brilliant colors of light forced us to remember the beauty and glory and greatness of God. In this moment, the firelight on Véronique's skin was stained glass – her body, my church.

Wrapped in crisp linen sheets, we didn't speak with our mouths but looked into each other's eyes. Touched each other's faces. For the first time since I'd been taken from my home I gazed deeply into another person's eyes and saw only acceptance. Truth. And love. With Véronique's love I could face anything. Even staying at the Chateau.

48

December 25, 1792

Unlike the previous year, Christmas of 1792 was a solemn affair. In the beginning, Madame invited guests. As the polite declines came in, for one excuse or another, Madame decided to save face and sent notice to everyone that she was canceling the festivities after all, in lieu of a quiet, intimate event while in mourning.

Of course, I could have told her that three months after the Duc du Brissac's disembodied head rolled across the floor at the last fête was too soon to have a party.

Perhaps it was because last Christmas was top of mind, du Brissac's absence—that I almost thought she'd gotten over—came over her like a heavy wool blanket. This Christmas day, no yule log burned in the fireplace. She forbade it. The burning yule log was supposed to be good luck. Not allowing that tradition put half of the house servants in a foul mood, believing the Chateau would be cursed for the coming year. It was an unpleasant indication of how the rest of the holiday would go.

Madame might have worn her festive, lacy black. Instead, she wore fabulously drab, funereal black, and ordered us to do the same. Most servants had more brown clothing than black, which stirred up two hours of her complaining that they didn't care enough for the good Duc to properly mourn him.

For the Christmas meal, this year, the general household servants weren't allowed to join the dinner. According to Madame, the Duc du Brissac's generosity in inviting everyone the year before was a courtesy; now proven to be undeserving of a household that didn't appreciate him.

Music wasn't allowed. She told me if she even caught a glimpse of my violin bow she would set the tip of it on fire and shove it up my backside.

"It was bad luck, us eating with the staff last year. It won't happen again, I'll tell you that," she had groused to me before instructing me to make sure she didn't have to see any of their faces during the dinner. Salanave made sure all the food was in warmers on the table and the buffet.

There were no traditional oysters. Madame said oysters were too festive for a household of ingrates. Though the general household was barred from dining, she demanded that Gaspard and I join her and her ladies for dinner. I would have preferred to eat with the serving staff, and I hated eating with them. I would have gladly taken my meal in my room.

Gaspard and I sat on either side of her, with her three ladies-in-waiting, all of us shoved to her end of the table; the other half of the dinner table empty of guests. We all sat there eating the small dinner of asparagus soup, roasted duck, plain roasted cauliflower, and bread. Madame said her signature velouté was only for happy occasions, so not even that to lighten the meal. And wine. Lots of wine. Tonight, it was red. She easily downed two or three glasses per course, swallowing it down like water.

We ate, silently, as the sound of her gulping wine echoed through the empty room along with the spitting, cracking fire, our silver sounding loud in the empty room. She filled her glass from the bottle, the splash from her sloppy pour spotting the tablecloth. At one point she gestured toward the bread sitting in the middle of the table with her fork.

"Gaspard, you will make sure that bread is fed to the pigs. Do you hear me? *None* of it is to go to the staff. Only hot ground meal for them today, *the ingrates!*" She yelled that last part, so her voice would carry.

It made no sense that she was taking out all of her ire on the staff, but she was in mourning and needed to blame someone for her misery. With a house full of staff to take the abuse, she seemed determined to take advantage.

I knew Salanave would quietly squirrel away bits of duck and vegetables to sneak to the staff. It didn't always happen, but it was Christmas. However, I would have to warn her that Gaspard was on the lookout, and I'd have to do *that* in secret, too.

We kept eating, afraid to speak. I had to keep drinking water to get the food down my throat. Discomfort made my mouth dry. Madame's eyes grew glassier with each course, until dessert.

Over the pâte à choux stuffed with the sweet, rich Bavarois crème, which took Salanave such a long while to make, Madame finally threw her head back and let out a long wail that devolved into wet, heaving sobs. Her ladies popped up from their seats and ran to her.

"Oh, my poor, poor dear!" Chon declared, reaching her first, followed by the other two, who circled Madame with their arms. They held and comforted Madame, who was now hiccupping and speaking drunken gibberish.

Both Gaspard and I, wordlessly, took the opportunity to slip away, quietly, in different directions, no longer needed. I found Salanave sneaking another whole duck out of the kitchen in a platter covered with a napkin. I mouthed to her that Gaspard was watching and pointed to the doorway. She looked panicked, so I walked over quickly to take the platter, moving as fast as I could out of the room, through the hallway to my room. I heard Gaspard enter the kitchen through the other door seconds after I left, his voice booming: "I better not catch you stealing food. Scraps go to the pigs, you hear me?"

Salanave came to my room later. We took the platter to a back room, grabbed some small plates, portioning out the meat so each plate had a bit. She went to retrieve some bread she had hidden away, and we put a lump on each of the plates. She added small sprigs of cauliflower but covered the meat and vegetables in a silky bearnaise sauce. Then, on the fourth quadrant of each plate, she put a tiny bit of choux pastry with a dollop of rich bavarois. We did all this in quiet, Salanave so concentrated the tip of her tongue came out through tense lips. She finished each plate with a sprig of holly. I carried the large platter of tiny plates and, together, the two of us snuck through the servants' quarters, quietly knocking on each door, then putting fingers to our lips so that everyone knew to keep it secret. Even the guards were hungry for meat and wouldn't dare tell Gaspard.

Madame's sadness permeated everyone's entire holiday season. It was especially difficult since many of the servants were away from their own families. Not being able to celebrate at the Chateau made it doubly hard. Most took their meals together in the communal servants' eating space, but the act of watching each other eat gruel for the twelve days of Christmas, forbidden to laugh or make any sounds related to the season, took its toll. We were all relieved when Madame and Gaspard left for England the next day.

A couple of days later, Véronique and I lay in her bed one morning. With things being so tense in the house, and me now fully in love, my protective instinct towards our new relationship was on high alert. There was no apparent threat, only my life history of having good things taken from me. In the back of my head, a little voice kept warning me that because I loved, someone would try to destroy it. So we were still keeping things secret, but it was hard.

"I will burn this world down for you," I breathed, and meant it.

She hesitated before speaking, not privy to the thought process that brought that comment on.

"Well, good morning to you, too. Thank you, but I don't want you to burn the world down for me. I want you to dance in the sun with me. On the banks of the river under the moonlight."

"What is it about that dirty river that enchants you?"

"Civilizations have been built on the water, you know. Where there's water…"

"Yes, yes. Water is the source of life, and all that. But it needs to be clean, doesn't it? The Seine is not clean."

"It's clean enough. It can be boiled to drink."

"Toss of bit of lye into it while you're at it and I may agree."

"Be quiet," she laughed gently, stroking my cheek. Her dark eyes were sparkling in the candlelight. "You don't have to drink it if you don't want to. It's nice that it's there. It's all of it. You and me in that little house with children running all around. You writing and me sewing. I can see it, clearly. And nothing has to be burned down for us to have it. We just need to decide when we're ready."

My breath hitched a little. She wasn't exactly right about that but I liked the sentiment. "I'll need my freedom before I can leave, but then you and I are off. Hopefully, a month or two. My speech went over well."

"It was a lovely speech."

I blushed. "But I'm a Paris man."

"I hear Croissy-sur-Seine is as close to Paris as we are right now. And I don't want that Paris fuss at our home. How about you work in Paris, but you come home to me in Croissy-sur-Seine?"

I could picture it, too. She was right. Paris was great, in doses. It was nice sometimes to get away from the noise.

"Maybe you'll come into town, occasionally. You have to meet people to sell your services."

"Ah, yes," she said, thoughtfully. "You might be right. And then, when I go into town maybe we'll take in a play or two. I've never been."

I smiled. "You'll love it. And maybe the opera. When Josephe comes back home a hero, I know he'll want to play at the Garnier Opera. He asked me to join his army of black soldiers, you know."

"Really?" she twisted to look at me. "Are you considering it?"

"I was," I said, carefully. "But I don't think Josephe or Thomas quite understand how battered my body is, or that I ache every time it rains. Besides... I have reasons I want to stay."

A pleased looked flashed across her face but I could tell she intentionally pinched her smile. "If you want to go ... I-I'll support you. I know how much you want to get away from here. I'll be all right. I don't want to hold you back."

My heart swelled. The fact that she would give me the gift of freedom was one of the things I loved about her. She was a genuinely good person."

I shrugged. "I think I'll stay here. I want to be close when slavery is abolished."

She was quiet for a moment. Then, "you really think it will happen soon? I'd love to tell my parents. We've developed our own code. It's almost fun writing to them. My mother picked it up quickly but my father never really learned how to read. So maman translates. And at the end of every letter she tells me how disappointed she is with my choice in life. We're writing in opposites. So when she tells me she's disappointed, it means she loves me. And when she tells me papa says my sewing is useless it means they are proud of what I'm doing. It turned out not to be so difficult, after all."

I was pleased she'd listened to me and was happy they'd found a way around it. Though there was no telling if anyone was reading their mail, it didn't hurt to be careful.

"I do think it will happen. Georges Danton says some of the French slave owners have been showing allegiance to Britain. They want to turn counter-revolutionary out of anger that the French government hasn't punished the enslaved people who revolted in Saint Domingue."

"They're lucky the enslaved people of Saint Domingue don't wipe *them* out for the abuse they level on them, constantly. Well, if slave owners turning against the new republic is what it takes for the new republic to turn on them, I'm happy for it. But even happier you'll be here with me when slavery is abolished. Maybe then we can go home to see my parents. They'll love you."

"When I'm free and have wed you, properly."

"In Saint Dominque slaves aren't allowed to marry. They marry under the eyes of God in their own ceremonies. It doesn't matter what society decides, Zamor, it doesn't stop enslaved people from living and loving each other and it won't stop us, if it takes longer for abolition to happen. We can't stop living our lives. Do you hear me?"

I smiled. "I hear you, Mademoiselle."

"Madame, to you."

"*Madame Zamor,* to me," I repeated, liking the sound of it.

She called me by my forgotten first name and it caught me off guard. I twisted to look at her this time. "Don't call me that," I said.

"But I thought..."

"I don't know why I wrote it. I didn't even remember it. I must have been drinking when I wrote that letter to pull that old name up. I don't—it doesn't resonate with me. It's like the name of somebody I used to know, that's all. That name was just ... a part of me that no one else has. That's why I wanted to give it to you. But it's not me anymore. You understand?"

She was silent.

"How do you think your parents will feel about me?" I changed the subject. "Do you think they'll like me?"

"Give them grandchildren and they'll love you forever."

"Funny. I'm no avocat like your last suitor. I'm a step down, Véronique, your father..."

"My father will take one look at you and be satisfied. You look like you can afford a household and you're black ... so that's good enough for him."

"Well, it might fool him for five minutes but eventually they'll learn the truth."

"The truth?" she looked at me and smiled. "The truth is you're loyal, loving, and brilliant. They'll love you because you love me."

I imagined what it must have been like in her home—how young Véronique must have been loved. "What were your Christmas's like?"

"Well, we didn't have much. If we had an animal to slaughter that wouldn't deplete our ability to keep making more, we would have it for dinner. We didn't douse our yule log in red wine, I tell you that," she smiled. "Papa would pull out this fruit mash drink he made from berries. Because we couldn't afford wine. After the morning's chores with the animals, we would take the day just to be with each other. It was plain, but it was special. I promised one day I'd make enough money to afford a galette des rois."

The galette des rois—*the king's cake*—was a traditional post-Christmas cake made of puff pastry with a surprise charm baked inside to celebrate the three kings who brought gifts to the baby Jésus-Christ.

She continued. "It was strange the first time I had that cake here at the Chateau without my parents. I almost wanted to wrap it up and send it in the post."

"We will get your parents a galette des rois."

"When you and I have our home, Christmas will be sacred. It will be celebrated," she said, resolutely. "Not like what we just had. Is Madame really planning to do the full year and a half of mourning for someone else's husband? And why do men only have to mourn for six months when their wives die?"

"Do you want me to bring it up at the Club?"

"There are more important issues related to women, if something is to be brought up. I know she's in mourning but did she have to take away our Christmas, as well? Christmas must go on, even in times of tragedy, no matter how difficult."

"So, you're saying if I die in November you'll still celebrate Christmas in December?"

"Absolutely. Christmas is about more than a party. It's about Jésus-Christ and our salvation. He died for us, the least we can do is celebrate Him on His day."

I didn't know how I felt about all that. I'd do it if she wanted but I didn't feel it the same way she did. Véronique had some internal belief system that I hadn't found yet, even though I was looking. I wasn't at all sure how God could let things happen to his flock. And I was suspicious of a God that would make a king of France His greatest thing.

But maybe she was right and God had his mysterious ways. Maybe it wasn't God who ordained the kings of France, as I'd been taught. And maybe He decided to finally put things right. Because the next evening, while in Paris, I learned that Louis XVI had just been convicted of treason and would be put to death.

49

────────

Madame was in Britain when word came down of the King's impending execution. On her return, she climbed from the carriage, still in mourning black.

"Why are you wearing black?" I asked as she stepped down. "Didn't you hear about the King? It looks like you're mourning the verdict."

"You know I was already in mourning, and what do I care what anyone thinks? They'd be right. We should all be mourning what they're doing to our King. You don't think they'll really put him to death, do you? This is just a threat, don't you think?"

"No, it's real."

"The poor King is going to be killed, not because he's a horrible king or for anything he did. He's going to be put to death because of *her*. She's destroyed the monarchy. They were saying it in England. Everyone knows it's true."

I was tired of hearing about how horrible the Queen was when, to my way of thinking, the King was the one who made the mistakes that put us where we were. I followed Madame into the house as she kept walking, picking her skirts up as she talked.

"Madame," Gaspard started.

"Enough from you!" she snapped.

"Madame?" Gaspard's face was stricken. "I was only..."

"Why didn't you tell me not to wear black? We stopped in Paris and I walked through town to the patisserie wearing these clothes. Louis-Benoit is right, they're going to gossip now. Why don't you ever think?"

I didn't know what had happened between them. I didn't care. I knew all along whatever they had going would end. It was the ending I was most worried about. Madame would be fine, but Gaspard was volatile in times of stress. And a drunkard, to boot.

"I-I..."

"*I-I-I*'..." she mocked him. "Get out of my sight."

I looked away, but not quickly enough. I saw how her words hurt him. He stalked away and I followed her into the house with her bags.

"*She* was never a good fit with France. Me, I'm a true daughter of France. I give to the poor. I volunteer to hand food to little beggar children. I have friends both in France and all over Europe. I've been the unofficial queen of this country since they left the Palace, and my people will remember that. Marie Antoinette has never been anything other than an Austrian who never appreciated this country."

We had reached her bedroom. She unpinned the hat from her head and sat down at her dressing table, looking at herself in the mirror as she went about undoing the multitude of pins holding her hair in place.

"I'll be for France what this country wishes she had been; that is the gift I will give to my people. And in the meantime, I will continue to show her kindness as a true lady. Goodness doesn't come from bloodline, Louis-Benoit. Goodness is a trait that she never had. But I do. I will show her goodness even in her time of terrible despair. I will show her how a true noble lady should behave. How a queen would behave. Maybe if she asks me nicely, I'll help her earn the respect of the French people again when she comes back. We can rebuild the royal court together."

Madame was looking at herself in the mirror, selling me her story, as if speaking before a group of people. This was how she got people to listen to her. But I now realized she was convincing herself as much as the people. Telling herself what she wanted to be true.

Belatedly, I considered her words. "Madame, if the King is put to death, it's very possible the Queen will be next. If that happens, the young Dauphin and his sister will be without their parents."

"Hmm?" She pulled her eyes away from her own reflection and looked at me as my words worked their way through her brain. The idea that the Queen might be in danger seemed new to her. She spun on her chair and looked at me, eyes swimming with emotion. "Oh, that poor child."

There were *two* children, but her thoughts were only on the future king.

"Once all this messiness is over, I'll need to return to Versailles to help him grow up to be a man his father and my dear, sweet, Louis, will be proud of. *I* will have to be his regent. There's no one else! *I'll* be the guardian he needs until he's old enough to rule."

Of course, there was someone else. Maybe not the King's first cousin—Josephe's friend the Duc d'Orléans had decided to side with the new republic—but the King had living siblings and aunts. Not to mention advisors and deputies and friends, any of whom could be a regent.

Her eyes were moving as she was thinking, no longer hearing me.

"Yes, the young king will need me after his parents are gone, just as you needed me when you came to me, a parent-less orphan. And I will be there at Versailles to receive him. I'll move in after the Queen is put to death. I will love him like he was my own son."

She turned back around to the mirror, picked up a puff and began to powder away the glow from her face, a face now shining with possibility. "I'll pray for the Queen, that in seeing her dear husband pay for her crimes she will repent for the cruelty she has shown to me all these years before she dies. I will never take it out on her child. You'll see."

GASPARD DIDN'T TAKE WELL to being humiliated in front of me. I was used to the occasional punch, but these days he was different. He was angrier all the time. The black eye he'd given to Salanave should have alerted me that things were different, but I was preoccupied and didn't notice what was happening with him.

The day after Madame returned, I had finished helping with the morning's chores, so I headed around back toward the stables. I almost walked full tilt into Henri, whose face was flushed.

Henri and I hadn't been speaking like we used to, so I was happy to see him. But his face was alarmed.

"Don't go out there, Zamor," he said. Henri was sometimes prone to teasing me so I brushed past him, heading outside to see what silliness he had in store for me.

"Nice try, but whatever you have for me I'm sure I can handle it and give back as well."

I expected a pail of water to come my way or to step in something unpleasant in my path as I continued toward the stables, but instead, my eyes were drawn to the group of men who stood a ways away, looking down at something. A horse is a large thing, so it shouldn't have taken so long for me to see it, but I was caught short by the expression on Gaspard's face, a smile that looked more like a grimace. Gaspard didn't smile, so the sight of it chilled me.

"Ah, Louis-Benoit," he called across to me, jovially. "This is truly a sad event but I am glad you are here."

The two guards standing nearby had expressions of distaste on their faces. A loud whinny from the ground pulled my eyes toward Lightning, lying on the ground, struggling to get up.

My horse. Lightning. My beautiful horse. *My horse.*

"Gaspard said the horse stepped in a hole, but she was in her pen all morning," Henri whispered from behind me. "She was in her pen when he sent me inside to grab some rags, but when I came out, she was over there with him and his guards on the ground."

"Poor girl," Gaspard called to me. His smile was gone and he looked at me, straight in the eyes. "Stepped into a hole."

Lightning whinnied, her voice panicked and pained. Her large head struggled to lift itself from the ground. I looked at her legs and saw that one of them was bent in the wrong spot at the wrong angle. Her eyes rolled around, searching around for relief.

It took a moment for my brain to grasp the situation. A horse couldn't live with a broken leg. My horse. My Lightning. My friend.

Cold washed through me from the top of my head down to my feet in a quick rush and I lost the feeling in my lips. I stepped forward, moving towards her. The guards stepped out of my way as I came closer to her.

"Hey, Lightning. It's okay, girl," I said, hands out, fingertips almost reaching her. It was a stupid thing to say but my brain was screaming at me and no other words came to me. "It's okay, Lightning," I mumbled through those numb lips as she lifted her head and her tail as she whinnied, panic stricken.

All I wanted was for her to see me so she wouldn't be so scared. All I wanted was to hold her and let her know I was there. But suddenly, when I was about a foot away from her, the sound of a large crack broke the air.

Lightning's head and tail dropped to the ground and a pool of blood suddenly erupted, spreading from under her head from the gunshot. The spray hit me like a balloon filled with water.

"There you go, friend," Gaspard's voice said, close to my ear from over my shoulder. "Put her out of her misery for you. Wouldn't have wanted the poor girl to suffer anymore. You're welcome, blackamoor. Don't you worry, these two will take care of the body, won't you, fellows? Cut her up, might make decent meat for some starving sans-culottes. Or the pigs. Same thing."

I stared down at her, incomprehension filling me. She was alive just seconds ago. Now, she was still and dead, like the life had been pulled from her by a string. Just seconds ago my Lightning had been waiting for me to comfort her. Now she was gone.

I heard Gaspard walk away and dropped to my knees beside her.

The guards didn't stop me. I laid my head on her large neck, spread my arms over her black coat. I heard the guards walking away from the pathetic scene, and I didn't care. I laid my head on her and fought to keep tears at bay. She had been my escape partner. She had been my friend. And I had been the only human she truly trusted.

"I'm sorry, Lightning," I told her, holding her until she grew cold in my arms.

50

———————

I dreamt of Lightning and our first escape attempt so many years ago. The wind on us as we flew through the night, thinking we'd escaped. Lightning and me, both of us feeling free for a brief time, living life as we were meant to. In my dream we didn't stop when surrounded. Instead, I pulled on her reins. Lightning's front legs rose up into the air and we flew up and over the ring of horses blocking our way, landing on the other side. And then we rode and kept riding. Kept riding. Kept riding...

But that was only a dream. When I woke up, Lightning was gone.

"Come on, we never talk anymore," Henri said when he saw me later in the day. He was right. I followed him outside and we ended up at the stables. It wouldn't have been my first choice of a place to talk, but it was where he worked, so I didn't complain.

"You're going to need another horse. How about this one? He's younger, anyway."

This horse was light brown and impressive.

"I'll think about it."

Henri brushed the horse with abnormal harshness, his eyes were red, as though he hadn't slept, shining with excitement.

"I can't believe they're putting the king to death. The Convention is more powerful than the King! I can't believe he'll lose his head like a common sans-culottes. I wonder if they'll cheer. They cheer a lot at the beheadings. Sanson is smart to draw it out so everyone has a chance to enjoy it."

It was macabre the way he spoke about it, but Henri had changed since his father died.

"I had no idea watching people die was so much fun to you."

"I didn't say *me*. But other people will like it. How many do you think that machine can kill in an hour?" He dropped his brush in a pail and began tapping against his thigh.

"Calm down, Henri. If anyone sees you like this they'll think you're celebrating."

He ran his hands through his hair. "Maybe I am. Why shouldn't I, what'd he ever do for me? Though it's a shame what happened to the Duc. You know they say he was on his way to trial when he was attacked by that gang. They found the rest of him, you know. They tore him to bits, Zamor, it wasn't a painless death. They say from the shape his hands were in he fought all the way. I don't know what I feel. I don't want people to die—I'm not a monster — but people have been suffering. Somebody's got to pay."

I was growing more and more uncomfortable with every word he said. Henri had a way of acting like a child, not paying attention to who was around or who might be listening.

"Why do you know all the details of all the terrible things, Henri?"

He picked up the brush again and went at the horse. "When do you think they'll put the King to death? I'll put money it will happen within the week." His brush pressed against the horse too harshly causing it to shuffle, but he still didn't notice. His eyes focused on the coat but he wasn't seeing, only speaking. "Maybe sooner. Six days, maybe five. Three is too soon, but four. What do you think, Z—"

"Shut up, Henri!" I said. His eyes jerked up to look at me, surprised. "Are you a fool? People may be listening! This place is full of royalists – how much of an idiot do you have to be..." The sudden hurt on his face stopped my words. "Henri, I'm sorry. I only meant—"

"I know what you meant." His face twisted with anger though his eyes were now wet. "No, I'm no idiot. I see what's happening. Now that you have your new friends, your new sans-culotte friends, you don't need me anymore. I'm no idiot. I was fine for you when you were just a blackamoor servant but now you're out in Paris with all your educated friends and I'm not good enough anymore."

"No, Henri, that's not true."

"You think I don't know they told you not to let me in to those taverns in Paris? Did you defend me, Zamor? Did you tell them if your friend Henri wasn't welcome, then you weren't coming?"

That seemed asinine to me, and I suppose it showed on my face because his face turned a deeper red and angrier.

"That's what I thought. Fine. You don't need to worry about me anymore. Because we aren't friends anymore. We just work here."

He threw his brush into the bucket and stalked off. I would catch up with him later, I decided, hopefully after he cooled off. But I didn't see him later that day.

～

THE NEXT MORNING, after my chores I went to Paris and tracked down George Grieve at a little café, sipping coffee and reading. Casting a shadow on his book he looked up, and then looked back at his book again.

"I came to tell you I'll do it," I said. "I'll be a witness for you against Citizenness du Barry."

"Too late," he mumbled.

"It can't be too late."

"I told you that if you continued to play games you'd lose your leverage, and you have. We have another household witness willing to speak against her."

My mind quickly ran through the ramifications of that. Who could it be?

"That witness isn't me," I reminded him. "No witness could possibly be as powerful as…"

He slapped his book closed and looked up. "No thank you, Monsieur. We don't need you. You've lost your usefulness. I don't know how many ways I can say it. Frankly, I think it's pathetic that it took you this long. How many years has that woman treated you like garbage? All those years she's made a fool of you and I have to convince you to do what's in your best interest? Go home."

I was disappointed. But I had rejected him too many times. It was a matter of his pride, now. But it was the only chip I had.

"I-I'm sorry I was rude to you before. But I'm ready now. Come, now, if you had enough evidence you would have arrested her, already. Tell Max..."

"You think I'm your errand boy? If Max wanted to speak with you he would summon you."

"You don't understand, things are getting ... tense at the Chateau. I need..."

"I don't know why you think I give an earthly care about your discomfort or your needs. You put up with the woman for this long and seem to like it. You like it so much that when given the opportunity to be free you chose to stay. You made your bed, lie in it. Maybe some people aren't ready for freedom."

My ignorant words, said to Véronique in relation to young Sally Hemings, came back at me, viciously. Said to me, I knew why Véronique had itched to slap me. The cruel, arrogant sound of those words, and all they meant, soured my stomach. She also told me things were different when you had more than yourself to worry about.

This man thought I wanted to be at the Chateau. He had no concept of why I hadn't quickly given up du Barry. But he also had no concept of what life could be like for a man like me. He continued, enjoying the turnabout.

"The case is no longer your concern. We cared more for your freedom than you cared for your own and now look. Poof," he made a demonstration with his fingers of something going up in smoke. "The chance is gone. Good-bye, page."

He opened his book again to read. I stood for a moment before walking away. I would get nowhere with Grieve. My excellent speech had earned me some attention, but not enough people to continue supporting my quest for overall abolition. And now, Gaspard was losing his mind and I had no plan.

I left Paris but wasn't ready to return to the Chateau. Instead, I went to the Palace to see who was still there. The servants I used to share and trade information with were long gone. There were no pastries laid out in the kitchen and I only saw one cook rifling in the dry goods room when I came through. The halls were quiet with only a few people here or there.

But it was the time of day when my old instructor, Barnier, would have just ended a lesson in the schoolroom, so I stopped in for a visit. He was packing up to leave and looked up when I entered the room.

"Bonjour, Zamor," he said, his face as friendly as always. "Did you hear about the revolt in the islands? The slaves have taken the government over; it's no longer a French colony. The people are calling it *Haiti*."

"What? When did you hear this?" The revolt was no secret, but Saint-Domingue was no longer a French colony? It now had its own name and was a sovereign country? Amazing! While I was rolling that over in my brain my eyes took in the bareness of the room. "Hey, are you packing, Barnier?"

He stopped and looked at me, rosy cheeks shiny, though his eyes were sad. "Ah, yes. I've gotten most of it but I'll be back tomorrow to get the rest. I'm sorry to have to say goodbye, Zamor. Being your instructor, being here to have some part in the development of your brilliant mind, has truly been the highlight of my career. I told my wife when you were a child that I'd never known a young mind as inquisitive as yours. Never before and never since."

This news was bittersweet. We were close when I was young.

"I've long stopped teaching you, I only come to Versailles at all in hopes of running into you, I so enjoy our stimulating conversations. It has been a pleasure to be around you. And more than brains, you have survival instinct. I do not. As you know, I rely on my wife's instinct, and she tells me it is time for me to go. There are only two

students these days—all the other nobles have fled to the country or
... *out* of the country."

He didn't have to explain to me. I nodded and watched him pack
up. "Wherever you go, don't go through Paris. Take the countryside."

"I wish I could take you with me," Barnier said. "I have asked
Madame, over the years, for freedom on your behalf. I've even—
forgive me for this—offered to buy you from her. I don't have much
but my wife and I were willing to tighten our belts if need be.
Madame always said she loved you too much to let you leave. I was
thinking of driving to the Chateau to ask her again before I go."

"It's okay, don't bother," I said, though I was surprised. "She will
say no again. She will always say no. But thank you for considering it.
And your wife. I'll have to get my freedom another way."

"I think she loves you. That's what she tells me, at least, with
much fervor. But, I admit, I discussed the situation with my wife and
she suggests that, perhaps, I have allowed my affection for Madame
du Barry to cloud my judgement. She says that denying you freedom
in the name of love is wrong. I knew that in my bones, but I told
myself that you were better off than most people. I told myself that
someday she would change her mind and make a way for you. I told
myself that it was okay because you eat well and sleep well and drink
fine wine—and have an education! But truly looking at it now, I see
it's not. It's a sin what they've done to you, son. What *we've* done to
you."

"I've known that since I was ten, Barnier," I said.

"I pray to God for forgiveness for my part in it. I ask you for your
forgiveness, now."

That softened me because Barnier was perhaps the only person
to ever ask for it. And he had no real part in my circumstances, at all.
"You gave me the education I needed to do what I can to free myself,
and books to make the time bearable. Of course, I forgive you." I hesitated and then said what was on my mind. Because very few people
were still around who knew me as a child. "He killed my horse, you
know."

"Lightning? Who would... oh. Manager Gaspard." He answered his own question.

"He did it just to hurt me, but no matter. He'll get his." I just wanted Barnier to know. Felt compelled to tell someone who knew my horse. Knew what she meant to me.

"I'm so sorry, son. My heart breaks for you."

I scoffed. "She was old and probably wouldn't have lasted much longer, anyway... *and all that*. I'm just mentioning it because I... I don't know why. I don't know why I said it. I—"

I was stopped by the man suddenly launching himself at me. His arms clutched me in a hug. I didn't know why he imagined I needed it, but I allowed him to hold me until he stepped away, looking slightly embarrassed. He cleared his throat and stepped back, running a hand over his shiny clean scalp.

"What will you do?" he asked.

"Me?" I shrugged. "I'll be honest with you, Barnier, I have no idea. Just between the two of us," I lowered my voice. "I'm already a Jacobin."

"I'm not surprised."

"Nothing else for me but to become part of the change, don't you think? Everything's happening so fast now, I don't know what's next for me. But like your wife, I feel it's time. It's time for something. I just don't yet know what."

51

January, 1793

"What is this merde?" Jean-Paul Marat said, slapping my sheaf of papers down onto the dusty printing room floor. I looked at the fluttering pages and made an attempt to gather them. "Don't bother, Zamor, those pages don't deserve the energy to pick them up off the ground."

I had changed my writing. Call it a conscience, but something of what Véronique had been saying had gotten to me. I took to heart what she had said about my words being a weapon. The power had been nice in the beginning, but now it felt like the world was getting a bit crazier every day. I didn't want any part of making things worse. That was not why I had gotten into all this for.

My knees creaked as I knelt to make a bed in the crook of one arm to gather my papers. Jean had already turned away, a look of annoyance on his face.

"What happened to you, Zamor? You used to be brave. A fighter with your words! Now you write like a mouse and expect me to pass it off as mine."

That made me do a double-take. I looked at him, slack-jawed, as he stood across the room, fists on his hips and fire in his eyes.

"You're joking, right? I'm only trying to be a responsible writer, what in the hell happened to you?" I gestured at him where he stood, his shirt little more than rags around him and his pants near to falling off. "When's the last time you've eaten or taken a bath? When's the last time you've even seen the sun? I'm writing words to help pull you back from the brink because you've gone so far outside of this world I don't even recognize you anymore. Your writing is dangerous. You're a doctor, for God's sake, don't you even see what's happening around us? You want that to continue?" I bent down to gather my papers.

"It has to continue," he said as he came across the room at me. I hesitated in gathering papers and put an arm up to protect myself from this new, frazzled, Jean-Paul, in case he planned to lash out at me. "It *must* continue if we're to *win* a revolution. You don't stop when it gets difficult, you push harder. You do more!"

"More," I snorted, pulling the last sheet into my pile and standing awkwardly. "There's such a thing as going too far, Jean. More isn't always better, especially at this point. No one can decide what to do. Look around at the world, Jean. It's burning; we don't need more kindling on the fire. We need a good bucket of water to cool everyone off."

"And I should listen to you, now, the filth monger? Filth! I thought the work you were doing for the republic was enough to counter that drivel and crap you write in pamphlets, but now you're pulling back from anything of quality. What good are you to me or France? Why don't you admit you're nothing but a Girondin! A weak, ball-less follower of Brissot – pretending you want a new republic when all you really want is to put the monarchy back on the throne. Missing the palace, aren't you? Missing your king to suck up to! You're a coward, Zamor, and a sore disappointment."

He had turned away from me dramatically, as if the sight of me hurt his eyes. It stung and angered me at the same time. A nerve twitched in my jaw.

I wasn't normally sensitive to insult but part of me wondered if he wasn't right. Not about putting the monarchy back, but the part about not wanting to do the things that people like he wanted to do. He had forsaken the Cordeliers and was now a fervent member of the Mountain.

"Someone has to think about something beyond themselves," I mumbled without conviction. Véronique's words kept playing in my head. I knew she was right but inside me it didn't feel right. It felt weak, just like he said. "I'm trying to look out for more than my own interests, Paul."

"Pffft," he looked at me with a smirk. "You've never thought of anything beyond yourself in your whole, pathetic life. You're a selfish man. Still thinking about yourself and your own hide. And if you think I'm publishing that nonsense under my name ... telling citizens to stay calm and try to turn down the heat ... you're not the man I thought you were. You've gone crazy or soft! As useless as friggin' Brissotins."

Hearing him compare me to Brissotin (or Girond) was alarming, being that he fashioned himself the arch enemy of Jacques Brissot. I'd never, technically, taken up the mantle of the Girondins, nor had I shirked it. Both the Gironds and the Cordeliers had good ideas, but they were slowly coming to loathe each other., while the Mountain loathed them both.

"Brissot is probably a spy like you," Marat spat the words at me. "You take your drivel and go peddle it to him – I have no use for you here."

Jacques Brissot had been writing, also. As much as Paul was railing about revolution, Jacques had been railing about anarchy. He and his Girondins believed the republic was rotting from within.

All that was annoying to the Mountain, but his biggest crime had been in urging calm and trying to prevent the republic from putting the King to death. I wouldn't admit it to Paul but a small part of me wondered if Brissot wasn't right. Not in stopping the monarchy but in killing the King before fighting off our enemies. Now the enemies of France had no reason to care how many French they killed.

But still, Marat's paper was the most popular in France. I needed him behind me for the time when I began to write for myself.

"Look," I tried, shoving my papers into my satchel. "I'll try again." I wouldn't write the fiery rhetoric he was starting to favor but I could be a bit edgier, maybe. "I'll try again..."

"Go home, Zamor! I don't want you to try again. The words used to come out of you as easily as sweat. If you have to work yourself up to putting out something worth reading you've lost your use to me. Now get out so I can go home. It's been a long day and this air is harsh against my skin."

I felt a flash of anger. I wasn't just his ghostwriter, after all, I was supposed to be his friend. I was starting to rethink that, with the many insults he was lobbing my way.

My chin went up. "I'll go, and let you come to your senses. I'll expect your apology the next time I see you."

"Then I guess we won't be seeing each other again because you'll not get one from me," he said.

"You've lost your mind," I told him. That was enough for me. I turned and left the print shop, letting the door slam behind me to express my annoyance, and headed straight to Sebastien's.

"You can't blame him." Sebastien had finished putting his kids to bed and we sat on the ground outside, in front of his front door, sipping brandy and watching the streets around us. It was evening but the streets were still busy. I remembered how it used to be, the year or so since I'd first met Sebastien. It used to be a pleasant, quiet street. Now there were vendors all hours of the day or night. News-boys handing out papers proclaiming news that seemed to change by the hour. The streets were alive.

Sebastien handed me a cigarette. I'd taken to smoking when in Paris. I took a long draw on it. "Bullshit," I coughed out.

"Not bullshit. He liked your work because you were fearless enough to say the things no one else dared. Things even he hadn't dared. You gave him the freedom to voice his own and influenced his writing. He might never have grown in popularity if he hadn't seen the world from your perspective, used a little of your voice in his works. You opened something up in him. And now you want to go back to writing pieces on how we just all need to get along. It's too late for that. It would destroy his reputation."

"I know what I did, but even a short while ago things were different. Everything's changed, Sebastien, everyone is crazy now. Now that the King is dead everyone's fighting for position and things are getting out of control."

"Everyone's always been crazy," Sebastien replied.

"No, this movement was driven by thought and reason, not this bizarre pandemonium."

"And underneath all that thought and reason has always been a bunch of crazy." He blew out exhaustion and took the cigarette back. "We had good intentions. But some people, when they see a little sliver of change, they're not content to let it be what it is. Something in their brain tells them all the rules of logic and civilization no longer apply. This revolution is a forest fire and nothing will heal until the whole damn thing is burned to the ground. You can't put water back into the spring. It does no one any good to bury their heads in the sand and pretend we can go back. You can't push the baby back into the womb..."

"Yes, Sebastien, 'we can't put the water back in the spring' or 'the baby back in the womb', but can we insert some logic and reason into where we are today? Start from now and make a change in another direction? I'm just saying we don't have to make it worse. We can direct some of this energy. For God's sake, we have to try, don't we?"

"Véronique's given you a conscience but it doesn't look as good on you as blind anger. Anger gave you clarity. Singularity of purpose. This," he used his hand to refer to my entire person. "This is new, and not nearly as effective. You can't make change without passion."

I stood up.

"Where are you going," he asked.

"Back to talk to Jean."

"He won't still be at the printer. He doesn't like to stay long after dark.

"I'll go to his apartment, maybe he'll be in a better mood. I'm no coward. He should apologize."

"Good luck with that," Sebastien said from where he sat on the ground, squinting up at me through craggy-skinned eyes and smoke. He raised his glass to me, taking a big swig. I heard his coughing as I walked down the street toward Jean's place.

I could make him see, just as words could rile, words could calm. In the calm he would see the logic, if I explained it correctly.

I veered off the street to the little alley that connected two main streets where halfway along the wall, a door opened up that led to the staircase to his place. At the door, I was surprised by a woman coming out so fast we bumped shoulders with each other.

"Pardon, Mademoiselle." I dipped my head slightly. A movement of her hands caught my attention. One hand was gloved, and the other, ungloved hand, held a knife, dripping with dark liquid. Both were shaking. I looked up and saw her eyes were wide and grey, lips parted as if she'd been caught in the middle of a sentence or a thought. We stared at each other for what seemed like forever, though I knew it was only seconds.

I can't explain why it took seconds for me to understand what I was seeing, but while I was working it out in my head, she moved past me, fled down the alley and into the street I'd just turned off. She put her hands up in the air, the knife still dripping in her hand, turned slowly, and stood there for a long moment, still staring at me. Then, when I would have thought a normal person would run, she sat herself down right on the dirty cobblestoned ground, dark brown billowing skirts floating delicately around her. She stared at me as if she were waiting, the blood dripping down her arm and staining her sleeve. I saw then there was more of it on her bodice and on her skirt, blending in with the dark brown fabric of the dress. She sat there on the street as if it were a fancy settee in a parlor.

But as I said, the streets weren't silent these days. Seconds later, I heard a voice yell, "That's blood on her hands. What did she do? Where did you come from? What did you do?"

I didn't know what was happening, but I knew I couldn't be there.

I secured my satchel more firmly on my shoulder and quickly jogged in the other direction. I turned the corner when I got to the end of the street and stood against the wall, listening, my heart beating hard in my chest. I heard more shouts as people came upon the woman with the bloody hands. Then, "David! David!" They called for the artist. "She came from the direction of Jean-Paul's apartment!" Everyone knew they were best friends. A woman's scream pierced the night.

I listened to the sound of footsteps as a group thundered into the alley and burst through the squeaky door that led to the staircase to Jean's apartment. I stayed to wait for Paul's voice, for him to come out, wounded but bloody. For him to come out angrier than he'd been earlier. I waited for him to tell them to arrest the woman. I waited. What I heard, instead, was David's wail through the open window, cutting through the night and the Paris streets.

My limbs began to shake. The sound of thundering feet and more shouts of "murder! murder!" pushed me farther down the street, away from the cacophony. I walked quietly, but fast, my head down, to the spot where I had tied up the horse behind a building. I wanted to tell Sebastien but I was shaken. David would let him know. But I had to get out of Paris. There was no telling what they might find in Jean-Paul's apartment and I wanted to be far away when they did.

The new horse wasn't like Lightning. He couldn't pick up on my feelings—didn't know when we should run simply by feeling the rigidity of my body. He was little more than a baby and I had to kick him on his sides to get him to move fast.

Soon, the sound of the horse's hooves clapping on the road seemed the loudest thing in the night as we galloped back to Louveciennes.

52

Paul Marat was dead. Killed by a woman named Charlotte Corday with a knife while taking one of the cool baths that soothed his sensitive skin. Apparently, Corday had been stopped by Paul's wife twice before Paul waved her inside, thinking she was a friend to the republic.

First on the scene to meet Paul's screaming wife was his friend, the artist David, and the man he was set to meet later that evening, George Grieve.

I read this in a paper over a week later. Paul's funeral was set up by the republican government, being that he was considered a hero and a close friend of Max. I thought about attending but I was still a bit worried that there might be pieces of me in his apartment, maybe a document or two with my name left on it. Or, maybe his wife knew about me?

According to the story, the murderer Charlotte Corday felt that the members of the Mountain were destroying the promising new republic. Under interrogation she claimed the death of Marat would mean others could live. Max Robespierre was livid.

In the paper they said the Marquis de Sade – or Citizen de Sade – gave the eulogy. I didn't know what to make of that.

Though things between Paul and I had gotten tense at the end, I was sad he was dead. One writer to another, I knew his need to be heard led him down a dangerous path. He'd paid for his radical ravings with his life. It was a lesson and a warning which I intended to heed. Each day that passed, I breathed easier because no one showed up at the door looking for Paul's accomplice.

As for Madame, her "mourning" didn't stop her from receiving guests. Later that evening I slipped into the dining room doorway just to listen to snippets of conversation.

"...I understand you barely escaped the revolt with your life," Madame was saying to a tall, thin man who sat at the opposite end of the table. I'd never seen him before and he moved with a level of discomfort that I'd noticed from guests unused to such formality at dinner. He had a shock of wild gray hair, a bushy gray mustache, and a way of avoiding eye contact that was curious and off-putting.

"How did you manage to work in the colonies for so long?" Madame continued, giving him the look that made its recipient feel like they were the most important person in the world. But everyone at the table seemed fascinated by his storytelling.

"Firm resolve, my good Comtesse," he said in broken French. I could tell he was American. "I barely got out with my life. Your good folks at the National Convention say I can't recoup any of the investment I made in Saint Domingue. The revolt was bad enough but now this new so-called republic is stealing my money and my property with their own home-grown Jacobins."

My ears pricked when I realized he was talking about Saint-Domingue and his "property"—the black people enslaved there. I knew it wasn't only French citizens who owned property in the islands but it had never occurred to me that foreigners would be slave owners in French territory.

Later that evening, musicians came into the grand salon and played strings for Handel's Water Music with baroque flute for Madame and her remaining guests. I stood in the room behind her but near enough that I could come if she called. I looked at the people in the room, all adorned in jewels and fancy dress, high wigs and breeches who sipped fine brandy and ate fancy hors d'oeuvres while the musicians played.

I remained long enough to be insulted by a visiting duchess who remarked to Madame that she was so kind to tolerate me in her presence—that at least as a child I was cute but I had none of that left to make it worth having me around. Madame simply smiled. I remarked that some might say I was kind to tolerate her many rude friends.

"Zamor, you can't speak to her that way! I'm so sorry, my dear."

Then the American spoke up. "This is why we don't educate them," he said to Madame. "It brings out their natural contrary nature. They can't help themselves – they aren't civilized. It's not their fault. They're like children. Or undomesticated animals."

"Yes, I have heard about how it is in America," Madame said, eyes wide, like she was hearing the most interesting gossip. A lick of anger took me.

"It's the enslaved people that lack discipline?" I asked. All eyes swung my way. "When we have a world of men who call themselves such, but force others to do their work for them. If a man cannot do his own work is he really a man at all?"

"Shut up," Gaspard said, his voice low and angry.

It surprised me. He normally stayed in his spot, glaring at me but keeping his mouth shut. But he was still angry at me, I knew. Angry because Madame was being kind to me, again.

"You, shut up," I said.

"Louis, am I going to have to ask you to leave? My apologies, Monsieur," Madame said to the guest. But the guest was staring at me. Before, I had noticed he didn't look at people directly when he spoke to them. Now, with his cold eyes on me, flashing with fire, I much preferred when he looked elsewhere.

"You let him speak like that? A nigger?"

It was a word I hadn't heard. Not far from what people around here called me when they were angry with me. Nègre was a step above blackamoor, but not this word he said. It was similar but it sounded different. The way he said it made me feel like a worm on the ground. His eyes confirmed the feeling as he looked away and spoke to her.

"I wouldn't dare to insult such a gracious, beautiful hostess, but I won't tolerate being spoken to by a slave. And I'm surprised you let him speak to your man that way."

Gaspard was near apoplectic but silent.

"That doesn't happen in the United States. You understand, Comtesse?" He dipped his head toward her, slightly. Color sprung to her cheeks and her pleasure was visible. He had bowed to her. Coming from the colonies, he probably didn't know not to bow to someone of her station. But bowing to her elevated her ego in a way that would never happen among citizens of France. Her eyes sparkled.

"You may leave, Louis-Benoit. Once again, you have overstayed your welcome."

I didn't need to be told twice. Once out into the hall, I realized Madame had followed me out. She came up to speak under her breath to me.

"Louis-Benoit, just a minute. Try to be kinder to Gaspard."

My temper flared. "He murdered my horse, I'm not being kinder to him. He's evil."

"He wouldn't want me to say anything, but you should know," she leaned in. "He's not himself because his youngest son was killed in the United States. He won't say anything, but his heart is broken."

Gaspard was unstable on a normal day. With his son gone, there was no telling when he would snap.

53

Dear Citizen,

On January 21, 1793, King Louis XVI was put to death by guillotine.

For a king who never had time to speak to the common man, from the time he took his first step onto the platform he didn't stop talking. Not when they were putting him into place. Not when they were laying him down. Not when his neck was secured in the bracket that was custom designed for his own neck.

He spoke to the people as if to make something normal out of the abnormal – as if to help himself cope with what was happening to and around him.

They gave him time to ramble for the entertainment factor, and plenty of people were laughing as he did. I didn't find any of it entertaining. The sound of that blade coming down rippled through my body. The hush ... swish...

And then, with a slam and a thud, we had no more king.

Le Roi est mort. The King is Dead. Long live the ...

My apologies. Habit .... and all that.

--Zamor, 1820

An impromptu Jacobin celebration had sprung up in the back room of a tavern. Some of the men in the room cried. A woman lifted her cup and gave the first smile I'd ever seen her give; a smile that spoke of decades—a lifetime—of feeling powerless and hopeless suddenly gone overnight.

"Everything's going to change now," a man was going on, sounding as if he almost didn't believe it had truly happened. "Our republic will be something the world has never seen. Men as equals. Wealth to the people. We have won, my friends!"

"He put my cousin in prison to die for nothing!" a man shouted. "I spit on his grave!"

It was a strange combination of gaiety and sadness, depending on the person. The servers were sent to bring another round.

"Come, let's go out into the streets and act like fools!" Sebastien said. But he'd been more somber lately. Drinking more and joking less. I wondered what was plaguing him that more and more often I was the one who had to cheer him up.

I allowed myself to be pulled along by my friend. Several others decided to leave, as well. There's only so much celebrating of death one could do. Working our way out of the back room, into the main hub of the tavern, we heard raised voices and commotion.

"Come on you drunken idiot, get out before I put you out ... and not so nicely!"

"Don't touch me!" came a voice. "I have a right!"

"You have no right to tear up my bar. Look at you, down there on the floor, a mess. This is why your wife left you, Gaspard. Taken up with a sans-culotte because you embarrass her like this. Two of your kids calling *him* their papa and the third gone around the world to be an abolitionist in another country just to get away from *you*. All while you spend your nights drunk on the floor of any bar you can find. Get out of here and do something useful. Maybe you can go find those missing jewels!"

I knew the third child of Gaspard who had gone round the world was the dead one. Now I knew why. Gone to be an abolitionist in the new U.S.; fighting for the rights of the black people his father despised. And now the boy was dead.

Revelers in the bar laughed. I had come out far enough to see Gaspard on the ground, lying by an overturned chair, looking belligerent and barely conscious. He babbled incoherently with his mouth wide, anguish mixing with speech. A long string of saliva fell from his bottom lip down to the floor. Tears sprang to his eyes as the laughter towards him grew.

"You w-won't speak th-that...!"

"I'll speak how I want in my tavern."

The barkeep and another man had reached down to try to pull him up.

"Don't touch me!" He swatted at them, wildly, hitting one, who cursed.

I felt a wave of pity towards him for a moment. Just a tiny moment.

The man he hit pulled back a fist to punch him, only to be stopped by the hand of the barkeep who had looked up and saw me.

"Hey, you, take this bag of merde back to Louveciennes before he gets himself hurt, oui?"

I, instinctively, sought to move backwards into the shadows to avoid him seeing me but it was too late. Gaspard's face whipped up, following the barkeep's look and he saw me standing there before I could disappear. I could almost see the thoughts running through his head in that moment, as I stood, flanked by my friends, sober and composed.

His eyes flashed. I was seeing him at his worst. I was watching him snivel on the ground like a scared, weak animal. Of all people, for me to see him this way was something worse than death to him;

that, I knew. But I also knew his son had just been killed. Death had a way of bringing people to their senses.

I didn't care to make anything easy on him, but I did care for this tavern, where I often came with my friends. And I didn't know what would happen if I ignored him. I didn't know how I would explain ignoring him to Madame, without giving myself away. And lastly, as one human being to another, maybe he had been changed by the tragedy? He was, clearly, broken. And as much as I hated him, I knew he loved his son and I knew what it felt like to lose people you loved. I was sure he loved his son at least as much as I loved Lightning. Maybe this was his price to pay, and if so, we were even now.

I stepped forward towards Gaspard as he watched me approach; eyes wide, face sodden from tears and saliva and snot. I reached out my hand to help him up onto his feet. He, instantly, slapped my hand away and exploded in fury, unleashing a stream of invectives the likes of which I'd never heard. I dropped my hand and stepped back. He stumbled onto his feet, looking at me like he was afraid to take his eyes off of me, lest I do something to him.

"Are you sure he's yours? The mongrel seems to bite!" somebody joked, seeing the whole affair. People laughed again, but it wasn't funny to me. He turned to the barkeep.

"How dare you, sans-culotte filth! Treating me less than a nègre blackamoor slave! I'll burn this place to the ground with you in it!"

"You try it and I'll have something waiting for you! You no longer have a king in your pocket, you worthless piece of skin. All those years, stealing from business owners trying to make ends meet and put food in their children's bellies. All those years throwing your weight around and threatening honest, tax-paying Frenchmen and women, like you had a right. Well, the age of kings is over now. You won't be stealing from any of us anymore," said the barkeep. "Now get out of my tavern!"

I averted my gaze as two men who took issue with Gaspard's words helped him out of the bar. Helped was too polite a word for how they maneuvered him. From inside, we could already hear the blows before the front door closed behind them.

Someone spat on the floor where Gaspard had sat. "To think, he used to be one of us. His parents are rolling in their graves to see what a sorry mess their son turned out to be. Dirty, fucking piece of scum."

"Will this cause trouble for you?" Sebastien asked, having come up beside me. "I imagine when he wakes up he won't even remember what happened tonight, he's so drunk."

"No luck of that," I mumbled. "No worries. Surviving Gaspard is what I do on a daily basis."

I bluffed because what else was I going to do?

I stayed at the bar for at least an hour more because I didn't want to run into my manager's prone body in the street. And when the tavern had cleared out, I left, I found the young male horse—I was trying to get used to it—and went back to Louveciennes.

I knew this newest public humiliation would come back to haunt me. We had turned a corner and I didn't want to know where we would go from here. I didn't believe it would be as simple as Sebastien did. I only knew I had to try harder to make change with this group of revolutionaries before Gaspard took his revenge.

But the first thing I did when I got back to the Chateau was to procure a steak knife from the kitchen and promptly hid it underneath my mattress, just in case.

54

Dear Citizen,

The year was already so unusual I forgive myself now for being off my game. Looking back I realize I was sloppy. The more time I spent away from Madame the more I felt like a human being with hopes, dreams, and a life.

And friends. I only had a few, and Sebastien was going through some sort of breakdown. I felt a need to help him.

--Zamor, 1820

"Seven people guillotined in two hours, and it took that long only because the executioner wanted to gin up the crowd between each one." Sebastien had consumed half a bottle of red wine and was huddled into a chair beside the fireplace in a tavern.

"Why do you watch them, Sebastien?"

"I have to! We put this in motion, we should have to see it! I teach my sons, they are responsible for what they cause. I can't be a hypocrite. You were right!"

Normally, a hard-to-shake personality, now my friend was trembling and trying desperately to hide it. But wine has a way of loosening the bounds of self-control, and his body gave away the inner turmoil of him having spent the day at the Place de la Révolution watching a steady stream of people being put to death under the blade of the monster in the middle of Paris.

"I'm not claiming this, nor should you. I'll remind you, some of those people deserve to be put to death."

"Sans-culottes, nobles, bourgeois ... everyone is being killed in equal measure, that's for sure. And I understand some of them deserve it, but not all. There's so much blood. Too much. I can't sit here."

We left the tavern. We were walking through the streets of Paris, and he seemed to be having difficulty raising his bloodshot-red eyes from the ground. He was skittish, jumping when I placed a hand on his shoulder, his eyes darting around as though afraid of something jumping out at him. But we kept walking through quieter streets, my hope being that fewer people around would calm his nerves.

Sebastien ran his hand through his short, choppy hair. His face was dark, with an uneven beard like he'd been shaving, haphazardly. I understood the fevered fear in his eyes, but I knew emotional instability was seen as weakness. Weakness could be interpreted as regret, softness toward the other side. Counter-revolutionary.

"Don't let anyone see you like this. Stay home if you must," I said low. "If watching what happens in the square does this to you, then never go again."

"And not look at what we're doing? What I've done?"

"Stop it, Sebastien," I snapped. "We are not sending people to their deaths by wanting a new republic. How that republic is implemented is not decided by you or by me, but something had to be done. Did you truly imagine there would be no bloodshed?"

He looked up and took a shuddering breath. "It's one thing to know it and another to see it and feel it. I understand street violence. There's a code to the streets. I understand that. But I don't understand death on a scale like this. We have trials but is *anyone* found innocent? The King is gone, shouldn't all of this be dying down by now?"

"Well, the King wasn't the only problem, was he? He didn't rule alone. He had his ministers and directors and a multitude of politicians on his side. And the wealthiest aristocrat supporters. The aristocrats were always pushing for him to do the things that made their lives the easiest. Always threatening to revolt if he gave even the least consideration to the common folk, and he folded every time." A glanced as Sebastien's face and he wasn't moved by my words. "When I was a child, just in the time it took to transport me from my home to this place I saw more violence than I ever care to see again. Senseless, needless, cruel violence. While we sit in taverns and back rooms talking about how the world should change, without ever expecting to have to sacrifice or get our hands dirty. Even now my brethren are still being bought and sold, murdered, and terrorized, daily. They're fighting back in Saint-Domingue and succeeding because they have the numbers. All of a sudden, blood matters when it's being shed by people with white skin instead of black. When I start to feel badly about what's happening in France, I remember how much worse it is for my people in the colonies, and that sets me right again. You think about it, too. Sans-culotte blood was already being shed under the monarchy, it just wasn't out in the open, in the center of Paris."

But the gore of the day wasn't lifting from him. Along a side road we were caught suddenly in the presence of a body shoved against the side of a building. The unfortunate man wore the short culotte pants of the elite, but his brilliantly colored satin jacket was stained with blood from a brutal beating. It was obvious he was dead, strange that he was alone. I tried to place his face but could not. In the meantime, Sebastien had doubled over to retch on the other side of the alleyway.

We kept walking as soon as he could stand, and when he did so, his eyes were wet.

"What kind of a world are we making, Zamor? I'm afraid for my children to leave the house every day, or my wife. Have I had a hand in destroying this country? Did I cause that?" He gestured behind us in the direction of the dead man. "And that smell. Can't get away from it. Does it smell in Louveciennes?"

It was the stench of death. The cemeteries of Paris were full, and there were places, like that enclosure where little Jean's body was tossed, all over the city now, filled with mass graves and not enough room or time to bury the bodies. The sweet stench of human decay lay over the city like a blanket.

"I remember that smell from when my grandfather died. I can't get away from it now. I never wanted my children to have to smell it but now I wonder if they'll ever breathe fresh air again. I pray to God at night and feel shame. I feel like we've unleashed something and it's no telling where it will end. I'm frightened, truly. But I can't show it. Not out in the world and not at home. I have to be strong for my family. I can't let them see me like this. But I'm a human being, I'm not made of stone. Where can I be human?"

We had reached a bridge over the Seine, in a quiet area.

"Here. Right here. Look," I gestured to the water, stealing from a wise woman I had mocked for loving the Seine. "It might be dirty, but water is life. When you feel you can't take a moment more, come look at the water. No matter what happens in the world those waves never end. There's death, but there's life, too. Stare at that water as long as you need to, and if I can, I'll stand beside you as I do tonight. That water teaches us that life doesn't end. It teaches us there's hope."

We leaned against the railing, staring down into the water while the time passed. Minutes or hours, it was hard to tell.

After a while, his limbs stopped trembling and his body lost its rigidity, as if talking and staring at that water had released all the poison from within him.

"All right," he sighed with a nod. "No more watching executions. He straightened, signaling he was okay, and we could leave. On our trip back to his house, when I gave his shoulders a firm shake, he returned a grateful smile.

"Thank you, friend," he said. "You are the best friend I've ever had. Thank you."

"Of course, that's what friends are…"

"Oh, one thing I meant to tell you, I've heard some rumors about Grieve. The word is going around that he and Madame know each other. That the two of them planned that jewelry theft. People are saying he was supposed to get a cut on the other side, in England, but was cut out of his due and now he's after her for revenge. Be careful with that one."

It was an interesting rumor and if any of it was true it meant Grieve was even less trustworthy than I thought. It meant that he'd plotted with Madame, knowing all along that she was setting me up as the culprit. It meant he was manipulating; using my desperation to get free of her against me. And now, he'd cut me out completely.

I was thinking about all this while Sebastien headed back inside and I walked the short way to find my parked horse. I knew it was late. But it was only after I climbed atop the horse and began the ride home, that I happened to notice the stillness in Paris. And then, on the road, when the sound of morning birds became louder than the yells and laughter of marauding gangs and late revelers, I stiffened on the horse.

The birds were singing? Dear God, it was morning.

Madame's chocolat…

55
____

Dear Citizen,

I forgot I was supposed to be small.

I forgot that to this country the King of France was its greatest thing. I had always known that, so long as France was ruled by a monarchy, I would always be a slave. But I expected that the death of the monarchy would be the death of my enslavement. Things hadn't worked like that. My brief moment of greatness had given way to this period of nothingness, while I was waiting for the republic to make me into a thing of greatness – a new citizen.

But the waiting is the thing. In the grey waiting period, we are most vulnerable. If France could behead its greatest thing for his extravagance, what would it do to a lowly slave who wore silk and was educated as if a king?

What would she—the magnificent Jeanne du Barry--do to the page who forgot that the world rose and set upon her satisfaction?

I missed delivering Madame's chocolat.

By the time I arrived, Gaspard and his guards had prepared the horses to come find me. Seeing me, he simply signaled to the others that the ride was cancelled. And then he looked at me — and I'll never forget that look — without anger or rage or disgust. He looked at me like he didn't even see me. His face was still marked and bruised from the beating he'd taken at the tavern in Paris days ago and his gaze was so unfocused I wondered if his mind was hovering above us, stuck in his own private hell.

When he turned and walked away, I felt a chill I'd never felt in all the years I'd known him.

I walked out to the perimeter of the manicured grounds to where the small patch of belladonna grew. With gloves on, I used a knife to cut a flower, its leaves and berries, and wrapped them in a piece of cloth I'd taken from the gardener's shed. I took the packet back to my room and while I would have liked to sit the berries on my windowsill to dry out, I couldn't risk someone seeing them. Instead, I put them away on a shelf in my wardrobe and hoped no one would find the poison before I could put it to use. I didn't know how to use it but thought a trip to the Palace the next day to scourge the dead King's botany books would fix that.

But I didn't have another day...

--Zamor, 1820

56

———————

I had been prevented from speaking to Madame the morning I missed the chocolat delivery. Chon was outside her door. She told me Madame didn't want to see me and would find me when she did. That didn't bode well, but I resigned myself to feeling her wrath later. I went back to my room to nap for an hour or so. Then, I dressed in fresh clothes and waited to be summoned. After a few minutes, I decided to dust, wondering if it was possible Madame had forgotten me or decided it wasn't worth the trouble. One could dream.

Later that day I took a seat at the kitchen table.

Though Salanave and I didn't speak much these days, we were close enough that simply being in the same space was of some solace to us. At least it was to me. I didn't want to make things difficult for her, but occasionally I would come to the kitchen, taking a tea or café or a piece of fruit, and just sit. She would stand at the stove and stir whatever hot liquid was in her pot. She never asked me to leave.

Sometimes I helped her carry heavy pans of meats or breads from the oven, as she wasn't getting any younger. She wouldn't respond, but would look at me, gratefully. It was comforting, being with Salanave, even if we couldn't speak.

So, I was at the table reading when heavy boots sounded in the door. Salanave looked panicked—she always looked afraid when Gaspard was around these days—but the manager's eyes were only for me as he strode in with two guards at his side. He marched in like he was on official business. His bruises were at their height, the discoloration of his face, along with the look in his eyes, making him appear a madman.

"You, blackamoor," he said, more calmly than usual. The calm made my hackles rise.

"What do you want?" I said, dubiously.

"You were late this morning and you worried Madame. On top of your normal impudence, your behavior will no longer be tolerated. The gentleman who visited the other day from the colonies, he gave me valuable advice on how to keep slaves in line."

His words caught up with me and I looked up at him as his face showed satisfaction. "I know you forget sometimes, who you are. We own you. You'll wish I put you down like your horse when I'm done."

"What are you saying?"

"Don't worry, I didn't forget Madame's instructions from so long ago. Way back when you were young, remember? She told me never to scar your beautiful face. I keep my promises."

I didn't know what he meant, I only knew his voice was too calm and his eyes too fevered. He had the blood lust. I looked back and forth between him and his guards, who looked uncomfortable, but avoided my eyes even as they were rigid and on alert. Gaspard walked towards me, and I stood up quickly, the chair falling from under me. He smiled a sick, delighted smile at the panic in my face. I walked away from him, going in the opposite direction, around the table to dodge him, but one of the guards blocked me in that direction as they spread out and flanked me.

"Hey," I said, hands out. "What is this? Wh—" someone grabbed me from behind. "Don't touch me..."

"What's happening?" Salanave cried out.

I was shoved over to Gaspard. His arms tightened around me like a vice. One of the guards tried to grab my legs and I kicked at him.

"Don't fight, Governor, you will only make things difficult. Come along now and don't make a fuss."

"Madame, Madame!" Salanave yelled, running from the room.

"No, no!" I yelled, fighting as hard as I could he half-carried, half-dragged me. I fought but they fought harder to take me. My boots scraped the ground as I struggled to stay upright, until one of them grabbed my legs. Again, I managed to kick my legs out of one of the arms holding them. But Gaspard still had me from behind, dragging me backwards, as another guard pushed me from the front. My hands grappled on the walls as I passed, trying to get a grip on the corners of the doorway, my fingernails breaking off against the stone, down below the quick, as I was ripped away. Pots and pans clamored to the ground as we tussled, making horrible noise. Surely, some guests would hear the racket and come to see? Surely, Madame would tell him to stop this madness?

Gaspard tightened his grip around me. I kicked. I bit. I fought. I even landed a strike or two, but soon I was dragged down the back hallway outside to a room off the main building used to butcher large animals. They slammed the door closed behind us and the two guards held me by my arms while Gaspard came around to the front of me and bent to speak into my face, spittle flying.

"You think you can humiliate me? Have people laughing at me? You laughing at me?" The stench of alcohol rose from his skin like he'd bathed in it. "All these years with your smart mouth and fancy ways. The King isn't here to protect you, is he? That's what they said to me that night, didn't they? While you laughed. But then I thought, *why, the King isn't here to protect* the blackamoor, *either*! Thinking you're such a big thing being favored by him. Thinking that put you over me."

He was talking nonsense, going on about Louis XV when it was XVI who had just been put to death. But his eyes were frantic in his head. Mind muddled with alcohol; I was sure.

"Let's see how smart you are today, blackamoor! Read me one of your sonnets! 'Oh, he reads so well!' she says. Like that means something. Like it matters. You're still a blackamoor. A small, weak one, like you've always been. From the moment I first lay eyes one you I knew you'd be trouble. Well, it's over now. See if you're smart enough to get out of this!" Gaspard said, backing up, quickly, before raising one of his beefy legs and landing the first kick into my stomach.

Immediately, the contents of my stomach rushed up my throat, emptying onto the stone floor as the other two held me aloft by my arms.

"Do it again!" came a voice from across the room.

I strained to look up to find the source of the strange voice and my vision focused on the American visitor standing in the doorway. It was the one who didn't like to be spoken to by a slave. He had come in so quietly, I didn't hear him. Now he was speaking to Gaspard like Barnier used to speak to me.

"Are you afraid, Manager? Stop drawing it out. Do what you have to do and put this nigger in his place! I thought you were the head of security? I told you what we do in the states to bucks who forget their place. A punch is fine ,but animals need to be kicked. *Do it*."

He kicked me again, this one higher, just a little under my ribs. This time there was nothing left in my stomach but I retched, anyway, my legs twisting under me as I twisted in agony.

"You let him get away with humiliating you in Paris? Oh, they told me about it in town, everybody's talking about it! You accept that? Your own people laughing at you? Everyone talking about what a failure and embarrassment you are because of him. Are you a man or a coward?"

"I'm a man! I'm a man!" He yelled, nodding with each statement, saliva dripping from his mouth like a rabid dog.

"Really? Does a man stand by and let a slave do what he's done? Walking in and out of a white woman's bedroom like he has a right? Without fear of punishment? Distorting and perverting the purity of a paragon of womanhood..."

My mind twisted to make sense of this through the pain. Gaspard *knew*. He knew it was never my choice. He knew she made me come to her room. Everyone knew. Even the Well-Beloved had known. She would have been angry if I *didn't*. I squinted up to look at him.

Gaspard looked feverish. He wiped a forearm across his sweaty brow. I could smell the liquor rolling off him in waves, but he caught my eye. We'd hated each other all our lives but this was something different. Altogether different.

"Gaspard—" I started, my voice husky and weak. "Don't—"

"—Don't you speak to him, boy!" The American landed a boot to my calf and I cried out in pain, falling due to my bad knee buckling from the sudden sideways blow. Trying to get off of the leg to shift to the other one at the same time, was fruitless. My chest was having trouble taking in air now, with the pain doubling up on itself.

"Him and his kind," the man said as he walked in front of me to yell at Gaspard. "He's an animal who doesn't know it. The kindest thing is to put them down, but if we can't do that then we put them in their place so they never forget. If we don't, it's *our* fault what they do to us. It's *our* fault they disobey us. *Our* fault they're intimate with our women. *Our* fault they revolt. Look what they did to your boy, who lost his life trying to save one of them. Did you forget?

Gaspard wailed like an animal in a cage. "My boy...!" he cried, his voice breaking like he'd never cried in his entire pathetic life.

"What did that darkie do after your boy saved him? He ran and left him, didn't he? Left him to be shot down like a dog in his place. Your good, white son, left crying in the road..."

I shook my head. "Gaspard," I gasped. "No. Not my fault. Not my..."

"Left your son in the road, crying while he ran to safety. Have you forgotten? Have you forgotten your boy?"

"Nooo!!" Gaspard yelled to the world, a second before the American stepped to the side and then we were facing each other again. His face was twisted and his voice ragged. "You son of a bitch. I'll kill you!"

He came at me, all red-faced fury and sweat. And then the blows started. So many fisted blows landed on my stomach, and torso, I couldn't tell what direction they were coming from. All while he sprayed me with snot and spit, garbling gibberish. The blows kept ... kept coming ... kept coming...

The guards released my arms and I fell to the ground. The blows kept coming, glancing off my shoulders and against my back when I fell to my hands. I tried to keep breathing, gasping at every blow.

The punches were bad, but then, the American reminded him to "use your feet, use your feet!" and each kick of his foot stuck like a dagger. The pain took the sound from me as my mouth gaped like a fish out of water, trying to breath air into my brutalized chest until I lost consciousness on the cold, wet stone floor.

I SLEPT. Or passed out – whatever it could be called.

In my dream, I was lying next to Véronique, her face so oddly silly, but at the same time so purely beautiful. I touched the skin of her cheek and put my lips to hers, my tongue tracing her teeth and the tiny, crooked tooth up front that managed, somehow, to make her more beautiful. I imagined this feeling was what heaven must be like. I wanted to be encompassed by her. I wanted to be in the space within her breath for the rest of my life.

She looked at me and I knew love. And I knew I loved her. The fact of it moved me to tears for the first time since a child. Oh, my Lord, thank you for this woman, I said to God. Oh, my Jesus, thank you for whatever life brought me to her, I said to His Son. Oh, my life, thank you for this perfect, perfect moment. A perfect moment as I have ever felt.

I WOKE to being dragged across the floor. I felt the hands gripping me under my arms from behind and saw my feet useless as I was dragged backwards. The floor gave way to gravel and I heard my own groan, my body feeling disconnected from me as sound rushed through my ears as if a great storm was in my head. Then, searing pain as I saw my feet bumping through another doorway. I tried to move my head to look. I said... "I don't feel right. What happened? Where are you taking me?" but the sound of my words in my ear sounded incoherent, my voice slurred beyond recognition. Then the screaming started from deep within my head. So loud it was deafening. Then it was burning. I was burning from the inside. And, suddenly, my vision blurred and my feet disappeared as the white stone fox was there staring into my eyes; staring like there was nothing else in the world but the two of us.

"No..." I shook my head. If I looked at it, I would die. But then it was closer, and the icy cold of it was a balm to the burning ball of fire that I was. "No!" I yelled, trying to move my head to the side. With my movement a hot slice ripped across me, jerking me away from the fox and away from consciousness. And I slept.

In my dream, the pain in my body was searing just like in my waking time. But in my dream I was baking under a burning sun. Yet, I was on fire within my skin. The heat was consuming me from inside as I lay on hard, earthen ground with two men holding me on either side, as the devil did his work within me, shredding the insides of me with sharp talons that felt like flames. As the devil flashed its talons and he was a she, going at me while giving me the most beautiful smile.

Josephe and Thomas were there. I raised my head to look up at them, over the head of the devil, my face awash in my own sweat. They gave me a look of pity and regret. They were both dressed in revolutionary soldier uniforms. Both armed for battle. Thomas sheathed his sword and Joseph lowered the little grill over his face. Then they turned and began walking away from me.

No! I shouted. I've changed my mind, I want to go now! Take me!

Josephe looked back once. I noticed the direction they were headed wasn't overtaken by the waves of heat that surrounded me. The orange sky and the parched earth that surrounded me gave way to blue sky and green grass and all the living healthy things that lived the farther they were from me. Thomas and Josephe walked off toward the blue and green and living things and away from me.

Don't go! Don't leave me. Don't leave me! Don't leave me...!

"Don't leave me ... don't leave me..." My eyelids fluttered open and I was in a room at the Chateau, being held down on a table, held on both sides by guards. A man I didn't recognize was perched over me as I struggled, the air thick with the stench of sweat and blood and something else I'd never smelled.

"Hold still!" came a bark from a man I was familiar with. It was the royal doctor, standing off to the side, yelling at me not to move, his rheumy eyes squinting and annoyed. But he wasn't the one standing over me. The man looking down on me was unfamiliar. He held one hand up and I noticed it was holding a knife already dripping with blood.

He was trying to kill me! I had to get up! But as I struggled against the hands holding my arms I felt a sudden, searing pain in my middle. Raising my head as best I could, I looked down and my eyes widened in horror as I saw my midsection laying open, saw my own insides that quivered with each movement as if they would spill out onto the floor at any second.

"Ahhhh! N-no, no ... no!" I heard my own voice, less of a voice than a sound that something makes when it's dying. The garbled sound coming from me, I was no more able to stop than I could end this nightmare.

"Hold his head to the table, I told you!"

Someone fell on the other side of the room, causing the large clatter of pans and utensils.

"Someone hold him down or he'll die! Put that leather in his mouth or get the spoon in so he won't swallow his tongue. Hurry!"

An arm was hooked around my neck and one forearm latched against my forehead to keep my head pinned to the table.

Someone mumbled—"Mon Dieu, I'm sorry. I'm sorry. God forgive me."—over and over in a litany.

Through watering eyes, I watched the piece of leather come towards me and felt it being shoved into my mouth. I struggled. Fear was all of me, now, wondering what was going to happen that I needed the leather in my mouth. A silver spoon was next, pressing down on my tongue as if the leather wasn't already doing it. Whimpers came from me as I struggled against all the hands that were holding me down. My veins felt like they were trying to escape my head, and the horrible, sickening feeling of open air inside my body widened my eyes in horror. I felt something foreign inside me. Searing pain hit, and I bucked, biting on that leather as inhuman sounds filled the room. I struggled as the devil's talons went at me again, sending me off to sleep with the sounds of my own screams, my only lullaby.

Véronique was running towards me, and the sight of her made me want to collapse in relief and happiness. To hold her was what I wanted most in the world. In the nighttime, we were in a field in the Louveciennes countryside, covered with red poppies, under the light of the moon. We ran toward each other, and suddenly her steps became labored and unsure. I called to her and ran towards her, but an invisible wall had sprung up between us. And yet, she still tried to reach me.

She was still moving towards me but going nowhere.

Looking down, I could no longer see her feet as they were sinking, swallowed up by the earth, turning to mud underneath her. She struggled as I called. The mud was up to her waist now, rising up over her pretty embroidered bodice. Her face, beautiful in the moonlight, was panicked as she reached toward me with arms wet with mud. Dripping with sodden wetness and the cloying sweet stench of death. Her skin turned slick with perspiration and panic.

And my cheeks were wet with tears as I reached toward her, uselessly, watching the cursed countryside take my Véronique of the East under, as if a blanket had been thrown over the sun. As if all light had been extinguished. As if the world, itself, had died... Noooo!

...but when I opened my eyes again it wasn't Véronique I saw.

My eyelids were almost glued together from gunk. My face was wet and I was still so hot I was burning. Now, through the gunk and the water, I could see Madame sitting on a small chair beside me, embroidering.

The room was quiet. It was so still, I tried to lift my head to search for sound, and pain rolled through me in waves, from my feet to my head. I labored to breathe and the movement caught her attention.

She glanced up, putting the material and needle on the table beside her. Her face was soft and sad.

"There you are. Oh, Dieu merci, I'm so happy to see your eyes, Louis. Mon cheri, how do you feel?"

It took me a moment to remember. I felt it coming back before the memories flooded me. How I was attacked by Gaspard and his guards. The American! The torture. Me open on the table.

"Madame ... what they did..." I ground out. "...what they did..."

"Oh, sweet Louis, please don't upset yourself. It will be all right. You're fine and I'm here now. I'm so sorry you were hurt, mon cher."

Her words brought relief to me. Somehow, they brought comfort to me. She was on my side, this time. She would get rid of him for good. She wasn't as heartless as I used to think.

She continued.

"Gaspard had promised to do only what he had to do to stop this need of yours to keep disobeying. The gentleman from the colonies said what he did will cure the sickness in you. It's not your fault, it's in your nature. I understand that, I didn't before. Now we've set the boundary, so you will know never to scare me like that again."

My eyelids blinked to see through the tears and the gunk and to clear the fog in my brain so I could see her. My mind must still have been in a nightmare because what I heard surely wasn't real. I watched her lips as she spoke so I could see that what I'd heard was a figment of my imagination, brought on by pain.

"We can't have you running, Louis-Benoit," her lips said. "When you're home by morning, I know all is well, but when you're not here in the morning, I can't tell you how frightened I get. It's like when you were a child and almost froze to death in the Labyrinth because you didn't know any better. You think you know the world but you don't. Whatever he had to do is just a *little* thing compared to a lifetime of happiness. You're awake and safe, just like he promised, and I don't ever have to worry about you breaking the rules, again. You can go to Paris to be with your little friends, but now I know you'll be back here *every* morning. We can be together, forever, and we can both be happy, as long as you follow the rules. You are the best gift the King ever gave me. You are the greatest thing in the world to me. You're all I have left, my Louis-Benoit. Don't you see? You and I are all that's left of the most glorious kingdom. And you and I are all we have left, for *each other.*"

She showed me the sweetest, most beautiful, smile before laying her head lightly on my chest. I couldn't catch my breath from the shock and the heat and her words.

Finally, after a lifetime of holding strong, I broke ... like the many things in the Palace I had broken over the years. I broke like the man I had barely had a chance to be. Like the person I had never had a chance to become. Like a headless body whose arms and legs still move, I broke like a dead thing that was alive one minute, and then, suddenly, dead before its body even realized it.

57

Dear Citizen,

*I fought delirium for four days. It was agony interspersed with
moments of dream and lucidity. I saw Véronique, Salanave, and
Madame in those dreams. Gaspard. Louis XV. The little boy I had
trailed during my voyage from free person to slave. And sometimes
I was in the Labyrinth at the Palace staring at the stone tableau of
those children and the leaping fox, caught in a white lightning
strike—the four of us frozen in time with the tall, tall trees
enclosing us in a wooded tomb.*

*Throughout it all, there were moments of pure horror when I
remembered it all clearly and prayed for delirium, again.*

--Zamor, 1820

Sleep was my only respite from the pain. But sleep came with
nightmares of being clawed open or even worse ones that
didn't feel like nightmares when I was having them, but the
second I woke I felt like screaming in horror. So, sometimes I forced

myself to stay awake. In the night, as I stared at the ceiling, I realized I wasn't in my own room. That I was in one of the empty back rooms they had pushed a bed into.

New room, strange people, and no one I knew around me. Now, the doctor walked into my room this morning without even a knock.

"You see?" he said to someone behind him.

Glancing over, I spied a man walking in behind him and recognized him as the one I'd only seen on that terrible night. He was the wielder of the knife who carved me up on the table.

I tried to raise up. It was in my mind to do him bodily harm and I grunted, struggling to force my resistant body to get to him; to give him a taste of whatever tools he carried in that bag like he'd done me. But sharp, overwhelming pain took my breath and forced me back down.

"I've told you not to move a thousand times." This time the doctor was speaking to me, his face a mask of disapproval as he frowned. "Any pain is your own fault."

I didn't remember seeing him a thousand times, but then I'd been out of my head a good bit since that night. The doctor turned to the other man.

"This one is obstinate, always has been. Fights people trying to help him, even in his sleep."

"You! You cut me...!" I gasped to the newcomer, who looked uncomfortable with being singled out. I jabbed a pointed finger in the air towards him. "*You* did it!"

"Amazing work," the doctor babbled on, sitting his own bag down on a chair and rolling up his sleeves. "I never knew a person could be cut open and live to tell about it. But when they came for me and described your belly, I knew you were as good as dead. But then, I remembered hearing about this man in Paris who was working in one of the new hospitals they opened up for the soldiers. That they were experimenting with ... what do you call it?"

"Internal surgery," the man completed, stepping over to me with reticence. "You were surely going to die. I could tell just by looking at you that one of your organs was likely bleeding *inside* your body. That's why your stomach was bloated."

"You looked like you were about to give birth!" The doctor declared. "Like a fish left to rot with its belly swelled up close to bursting!"

"That's what happens when one of the organs is damaged," the stranger said. He looked young to be so confident about what was going on inside my body. "A little leak can spread into a big one," the surgeon demonstrated with his hands in claws, radiating outward. "It fills your body with blood. It was a ruptured spleen. I was able to remove it and tie everything up to stop the bleeding."

"What the hell is a spleen?" I groused.

"Come, try to sit up a little so we can remove these bandages and see what we've got."

I looked at them both sideways. I grimaced again in anticipation of the pain, knowing they wouldn't leave until having a look.

Though, packed up in cloth as I was, I knew I'd soiled myself. They didn't seem to care, unwrapping my torso while I perched myself up on my elbows, feeling as weak as a babe and shuddering with every breath. When they came to the layer closest to my body it was yellow and pinkish white and wet. Pulling it away, I groaned at the sight of me. From one side to the other, the ugly cut was secured with threads crisscrossing over the incision. I looked like a monster. They "*ahh-ed*" in appreciation.

They kept unwrapping and when they undid the cloths swaddling me like a baby's diaper, I noticed the whole of me, from the cut down to my groin, was swollen.

"It will go down, don't worry," the doctor said. "They didn't take your manhood, they only damaged it. The surgeon here had to remove a testicle and stitch up a tear so there's some scarring. You won't make children with it, but you can obviously still pee, from the smell of you."

"Wait, what did you say? I can't make babies?"

"You're lucky to be alive, that's all that matters. Besides, making children is little to worry about for you, I'd think. It's not like *you* would ever need them. Unless, of course ... Madame did *so* enjoy you when you were young and would tumble around entertaining the court. You used to get into everything! You were a cute little thing. Now that you're grown, maybe she would have liked to breed another little one to play with..."

His words hit me like a brick. He turned to chatter with the other man about nothing as heat rose up inside me.

"Get out," I croaked.

"What? We're not finished..."

"Get your bag and get out. Get out." He looked at me like he couldn't understand French. As he watched, I reached over—I tried to do it fast but my body made it happen slowly—and grabbed the teacup from last night's tea that hadn't been cleared away, and managed to throw it at him with vigor. His eyes widened and he ducked. It crashed against the far wall.

"Are you mad?" he asked, flushed and indignant. He looked at the other man. "Come on. He doesn't know how to be grateful. You wasted a miracle on him."

"Get out, get out!"

Grabbing his bag the doctor left but the other man lagged behind, his face looking like he didn't know if he should speak.

"It's a shock, I know. I'm sorry for your loss. But, you truly are a miracle, Monsieur. Thank you for allowing me to do what was considered impossible, even six months ago." He gave a small smile.

My face twisted. "I didn't *allow* you to do anything. I had no say in the matter. Now, I'm a freak!"

"Madame sent word that every attempt be made to save you. No matter how experimental. She said—"

"—oh, by all means, if *she* says to torture the page than have at it! I'm not a human being. I don't feel pain. I don't have a say." My head went back and forth at each point, rife with angry sarcasm. "Do anything you want to him, he's nothing! That's what you all think of me, isn't it? First, she tells them to hold me down to beat me almost to death. And then you doctors are called to save the day, and what happens? She tells *you* to hold me down and carve me like a beast to slaughter! It's unnatural for a human being to see inside his own body! And all because *Madame* wanted it? Jeanne du Barry wasn't the one under the knife, was she?"

"I thought, surely, you'd want to any chance to live..."

This man didn't understand. A body can withstand much if it's accepting of what's happening. But a body—my body—never felt more inhuman than when I was being cut on without even a chance to understand. Feeling like I was watching my own murder.

"I've never felt pain like that in all my days. I never imagined a human body could stand that much pain and still live." Even remembering a little of it caused a bubble of bile to rise in my throat and my eyelid ticked. "There are people in this house who care about me. Where were they to speak for me or pray over me?".

"I just did what I was told, Monsieur..."

"Don't say it again!"

I remembered that roomful of strangers who thought nothing of me, looking down on me while I writhed and screamed and whimpered and begged. Like I was a specimen; a thing wiggling under the magnification of the dead King's microscope. Like I was nothing.

It was me laying on the Palace floor all over again. Me, having to escape my brain by embracing the death siren of the stone-cold fox of my nightmares. I would rather have died.

"It's my body, dammit!" I slapped the sheets beside me. "Any one of the times I woke up you might have asked me. You might have told me what you were doing so I wouldn't have..." *been so frightened*, I stopped myself from saying aloud. "It was unnatural, what you did. I'll look like this for the rest of my life. And now you walk in here with that satisfied smirk on your face, expecting me to praise you. To thank you. Like you did it for me. You were thrilled to have a body to play with, weren't you? Someone to experiment on without repercussion. You wouldn't have done that to a white man on the say of one woman, would you? People like you just do what you want, don't you? All of you. Treat people like we're all your personal playthings. Well, somebody will pay for making me see my insides! You're no better than the piece of filth that just left. The miracle is yours, Monsieur, that I don't have the strength to take a knife and plunge it inside of *you*! If I see your face again, I will gut you like you gutted me. Get out. Get out!"

I leaned over in a repeat slow move, this time to grab the little matching saucer to throw. Reaching for it so suddenly made me grimace in pain.

"I'm sorry, Monsieur," he said, quickly leaving, just as the saucer I threw at him crashed and shattered against the far wall. I lay back down, exhausted, water leaking from the corners of my eyes onto my pillow. A few minutes later, a woman came in to change my soiled clothes, clean me like a baby, and wrap me back up.

By the time she finished, my eyes were no longer wet.

58

———————

Dear Citizen,

Shortly thereafter I decided to allow myself to sleep at night. The nightmare of being clawed apart came less frequently and the other nightmare increased until I was having it almost every night.

In my new nightmare, I dreamt of Véronique and me, married and living in Paris. Enjoying the theatre and Josephe's orchestra while her parents watched the children. Or the two of us in that little house in Croissy-Sur-Seine she kept going on about, tucking our children into bed at night, kissing their little brown faces. Little brown free *faces.*

It doesn't sound like a nightmare, I know. But every morning, after waking from it, I would open my eyes and realize, afresh and anew, that I would never make those little babies. I would never give Véronique the life we both wanted so badly. And then my mouth would open wide in a soundless scream, all on its own. My hands would twist the bedsheets in my fists and I would groan in agony while, inwardly, cursing my own body. Every morning after that dream, I felt the same horror upon waking.

I didn't know what a spleen was or what it did, but I would swear to anyone that I felt the empty hole where it had once been. Perhaps the emptiness was that missing organ. Perhaps the spleen is where my hope had lived.

I began to hate myself for my own stupidity. Knowing who those people were, I had let my guard down. Knowing what they were capable of, I'd strutted around as cocky and arrogant as a white nobleman. It didn't matter that those traits were central to my personality from birth – I was supposed to pretend to be less. I forgot the very tenant Salanave taught me all those years ago. I forgot to be small. I forgot to save who I was for the places where I was safe. And now look at what I'd lost.

I had known Jeanne du Barry from ten years old. Throughout my life she'd shown a kindness here or there. Because of those few instances I forgave her many things. Overlooked many things. Rationalized many things. But I never anticipated how far she would go to keep me. I never believed she'd mortally wound me until the moment she looked me in my eyes and told me she had willingly participated in my mutilation.

Naïveté is only a small part of why I had deluded myself. The greater truth is that it's necessary to one's sanity to grab hold of whatever hope there might be. Because how could a person truly reconcile the idea that the entire world thought that person to be little more than a thing to be had? I had given Madame the benefit of the doubt for my own sanity until the very moment when she almost destroyed both.

There were moments I wished I had died on that cold floor. Wished that instead of curling up to protect all my soft parts I had lay, spread eagle, and let them do everything they wanted. I'd be dead, but I wouldn't have to feel what I felt now.

It was at this point in my life that I realized the truth. Madame was the devil. Every time she fed me a bit of spite, anger, general meanness, it was like one of those little berries of a belladonna, no less dangerous because the plant was beautiful. I had only to look at what she'd done to me. She'd killed every hope I ever had, or sent others to do it. Like I said, the devil.

Oh, I know reading this you must be thinking I'd lost my mind at this point.

Far from it. I tell you, Dear Citizen, as the pain in my body lessened a little bit every day, I thought about what Sebastien had said. I had gotten soft. I was at my best when I was hard. The hellfire rained down upon me had given me clarity of thought and purpose.

Why should I hate myself? Hate myself for being human? Hate myself for expecting decency from others? Hate myself for having, for a brief bit of time, been lost in the possibility of something more for me? Hate myself for wanting to walk in the sun? Hate myself for wanting to be free?

For a brief moment I had reverted back to the scared child I used to be, but that child taught himself how to survive. Taught himself that when at one's worst, one can always feed on the pain of others to become strong again!

I would not hate myself!

I thought of my mother's words—that I was the greatest thing God put on earth. If there was greatness in me, there was no room for hatred towards myself. Hatred was theirs to hold. Gaspard should hate himself. *Madame should hate* herself. *They should both suffer. And me, I should feed on their pain. And I would. There was nothing to be done for it, they set it up... and all that.*

Paul Marat was right. Chloe was, too. I had grown soft before getting the job done. No different from Louis XVI, feeling relaxed enough to get out of that carriage and walk around freely, minutes from escape. I had allowed myself to get complacent, walking through life like I was a free man before freedom was in my grasp.

My previous worry about timing and losing my leverage disappeared. Yes, I wanted my freedom. But I was going to get rid of her, with or without it. It would be my gift to the world. And since she could possibly have set it up to pass me on to him—as inheritance, along with the pots and pans, should anything happen to her—I had to get rid of them both. It was the only smart thing to do.

The small seedling inside of me that delighted in the pain of the people who had pained me--it was now a thriving plant. Even though it was hungry, it was growing stronger with each day I lay recuperating in bed.

The doctor told me to lay still but my body told me to move as much as possible. I walked in circles in the room because every time I opened the door a guard was standing outside it to stop me from leaving. So I built my strength in solitude. And the warrior feeders of my own personal levain grew angrier and hungrier. They would have their season soon.

I would have blood, of that I vowed.

It was the oddest thing. Once the decision was made, I began to sleep like a baby. Dreams of a future with Véronique died as if they knew they were no longer wanted. Now, I dreamt of the death of my enemies and woke up each morning refreshed and looking forward to the day. No more silent screams as I allowed my old dreams to die.

Dear Citizen,

People give you poison and say they love you in the same breath. They grow death and hand it to you like a platter of the sweetest, most delicious fruit. Or they slip it to you daily, one beautiful berry at a time, knowing the poison will build upon itself in your tenderest spots; every day with the most sincere gaze in their eyes. They smile while you slowly melt into a puddle of decaying flesh. And when you look up at them from the puddle you have become on the ground, they look down, smile, and say, 'I love you. You are mine. But you are the Devil and must be tamed'.

I knew who the Devil was. It was my mission to make her eat her own damned berries. Eat them or choke on them, either way was fine with me.

It's like I always say, at the end of every day, every fox must survive its own hunt ...

...And all that.

-Zamor

SOON TO COME

Over 200 years after the death of Louis-Benoit Zamor, the story inspired by his life comes to an end.

In the midst of the *Reign of Terror*, Louis-Benoit Zamor finally escapes the dying Ancien Régime. But his freedom will come at a cost. Though plagued by regrets and ghosts of the past, Zamor will forge ahead, embarking on a journey of self-discovery.

Who is Louis-Benoit Zamor without his family, the royals, or his friends? Who is the Page without a Favorite to serve? Is he the traitor of the Ancien Régime that all of France is calling him? Is he the survivor of the Révolution left to tell the tale?

He was a person before he was a slave. Before he was a toy. Before he was a page. Before he was a revolutionary.

When all is said and done, every fox must survive its own hunt.

∼

Through the eyes of a man who straddled times and worlds, read the final book in the trilogy re-imagining the unexplored life of Louis-Benoit Zamor. Stay tuned for...

The Truest Son of France
(The Last Favorite's Page: Book Three)

AFTERWORD

Dear Reader,

Of the three books in *The Last Favorite's Page* trilogy, *The Devil's Berries* was the most difficult (I say that now before I tackle the revision of book three!). Whereas the first book was mostly fiction this second book had a good bit of history.

I want to acknowledge, again, that this is a work of fiction. Some characters have been changed and a few dates fudged (though, not as many as you might imagine). I will go into the characterization at the end of book three.

I wrote most of this trilogy during the pandemic, when our world was changing. Probably not the best idea to tackle such heavy fiction during a time of heavy real-life, but we go where the pen (or the keyboard) takes us.

I couldn't stop thinking, when the world is going through drastic changes, how much worse it is for people who have the least control, even over themselves.

I decided to tackle the research from three angles: 1) I found everything I could about Zamor on the internet, 2) I studied the French Revolution and its causes, and 3) I researched slavery in France. I was fortunate to have some help from actual historians and researchers. Any inaccuracy in my interpretation of events of the time should not be attributed to them, but to my own lay-person misunderstanding. Or, it might be intentional for the sake of the story. Interestingly enough, quite a few things you might think I made up actually happened.

There are questions and controversies surrounding Zamor that I'd love to discuss. But with one more book left, I'll leave it till then. Hope you stay to the end.

READING LIST

Here are some of the sources and reading materials that shaped the direction of the story or rounded out my understanding of what was happening in the world during this time. Additional materials will be cited at the end of Book Three.

<u>**Resources & databases**</u>

Wikipedia

Researchers at the Bibliothèque Nationale de France, BnF (The National Library of France), and the BnF research database, Gallica

<u>**Articles**</u>
Zamor: the tale of a Bengali in the French Revolution, Faiaz, Zarif, Medium, September 28, 2019
https://zarif-faiaz.medium.com/zamor-the-tale-of-a-bengali-in-the-french-revolution-d200de306f1f

Zamor, the slave boy from Bengal played a major role in bringing

down Bastille during French Revolution, Get Bengal, December 30, 2021
https://www.getbengal.com/details/zamor-the-slave-boy-from-bengal-played-a-major-role-in-bringing-down-bastille-during-french-revolution

How an Indian man taken to Europe as a slave played a role in the French Revolution, Bose, Arghya, July 14, 2020, Scroll.in
https://scroll.in/article/967343/how-an-indian-man-taken-to-europe-as-a-slave-played-a-role-in-the-french-revolution

In Paris, Offspring of the Revolution, Mikelbank, Peter, Mary 16, 1989, Washington Post

Books

Venus Noire: Black Women and Colonial Fantasies in Nineteenth-Century France (Race in the Atlantic World, 1700-1900 Ser.), Robin Mitchell, University of Georgia Press, January 1, 2020

African Europeans: An Untold History, Olivette Otele, Basic Books, August 29, 2023

"There are no Slaves in France": The Political Culture of Race and Slavery in the Ancien Régime, Sue Peabody, Oxford University Press, September 26, 2002

Plays

L'Escalavage des Noirs, ou L'Heureux Naufrage, MMe Olympe de Gouges, performed Dec 1789, La Comédie Française (translation by Hannah Palmer)

Alzire, Voltaire (translation by William F. Fleming), First Start Publishing e-book edition, October 2012

Academic journals & papers

Bishop, Cécile. "Seeing Race, Seeing Ghosts: Zamor, Ourika, and the Specter of Blackness." *L'Esprit Créateur* 59, no. 2 (2019): 56-71. https://doi.org/10.1353/esp.2019.0016.

Brixius, Dorit. 2020. "From Ethnobotany to Emancipation: Slaves, Plant Knowledge, and Gardens on Eighteenth-Century Isle de France." *History of Science* 58 (1): 51–75. doi:10.1177/0073275319835431.

Hammersley, Rachel. 2015. "Concepts of Citizenship in France during the Long Eighteenth Century." *European Review of History* 22 (3): 468–85. doi:10.1080/13507486.2015.1036231.

Mccloy, Shelby Thomas. 1945. "Negroes and Mulattoes in Eighteenth-Century France." *Journal of Negro History* 30 (July): 276–92. doi:10.2307/2715112.

Parrish JN, Leary JPO. The French Revolution and the Rise of Surgery. The American Surgeon™. 2000;66(1):94-95. doi:10.1177/000313480006600120

Sarti, Raffaella. 2022. "From Slaves and Servants to Citizens? Regulating Dependency, Race, and Gender in Revolutionary France and the French West Indies." *International Review of Social History* 67 (1): 65–95. doi:10.1017/S0020859021000432.

Schreier, Lise. 2016. "Zamore 'the African' and the Haunting of France's Collective Consciousness." *Nineteenth-Century Contexts* 38 (2): 123–39. doi:10.1080/08905495.2016.1135290.

www.ingramcontent.com/pod-product-compliance
Lightning Source LLC
Chambersburg PA
CBHW060608300726
48975CB00005B/1489